Lost and Found Family Novella Collection

Janet Koops

Brown House Books

Book Cover by: 100 Covers
1st print edition 2024 by: Brown House Books

Lost and Found Family Novella Collection (print): 978-1-963745-01-6 (ebook): 979-8-9865521-7-0
Homing Instinct (ebook): 979-8-9865521-2-5
Six Weeks With You (ebook): 979-8-9865521-0-1
Rules of Disengagement (ebook): 979-8-9865521-1-8

Books in the Lost and Found Family Series

Homing Instinct
Six Weeks With You
Rules of Disengagement
Family Friends
Then I Met You

For a complete list of all of Janet's books, please scan the QR code or visit
janetkoops.com

JANET KOOPS

Homing Instinct

Sometimes home isn't a place

1

THERE WEREN'T MANY THINGS that could render Darcy speechless, but the surprise of a nearly naked man in Becks' kitchen was one of them. Make that completely naked because his surprise equaled hers, causing him to drop the towel he held around his waist.

Thinking quickly, she grabbed the empty coffee pot off the counter and wielded it above her head. If she was going to go down, she would go down with a fight. Or kick his ass. "Who are you? What are you doing here?" she asked, her eyes locked on his.

"Me? Who the hell are you?" Even though the intruder was vulnerable, Darcy saw no sign of fear. His back was straight, his feet were in line with his hips, and he held her gaze with an intensity equaling her own. With his forehead furrowed and his mouth pinched tight, he looked both mad and confused.

Had she walked into the wrong apartment? Her eyes darted around the room, searching for proof of Becks. Sure enough, pictures covered the fridge, one of which included her. Peaches, the cat—the reason she was there—was sunning herself on the window ledge behind Mr. Naked Intruder, clearly not interested in either of them. And, of course, Darcy had used the key to let herself in. Yup, all evidence indicated she was indeed in the right apartment. So what was going on?

Unless... "Oh my God, is Becks back? Are you and her..." She shook her head. That made no sense. Becks was out of town with her boyfriend. They'd only left yesterday. Could things have changed that fast?

"No, no. Nothing like what you're thinking. She's letting me crash here for a few days," the intruder said, his facial muscles relaxing, changing his expression from angry to perplexed.

"Well, she didn't tell me."

"Yeah. I'm getting that." He squatted down slowly, picked up his towel, then stood to wrap it around his waist. Not once had his eyes deviated from hers, as if he thought her a cornered animal, waiting to pounce. Darcy almost laughed.

"And you are?" he asked.

"A friend. I'm taking care of her cat while she's away for the week."

He nodded slightly. "Sounds like Becks, no? Forgetting to provide all the details."

"Um, yeah. It kind of does. But still, how do I know you're telling the truth, and you didn't break in."

"You think I broke in to take a shower?"

Darcy gave him a one-shoulder shrug as she still held the coffee pot menacingly, or so she hoped. "People commit crimes for stranger reasons."

"Tell you what, you put down your weapon, and we'll figure this out."

Darcy didn't move.

"Oh mon Dieu, really? I have my own key."

"Right. Why would you have a key?"

"Because she always lets me stay here when I'm in town."

"Uh-huh."

"Look, my name is François. Rebecca and I were neighbors growing up. We have been friends forever, even going to Camp Wanakeeta together when we were kids. Her cat is named Peaches, and she's dating a guy named Jason. Her middle name is Mabel, and if you ever call her that, she will hit you. Hard. Does that prove anything?"

"Yes. You're a stalker."

He removed one hand from his tight grip on the towel to rub his temple, mumbling to himself in French.

Fortunately, Darcy understood French. Especially the expletives. "Well, boohoo for you. All I wanted was to feed her cat and watch some cable TV, but now I have to call the cops and make a statement, and I'll probably go to the station. So thanks to you, my night is ruined."

"The cops? Are you kidding me?"

"Yeah." Darcy smiled and put down the coffee pot. "I'm totally fucking with you. She's mentioned you before. But she didn't mention anything about you staying here. And you're right, that is classic Becks. Now get dressed." She dismissed him with a wave of her hands.

"Yes, ma'am." He saluted her, then walked past her towards the bedroom, passing close enough for her to smell vanilla bean and citrus off his damp skin. He didn't strike her as the vanilla bean type, so he must have used Becks' soap.

The moment the bedroom door closed, the tight spring holding Darcy together loosened, allowing her to exhale some tension and process the last few minutes. Her adrenaline shot through the roof when she first realized she wasn't alone, and when she thought he might be a threat, her mind went directly to the worst possible scenario.

If this was the end, what of her life? She'd not yet hiked the Pacific Crest Trail, learned to skate, stayed at the Ice Hotel, fallen in love, or put down roots.

Darcy leaned over the sink and drank water straight from the tap. No harm done. Time to forget about it and laugh. Still, what if time was running out? A slight tremor shook her body.

"I never got your name," François said, suddenly back in the kitchen and scaring the wits out of her. Again. Quickly lifting her head away from the tap so she could face him, Darcy smacked it on the cupboard above the sink.

"Holy mother..." She took a deep breath, then another, rubbing her head. "So you are trying to kill me."

"No. Of course not." Were his lips turning upwards? Was he about to laugh? "Sorry." He covered his smile with a hand.

Darcy ground her teeth while glaring at him. She wasn't mad. She probably would have wanted to laugh if roles were reversed. Laughter relieved tension. Everyone knew that. But why not try and make François sweat for a bit? Plus, it gave her an opportunity to check him out. Fear of death had prevented her from taking in his appearance earlier, and holy cow, he was cute. Ugh, she hated the word cute. It was so middle school, but it described him perfectly, at least dressed, with his towel-dried hair and deep blue eyes. She'd pull up his naked form later, the image no doubt burned into her long-term memory. Luckily, he'd never guess what she was thinking. She was great at poker for a reason.

"You remembering me naked?"

A sound that was part shock and part laugh burst out of Darcy. Unable to maintain her death stare, she began laughing in earnest. François soon joined her.

"I'm sorry for laughing when you bumped your head," he eventually said.

"You're forgiven. It was kind of funny. In fact, this entire situation is funny. And my name is Darcy, by the way."

"Well, nice to meet you, Darcy." He opened the freezer and offered her a bag of frozen peas for her head, which she waved off.

"Beer then?" He held one out to her.

"Yeah. Thanks." She took it, chugging down about half. It was wonderfully cold.

"I take it you're thirsty," he said with a wry little smile, leaning back against the counter with his legs crossed at his ankles. He was so...relaxed. So comfortable.

She took in her own posture. Even with her tension gone and after laughing, her back was ramrod straight. Her arms crossed. Her stance might be interpreted in several ways, but not one of them would be relaxed.

Was she always like this? She'd lived all over the world and grown accustomed to meeting new people. If anyone should be relaxed, it should be her—except she was a constant stranger, always focusing on what to say, what to ask, how to fit in.

Not the right time for self-reflection, she took a long sip of beer, trying to drown her thoughts. "You know, you're lucky. I have a black belt in Taekwondo. I could have seriously injured you if I wanted." Why did she tell him that? She rarely told anyone about her black belt. Maybe she hit her head harder than she thought.

"They teach you the coffee pot move?"

"Very funny." She finished her beer, then rested the empty bottle on the counter. In for a penny, in for a pound. "Stand back. I'm going to do a Poomsae." Darcy moved into the middle of the room and performed a sequence of kicks and punches. Impressive, considering the size of Becks' kitchen.

"Wow. You're serious."

"Sure am."

"Well, I'm impressed. Except you forgot the coffee pot."

"I think you've beaten that joke to death, don't you?"

"Not quite yet," he said with a grin and eyebrow wiggle. "But seriously, I admire the dedication. What inspired you to achieve such a level of expertise?"

"I liked the focus and the hard training. I also like being able to take care of myself. Plus, no matter where we lived, we always found a martial arts school."

"You moved a lot?"

"You could say that. Honk Kong, Holland, England, Germany, Mexico, British Columbia, New Jersey, D.C., and Oregon."

"Oh wow. Those are big moves. What are some of your favorite places? I've been traveling for about a year and have visited some of those countries. Soon I'm off to Mexico. Who knows where I'll be for the new millennium."

"So you're gonna party like it's—"

"Don't say it." He stepped forward and clasped his hand over her mouth before she could finish.

She laughed, pulling it off. "I was going to say it, but now I'm going to sing it." And she did. That one line. That's all, but oh boy, she certainly must have hit her head hard.

Darcy accepted a second beer, more than happy to continue the conversation. She loved talking about her travels but didn't do it as much as she would have liked. While some people talked about their hometown, Darcy had this. She'd been to some fantastic places and done some amazing things but hesitated to talk about it for fear of coming across as a showoff. But with François, it was a two-way street. They'd visited some of the same locations. And in one city, they'd eaten at the same restaurant.

"So now your family is here in Montreal?" François asked.

"Nope. Just me. My parents are in Yakima, Washington."

"Where's Yakima? Near Seattle?"

"It's about a two-hour drive east over the Cascade mountains."

"And you came here for work? School?"

"None of the above. I was born here."

"Ah. I get it. You came home."

She nodded, picking at the label on her beer bottle. "Yeah. I guess." Can you call somewhere you lived as an infant home? That was twenty-five years ago. "But Montreal is no different from any other place I've lived because I started from scratch. Meeting people. Learning the lay of the land. Stuff like that."

"And how's it going?"

"I don't know. Okay." Was it, though? She hoped she'd masked the uncertainty in her voice. After one year, what had changed? A big fat nothing, that's what. She still didn't find herself attached to anything or anyone.

"I'm going to order pizza. Want to stay and have dinner with me and Peaches?" François asked, looking down at Peaches. She'd become very vocal, winding her way back and forth against both of their legs.

Darcy looked down too, then wished she hadn't. Because the plan had been to hang out with Peaches and watch some TV, she'd worn her old comfortable sweats. They were frayed at the bottom and a bit too short, so her mismatched socks were obvious. Something she hadn't noticed until she kicked off her shoes upon arrival. But, of course, it didn't matter then because she was alone, or so she'd thought.

"So? What'll it be?"

"What? Oh, no thanks. I got a thing." She pointed at the door with her beer bottle.

"You're sure?" he asked, bending to pick up Peaches, who was right by Darcy's feet—her mismatching sock-clad feet.

"Yeah, I'm sure."

"Well, another time then. Maybe when I'm back from Mexico."

"Sure. Sounds good."

Darcy gave him a bow and then pulled the door shut behind her. Her final image was of him picking up the receiver of Becks' lip-shaped phone in one hand while holding Peaches in his other. Had she not thought him cute already, this would have done it.

She made her way down the street to her car. Leaning back against her seat, she gave her tiny stuffed pig, Glücksschwein, a poke in the belly, watching him swing back and forth from her rear-view mirror. She could have stayed, she'd enjoyed talking to him, but tonight had forced her to face some truths. She was stuck in a rut, and her efforts to make Montreal her home had stalled.

"All right Glücksschwein." Yes, she was speaking to her pig. "Tonight, I choose a paint color. Let's go to the store." And if she chose the wrong color, so what? She could paint over it. Had life not taught her that nothing was permanent?

Is that what scared her?

2

Finding a naked guy in Becks' apartment earlier was less of an ordeal than the one Darcy now faced. She confronted her opponent head-on, her body tense, her brow furrowed. Three painted stripes on the wall stared back, mocking her. *Oh my God, pick one already.* This should be easy. None of the colors were bold. None were outrageous. In fact, one was white—warmer than the awful ice-blue white that made her apartment feel cold—but still, you know, white.

Never one to step away from a challenge, she loathed the thought of giving up, but at what point could she graciously admit defeat?

Darcy pulled a tub of ice cream out of the freezer and dug in. She had dreamed of having her own place for so long, and now that that had come true, why couldn't she choose a paint color? No one would describe her as indecisive. Heck, she signed the lease for this place after seeing only two others. Her mother loved it, excited about decorating such a "wonderful blank canvas." Darcy saw it more as a box with a bathroom, but she agreed with her mother about the "blank" bit.

Not that she was complaining. It was a practical space, a temporary space, and most importantly, an inexpensive space, allowing her to build up her savings account. One day she would buy a house, anchoring her somewhere. A girl could dream.

The phone rang, interrupting her from staring at the colors as they merged into one giant blob.

"Hey, Darce. It's Krista. We're heading to The Sanitorium. One-dollar shooters until midnight. You coming?"

"Of course, I'm coming."

"I knew it. You never say no. We're all meeting here. Come when you're ready."

"Okay. Be there soon." Darcy hung up and walked over to her paint samples. Why didn't she say no? The paint colors weren't going to choose amongst themselves, and she had a new book she was dying to start, but she'd learned long ago that being social was the key to fitting in.

"Sorry," she said to the wall, running her hand across the colors. "It's not you. It's me."

"Don't blame me for your wicked hangover tomorrow. Blame the bartender. These were on the house," Krista said as she passed out the shooters. Going out with Krista usually saved Darcy money, and this night was no exception. It was no mystery why. Even handing out the shots, Krista oozed sex appeal.

Darcy studied her movements like she was studying an animal in the wild. Sure, Krista was beautiful. She was tall with thick brown hair and piercing green eyes, not to mention she had curves like a fifties pin-up girl. But lots of women were beautiful. There was an element to Krista beyond pure beauty. Her graceful and welcoming movements were part of it, but there remained an ethereal quality that eluded Darcy. How did Krista's action of pulling her hair back while leaning across the table to pass Darcy a drink evoke intimacy?

Krista shimmered like a beautiful butterfly. Darcy was a redheaded stick bug covered in freckles.

And like a stick bug, Darcy protected herself through camouflage. She held up her drink. "All right, ladies. Here's to a night of fun, drinks, and meeting some good-looking guys, except for Krista, of course." She placed her hand over her heart and batted her eyelashes, hiding her true feelings behind her teasing. "She's in loooove." What did that feel like?

"Cheers to that," said Carrie, Krista's best friend, and downed the shot. Her face scrunched up as if she'd sucked a lemon, making her signature red lips pucker, the blacklight turning them dark, unlike her platinum pixie cut, which glowed.

"I wish I had a camera right now," Darcy said to her.

"Me too," said Amber, Krista's cousin. "Your face is priceless."

"Oh yeah? Let's see how you guys do with that nasty stuff." Carrie glanced around the table. "Well? What are you chickenshits waiting for?"

"We don't all have the liver of a biker like you," replied Krista, laughing as she downed the shot.

"Yeah, you've drunken us all under the table at least once. You're amazing. What are you, like ninety pounds?" asked Darcy.

"Very funny," Carrie said. "It's not my fault you girls are jealous of my liver. I have a gift. I'm not going to waste it."

Laughing, Amber and Darcy knocked back their shots.

"That's gross," Darcy said. "It tastes like paint thinner."

"Speaking of paint, didn't you mention earlier we rescued you from painting?" Krista asked. "Are you nearly done?"

"Not exactly."

"Really? You always tell us how small your place is. What were you doing all day?" Krista's question provided a golden opportunity to bring up the François story. Not that she needed it. The story was hilarious. Most people would have told their friends the moment they saw them. So why was she keeping quiet?

"I'll be right back with more shooters, ladies." A waitress said as she cleared away their glasses. "Guys over there just bought you another round." She pointed left with her chin.

"Wow. Big spenders," Carrie said. "I know it's likely you they want, Kris, but I'm going to give them a wave before you shut them down." She turned towards the men, then turned back to Krista, grabbing her arm. "I think we went to school with those guys. Tony..." she waved her hands near her head, trying to conjure up his name like a magician. "Tony Harper and Mick Price."

"Oh my God, yes," Amber said, then leaned closer to Darcy. "Most girls had crushes on those guys at one time or another. I'm going to wave them over."

"Should be fun," Darcy said when she wanted to say, *please don't*. She knew what was coming. It was hard enough to fit into a group that had grown up together, but at least they'd all worked a few years and no longer lived in the same neighborhood. The fact that Darcy and Krista worked side by side gave them something in common. But running into old friends, well, that typically resulted in a trip down memory lane.

And she wasn't wrong. Other than amusing her friends by pulling out a party trick and pretending to be Australian during introductions, she barely said a word. Smile and nod, smile and nod. When she had toasted to meeting some guys, this wasn't what she'd intended. God, where was that shot?

Finally, she thought as she turned to the tap on her shoulder, expecting the waitress. Instead, she faced Stefan, her kind-of-ex.

Okay, she was never making another toast again.

"Hey, Darce."

"Hey, yourself," she said, stepping away from the table so as not to give away the fact that she was not Australian. Not that anyone took notice. She couldn't pop the bubble of shared history. Inhaling deeply to recharge her confidence, she got a lungful of smoke instead. Coughing, she stepped into a hug. "It's great to see you. I hardly recognize you without the beard."

"Yeah, it was time for a change." He smiled, running a hand across his chin. "I'm really glad you're here. I can't believe I haven't seen you since you left the university." Nice, but he couldn't have missed her that much. He did have her number and could have called anytime in the past few months. Then again, so could she have.

"The joys of contract work," she said. "Here today, gone tomorrow. Tell me how your thesis is going?"

"Oh, you know. Same as always. Slow." He moved closer. Intimately closer. "So I was wondering," he said, tilting his head to the side, giving her a coy smile, "would you want to go dance or something? We can catch up."

Darcy knew *catching up* translated to *going back to his place*. What to do? What to do? Remain on the outskirts with this group of people or go down a memory lane of her own? She decided when he reached out and took her hand. It was warm and familiar, and she needed that right now. "Yeah, okay, I like that idea." She smiled, squeezing his hand before letting it go. "Just let me tell my friends."

She leaned against Krista, speaking directly into her ear. "A friend of mine, Stefan, from my last job, is here, so we're going to catch up."

Krista's eyebrows raised as she peered over Darcy's shoulder. "He's cute. What kind of friend are we talking about here? The kind with benefits?"

"Something like that."

"And why haven't you mentioned him before?"

"I don't know. I haven't seen him in a while."

"Well, have fun, but tell me if you're leaving with him so I don't worry."

"Yeah, I'm pretty sure we're headed there, so I'll see you at work Monday."

"You sure? You don't seem excited."

Darcy forced a grin and winked. "I know what I'm doing."

Stefan led her onto the dance floor. Was this his way of pretending that asking her to dance wasn't code for "let's have sex"? They both understood what they were to one another. Why waste time? The sooner they left, the sooner they got it over with.

Wait. That attitude can't be healthy.

She attempted to swallow down the thought, but it lodged in her throat, and despite the stifling hot air on the dance floor, Darcy's blood turned cold. The bass pounded through every cell of her body, churning up the watermelon schnapps in her stomach. Her head throbbed. As another song started, she wondered how much more jostling she could take.

Stefan moved closer and closer until their bodies were pressed together, then he leaned in and kissed her. Finally, they were getting down to business. Darcy waited for her body to respond. It didn't. Not that she pulled away. Maybe it would take a while for things to heat up. Like her car in winter.

She tried summoning the excitement of those first heady nights together, how he brought light to weeks and months of darkness. Remembering how their intimacy kept her loneliness at bay. But tonight, his kiss fell flat. Sure, she looked like the Darcy he'd known, but it was a shell, and inside was hollow.

Dramatic much? What the hell was wrong with her?

He pulled back from the kiss, grabbing her hips and grinding against her as he nuzzled against her ear. "God, you turn me on so much," he whispered.

Why? How? Surely kissing her right now was like kissing a statue.

He continued, "I'd forgotten how good we are together."

Apparently, so had she. Maybe she should try again. "Yeah, me too," she said, hoping to convince herself as she wrapped her arms around Stefan's neck and kissed him.

Still nothing.

"You want to get going?" he asked. His words fell like a guillotine, severing a tiny piece of her heart. He couldn't tell that her kisses were devoid of desire. All that mattered was the mechanics of kissing and, later, access to her body. That was pretty much it. She was replaceable. It had always been that way. Why was it bothering her tonight?

Her knees almost gave out from the weight of her baggage. With her arms still around his neck, she hung on like a person drowning. Had that piece of her heart lodged in her brain? Because she was definitely losing it.

"You okay?" he asked when she took too long to reply.

"I actually feel kind of sick. We had a lot of the one-dollar shooters. I better go home." She'd only had two shooters.

"You don't think it'll pass? I can get you some water."

"I wish, but I don't want you to spend the night holding my hair back as I vomit into your toilet." It saddened her how easily the lie came.

"I don't get it. You're not acting wasted." He ran a hand up and down her arm, remaining hopeful.

"I'm not. It's the mixing of schnapps with the sushi I had earlier." Another lie.

"Ew. Yeah. Bad combination. You'll be okay getting home then?"

She smiled and laid a hand on his chest, giving him one more quick kiss. "I'm good, thanks." And she was. At least with this particular decision.

Outside the bar, the streets were busy with Saturday night traffic, so she walked home, past bars and restaurants and groups of friends, like she had in cities across the globe. This time, as in her move to Montreal, was supposed to be different, so why had she never felt as lonely as in the place she wanted to call home? At least she had turned down a night with Stefan. As funny and kind as he was, leaving with him would have meant taking a step backward. And thanks to the surprise of a naked guy in Becks' apartment, she realized that's precisely where she didn't want to go.

3

A week later, Darcy found herself once again at Becks' apartment. The aroma of Thai food greeted her at the door. Not a problem. She loved Thai food.

Becks opened the door and welcomed her in. "Thanks again for taking care of my princess."

"Anytime." Darcy kicked off her shoes and walked into the kitchen. "But next time, give me some warning if someone else is staying here. I caught François by surprise as he walked out of the shower. Poor guy dropped his towel."

Becks tilted her head back and laughed. "Oh yeah. Oops. But if François still has that awesome bod, I did you a favor. So you're welcome."

Darcy raised an eyebrow. "Did you and François ever...?"

"Nah." She waved her hands dismissively. "Not my type."

"Every guy is your type, no?"

"Funny. And it depends. As far as François is concerned, I guess we were friends for too long, not to mention the pictures of us as toddlers, naked together in a kiddie pool." Becks shivered, assumably with disgust. "So yeah, we never went there."

"Makes sense," Darcy said as Becks passed her a martini.

"Here, santé." Becks clinked her glass against Darcy's, and they each took a sip.

"You and Jason have fun?"

"Yeah. It was fine." Becks grabbed two plates off the counter and placed them on her small table.

"Fine is hardly a ringing endorsement."

Becks gave a slight shrug, pulled out a chair, and sat at the table, signaling with a tilt of her head for Darcy to do the same. "We had fun. We ate. We skied. We had sex."

"Stop." Darcy held up her hand. "I don't want you to tell me the details."

"Who me? Never," Becks replied, causing them both to laugh.

"So, where's Jason now?" Darcy asked.

"At the lab. Where he always is." Becks rolled her eyes. "I'll be so glad when he finally gets around to finishing experiments and can begin writing up his PhD."

"You did meet at the lab. Surely you knew what you were getting into."

"Yeah, but still." Becks sighed and began opening the takeout containers. "Enough about that. I have exciting news." Becks reached behind the Pad Thai and slid a pamphlet over to Darcy.

"It's a real estate flyer," Darcy said, preferring to have been passed some food.

"No shit."

"Wait. Are you buying a house?" At the thought of this possibility, several conflicting emotions crashed around Darcy's brain like bumper cars. Jealousy, because that was a significant step towards building her life and relief because it wasn't her. As much as she wanted it, the paperwork alone gave her anxiety.

"No. We're buying a house. Well, not an entire house, the middle floor of a triplex."

"By we, you mean you and Jason, right?" She knew from the intensity of Becks' stare that that was not, in fact, who *we* referred to. Jealousy and relief disappeared to be wholly replaced with some solid old-fashioned fear.

"No, ma'am." Becks pointed to Darcy, then herself. "You and me, babe. You and me."

"That's crazy."

"Smart. Not crazy. My parents are friends with the sellers. We'll get an amazing deal and no fees because we don't need a real estate agent. My mom's a lawyer. She'll review the contract and stuff."

"I don't have money for a house."

"Uh, yeah. You do. That account or bond or whatever it is you said your parents had for you for this specific reason."

Shit. When did she tell Becks that? Swallowing was hard, and the back of her neck prickled with heat. "This is a lot to ask." What was wrong with her voice?

"Relax. I didn't propose to you. We both need a place to live, right? Instead of wasting money on rent, we'll now have an investment. Money makes money." Becks rubbed her thumb against her first two fingers.

Why did she have to be so logical? Darcy knew her parents would agree with Becks one hundred percent. And isn't that why Darcy moved here? To put down roots? Was she not lamenting her lack of progress earlier this week? "What if we don't get along?"

"It'll work out fine. Neither of us is the touchy-feely-over-emotional-I-have-to-tell-my-friend-everything type, and my mom will write out the terms and conditions for when one of us wants to sell. We'd be crazy not to take this place. I mean, look at it."

Darcy scanned the photos. Exposed brick, hardwood floors, soaker tub. They made her apartment look like a storage locker. "I'll have to think about it."

"Of course, now eat up. My mom is picking us up in thirty minutes to view the place."

Darcy choked on her martini.

Becks shook her head as she patted Darcy on the back with one hand and passed her some food with the other. "I thought living all over the world made you adventurous. Little did I know that one apartment viewing could bring you to your knees." She was teasing, her tone friendly, but Becks liked getting her way. And she usually did. Once Becks had a plan, it was much easier to go along than fight it, so Darcy would humor her and go on the tour. They weren't going to sign anything, right?

Wrong.

"How?" she asked the universe. No one answered. Not even Peaches, who sat sunning herself in Darcy's window. *How did I go from seeing this apartment six weeks ago to waking up here for the first time?* Darcy leaped out of bed, preventing herself from going down a spiral of self-doubt, reminding herself that this was what she wanted. Wasn't it? A permanent place to call home? Yes. Yes. Of course. Just keep moving forward, and if she couldn't do it mentally, she'd do it physically.

It was time to explore the neighborhood. "I'm going to go walk around and find a coffee shop. Want to come?" she said to Becks, who was sitting at the kitchen island blowing on freshly painted nails.

"What? No. I invited a bunch of people over for a housewarming and need to grab some stuff."

"For tonight?"

"Yeah. It'll be fun. Our first party."

"You should have said something. I was looking forward to a soak in that awesome tub with a book."

"Oh, come on. Don't be so boring. This will be much better."

"I don't have much choice, do I?"

"Nope. Now give me a few more minutes to let my nails dry, and we'll head out. I could use the extra set of hands." She held her fingers out for inspection. "Like the color? It goes perfectly with the top I'm wearing tonight." She wiggled her fingers at Darcy.

"Yeah. Nice," Darcy said as Becks hopped off the stool and disappeared into her bedroom.

Darcy sighed, poured herself the cold dregs at the bottom of the coffee pot, and put her mug in the microwave. Hardly the cafe au lait she'd been thinking about five minutes ago. Still, even the dregs tasted better in her exposed brick kitchen. She drank it in peace and then put it in the dishwasher, along with Becks' breakfast dishes. They had a dishwasher. She ran her hand over the controls. "I love you," she said to it.

"Hate to interrupt your moment, but let's go," Becks said as she walked to the hall closet. "And grab that list off the island. I don't want to forget anything."

Darcy scanned the list. "Holy, how many people are we feeding tonight?"

"We don't have to buy everything. I was brainstorming."

"Well, I was going to suggest we walk, but there's no way we can carry all this."

Becks snatched the list away, and Darcy grabbed her car keys before stepping outside and locking the door. As they descended the stairs to the street, *their* street, the sun poked out from behind puffy white clouds. Suddenly a party didn't seem like such a bad idea. Why not celebrate? She'd call Krista, Carrie, and Amber when she got back.

Jason arrived first, bringing a few bottles of wine and a houseplant. Even though he'd helped them move in, Becks gave him another tour of her bedroom with the door closed, so Darcy was left alone to welcome guests. Within thirty minutes, the place was packed. How many friends did Becks have, and when was she coming back out?

Darcy had just shut the front door when she heard another knock. She opened it to a grinning François.

"What are you doing here?" she asked, her tone unintentionally brisk. Wasn't he supposed to be in Mexico?

"Uh, Becks invited me."

"Yes. Of course. I meant...I thought you were traveling. Oh, never mind." She grabbed his arm and pulled him in. "Thank God you're here. I could use the help."

"It never hurts to be wanted, even if it is only to be put to work," he said, leaning in to kiss both her cheeks.

As his stubble brushed against her and his warm lips made brief contact with her cheeks, her blood was replaced by something warm, velvety, and chocolatey sweet.

Interesting. Maybe she'd had too much to drink. Or not enough.

She blinked and realized he was holding out a bottle of wine and a can of cat food with a bow on it, expecting her to take them. Dear Lord, he'd brought Peaches a housewarming gift.

Darcy reached out, taking the wine and cat food. "Peaches is in my bedroom tonight, but I'll make sure to tell her about your gift."

"I'd hate for her to forget about me," he said, giving her a goofy grin.

She stared at him. Something was different.

"It's my tooth," he said. "I lost the crown in Mexico and haven't seen the dentist yet."

"How'd you do that, the chip, originally?"

"Hockey."

"Of course." He answered her question, but she continued to stare. "I see it now, the hockey player, the scar under your eye, the one on your chin, and if I'm not mistaken, you've had your nose broken."

"Twice."

"Huh." As interesting as all that was, it was his blue eyes that drew her in. She'd noticed them the first time they'd met, and they captivated her now. They were open, metaphorically, in that they weren't afraid to reveal who he was. Could they see other people as deeply? Could he see her?

It wasn't until he gave her a slow blink while raising his eyebrows that she realized her hand rested on his cheek and snapped herself out of her trance. "I'm so sorry," she said, taking a step back. "I hope I didn't embarrass you."

"All good. How about a tour?"

"That's going to have to wait. Becks and Jason disappeared into her room, and now I'm playing hostess to all these people," she said. "Although this is pretty much the entire place. You can see the whole flat minus the bathroom and bedrooms."

"Flat. That's not commonly used here."

"Well, like I said when we first met, I'm not from here, well, born here, but then we moved, oh, you know what I mean. Now, come on in and have a drink. I could sure use one."

"Rough night?"

"Not exactly, but it would be better if Becks came up for air. These are her friends, after all." Amber and Carrie were both busy. Krista was going to try to stop by.

"You said at the door you needed my help. What can I do?"

"Don't offer unless you are willing to help. I will take you up on it."

"I only know you and Becks, so this will give me something to do."

"Okay. How are you at making drinks? Most people brought their own beer and stuff, there's a cooler in the kitchen and one on the balcony, but Becks wanted a signature cocktail. Can you make a crantini?"

"Can't be too hard. Point me in the right direction."

She led him into the kitchen where Becks had set up a makeshift bar, and he picked up a piece of paper with the drink recipe. "I got this. Don't you worry."

"I owe you one," she said and turned back towards the door, just as Becks and Jason emerged. "Finally," she whispered to Becks. "Your turn on door duty."

"Yes, Mom," Becks said and walked into the living room with Jason, who looked more and more like a lumberjack than a scientist since Becks had asked him to grow a beard.

Maybe now she could relax a bit.

"Here," she felt a nudge and turned. François held a drink out to her. "Tell me how I did."

She took a sip. It was strong and exactly what she needed. "Almost as good as the ones Becks makes. Cheers." She downed the entire drink like it was a shot. "More please," she said and passed him the empty glass.

"Easy, there. That was two ounces of booze."

"Like I said, more, please."

Knowing her limit, Darcy took her time with the second crantini, then switched to water. Tomorrow she would explore the neighborhood, and she didn't want to do that with a hangover.

Crowds of strangers never intimidated her. She'd walked into enough new classrooms and situations to overcome that fear. Still, she was glad to see Krista and Marco walk through the door.

Darcy excused herself from a conversation about the upcoming jazz festival and greeted them.

"I'm so glad you called," Krista said. "I never saw your old place."

"Well, that's because it was nothing like this one. Like I've said, it was way too small for more than one person. Come on, let me get you both a drink." Darcy directed them towards the martini station.

François gave her a quick nod but said nothing because he was mixing drinks for a couple. There was something familiar about them. No. Not the couple, the man. Darcy stopped abruptly, causing Krista to plow right into her. Of course Stefan would be here. She'd met him through Becks.

"What's wrong?" asked Krista.

Darcy, too fixated on Stefan, couldn't reply.

"Wait, is that the guy from..." Krista asked. Darcy nodded her answer. She'd never admitted to Krista what really happened that night. Not that it mattered now.

"Oh," was all Krista could say.

Stefan's arm encircled the woman's shoulders possessively like he was staking a claim. The woman was no different, with her hand in a back pocket of his jeans. François said something, and the three of them laughed, then Stefan leaned his head against the woman's, whispering something that made her laugh harder. Then he kissed the top of her head. Such a small gesture, but even Darcy could tell it was laden with deep emotion. The man who swore he'd never be tied down was in love. He'd never looked at Darcy like that. Not even close. Hell, no one had. She was supposed to be the one moving forward. How was this fair?

4

Sometimes life could really knock you down with a surprise punch. The thing was, to be a competitor, you had to pull yourself up and continue on. Even if you felt outmatched.

Darcy had never prepared for this outcome of events. Not that she longed for Stefan. That wasn't the point. The point was...well, therein lay the problem: she wasn't sure. And if you weren't sure of the problem, how could you fix it?

"Fuck it." Darcy marched over to François and slid an arm around his waist. All logic went out the window as her emotions collided at the intersection of indignation and indifference. "Hey babe, miss me?"

He looked down at her, raising an eyebrow. She gave him a strained smile as the warm tingling of perspiration began across her hairline. If he didn't play along, she'd have no choice but to move. Far, far away. "I wanted to introduce you to some friends, but as it turns out, I also know Stefan."

His expression changed from confusion to understanding, and he slid an arm around her. Relief and gratitude hit her like a tsunami, and when he gave her a tiny squeeze of support, she melted against him.

"Congratulations, Darce. Becks told us you were a co-owner with her. This place is great," Stefan said, not acting the slightest bit uncomfortable. And why would he? "Oh hey, this is Clara. She's in the lab next to mine."

"Nice to meet you," Darcy said. "I hope your bench work goes faster than his. You'd think he was doing a joint thesis in biochemistry and theology with the number of prayers he says for his experiments."

"That sounds like him," Clara said. "And if he's not praying for results, he's cursing the ones he gets."

Stefan laughed "Well, everything helps."

"So, whose lab are you in?" Clara asked.

"None. I was there as a temp in the biochemistry department office."

"Huh, too bad you're not there anymore. I've been there several times this week trying to sort some stuff out. I could use a friend."

"Yeah. Too bad. Anyway, do you mind if I steal this guy away now that you have drinks?"

"François was telling us about his trip to Mexico. Sounds amazing. Were you with him?" Stefan asked with nothing but genuine curiosity, making her want to kick him in the shins. "Clara and I were thinking of going down there sometime soon."

Darcy opened her mouth without any idea what to say, but François began talking before she could reply. "No, I already had the trip booked before we met. I'm lucky, though, because she was able to tell me about some amazing places to visit. The kind of places that locals go to."

"Oh yeah? I didn't know you've been to Mexico," Stefan said. Had she told him she'd lived there? She wasn't sure. Their interactions were never about talking.

"Are you kidding?" François said. "Darcy used to live there. Having her there would have made the trip so much better, but as it was, I had to settle for following her recommendations, all the while missing her but feeling so connected because she'd walked where I was walking and had seen what I was seeing."

"Oh honey, you're so sweet," she said and impulsively stood on her toes to kiss him. Mistake. A bolt of electricity shocked her entire body the moment their lips touched. The arm François wrapped around her waist tightened, drawing her against him. Hers did the same while her pulse quickened at their closeness. As his other hand slid up her arm, it left a trail of fire before cupping her face, his fingers in her hair, the pad of his thumb caressing her cheek. God, she wanted more and leaned in, deepening the kiss until her entire body tingled with high-voltage power. Surely, she must be glowing. Darcy had never understood the reference to sparks or chemistry until now.

Whoa.

By the time they parted, Stefan and Clara had moved on.

"Thanks," she said, trying to calm her heartbeat and control her breathing.

"Yeah. Anytime," François said, leaning his head against hers. "I hope I didn't overdo that last part."

"No. It was perfect." She smiled reassuringly while wondering if he meant the kiss or his comments on Mexico.

"Hey," Krista said as she stood before Darcy, eyeing François. "Is it hot in here, or is it just me?" She fanned herself with her hand. "So you going to introduce us to your friend here?"

"Oh yeah. Sorry. Krista, this is François. Krista and I work side by side at the fracture clinic. And this is Marco, her fiancé."

"Pleasure to meet you both," said François.

"You too," said Marco.

"I hope we can find a place this awesome. You did well, girl." Krista turned to François. "So was her old place really as small as she claims?"

"I've never seen it."

"Never?" Krista's eyebrows scrunch together in confusion.

"Nope," said Darcy. "We barely know each other. He's Becks' friend." And yet, she hadn't withdrawn her arm from around his waist.

"So if you two aren't...close, how'd you figure out what she wanted from you just now?"

He shrugged. "I'm no rocket scientist, but when someone pretends to be your girlfriend, you better go along. Although now I'm curious what that guy means to her."

"He doesn't mean anything."

"Ah, so you were looking for an excuse to kiss me."

With the arm that remained around his waist, despite her telling it to let him go, she gave him a pinch.

"Ow." He laughed while rubbing his side. "Violence won't curtail my curiosity."

"He means nothing. It was my pride I was protecting. Happy now?"

"Interesting," Krista said. "Well, whatever's going on, I'll be the last to find out. She never tells me anything even though we sit side by side every darn day, right, Darcy? Trust me, you need to pry out every bit of information with this girl."

Darcy gave the three of them a shrug because Krista wasn't wrong.

5

ONE OF THE BEST things Darcy did when she moved to Montreal was to start volunteering at the animal shelter. As a child, she'd taken in a stray and knew firsthand the difference a dog could make in someone's life. Now, as an adult, she could make an even bigger impact. And thanks to that determination, she never missed a shift. Not even in the kind of driving rain that beat down on her car as she pulled into the parking lot.

"Hold on," Darcy yelled as she ran towards the doors.

Annique, the shelter's office manager, was about to lock up. Luckily she heard Darcy call out and opened the door so she could run in. "I don't know how you find the energy to work then come here to volunteer. Especially on a night like this," Annique said.

Darcy shrugged. "It's peaceful, and the data entry is not hard, just tedious." She kept "and it's better than sitting at home with nothing to do" to herself.

Not that she didn't like her new flat, she did. In fact, she loved it. But one month in, she still felt something was missing from her new life. For starters, living with Becks left her as lonely as before. Not that she expected Becks to babysit her, but the girl was never home. And sure, exploring the new neighborhood had introduced her to new stores and a funky coffee shop, but she remained an outsider. So, to compensate, she increased her time volunteering at the animal shelter.

"Well, better you than me," Annique said, grabbing her coat and purse. "I only managed to work on the database for about fifteen minutes today. We were busier than normal, and two dogs got adopted."

"Fantastic," Darcy said, removing her wet jean jacket and hanging it on the back of her chair. Nothing was more rewarding than helping an animal find its forever family. "I love a happy ending."

"Fingers crossed they aren't returned," Annique said with a wave as she left.

Darcy clenched her jaw, incensed by human nature. Animals were not ill-fitting articles of clothing to be returned, exchanged, or discarded. Of course, she realized that on occasion, situations arose in which a beloved pet needed rehoming, but some people thought of pets as nothing more than accessories, surprised at the amount of work and unwilling to do it. Those people drove her nuts. Dogs, cats, bunnies, and guinea pigs deserved a forever home.

With Annique gone for the day, Darcy retrieved a stack of folders, trying to remain undaunted by the fact that there was paper everywhere. It was 1999, not 1979. Having information in a database (her initiative) would save so much time. Why could Annique not see that? Darcy dreamed of having a job like Annique's, managing an animal shelter. Waking up every day with an opportunity to transform the lives of animals and the humans who adopted them would be a chance Darcy would never refuse. She would do it even if it meant a permanent position over her preference for contract work. Why didn't Annique realize how lucky she was? Why didn't she try harder? These questions stuck in Darcy's brain every time she found a process that needed improving, which was frequent.

Darcy stretched, hoping to release her frustrations, before firing up the database. She had yet to open the first file when a cat started meowing. Unable to focus, she walked down the hall to the kitty condo—the name she invented for the bank of cat cages close to the reception desk. Darcy located the unhappy cat and opened the cage.

"Why hello there, Mr. Fluff," she said as she picked up the tiny, cuddly ball of grey fur. The meowing stopped immediately. "Oh, is that why you were meowing? You were lonely? Well, why don't you hang out with me for a while?"

Darcy made him a bed from a discarded cardigan draped over the arm of the chair next to hers. As soon as she put the cat down, he gave his face a quick wash, curled up, and fell asleep. With Mr. Fluff settled, Darcy worked almost solidly until eight-thirty; her only interruption was a night technician searching for an escaped rabbit with a broken foot.

She was in the middle of entering her last file when a flash of lightning was followed immediately by a clap of thunder, shaking the building and leaving them in utter darkness. "You've got to be kidding," Darcy said to the dark. "I can't remember when I last hit save." When the auxiliary lights powered on, at last, she carried Mr. Fluff back to his cage and then organized the desk for tomorrow morning. Whatever files she didn't save were gone—nothing could be done about it now.

She went to the back, waving goodbye to the technicians, then stepping out into the darkness and rain. She pulled her jacket over her head and ran to her car, regretting her decision to park out front. Thanks to the blackout, she stepped in puddles the size of small lakes and nearly walked into a lamp post, but she made it.

"All right, Glücksschwein, we need some better weather." She reached up to give her lucky pig a poke in the belly, but he was no longer hanging from her mirror. "Glücksschwein!" In a panic, she turned on the interior lights, rifling through everything, nearly tearing her car apart. "Oh my God, wo ist mein schwein?"

She found him on the driver-side floor, wet and dirty from her feet. "Don't scare me like that." Glücksschwein had traveled with her since she was eight. She couldn't lose him now. Darcy futilely tried to wipe the mud off his body using her jeans, but it smudged instead. Giving up, she poked his belly and placed him on the dashboard. Immediately the rain began to lessen. "Why, thank you, Glücksschwein," she said. "I guess you felt like you owed me one for the panic attack."

The dim interior light highlighted all the fur Mr. Fluff left on her shirt. Of course, she'd worn black, and it would take a miracle to get all the fur off, but a cuddle with a cat was worth it. Maybe she'd double-up and have Peaches sit on her lap for a while when she got home.

The image of François holding Peaches in Becks' old apartment popped into her head, as did his thoughtfulness of bringing the cat a housewarming gift and, oh God, that kiss. She thought of that often. Unfortunately, the reason why they kissed soon followed.

The weight of emotions that night evoked fell heavier than the rain. Is that why she didn't ask for his number? Was she afraid of feeling deeply? Because she would fall for him if she let herself, and being casual wouldn't suffice. She wanted more. She wanted...ugh, she refused to think of the word. Considering life had shown her time and time again that nothing was permanent, it was hardly surprising.

Self-awareness sucked.

"Well, Glücksschwein, any advice?"

Fortunately, Glücksschwein had the good sense to remain silent.

6

Darcy awoke to Peaches perched on her chest, staring at her with big green eyes. So much for sleeping in. "You know, Becks lives here too. You could go back to waking her up," Darcy said to the cat, knowing she would do no such thing. "Hey, it's not my fault that waking Becks up is like waking the dead." Peaches lifted a paw and tapped Darcy on the cheek. "Fine. I'll get up." Gently rolling over forced Peaches to jump off, landing gracefully on the floor and instantly meowing. "A little patience, please."

The kitchen was bright with morning sun, last night's thunderstorm long gone. "Isn't it beautiful," she said as she gave the impatient Peaches a scoop of food and fresh water before making a pot of coffee to the sound of contented crunching.

Fresh air blew in an open window, bringing with it the scent of lilac and the sound of bird song. Everything felt better in the sunshine. Last night was a blip in her programming. The storm messed with her the way it had with her database. Move forward. That's all she could do.

While she sat at the island waiting for the coffee to finish brewing, basking in a beam of sunlight, and enjoying spring's fragrance, she wondered what all the seasons would be like here. Where would they put the Christmas tree? Would they host a Thanksgiving dinner? Dreams of creating a home, not just a house, warmed her more than the sun. Even after a month, she still couldn't believe her luck. She'd moved from her blank box to here, and not only that, it was hers, or at least half of it was. Yes, indeed, Glücksschwein had come through again.

As the coffee maker sputtered to a stop, Darcy grabbed her favorite mug, filled it with coffee and milk, and continued to savor the morning's tranquility.

Unfortunately, her peaceful morning didn't last long. Becks came out of her room and straight for the coffee maker. Luckily Becks wasn't a talker in the morning. Darcy heard the bathroom door close and knew Jason must also be there. She liked Jason, not that she knew him well, but he genuinely cared about Becks, and given Becks' dating history, that wasn't typical.

As soon as the shower turned on, Becks began talking. "So Jason has almost finished his experiments and will be writing his thesis soon."

"That's great. He must be happy about that."

"Yeah, well, he's been looking at post-docs and is planning on going to Europe. Most likely Germany."

Darcy's stomach knotted. She had a feeling as to where this conversation was going based on how Becks nervously played with the mug in her hands. "Germany is a fun place to live."

"That's why I want to go with him." Becks looked up from her coffee. "He asked me to go last night. He also asked me to move in with him for the remaining time we're here."

"Oh, wow. When's he moving in?"

"Actually, I'm going to move into his place. And don't worry. I'll find you a roommate, so my half of the mortgage will be covered."

"Thanks, but I didn't think you liked his place." Darcy swallowed hard, hoping her voice sounded normal, hiding the ball of dread that formed in her belly, increasing in size by the second.

Becks leaned closer and whispered. "I don't, but it's not for long. Plus, I have this place to return to if it doesn't work out."

"Makes sense, I guess," Darcy said, forcing a smile. "Congratulations."

"Thanks, I knew you'd understand." Becks topped up her coffee. "There's one more thing. Can Peaches stay here? Jason is allergic to cats." As if choreographed, they heard Jason sneezing from the bathroom. Becks gave her a weak smile. "He hasn't taken any allergy meds this morning."

"Of course Peaches can stay."

"Yay. You're the best." Becks gave Darcy a kiss on the head as she walked by her and returned to her room. Darcy topped off her coffee and retreated to her room, avoiding Becks and Jason.

She sat on her bed, not realizing Peaches had followed her until she jumped up on the bed and curled into a ball. Absentmindedly, she scratched Peaches on the head. Why was her throat burning? Her eyes blurring? Was it because Becks was the closest Darcy had come to having a best friend? Maybe. So what if they didn't share their emotions or reveal their secrets like TV best friends did. Her leaving still stung. But hey, they were both adults, and Becks could do what she wanted. And so long as Becks met her financial obligations regarding the mortgage, did it matter who Darcy lived with? No.

Yes.

Sort of. Because as Darcy laid back on the bed, with the warmth of a cat at her side, she couldn't help but fear that her long-time dream had gone up in smoke. She thought owning a house in the city where she was born would give her a sense of belonging. Home. Friends. Community.

"It's all an illusion, isn't it, Peaches? At least for me. Nothing around me sticks."

Peaches replied with a stretch, remaining at her side, unlike Becks.

Later that night, Darcy returned from her volunteer shift at the shelter to find Becks at home. Still buzzing from a successful Saturday, as three dogs and two cats were adopted, Darcy longed to share the sense of fulfillment this brought her. What could be more rewarding than watching a dog's reaction when it realizes it had a forever home? How they knew was a mystery, but they must, judging by their changed facial expressions and tail wags. It made all the hard work worth it.

She might have opened up to Becks had Becks not told her she was moving out. Not that it mattered, Darcy never got past hello before Becks leaped off the couch and said, "Guess what? I have awesome news."

Darcy wasn't sure how much more of Becks' news she could take. "Oh yeah? What's that?"

"I found you the perfect roommate."

"Seriously? That was fast. I thought we agreed to let me meet them first."

"You already did." Becks practically vibrated with excitement. "It's François."

"François?" It was nearly a yell. "As in your childhood friend?"

"Yeah. He needs a place and is looking for a job. Not many landlords will let you sign a lease while unemployed."

"Can't he live with his parents or something?" Anything but move in here. Being attracted to her new roommate was far from ideal. He'd probably be a good roommate too. He was funny. He liked the cat. And he made a good martini. Dammit. Could she keep her attraction hidden? She wasn't that good of an actor.

"They live in a tiny condo, and his brother lives in Ottawa. This place is perfect."

Darcy swallowed down panic. "I guess. So how long is it for?"

"I don't know. Hopefully he'll like it here and stay long-term. I thought you'd be happy about this, but you have the weirdest look on your face."

Darcy made a conscious effort to relax and force a smile. "No. It's fine. I mean, great. I like him. We get along. I'm just tired from a long day at the shelter."

Her desire to talk about her day was gone. What she needed was a drink. Or two. Oh, and they needed to be strong. Very strong. "How about you make me a martini to celebrate. I'm going to miss those when you're gone," she said to Becks, leaving her in the kitchen. Darcy needed to sit down. She kicked off her shoes and collapsed onto the sofa, hoping it wouldn't take long for that martini.

At least that wish came true. Becks delivered her drink within minutes and then sat beside her, putting her feet on the coffee table. "Cheers, Darce. Here's to Jason and me and you and François."

"Cheers." Darcy took a big swallow. François. Moving in. Yikes.

7

In less than a week, Becks had moved out, and Darcy found herself standing on the landing outside her front door, tense with the expectation that François would be on the other side. They were to be roommates. Nothing more. Besides, as far as she could tell, François had not demonstrated any attraction toward her. Not that she was a mind reader, but he'd made no effort to contact her since the party. Despite the fireworks he'd set off within Darcy, their kiss had been for show, so roommates, friends, or whatever platonic relationship they ended up having, Darcy would deal.

But first, she had to open the door and walk in. Challenge accepted.

"Hey, roomy," François said, drilling in the whole roommate situation. He turned off the TV and walked over to greet her.

"Hey, you," Darcy replied. "Becks told me you were moving in today. I hope everything went well."

"Not much to move. Just my clothes."

"That makes it easy, I guess." Craving beer, she opened the fridge, finding it stuffed with enough food to feed her for a week. No, make that a month. "I think you brought more than clothes." She dug her beer out from the back and chugged down about half, wondering why his presence made her thirsty.

"Yeah. I had time to shop," François said, standing beside her, close enough for her to feel the heat radiate off his body. Her skin broke into goosebumps, and she took a few more long sips of beer.

"I thought I'd make dinner for you since it's my first night here," François continued.

"Just me or an army?"

"It's not all for tonight. What can I say? I like my food." He let out a small laugh. "Although, without hockey and all the recent hiking, I should probably cut back." He tapped his stomach, then turned sideways, running his hand down his torso. "Looking this fine takes work."

"I bet," Darcy said with a wry smile. "Speaking of hockey, you got your tooth fixed."

"I did." He gave her a big grin. "The best part was when the dentist held up a chart of yellowy-whites so it would blend in with my real teeth."

Darcy nearly snorted beer out her nose, and soon they were both laughing. "I'm sorry," Darcy said when the laughter died, wiping a tear from her eye. "Something about that struck me as funny." More than that, although she'd hardly tell François. She'd needed that release of tension and felt all the better for it. "So, how much hockey did you play exactly? Most kids don't have as many battle scars."

"Yeah, I guess not. I played for the Mont-Laurier Royales. They're a professional—"

She held up her hand for him to stop. "Don't worry. Even I'm aware of who they are. So you've got some talent."

"Well, not enough for the NHL, but yeah, I do okay. Or did. When I aged out of junior hockey, I went to university, worked a few months after graduation, before—" He abruptly stopped talking to grab a glass of water. "Before deciding to travel. And there's my life in a nutshell, not that you asked."

"Except for why you returned early from Mexico. You never said why you came back at the housewarming. I assumed you would be taking off again," Darcy said, picking at the label on her beer bottle. Wanting to sit in the kitchen all night learning about his childhood, hockey, and anything else was completely normal, right? Surely, roommates did that.

"Oh right, well, my friend had had enough. We'd traveled for a year, then came back here, and I think that's when his attitude towards the next leg of our trip began to change. After a month in Mexico, he admitted he wanted to go home, and, to be honest, I kind of felt the same way. It was time to get back to the real world. And here we are."

Darcy nodded as if she understood the draw of home.

"So come on, sit and relax while I work my magic in the kitchen as thanks for letting me move in."

"That was all Becks, but who am I to argue?"

Darcy had another beer while François cooked. Her roommate had an easy way about him, and they chatted about his last few weeks traveling while he prepared the food. He insisted dinner was simple, fettuccine noodles with fresh garlic, tomatoes, and spinach, gently heated and broken down into a creamy sauce. However, most things that took more than a few minutes in the microwave seemed complicated to Darcy.

When dinner was ready, he opened some wine, poured them a glass, and placed two dinner plates on the island.

"This smells so delicious," Darcy said. Her mouth may or may not have been watering.

"Oh, I almost forgot Miss Peach. That's the level of friendship we're at now, nicknames."

"Oh yeah? What's hers for you?"

"It's hard to say because some of it becomes lost in translation, but I'm pretty sure it's *Hey, I'm Hungry*." He put a scoop of food into Peaches' bowl, along with a few treats. "Peaches, dinner," he called out as he sat. "Got to impress two ladies tonight, don't I?"

"Cheers to that." Darcy held up her wine glass and tapped it against François'. "I'd say you're off to a decent start."

And it was true. The food was terrific. So was the conversation; before Darcy realized it, they'd finished the bottle of wine and part of another. She yawned and looked at the time. How could it be eleven already? Maybe talking all evening was normal for roommates.

She got up and began loading the dishwasher. "It's late. I better go to bed."

"Don't worry," he said, carrying his plate over. "I'll clean up. I don't have anywhere to be tomorrow."

"That's not fair."

"Trust me. You go to bed. Peaches and I are going to clean up and watch some TV. We'll see you tomorrow."

"Well, I'm not one to argue with that logic. Thanks again for dinner."

"Any time, roomy."

She smiled as she walked to the bathroom. Dishes clinked together as the dishwasher was loaded. *François cleans up faster than Becks, cooks better than Becks, and I didn't once think of that kiss.* As long as they remained strictly roommates, everything would work out perfectly.

That Sunday, the rain pelted down so hard that Darcy and François were soaked when they reached Darcy's car. The falling rain did nothing to lift her mood. She hated grocery shopping and wanted it over as quickly as possible, but despite her grumpiness, seeing François wedged into her car caused her to laugh. Not only were his knees butted up against the dash, his right side was also pressed against the passenger-side door, and he only had about one inch of clearance above his head.

"What's so funny?"

"I'm sorry. You just look like you're in a clown car or something. Chevettes weren't made for hockey players, I guess." Darcy put the key in the ignition, poked Glücksschwein, and started the car. The pig swung back and forth in time with the windshield wipers.

"Cute pig."

"Thank you. His name is Glücksschwein. It means lucky pig."

"I take it you got him in Germany."

"You should be a detective," Darcy said as she pulled into traffic.

"I never took you as the superstitious type. Does this mean you count on luck to reach a destination in this little tin can of a car?"

"You could get out and walk."

He held up his hands in surrender. "I'm kidding. I appreciate the ride. Very thankful that you have a car. Especially in this weather."

Darcy glanced at Glücksschwein. She wasn't superstitious. So what if she'd always liked having his smiling, little face nearby? She used to carry him in her backpack or her purse. Sometimes in her pocket. Now, he rode in her car, and maybe she did talk to him on occasion and developed a habit of poking him in the belly for—*oh shit*—luck.

Darcy pulled into a parking spot as close to the store as possible.

"Ready? We're going to have to run." François had his hand on the door handle. "Race you."

They ran through the pouring rain into the grocery store. The automatic doors welcomed them in with a swish and rush of cold air.

"I win," said Darcy, stopping by the carts to wipe the rain off her jacket.

"We tied."

"Nope. Your door was closer, so you got a head start."

"Really?"

"Yes, really." Her hands went to her hips, and they stared at one another in mock seriousness.

Finally, François caved in, giving her a lop-sided grin. "Okay, I'll let you have this one. So, back to grocery shopping, I was thinking," François said as he wrestled with a cart, trying to release it from the one it was linked to. "Mon Dieu." He gave one hard yank, and as his arm flexed and released, Darcy became hyper-aware of his strength, his beefy muscles, the visible veins, the dark hair, and imagined how they might feel wrapped around her body. Her mouth went dry. Great. Thirsty again.

"Oh, there we go," François said as he freed the cart. "What was I saying? Oh yeah, I thought if we buy food together, we'll save some money."

Together? That snapped Darcy out of her dream. She'd never done *together*. "Perhaps in theory, but we don't eat the same amount. We don't even know if we like the same food."

"I thought of that. Think of this week as an experiment. As we walk through the store, we'll be learning about each other's tastes. We can divide the cost by two-thirds for me and one-third for you and see how this week plays out. If I owe you money, I'll pay up. Ça va?"

Darcy stood in the produce section, chewing on the inside of her cheek. Nothing so simple should take this much thought. Why did sharing food with him feel so...intimate? *Stop being ridiculous. Roommates do this kind of thing all the time.* "Fine. One week."

"Super," François said, pulling a grocery list out of his front pocket.

"You have a list? What are you? A suburban mom?"

He shrugged and pushed the cart towards the vegetables. "Okay, I'll admit, I'm a bit of a nerd, but planning saves money, and with a list, I won't forget anything. I don't want to be coming to the store every day."

Darcy shook her head in disbelief. He was tidy, organized, liked to cook, was sweet to Peaches, and made her laugh. Yup, he was perfect for...a roommate.

"You okay, Darce? You're staring at that head of lettuce like it's a crystal ball."

"What?" She blinked a few times, and sure enough, she was standing there holding lettuce. "Just making sure there's no bruising." Did lettuce even bruise? She turned it over, pretending to examine it, before placing it in the cart before she made a bigger fool of herself. François put in two more, along with some red peppers, tomatoes, carrots, and cucumber.

Too aware of his presence for her liking, she stiffened as he leaned against her and showed her the list. He'd written a meal plan at the top, the ingredients categorized below. "Want to divide and conquer?"

Darcy prided herself on being organized and efficient in most areas of her life, but her food shopping style was not among them. Despite how much she hated grocery shopping, she was the person who stopped at the store each day, and her purchases usually came from the frozen food aisle. She ran in, picked out a few things, and ran out. Now she was stuck wandering through the store and filling a cart with a handsome ex-hockey player with a voracious appetite who happened to be her roommate. Whatever.

This system wouldn't last, but she wasn't one to shy away from a challenge. She could handle one week.

"Okay, so here's the deal," François said as he shut the fridge. "While I'm not working, I'll cook. When we're both working, we'll take turns."

"I'm not really a cook, and with my contract ending soon, you might regret your suggestion."

"Your contract?"

"Yeah. I'm on a maternity leave contract. I should be done already, but the person took an extra month of vacation. I usually have something else lined up but haven't had any luck so far."

"Sounds like you always work on contract."

"Yeah. You're never bored because you're always learning, going new places, and meeting new people."

"Huh, I never thought of it that way. Not that I plan to work at the same place for my entire career, but I like the idea of getting to know a place and the people. Becoming proficient and building connections. Not to mention the appeal of a regular paycheck. But let's return to cooking. What can you make?"

"Um, spaghetti, omelettes, schnitzel." Darcy counted them out on her fingers. "Dutch apple cake, burritos." Yup, that was five.

"So when it's your turn, you make those things. They all sound delicious to me." He bit into an apple. "I love schnitzel, by the way."

Darcy walked to the sink, filling the kettle. Making tea relaxed her. A habit inherited from her mother. "I appreciate the effort here, but honestly, I can't imagine this working." She opened a drawer and pulled out a teabag. "Tea?"

"No thanks."

"I don't sit down and eat dinner. I grab something quick, microwave it, and watch TV or read a book, especially if I'm home late from the animal shelter where I volunteer."

"Fair enough. But I'm not saying we have to have a sit-down dinner with candles and placemats—unless, of course, you want to."

What?

He had his back to her, reaching into a cupboard so she couldn't see his face. Darcy wanted him to be flirting, or at least she thought she did. Unrequited feelings were one thing, but if he liked her back? Her stomach knotted with the thought.

"Let's say, for example, I make a lasagne tonight." François continued to talk. "I'll eat dinner and then put the leftovers in the fridge. When you're ready, you take a piece and reheat it."

Darn him for making that sound reasonable and practical and not flirty at all. "Fine." She poured the hot water into her mug, wrapping her hands around it. "I'm freezing from the rain, which is crazy considering it's summer. Do you need the bathroom because I think that soaker tub is calling my name."

"Nope. Go ahead."

She grabbed her book and left François in the kitchen, needing a distraction from her thoughts. But as she sank into the hot water, she could hear music, cupboards opening and closing, and something sizzling. They were warm, comforting, domestic sounds.

They were the sounds of home.

Even submerged in hot water, Darcy shivered.

8

As much as Darcy loved volunteering at the animal shelter, the temperamental air conditioning had her longing to go home. At least that's what she told herself. It had nothing to do with wanting to hang out with François. For all she knew, he wasn't even there. She didn't ask him his plans, not wanting to appear nosy.

The desktop fan, which did little more than blow hot air at her, made so much noise that hearing people over the phone proved challenging. "Sorry, did you just say there is a dog under your shed that's not yours?" she asked into the phone.

"Right. Not mine. She won't come out, and her belly is huge. She must be pregnant or sick or something."

"You're sure?"

"Oh yeah, I'm sure. I had a dog as a kid. Can you send someone to get her?"

"Sir, can you hang on for a minute? Let me see what we can do." Darcy placed the call on hold and turned to Sarah, one of the part-time staff members. "Who's working in rescue today? We need to help a pregnant dog under a guy's shed."

"I'll go to the back and see what we can do, but I don't think we have room for a dog and puppies. We're maxed out right now."

"Well, we can't leave her there. At least let's bring her here. I can start calling foster families we've used in the past and see if anyone can help us. Even temporarily." It wasn't Darcy's place to boss around an employee while she was a volunteer, but someone had to do something.

"I don't know if it'll work out, but I'll go to the back and talk to them."

45

Wow. Don't try too hard. Frustrated with Sarah's lack of enthusiasm, Darcy picked up the phone as soon as she was out of earshot. "Hi. Sorry for the hold. Can you give me your address? Someone will be over in the next little while to get her."

"Thank you so much."

Darcy took down the address and was standing when Sarah returned to the desk. "Philip said he'd go pick her up, but he'll likely need some help. I'll call around to see if anyone can come in."

"I'll go with him."

"You can't. We need you to find a foster family. Like I said, we don't have room."

"I'll take her. I'll foster her."

Sarah's eyes opened wide, and Darcy wondered if hers had done the same because she was as surprised as Sarah when the words popped out. If she'd been thinking them, it was on a subliminal level, but now that they were out, they felt right. But why this dog? And why now? They always needed foster families, and she'd never volunteered before. Darcy shook her head in an effort to clear her mind. Her introspection would have to wait.

"Darcy, that's kind of you, but can you handle it?"

"Of course." She'd have to. And maybe François could help. Oh shit. François. Should she have checked with him first? Probably. Yes. But she couldn't back down now. Well, she could, but she wouldn't. How did everything get so complicated? She simply wanted to help this dog. "I think the best thing to do would be to bring her back here and give her a physical. While that's happening, I'll go out and get the supplies I need. When she's given the okay, she can get dropped off at my place, or I'll return and get her myself. So, that means, while I'm out, you need to get me a list of essential items and instructions on what to do leading up to, during, and after birth." She cringed at the sharpness in her voice and because she sounded like Sarah's boss.

"Try to understand that we can't help them all."

Oh my God. Darcy forced a small smile and tried to sound relaxed. Sarah meant well. Part of her job included assessing potential foster families. It wasn't personal." I know that. I really do, but we don't have to turn her away because I can help that dog and her puppies. So, how about you help me do that."

Sarah sighed but sat down at the desk and picked up the phone, turning towards Darcy before dialing. "I'll let the vet know she's coming in. It's great you're doing this. I just hope you know what you're getting into."

"Trust me on this. I've fostered a dog before." Darcy wasn't going to admit that she was a child at the time. She wanted Sarah to believe she could handle it, even if her confidence was a façade.

Darcy tucked the address into her pocket and headed to the back to find Philip. Someone needed to light a fire under Sarah's ass. Okay, that was harsh and not entirely fair. In fact, by allowing Darcy to take the dog, Sarah was breaking protocol. But sometimes, that's what it took. This wasn't just a job where you answered phones and filed papers. You needed someone with a solid commitment to making things better. Someone willing to go the extra mile when they could. Someone, well, someone like Darcy.

Darcy pushed open the door to the back with so much force it banged against the wall. "Oops, sorry, Phil, just excited about helping this dog. Let's go. I have the address, and I'm coming with you. I'll explain what we're doing on the way."

"Yes, ma'am," Philip said, giving her a mock salute and grabbing a set of keys off the wall.

Darcy followed, determined to help this dog.

Darcy returned home with her new house guest a couple hours later. Both were nervous. At least Darcy was. She'd bought a large dog bed and tried to create a cozy spot. Darcy sat on the floor, close but not too close, allowing the dog to acclimate to her new surroundings.

The jostling sound of a key in the door had them both turn. Darcy should have checked if François had dog allergies. Or if he minded having a pregnant dog in the flat. Hopefully, the dog took less time to adjust to her new roommates than Darcy did.

She braced for confrontation. If François didn't like having a dog in the apartment, it was too late now. She was committed.

"Oh wow. What's going on here?" he asked as he kicked off his shoes.

The pregnant dog, affectionately named Cookie, followed him with her eyes as he approached, stepping around a large kiddie pool for when she gave birth, a stuffed bear, a food dish, and some water. A box in the corner contained everything else required for the day the puppies arrived.

"I'm fostering her. I'm sorry if that bothers you." Darcy heard the brittleness in her tone. Great. She would hardly win him over with that attitude.

François didn't reply. Instead, he squatted next to Cookie and let her sniff him before reaching out to give her head a gentle scratch. "Hi, beautiful. How are you?"

Cookie licked François' hand. "Thanks for the kisses. I bet Peaches is jealous of all the attention you're giving me." He stood up. "Where is Peaches anyway?"

"In your room. They met earlier. She wasn't particularly bothered, and it won't be for long. The dog is only going to be here until her puppies get adopted. Or sooner, if the shelter can take her."

"Don't send her away before the puppies arrive. Certainly here is much better, no?"

"Well, yeah. That's what I thought too." He didn't mind? What was with this guy? Why did he have to be so freaking accommodating? How could she stop thinking about him when he was always so damn perfect?

"So why do you look angry? Did they pressure you into taking her?"

"Of course not. It was my idea." If her tone was any colder, she could spit out ice cubes.

"So...?" He walked into the kitchen and opened a bottle of wine.

"I'm not angry. I do not have an angry look on my face." Darcy got up and joined him, thinking wine might not be a bad idea.

"If you say so." He passed her a wine glass. "Cheers to the dog. What's her name?"

"Cookie. Because we could only coax her out of hiding with a dog biscuit."

"Well then, here's to Cookie."

She took a sip, another, then another. All the while, François kept those intense blue eyes on her as if waiting for her to admit she was angry. "What?" she finally asked.

"Just trying to figure you out." He gave her such a small smile her heart hurt.

Not fair. This was so far out of her wheelhouse that she could do nothing but tell him the truth, more or less. "I'm not angry. It's just that I expected you to protest or at least be less than thrilled I'd brought home a pregnant dog, and it would lead to an argument or something."

He put his wine glass on the table, gently rocking it so the contents swirled around as he stared into it as if expecting a secret to be revealed. He seemed so lost in thought, Darcy wondered if he'd forgotten about her. "First of all, I like dogs. Second, it's your house. And third, please do not presume to know what I'm thinking without talking to me. I don't like it when people jump to conclusions."

Darcy clenched her jaw, longing to cling to anger because it was a simple emotion and one she understood. But François was right. She'd totally jumped to conclusions. "Here's the thing. I'm used to being on my own and doing things my way. Until I moved in with Becks, I'd never had a roommate, and just when I get used to her, she moves out, and you move in. Then, before I know it, we're cooking together...and...and I know it sounds lame, but it's a lot for me." No, her voice did not crack, and no, her eyes weren't beginning to–nope. No way. What the hell was wrong with her? It wasn't as if Becks' leaving hurt. Nor did it have anything to do with her fear that if she grew close to François, he'd do the same thing. And by growing close, it would be as friends because why would kind and caring François be even remotely interested in someone as cranky and rude as her?

She walked over to the couch, plopped down heavily, and pulled a blanket over her lap despite the heat, wishing she could pull it over her head. So many feelings she didn't want to deal with. Had someone opened the drawer where she kept her emotions and dumped them all onto the floor? How would she ever sort through the mess? She'd just have to act normal. *Act* being the operative word. "I have a lot of reading to do," she called over the couch. "The vet thought she might go into labor any day now, and I want to be ready."

"What will you do if you're at work and she goes into labor?"

"Yesterday was my last day. My contract is over." Did he just sigh?

"You told me it was ending soon a while ago, but you don't share many details, do you?"

His tone was different somehow. Confusion? Hurt? Tenderness? Whatever it was, it had an emotional component, making her all the more uncomfortable, so she turned towards the kitchen and scowled at him. Again. All part of acting normal when what she really wanted to do was hug him.

François held his hands up in surrender.

Kitchen noises filled the silence as she tried to read a pamphlet the shelter vet had given her, and before she knew it, François placed a sandwich, her wine glass, and a bowl of chips on the coffee table. Before she could thank him, he walked away. Darcy felt that damn prickling sensation in the corners of her eyes again. She didn't deserve his thoughtfulness. She'd acted horribly.

Cookie sighed contentedly. What a difference to when they'd found her. She'd growled and snapped when they first approached her, on the defensive, afraid to trust.

The light clicked on in Darcy's mind as François sat beside her with his own sandwich and the bottle of wine.

"I'm sorry," Darcy blurted out, and François turned to her. "I feel all jumbled up inside, and that's a specific medical term, in case you were wondering. I acted on impulse to foster Cookie. I don't know why. Now I'm nervous and questioning myself, and it's making me defensive, by which I mean rude, in case you haven't noticed."

This elicited a small smile from him, encouraging her to tell him more, but where to start? By admitting that opening up scared her? Sharing involved forging relationships, growing closer, and building trust. And as lovely as all that sounded, it usually led to pain and sadness because nothing was permanent. Nothing lasted. At least not for her. And if nothing lasted, it meant her dream of a home and roots would never come true.

Yes, she was exactly like Cookie. Fear caused her to snap and growl. Except Cookie had taken a leap of faith. And now look at her. She was safe and content and much, much braver than Darcy.

"So what are you making us for dinner tomorrow?" he asked, pulling her out of her thoughts.

"What? Dinner? Me?"

"Did you not say your contract is over?"

"Ummm, maybe."

"And...?"

"You made the menu. What's on the list?"

"I'd be more than happy to buy ingredients for schnitzel."

"Seriously?"

"Yeah. I've been waiting for this moment. Now pass me one of your books. Is there a *What to Expect When You're Expecting* for dogs?"

"Hardy, har."

"No, seriously. What can I read? I need to be prepared too."

"I told you, I..." he stopped her talking by shoving a chip in her mouth.

"I know. You're used to doing things on your own. But you don't have to. We're friends. Friends help each other. And if you don't like it, you can finally get that argument you had your heart set on."

Friends. Right. She stuck her tongue out at him, then passed him a book.

"Oh, and even though it's not my business, I think you chose to foster a dog now because you finally feel at home. And what a better way to show that than to give back to the community."

Darcy opened her mouth to protest, but nothing came out. Maybe there was hope for her after all.

The next afternoon Darcy returned from the grocery store to find François sitting at the island working on his laptop. He was fixated on the screen, typing intensely, so much so that he didn't realize she'd come in. She had the ingredients for schnitzel and wanted to surprise him. Even though he'd hinted last night, she doubted he thought she'd actually make it.

With François in the kitchen, dinner would no longer be a surprise, but she would still prove to him she could be a considerate roommate, a friend, and not only a snippy crank.

François sighed, ran his fingers through his hair, then startled, suddenly aware of her standing by the door.

"Darce, you scared me," he said, placing a hand over his heart. "I didn't hear you come in."

"So I noticed," she said, walking into the kitchen and placing the bags on the counter. "What are you working on?"

He let out a long sigh. "I'm trying to write a cover letter. I don't know why it's so hard. I mean, I have a basic one I modify for each job, but somehow I still end up working on it for hours."

"Want me to take a look? A fresh set of eyes might help."

He straightened his back and stretched his arms above his head. "You wouldn't mind?"

"No. Of course not." See, helpful roommate.

"All right, thanks. I appreciate it, but how about a bit later on? I need to take a break, and I see you've been shopping."

"My turn to make dinner, right?" She began to unpack the groceries.

"What'd you buy?" He sounded excited, which alone would make the entire schnitzel-making process worthwhile.

Darcy turned toward him and leaned against the counter, smiling. "How about you help me put away the groceries and see if you can guess what I'm making."

"Sounds fun." He slid off the stool and joined her. "Wait. Is this just a way to get me to do the work?"

"No. Of course not," she said teasingly while passing him a bag.

"Okay. Let's see." He began to pull ingredients out. "Romaine lettuce, croutons, bacon, ice cream. No idea yet," he said as he put away the ice cream and bacon. "Okay, next bag, please."

Darcy handed it to him.

"Lemons, bread crumbs." He turned to her, raised one eyebrow, and gave her a smile so big, that the corners of his eyes crinkled.

This caused her to smile back, making her chest fill with sparkles and warmth. "Keep going."

"Boneless pork chops, cream, eggs. Yes! Thank you. You're making schnitzel, right?" His arms wrapped around her, pulling her against his chest and lifting her off the ground. "Whoo hoo," he said, spinning them in a circle. Then he placed her back on the ground. "Sorry. I just love schnitzel."

"I see that," she said, laughing. "I should warn you, though. It's been a while since I made it." She couldn't remember the last time, definitely not since she moved to Montreal. "There's another bag with some hummus and veggies. Sort of an appetizer because I think this might take me a while."

"I don't mind waiting. Need any help?"

"Oh no. It's my turn to cook. You more than deserve the night off." Darcy opened the fridge, wanting to climb in and lower her body temperature. *Oh my God*, she mouthed to the orange juice as she searched for wine. What could she do to get pressed up against his chest again? How hard would it be to make schnitzel every night?

She pulled out a bottle of white and found herself humming as she twisted the corkscrew. Humming? She stopped immediately. Interesting. As was the lightness in her head, almost like she was buzzed. But she hadn't opened the wine yet, let alone had any.

Darcy froze. One simple, playful embrace with François couldn't have caused this. Could it? Some kind of brain chemical release? Oxytocin? Dopamine?

"What are you thinking?" François asked.

"Oh, um, dinner is my way of apologizing for my behavior last night."

"Thanks, but you don't have to apologize. Once you told me why you were acting so angry, I understood. We all deal with stress in different ways."

She gave him a small smile and nodded. Quite true, even if he didn't know all the reasons behind her stress. A desire to admit the truth washed over her. If she revealed that Becks moving out had been difficult and that she feared he'd do the same, he'd probably understand, at least about Becks. But what if he thought her crazy for worrying about him? He didn't owe her anything. He was simply subletting the place. They barely knew each other. See? Crazy. "Well, thanks, but I still want to do this for you. Wine?"

"Sure."

She poured them both a glass. "Cheers," she said. Time to change the subject. "Do you think Cookie needs a walk? Where is she anyway?"

"She's okay. I took her out about an hour ago. Now she and Peaches are curled up in the corner of the couch."

"Together? Are you serious?"

"Yeah. Funny right? They seem to have hit it off."

Darcy put down her glass and moved toward the couch as quietly as possible, peering over the back. Sure enough, Cookie was stretched out, and Peaches was curled up, nestled under the dog's neck.

She returned to the kitchen. "How cute are they?"

"Oh yeah. Funny how sometimes there's an instant connection."

"Yeah. Funny." Darcy took a long sip of her wine, watching François carry his laptop into his bedroom. Memories of their kiss reminded her exactly how much she understood instant connections. Too bad she was the only one.

9

Instead of waking up to her furry alarm clock swatting her face, Darcy opened her eyes to François gently tapping her shoulder.

"Sorry to wake you, but you have a phone call. They said it was urgent."

Darcy bolted straight up. "Is it my parents? Are they okay?"

"I don't think it's your parents. The voice was younger."

"Oh, thank God." Darcy got up and stumbled down the hall to the phone. The news wasn't good, but without caffeination, she couldn't process everything yet. She poured herself a coffee, sat deflated at the kitchen island, and reviewed the brief conversation. Her date for Krista's wedding was sick, and now she'd be going alone. Okay, technically, he wasn't her date. They were two colleagues, both invited to the wedding, who thought it would be easier to go together than find dates. Disappointment filled her, not to mention nerves. Her first wedding in Montreal, and she'd have to go alone. It shouldn't be a big deal except that Darcy saw Krista's wedding as a giant step toward being part of a group of friends, friends that celebrated milestones together, dropped by unannounced, and offered career advice. Not just people to go out drinking with.

Because she'd attached so much significance to this one event, she feared her nerves would get the better of her, and having someone to go with would have helped with that.

"Shit."

"What's wrong?" François' voice startled her even though she'd sat beside him.

"Nothing."

"Right. I always curse when nothing is wrong," he said without glancing up from reading the newspaper.

"Very funny, and how come you're up so early?"

"Cookie and I went for a walk to buy this." He tapped the newspaper. "I thought I'd look at the classifieds, knowing full well that I have a better chance online." He shrugged. "Who knows, maybe someone like my dad, who hates the internet, ran an ad." François shut the paper and walked to the toaster, dropping in a bagel. "Are you going to tell me what had you swearing before breakfast?"

She took a sip of coffee. "Remember me telling you that Krista's wedding is today? Well, my plus one bailed on me."

"Wow. What a jerk."

"No. It's not like that. He didn't stand me up. We worked together at the fracture clinic and were both invited to her wedding, so we thought we'd go together. I believe him when he says he's sick. He sounded terrible." She sighed and finished her coffee. "It's not a big deal, there are a few people from the fracture clinic going, but I thought it would be easier to show up with someone. Most of my life was spent going to things solo. I can do it. I'm just tired of it." How many times had she entered a room full of people she didn't know? *Go on in, Darcy, just start talking to someone. Come on, Darcy, there's nothing to be nervous about. You have to go in, Darcy.* School, clubs, Taekwondo. Over and over again.

"At least you know people. It won't be so bad this time." François' bagel popped out of the toaster. "Want me to stick one in for you?"

"Sure." His back was to her as he spread cream cheese on his breakfast. Darcy noted how his movements were unhurried and attentive, unlike her own, which usually involved her rushing from task to task. She ignored, or tried to ignore, how his old, frayed blue T-shirt sleeves were taut around his arms, highlighting his biceps, and how his cargo shorts hung low on his hips, revealing an inch of skin between his waistband and the bottom of his shirt. She licked her lips—it couldn't be helped. He always looked so darn good, no matter what he wore. Shorts. Jeans. A suit. Not that she'd seen him in a suit, but yes. He would look darn good. Especially at a wedding. What if she asked...no. Should she? No.

Maybe. It'd be better than going alone. She fiddled with her coffee cup, grateful his attention was on his bagel. "So listen, I know it's short notice, but if you're not busy, would you be my plus one?"

François stilled, and a cold silence filled the space between them.

He didn't want to be her date. "Never mind. Forget it." Embarrassed, she jumped off the stool, straightened her posture, pulled her shoulders back, and walked swiftly into the living room on a tidy-up mission. She found Cookie's blanket, balled up on the floor, with Peaches right in the middle, sound asleep. Gently removing Peaches from her spot, she began folding. If she kept busy, he wouldn't realize she was hurt because she shouldn't be. Absolutely not.

"Look, Darce, I'd like to help you, but weddings aren't really my thing. If it were anything else, sure."

"They're not my thing either."

"Great. Then you understand why I don't want to go." He joined her in the living room and picked up the free end of the blanket. Or tried to, without success, because Darcy snatched it out of his hands.

"I can manage by myself. Thank you very much."

He rubbed his forehead while she continued to fold the blanket. "I don't understand why you're mad."

Neither did she, at least, not entirely. There was so much going on in her heart and in her head that she struggled to make sense of it all. The weight of her emotions, both acknowledged and unacknowledged, was suddenly too much to bear, and she collapsed on the couch.

One of those emotions, romantic desire and the daily challenge to hide it, exhausted her. She longed to be more than friends and didn't know how much longer she could hide her feelings. But as François faced her, revealing genuine confusion and concern, Darcy knew that if maintaining their friendship meant forever concealing her secret, she'd do it. And it would be worth it.

She looked up and tried to smile. "It's not you I'm angry with. I'm frustrated with the situation. And, as we discussed the other night, when I'm stressed or defensive or anxious or embarrassed, getting mad is what I do. My mother says it's some kind of self-defense mechanism. It's not like she's a psychologist or anything, but she probably bore the brunt of my outbursts while I was growing up."

He sat down beside her, probably stunned at her openness.

"This is the first wedding I've been invited to since I moved here, and I've been looking forward to it. Don't laugh, but to me, going to Krista's wedding means I am more than a drinking buddy—like I'm becoming part of her life." Darcy's head dropped, and she stared at the blanket in her hands. "It sounds stupid when I say it out loud. Anyway, I overreacted, and I'm sorry, but I'm okay now." It took all her strength to push her shoulders back with faux confidence and flash him a big smile.

François put his arm around her and squeezed. "So we're good?"

"Yeah, we're good."

He gave her another quick squeeze and kissed her on the head. "Thanks for telling me."

"Don't get used to it. You caught me at a weak moment." She slapped him on the knee, tossed the blanket onto his lap, and stood. "I better go shower."

They might be good, but *she* wasn't. Darcy was a wreck, crying even. Luckily, the water hitting her face hid all evidence of tears.

Hot, cried out, and wrinkled like a prune, she finally turned off the water. Now, simply wanting to get the day over without further complications, she quickly dried off and pulled on her robe. What time was it? She never checked. What if she was late? She better hurry. Throwing the bathroom door open, she rushed out, tripped, and fell hard.

"Oh my God, I'm sorry," François said, also from the hall floor.

Darcy rolled over. Stunned. The day kept getting better and better. "What the hell are you doing there? You tripped me."

"I didn't mean to. I was waiting for you to get out of the shower. Again, I'm so sorry."

"You could have waited in the kitchen like a normal person. Instead, you chose the floor outside the bathroom. Who does that?" She looked at the new bloody graze on her knee. "Great. Now I get to wear an unsightly bandage. Do they come in blue to match my dress?"

"Let me help you up." He got off the floor and held out his hand.

"No thanks." She stood and returned to the bathroom to find a bandage.

"Look, Darcy…"

She held up a hand, indicating stop.

"I'm—"

"I don't want to hear it, François. Now, where are the bandages?"

He continued to talk, despite her attempt to ignore him. "I really don't feel comfortable at weddings, but I'll go with you if you still want me to. That's why I was sitting there—that sounds weird, but Peaches was sitting there first, and then I squatted down to pat her. She left, but the water turned off, so I sat down to wait because I wanted to tell you right away before you had a chance to ask anyone else. And I'm going to stop talking now."

Like she had anyone else to ask. She sat on the tub's edge and stuck the bandage over her knee. "Forget it. I'm uncomfortable making you do something you don't want to, especially since it will be a pity date."

"It's not pity. It's friendship. We're friends, right? That's what friends do."

Her jaw clenched so hard she thought her teeth might crack. Friends. Yes, of course. Friends. Did he have to beat her over the head with it? "I appreciate the offer, but no thanks. Now, if you'll excuse me, I need to get ready." She stood up to leave, but his annoyingly big frame blocked the door. "Move out of my way."

He took a step to the side. "At least consider it."

Unable to answer, she stomped by him and returned to her room to get ready.

Darcy yanked her dress out of the closet. Life would be so much easier if jeans and T-shirts could be worn to weddings. Who makes these rules anyway? And why do they make dresses so hard to put on? She slid the dress over her head, realizing too late that she'd missed the spaghetti strap on her right side and had to wiggle it half off to get her arm through. *Stupid dress. Stupid François. Stupid me.*

Darcy drew her hair into a loose bun, then applied mascara and lip gloss. It was minimal but the best she could do, even for a wedding. She hated makeup almost as much as she hated her strapless bra, which wasted no time to begin digging into her skin. Screw it. She refused to spend the day being uncomfortable—at least physically. No siree. She undid the bra and tossed it back into her dresser. No one would notice under the loose fabric. One of the advantages of an A cup.

With comfort restored, she took a deep breath and opened her bedroom door. She could do this.

She almost missed François in the kitchen as she whizzed by to call a taxi. He was leaning against the counter. Eating, of course.

She stopped abruptly. He was wearing a suit.

She turned to get a better look and noticed his eyes widen as he straightened up. "Holy shit, Darce. You look amazing."

A burst of hot lava began in her chest and climbed up to her face. He noticed her—and seemed to like it. Great. Another thing to mess with her mind.

"Look," François said, "This is my last attempt. Let me come with you. You won't regret it." He wiggled his eyebrows.

"Someone needs to stay here with Cookie in case she goes into labor and that someone is you."

"Becks said she'd come by."

"I never talked to her."

"I did."

"What? Why?"

He gave her a one-shoulder shrug. "Just in case."

Darcy's emotions fell to the floor like a dropped puzzle, and she didn't know what piece to pick up first. Was she angry because he'd arranged things behind her back or flattered because no one had ever tried so hard for her? Would it be rude to decline since he'd gone to so much effort? Was it selfish to accept his offer? Dammit. If being alone all night made her miserable, she had no one to blame but herself. And she certainly didn't like doing that. She gave him a small smile. "Thanks. We should call a cab."

He better be right—she better not regret it.

By the time they arrived at the reception hall, Darcy already didn't regret having François there. The church had been packed, people talking and hugging, and Darcy didn't spot a single person from work, so she was thankful to have François to sit beside. Even if he was restless. Maybe he was as uncomfortable in a suit as she was in a dress.

"Do you think the taxi driver heard my stomach growl?" she asked as they walked toward the reception hall.

"I think half the city did," François said.

"You're lucky I'm in heels, or I'd give you a roundhouse kick right now."

He took a giant step away from her, holding his hands out in self-defense.

She laughed and ran to catch up. "Seriously, we should have stopped for a snack on the way here. And if I'm hungry, I can't imagine how you must be feeling."

"I came prepared," he said, pulling a granola bar from his inside jacket pocket. "I've already had three."

"What? When? How did I not notice?"

"I don't know. Guess you're not that observant."

She gave him a quick elbow to the gut. "Hand it over."

He passed her a granola bar, playfully rubbing his stomach. Darcy moved into an alcove beside the doors and ate quickly.

"You don't have to hide. You're not doing anything illegal," François said, prompting Darcy to move her hand in a chopping motion. He held up his hands in surrender. "Never mind."

She stuck the granola bar wrapper into his jacket pocket, then they walked inside and found their seats before heading to the bar. Conversation and laughter grew in volume, nearly drowning out the jazz trio. Darcy scanned the room for her old colleagues but still didn't recognize anyone. Carrie and Amber, the only other people she knew, were in the bridal party and hadn't arrived yet.

Carrie and Amber were part of Krista's day, and Darcy was in the last row of tables at the back of the room. Despite the few weddings Darcy had been to, it didn't take a rocket scientist to know that the closer you were to the bride and/or groom, the closer you sat to the head table.

Something tugged at her, deep inside. There was no reason she should be feeling jealous or ignored. She'd only known Krista for six months and couldn't compete with Krista's long-time friends, but she thought her invitation was a step forward. Clearly, this wasn't the case. What if she never developed close friendships? What if, after years of moving around, she didn't know how?

"I need to sit down," she told François as he passed her a glass of wine. Her limbs were heavy, and her throat tightened as fear coiled around her and squeezed. What if she spent her entire life alone?

"You okay?" François asked.

"Yeah. Fine." She tried to sound upbeat but must have failed because François intertwined his fingers with hers, giving her hand a squeeze as he led her to their table. This simple reassurance (Darcy refused to read more into it) warmed her from the bottom of her feet to the top of her head. She glanced down at their clasped hands—connection—the one thing she needed at the moment more than anything in the world.

Thank God he was there.

Just as they sat down, a few people from the fracture clinic joined them at the table, none of whom Darcy knew well. At least she remembered their names, unlike her colleagues, who didn't remember hers. One didn't realize Darcy had worked there. So any relief at the familiar faces quickly evaporated, replaced by what felt like exhaustion, but she wasn't tired. Instead of leading the conversation, as she'd learned to do in this type of situation, she barely had the energy to answer questions, and soon she wasn't listening.

She detached from the present, letting her thoughts carry her away so she could observe the activity from a distance. But it wasn't only today. Only this wedding. Similar moments throughout her life flashed through her mind. Birthday parties. School trips. Dances. Graduation. A participant, yes, but on the periphery of belonging. None of it memorable or significant because she was never engaged. Never invested. Never truly involved.

A waiter placing a plate of food in front of her snapped her back to the present. "So we're on call tonight in case the puppies arrive," François said, turning to Darcy, expecting her to join in. When all she did was nod, François continued talking. "And the funniest part of it all is the way the cat..."

His voice faded as Darcy tuned out for the remainder of the meal, occasionally nodding, mostly picking at her food. What was the point of it all? When a concerned François squeezed her knee and gave her a wink, she nearly burst into tears.

When at long last, the wedding cake was wheeled out, relief flooded every cell of her body. Cake cutting, first dance, an obligatory dance or two, and then they could politely go. Darcy followed along as the guests circled the couple for the first dance. Krista and Marco had large families and many friends, their community literally surrounding them. She was so happy for them but also a tiny bit envious. She'd tried to make friends and build a community. Hell, she'd even bought a house, but if you removed her from the equation, nothing would change. No one would miss her. No one would notice her gone.

"Come on, let's dance." François took her hand and led her to the dance floor before she had a chance to protest. With one hand holding hers and another on her back, they swayed to "Alone" by Heart, and Darcy nearly laughed at the irony.

But tonight, she wasn't alone. François had stepped up, despite his reluctance, despite her anger, and been there for her. She leaned into him, grateful for his presence, for his arm around her. Without François holding her, she'd have come undone.

"What's bothering you?" he whispered against her ear.

"Nothing."

"So how come you're not your normal self?"

"My feet hurt."

"Sure they do."

"They do, honest."

"Perhaps, but there's more to it." They danced in silence for the remainder of the song and continued as "Feels Like Home" began. Indeed, the cosmos was having a good laugh at her expense.

But even though the lyrics mocked her, they also moved her. Darcy didn't consider herself a romantic. She trusted her brain, not her heart, so why were both of them insisting that as long as she was with François, she'd be okay? Because living with him, she was part of something. He made her flat a home.

"So tell me, of all the places you've been to, how has this wedding compared? What are some unique traditions you've seen?" François asked, breaking the silence.

Darcy took a deep breath, grateful to be drawn out of her thoughts. "I thought you didn't like weddings."

"Maybe having such a beautiful date is changing my mind," he whispered against her ear. Oh God, he was simply being sweet, trying to make her feel better, but wow. Her heart lodged in her throat, so instead of thanking him, she tried to convey her gratitude with a squeeze.

"Come on, tell me something interesting," he said, so close to her, his five-o'clock shadow grazed the top of her earlobe, making a shiver run up her spine.

Darcy longed to freeze this perfect moment and save it in a box she could take with her, no matter what happened or where she went. Instead, she cleared the emotion from her throat. "Honestly, I've not been to many weddings, and those I have been to were similar. One in England. One in America. In England, we were only invited to the reception, not the church. Apparently, that's pretty normal. The one in the US was pretty much the same as tonight, except the couple danced when they first entered the reception hall. Although, I'm hardly an expert. This is my first wedding here."

"Wow. One year I went to five, but this is my first since—" François paused, swallowed hard, then coughed. "Sorry, something was tickling my throat. As I was saying, this is my first since traveling."

She pushed away slightly. "Well, I haven't been here that long."

He pulled her closer again. "Darce, don't be defensive. It must be hard always moving to new places and having to start over making friends."

"It is." She tried to suppress the swell of emotion needing release. "People always say they will keep in touch, but they don't. Out of sight, out of mind."

"That's harsh."

She stopped dancing and took a step back. "Well, it's true. If you're not going to stay in touch, don't say it. Just rip that bandage off. Say *have a nice life* because nothing is more heartbreaking than waiting for a reply to a letter that never comes or a phone call that's never returned." She left the dance floor, heading towards the bar. She didn't have to turn around to know that François was following her.

"I don't need a babysitter. I'm fine," she snapped.

"I'm not your babysitter. I'm your date, and I care about you, but I'll leave if you don't want me here. I'm sorry I insisted I come with you. I was only trying to help."

"No, please. Wait." Darcy pinched the bridge of her nose. God, this was hard. "The truth is, I'm glad you're here. I couldn't have gotten through tonight without you. And I mean you specifically. Not some guy I used to work with. You're a better friend than I deserve."

He held her gaze, searching for something. Darcy wasn't sure what, but if he was after sincerity, he would find it because she'd never been so honest. Eventually, he gave a brief nod and continued to the bar.

Darcy waited until a conga line began before telling François she wanted to leave. They found Krista and her husband, both with ear-to-ear grins. Their joy radiated in all directions. Its gravitational pull so powerful that even Darcy couldn't resist the happiness—until Krista introduced her to her mother as "someone I used to work with." A slap in the face would have hurt less, and it was all Darcy could do to wish them the best before turning and bolting for the door.

François caught up to her as she stepped outside into the warm night. He held his hand out to her, and she took it without hesitation. Thinking of its warmth and how their fingers entwined was better than thinking of the riptide of emotion that had caught her completely off guard tonight. She didn't like contemplation, introspection, or whatever her mind was doing. No, she preferred focusing on the here and now.

"Since we're all dressed up, is there anywhere you want to go?" François asked.

"No. Home sounds perfect to me." The two of them, maybe watching TV or playing with Peaches, all while Cookie snuggled close by, was all she wanted. And after tonight, she knew that as long as François was there, there was no place she'd rather be.

10

Darcy threw open the door and moaned as she kicked off her shoes.

"Hey, Becks," said François. "No issues?"

"All quiet," Becks said from the couch. "You two look fantastic. Fun time?"

"Yeah, it was fine. Jason not here?" Darcy asked.

"Nope. Back at the lab."

"Wow. That guy sure does work hard." Darcy filled the kettle, longing for a cup of raspberry tea and a return to normal.

Becks shrugged. "Yeah, but it's not so bad. I got to spend the evening with my princess, didn't I, Peaches?" Becks gave the cat a big kiss and then joined Darcy in the kitchen. "She likes the dog a lot. The dog likes her too, which is weird. They were curled up in that pool for most of the night."

"Well, Cookie is a sweet little thing. It's hard not to like her," François said. "How are you getting home? You're not walking, are you?"

"Walk? Yeah, right." Becks turned to Darcy. "Can't one of you drive me?"

Before Darcy could respond, François said, "We've had too much to drink. Let me call you a cab." He picked up the phone and called the taxi company. "Ten minutes, they said."

"Sounds good," Becks said through a yawn. "I think I'll go wait outside. It's a gorgeous night."

"I'll walk down with you," François said. "I should take Cookie for a quick walk."

"No need," Becks opened the door. "I took her out shortly before you got home."

"Oh yeah? Thanks."

"Peaches might need a leash now too. She didn't appreciate being left behind. Anyway, I'll send you my bill." She laughed. "Night all."

Darcy gave her a quick wave before François closed the door behind her. If Becks noticed Darcy's unusual silence, she kept it to herself.

Unplugging the kettle, Darcy poured hot water into her mug and watched François as he scratched under Cookie's chin.

"How's my sweet girl doing?" he asked, and Cookie replied by licking his hand. "And don't worry. I didn't forget about you, Miss Peach." He picked the cat up and scratched her head before placing her beside Cookie. The two of them curled up together and went to sleep. "They've become the best of friends. So funny."

All Darcy could do was nod. Her mind wasn't on the two animals. It was on how loving he was towards them, how gentle, how kind.

"That's the first genuine smile you've had in hours. Those two are quite the pair, aren't they?" He came and stood beside her, leaning against the counter.

She watched the steam rise out of her mug, speaking softly. "It's not them. It's you. You can tell a lot about a person by how they treat animals."

"I hope it says good things about me."

"It does, but I've known that since the first night we met." She gave him a wistful lopsided smile. He swallowed hard and began to undo his tie. Great. She'd embarrassed him.

But he didn't leave the room.

Unable to maintain eye contact, Darcy focused on his fingers as he loosened the knot. Strong fingers that squeezed her knee, held her hand, and pressed against her back when they danced. They were comforting and reassuring, and as he finally undid his tie, he undid her resolve.

She grabbed two fistfuls of his shirt and pulled him into a deep, long kiss. All those electric currents she'd felt at the housewarming party recharged and surged throughout her body, leaving her breathless.

"What was that for?" he asked when they broke apart, his forehead pressed against hers.

"I wanted to see...never mind." She looked down at her hands as they grasped his shirt like a lifeline.

"Tell me. See what?" He took her hands off his chest, closing his eyes as he brought them to his lips.

The strength in his hands, and the softness of his kiss, made her knees weak, and she wasn't sure she could talk. "If I imagined the...the sparks when we kissed at the housewarming party."

"I thought it was just me," he said, opening his eyes and locking them onto hers. They were bluer, warmer, and dilated with arousal, but they also expressed something more, something unfamiliar, something beyond carnal impulses.

She turned her head, wanting to run, not because she didn't want this—because she did. Oh, how she did, but until tonight, she'd never connected with someone emotionally *and* physically. And it terrified her.

"Darce, please don't look away." His voice, so soft and earnest, revealed something at risk for him too. And if he could do it, so could she because Darcy didn't back away from a challenge.

With that decision made, she faced him, opening herself up to the moment. To him.

François slowly ran his hands up her bare arms, her collar bone, her neck until he cupped her head, the pads of his thumbs caressing her cheeks, his fingers on the back of her neck. A warmth began in her belly, melting away the earlier tension and replacing it with something sweet and decadent, like melted chocolate. She embraced the sensation as it flowed through her body, luxuriating in its heat, licking her lips, wanting more. Her head fell back against his hands, and she moaned his name as his lips brushed against her skin, his breath caressing her like the softest feather.

Darcy wanted to touch him, wanted him to feel as she did, but before she could even move, his tongue, oh God, his tongue, traced the neckline of her dress, eliciting a tingling sensation that began on the top of her head, then continued down her body, trickling into her arms and along her spine. Her knees gave out, and she grabbed his arms to steady herself.

"Tell me what you want," he whispered against her ear.

What she wanted was him. All of him. Today. Tomorrow. All her instincts were screaming that she was right where she belonged. So she listened. They'd never failed her before.

Only when he began to pull away did she realize she hadn't spoken. "Don't," she whispered, tightening her grip on his arms. The shaking in his hands was almost imperceptible, but she felt it, so she looked up and saw...insecurity. Couldn't he see her desire? Her longing? "I want you," she said, her voice husky and raw. "I've wanted you for so long."

Darcy took a step back and slid the straps of her dress off her shoulders. The bodice fell to her waist, revealing her naked breasts, causing his breath to hitch. Burning with need, she somehow shimmied the dress down past her waist, and the second it hit the ground, pooling at her feet, the tempo changed.

She yanked him against her, her mouth on his, their kisses hard, feverish, and desperate. Her hands were in his hair. On his shoulders. His ass. His shirt brushed her chest. His belt rubbed her stomach. But he wasn't close enough. Her fingers struggled with his buttons while he fumbled with his pants. Why couldn't they move faster? Would they make it to the bedroom? Would it matter?

Dear God. Nothing had prepared her for the supernova effects of combining the physical and metaphysical. It was intense. It was hot. It was all-consuming.

The problem was that while a supernova burnt bright and hot, it quickly burnt out.

Darcy awoke the following day to the angry sounds of a hungry Peaches. The cat marched back and forth beside the bed, meowing like her life depended on one of them getting up. Darcy stretched, then the arm that had been holding her all night gave her a squeeze.

"Don't worry. I'll get it," François said and kissed the back of her neck.

Cool air hit her skin as he drew back the covers and climbed out of bed. His feet padded on the hardwood as Peaches intensified her meowing.

"Hang on, Miss Peach," he said. "Darce, do you know where...oh, there we are."

She rolled over to see him balancing on one leg, nearly falling as he pulled on his boxers. "Smooth."

He threw a pillow at her.

Once he left, a meowing Peaches trailing after him, she closed her eyes again. What an incredible night, but what now? She cringed with embarrassment at the thought of her behavior at the wedding. So freaking emotional. Weddings cause that, though, don't they? Isn't that a universal truth?

Could that also explain what happened after the wedding, or was it all in her imagination? Not the sex, that had definitely happened. But was there really an emotional connection, or was Darcy reading too much into it? What if François had just been drunk or horny or feeling sorry for her? Then what? Darcy pulled the covers over her head. All this second-guessing sucked. No wonder she never let herself get involved.

She would pretend like nothing had changed. Who knows? Maybe it hadn't.

"Rise and shine, sleepyhead." The mattress depressed as François sat down on the bed.

Had she dozed off? "Why are you waking me up so early?"

"Early? It's noon. I took Cookie for a short walk, and now I'm going to go for a run, but I brought you some coffee first. I know how cranky you get without it."

She grabbed the pillow he'd thrown at her and hit him with it. "I am not cranky."

"Not at all."

"Go away."

"Again. You prove my point."

She pulled the covers back over her head.

"All right." He attempted to peel back the duvet, but her grip was firm. "I'll leave you alone, providing you tell me about the tattoo."

"I don't know what you're talking about," she said, popping her head out.

He opened the blinds, letting daylight pour into the room.

She rolled over, away from the window. "You're evil."

"Tell me why you have a tattoo of Glücksschwein on your hip, and I'll leave you in peace."

"It's nothing."

He lay down beside her and kissed the back of her neck. "If nothing, why all the secrecy?"

Instead of answering, she rolled towards him and kissed him back. So much for pretending nothing had changed. His gravitational pull proved too strong for her to resist. Even so, it wasn't strong enough to draw the tattoo story out of her.

She pulled down the sheets revealing her naked body, reaching for him and running her fingers along the inside of the waistband of his shorts.

He raised an eyebrow. "Are you trying to distract me?"

"Who me?" she asked innocently, biting her lower lip as she began tugging his shorts down. She considered telling him about the tattoo for the briefest of moments—it was hardly a deep, dark secret. And she would, eventually, but unfamiliar with openness, she knew she needed to take baby steps.

Darcy wrapped her arms around him, pulling him against her and tossing a leg over his waist. Hearing his breathing change caused her heart to beat faster. She wanted to make him happy. She wanted to keep him close.

There was no denying it. Everything had changed, and there was no going back.

11

Several days later, François burst into her bedroom, yelling, "Darcy! Le chien! Le chien!"

She bolted straight up like the house was on fire. "Are you sure?"

"Yes. I'm sure. It's time." And he was gone.

She glanced at her alarm clock. Seven. Too early to call the vet unless there was an emergency, which there wasn't. Besides, she was prepared. She had been over all the reading material, going so far as asking François to quiz her. She could handle it—barring any major issue, of course.

Pulling on sweats and one of François' T-shirts, she stumbled into the living room, wiping the remnants of sleep from her eyes. Even through the thick fog of morning, she could smell François on the shirt, or maybe his scent came from her skin since they now spent every night together. Overnight, they'd become a couple, living together. The speed with which that happened should have set off alarm bells. Instead, Darcy's corner of the world had lost some of its hard edges and been turned upside down. They fit together perfectly. Connecting with him filled her with joy and light and color. If cut, bleeding rainbows would not shock her.

She grinned as François rushed around, getting everything into place. Together they would witness the miracle of life.

Enough sitting around. Darcy needed to help him. But not a lot needed doing if anything. Cookie laid in the kiddie pool lined with newspapers, with the heat lamp close by. Towels were piled at the end of the couch. A pot of water was

73

being brought to boil in case scissors needed sterilizing to help Cookie tear the birth sacs. He'd done it all.

"Ready?" François asked her.

"As I'll ever be." She wrapped her arms around him and pulled him into a kiss. "Thanks for doing all this."

He gave her a tight hug. "Go be with her. I'll bring you some coffee."

Too tired to argue, Darcy agreed and dropped onto the couch. Peaches joined her, alert cat eyes focused on Cookie. Peaches seemed as anxious about her best friend as she and François were. As they watched her, Cookie's abdomen contracted.

François leaned over the back of the couch and handed Darcy a large mug, that goofy grin back on her face. He treated her like a queen, though she felt undeserving.

"Poor Cookie must have been in labor during the night," Darcy said, and, as she spoke, clear fluid ran onto the newspaper. "Oh my gosh. Already? See that? This is it. Puppies are on the way." Her heart pounded with anticipation, and she wondered if Cookie could hear it.

François rushed around the couch and sat beside her, leaning forward, elbows on his knees. Cookie did everything by the book. Biting through the sac and umbilical cord, then licking the puppy clean.

"We need to breathe," she said. "We're both holding our breath. We can't help if were both passed out."

"You're right. It's just so…" his voice trailed off as they heard the puppy breathe. "Good girl, Cookie, you did it. That's one down."

The little puppy squirmed around, so tiny, helpless, and absolutely beautiful. Darcy leaned back, mentally exhausted, and all she had to do was watch. "That was amazing," she whispered. François nodded. Still leaning forward, he wiped a tear off his cheek. Darcy closed her eyes and, full of affection, wrapped her arms around his waist.

The next puppy came along ten minutes later. After that, things slowed down, and Cookie rested, letting the first two nurse.

"Okay, this is normal. So far, it's been a textbook delivery," Darcy said.

"Yeah, our girl is doing great. Hear that, Peaches?"

Peaches hadn't moved an inch since Cookie went into labor.

"I'm going to take a quick shower," François said through a yawn. "Want to join me?"

"Very tempting, but one of us should be here."

"You're right. It's just so hard to keep my hands off you." He pulled her onto his lap, causing Darcy to giggle. She hadn't giggled since she was a kid.

"Get going, or you're going to run out of time, and I'll throw a bagel in the toaster for you."

"Oh fine," he said, standing up, keeping Darcy in his arms until they reached the kitchen.

After an hour, Cookie showed signs that the next puppies were coming.

"Oh no. It's coming out tail first," Darcy said. "What did the book say again? Only help if it gets stuck? Is that right?"

François grabbed the book. "Yeah," he replied, then put the book down. "We know this stuff, Darce, but nerves are making my mind go blank."

"I know. Me too." Darcy perched on the edge of the couch. "It's not coming. I'm going to wash my hands in case Cookie needs help."

She returned from the sink, her hands shaking. "What if I can't do it? Should we call the vet?"

"You got this. You'll be fine."

Darcy nodded and took a deep breath, hoping to steady her hands. She moved closer to Cookie, and as she was squatting down, the puppy made it out unassisted. "Oh my God, she did it. Did you see that? She did it." Darcy jumped up and kissed Peaches on the head before collapsing next to François.

Five minutes later, all four puppies were nursing. Cookie looked tired but protective and Peaches, now perched on the arm of the sofa, acted like a sentry.

François's light snoring began before Darcy finished her conversation with the shelter vet, arranging a time when he would stop by. Once she hung up the phone, she retrieved a blanket from her room and gently laid it over him, his hair messy, his mouth slightly open. She remembered the tear he wiped away and his confidence in her. She also thought of how he'd waited to wake her up until he'd prepped everything and made Cookie comfortable.

The puppies made a noise, so Darcy turned to check on them. All good. They'd done it. They'd cared for Cookie, given her a safe and comfortable home to have her puppies, all of which seemed healthy.

After years of handling things alone, that last thought stopped her in her tracks. *She* hadn't done it. *They'd* done it. Together. As a team.

She was no longer alone.

Darcy's throat tightened, and her eyes blurred. *Not now. Get a grip.* She attempted to distract herself by focusing on tangible actions. The kitchen needed tidying. She should shower. Peaches required breakfast.

Why wouldn't her body comply? Why did it refuse to walk away from where François slept? Or didn't sleep because even though his eyes were closed, he lifted the blanket, indicating she should join him. This, her body complied with; the pull to entwine herself amongst François' heavy limbs was too hard to resist.

This would take some getting used to, but, as always, she never backed away from a challenge.

12

Impatience meant that instead of making two trips, Darcy's arms were overloaded with supplies, causing her to stumble while opening her door and fall in with a crash. "Look what the shelter lent us," she called out from the floor.

She was getting back to her feet as François rushed out of the bedroom with a puppy in his hand, his hair disheveled, and Peaches at his feet.

"You okay? What was that crash?"

"I tripped carrying this." She pointed to fence panels at her feet. "It's a corral for the puppies."

"Seriously? You just made my day," he said, leaning down to kiss her. Being welcomed home by François would never grow old, making her wonder if the butterflies in her stomach were due to their chemistry or her fear that it would end too soon.

She swallowed down her emotions as she carried the pieces of the pen over to the center of the living room and began assembling them. Things had become quite unpredictable and chaotic in the two weeks since the puppies were born, making job hunting particularly hard. Her parents had drilled it into her head since her first job to save enough money to live on for three months. So she did, but she hated watching her savings dwindle. Restoring order would help, and the way to do that was to keep the anarchy contained.

A few F-bombs and one cut finger later, Darcy smiled at the puppies, now safely behind bars. Immediately, Cookie joined Peaches on the couch and fell asleep.

"Looks like momma's happy too," François said, scratching the top of Cookie's head. "And now that I can think for a minute, there's a message for you from that charity on the south shore. You got an interview. Which is awesome, but I thought you weren't applying because it wasn't a contract."

"You know I think it's a good cause, so I figured it doesn't hurt to apply. But I can't believe they called. It was a long shot."

"I think you'd be great at it."

"Thanks. I know I have the office managerial skills, but what if I get bored after a year or so and want to quit?"

"So then you find a new job. But come on, they train support and therapy dogs. You'd love it from what you've told me about the animal shelter."

"I do love being a part of matching dogs with the right family." While she wouldn't be working directly with the dogs, playing a role in the process of matching a dog with a person in need would be reward enough—she knew that from experience.

"And if you get it, and something opens up in their HR department, you can recommend me." He wiggled his eyebrows at her.

"I think their HR department is a department of one, and they mostly coordinate volunteers. It's similar to the animal shelter. If that's something you're interested in, I could introduce you to the volunteer coordinator at the shelter. She could tell you what a job like that entails."

"That would be awesome. I would really appreciate that."

She stared at him while he peeled a banana and took a bite. "What?" he asked with his mouth full.

Darcy shrugged. "You'd be good at a job like that. You're outgoing, friendly, and well organized. A big part of getting volunteers to return is making them feel like they are part of a team and contributing. I should know. I entered the answers to our recent volunteer survey into a spreadsheet."

"And you think I'd be good at that?"

"Yeah. You have this way about you that makes people feel welcome and part of a team. Okay, so maybe I'm basing this on a study of one, i.e., me. But you moved in here and got me cooking and buying food with you, and even that first night we met, I loved talking to you." Her cheeks turned hot. Maybe she should add that he made even the most reluctant people open up.

He looked at his feet, but Darcy could make out a smile on his face. After a few seconds, he turned that warm smile toward her. "I loved talking to you that night too."

As if her cheeks weren't red enough already. She coughed to clear her throat, knowing it was clogged with emotion. "See, that's what I mean. You make people feel special." She stepped in front of the fridge, wanting to shove her face inside so he wouldn't see the need she had to be the only one he made feel special.

As she reached for the fridge door, François wrapped his arms around her from behind, giving her a squeeze, conveying more in his touch than in words. The heat from her face flowed into her heart, nearly causing her to melt.

She tugged the fridge door open and began pulling out dinner ingredients.

François poked his head over her shoulder. "Schnitzel?"

"No. I can make other things, you know."

"But I love your schnitzel," he whispered, kissing her neck.

"Did you just try turning schnitzel into something dirty?"

"Maybe. Did it work?"

"No," she said, laughing.

He released her from his embrace and leaned against the island. "Can't blame a guy for trying. So what are you making?"

"Chicken Parmesan. At least, I hope to. I got the recipe from my mom when she called the other day."

He wiped at a fake tear. "They grow up so fast. Just last month you could only make five things. Now look at you, making Chicken Parmesan."

"Very funny. Did you put *smart ass* under your skills on your resume?" She grabbed a tea towel, twisted it, and snapped it in his direction. François ran for shelter to the opposite side of the kitchen island. She was winding up for a second shot when they both stopped and turned toward Peaches' frustrated meow.

She was near the front door, nudging a puppy towards the pen, like a dung beetle rolling a ball of poop.

Darcy let out a small laugh. "You can deal with that. I'm making dinner." Back by the sink, she opened the window blinds, immediately struck by how the sun filled the flat with gold. She closed her eyes, enjoying the warmth on her face, the gentle breeze on her skin, and the sounds of life behind her. She opened her eyes as François picked up the wayward puppy.

"How the hell did this happen?" he asked.

She had no idea.

Three days later, Darcy had barely pulled to a stop in front of her flat when François' face appeared in the passenger side window. He was still in a shirt and tie from an interview. "How'd it go?" he asked as he opened the door, flipping the seat forward and leaning into the back to grab the pet carrier. The four puppies squirmed and yipped.

"A-plus. They got their shots, and Dr. Tremblay said they are all doing well," she said. "Me, on the other hand, I am completely exhausted. All I want to do is put my feet up and relax. Remind me next time to reschedule if you can't make it."

"Yeah. That'd be great. I can't believe I've never been to the shelter yet. I feel like I know it already."

"That reminds me, Denise, the volunteer coordinator, is going on vacation for two weeks, but she'd love to talk to you when she gets back—if you still want to. How did the interview go?"

"Okay, I guess. It's hard to tell." He leaned down and gave her a kiss. "Imagine if these were kids. I don't know how my brother and his wife manage three."

"Wow. Yeah," Darcy managed to say. Any hidden meaning in his comment seemed unlikely, yet her mind took a direct route to Future Town. She'd never thought of kids before, at least not in a specific way with an actual person. But she did now. Hockey practices. Taekwondo classes. Swimming. School. Holidays. Whoa. She was getting ahead of things. Way too far ahead. She swallowed those thoughts down for later. Right now, she had more pressing things to deal with.

With François carrying the puppies, she pulled out a box full of supplies, locked the car, followed François up the stairs, and was greeted warmly by Cookie.

Once inside, she kicked the front door shut and put the box down. François walked over to the pen. "Release the hounds," he said, laughing at his joke as he opened the carrier.

He was so darn cute.

"So what's in the box?" he asked, lifting it off the floor and placing it on the island.

"Lots of goodies," Darcy replied as she walked to the kitchen counter and filled the kettle. "Wasn't it just summer? Do the weather gods have a switch, like, hey, today's October first, let's set the temperature to near-freezing."

"I know a way to warm you up," he wiggled his eyebrows at her.

"Oh yeah?" She wrapped her arms around his neck. "What do you have in mind because I'm very, very cold."

"Well—" The phone ringing cut him off. Darcy turned to get it, but he held her close. "Let the machine get it." She didn't protest because he'd begun kissing her neck.

"Hey, Krista here. I talked to Marco, and we're both free for dinner tomorrow. So we'll see you then. Let me know if we can bring anything."

Darcy froze and pushed him away. "Dinner? What dinner?"

"Yeah, she called while you were out, said she'd left two messages, and you haven't called back. I told her it must be because we are up to our ears with puppy care, and then I invited her and Marco for dinner on Saturday."

He what? Her hands flew to her hips. "You had no right to do that."

He scratched his head, looking uncertain. "We were talking, and it just kind of happened, but you guys are friends. I don't understand why you're so angry."

Good question. When Darcy didn't say anything, he reached for her, but she held her hand out in a stop gesture. "Give me a minute, okay?"

He nodded, even moving away to give her space.

She stared out the window to the street below while she heard him unplug the kettle that was whistling at an annoying pitch. She'd been avoiding Krista, Carrie, and Amber since the wedding. Being on the fringes stung, and she wanted to show that it didn't matter, that their friendship didn't matter, but here Krista was, calling her several times now.

"I've never had people over for dinner before," she said softly.

"Sorry, what?"

"I said, I've never had people over for dinner before." She was so loud that the puppies stopped yipping.

"Never?"

"Isn't that what I said?" She clenched her jaw and crossed her arms, waiting for ridicule. Instead, he walked over, carrying her a mug of tea, holding it out like a peace offering. She took it reluctantly, wrapping both hands around it, warming them up.

"Tell you what, since I got us into this, I'll call and cancel."

His kindness made her want to lash out or run—embarrassment did that to her. Instead, she remained still. If she were being honest, she was kind of tired of doing both. At least she allowed herself to sigh dramatically. "No. I want to do it." She took a sip of tea. "My other apartments...they were always too small. Before that, I lived with my parents. I've never had the chance." Not exactly true, but not a lie.

"You don't need to come up with excuses. What does it matter?" He took her mug and placed it on the window ledge, pulling her close. "We're all different, Darcy."

"I know."

"Permission to speak freely?" he asked.

She nodded reluctantly.

"You're not good at letting people in. Hold on," he said as she stiffened. "It just means that the people you do let in mean something to you. There's nothing wrong with that."

His words weighed heavy on her shoulders, but instead of brushing them off, she let them sink in. She wanted a closer relationship with Krista; avoiding her would not accomplish that goal. That's how you put down roots and build a community. It sounded logical, didn't it?

François began kissing her neck. "Now, where were we before the phone rang?"

"No way," she said, pushing him away. "If this is to be my first dinner party, it's going to be freaking awesome. Now, where's that cookbook of yours? We've got things to do."

Darcy took one last look in the mirror, making sure François couldn't see her as she sniffed her armpits. She'd applied antiperspirant. Why did she feel so clammy? She'd never been nervous like this for any job interview, and trying for her black belt had been less stressful. All she had to do was survive the night. No—it had to be perfect.

She ran through the checklist in her head. Lasagne in the oven? Check. Wine chilling? Check. Dessert? Check. Appetizers? Check. Music? Uh-oh. She'd forgotten music. She turned around, plowing right into François. "Move it. I forgot to pull out some CDs."

She selected two jazz albums and one classical guitar. She opened the CD player, put the first one in, dimmed the overhead lights, turned on lamps, and lit a few candles.

One puppy was sleeping while two were wrestling, and one was trying to dig its way through the area rug. Peaches and Cookie were curled up together, asleep. "Make me look good. Okay, ladies? And Cookie, no farting." Cookie replied with an ear twitch.

"Looks great in here, Darce. How come you never light candles for me?"

"You get to see me naked."

"Fair enough. Want some wine?"

"Yes, yes, and yes."

"Okay then." François finished pouring the wine as they heard a knock on the door. Darcy opened it, and Krista immediately embraced her, rocking her back and forth. "Where've you been, my friend?"

My friend. Not someone I used to work with. Good lord, Darcy acted like such an idiot avoiding her. She would do better. "The puppies." Darcy tilted her head in their direction. "Kinda crazy, you know."

"Oh yeah. I remember when my dog was a puppy. I can't imagine an entire litter of them. Wow."

"I didn't know you had a dog."

"No. Not anymore. We had to put Ollie down a few years ago. He was twelve and had cancer. I still miss him."

Marco placed an arm around Krista's shoulders. "She still has a framed picture of him, don't you?" he said.

"You bet. He was family." She passed Darcy her coat. "And what's cooking? It smells amazing."

"Darcy made her world-famous lasagne," François said. "Can I get anyone anything to drink?"

"I'll take a red wine," said Marco. "Babe, white for you?"

"Yes, unless Darcy has watermelon schnapps."

"Oh no, never again," Darcy said, then turned to François. "One-dollar shooters at the Sanatorium. Need I say more?"

He shook his head.

"Now, come on into the kitchen."

They stood around the island as François handed out the wine. "Cheers."

"So what makes the lasagne world famous?" Krista asked, taking a sip of wine.

"François thinks he's funny. I've never made it before." She turned to him, giving him the stink eye. "Why don't we go sit? He'll bring out the appetizers. We couldn't put them out in case Cookie or Peaches got into them."

François put the charcuterie tray on the coffee table and sat down beside Darcy, wrapping his arm around her.

Krista's eyes went wide, and she wagged her finger between them. "What's going on here? Last time we were over, you barely knew each other, then at the wedding, you said you were roommates, and now..."

Darcy shrugged as a smile grew on her face. She turned to François. "Things changed."

Krista smacked Marco in the stomach. "See. I told you. I knew at the housewarming that there was chemistry between these two. Didn't I say that?"

Marco looked at Darcy. "She did."

"So, you're a friend of Darcy's original roommate, right?" Krista said to François.

"Correct, we first met before they bought this place. Darcy was feeding Becks' cat while she was away, and I was crashing there for a few days. Becks forgot to mention Darcy to me and vice-versa. Didn't Darce tell you what happened?"

"No. But I think I want to hear it."

"You want to tell it?" he asked Darcy.

"Nope. Go ahead."

"Okay, so as I said, I was at Becks'. I had returned from a run and just showered. I walk out of the bathroom with only a towel around my waist to see this crazy woman in the kitchen wielding a coffee pot at me. She scared me half to death, the towel dropped to the floor, and well, for her, I assume it was love at first sight."

Darcy's elbow made contact with his ribs.

"Weren't you afraid, Darcy?" asked Marco. "To face a stranger like that? He's so much bigger than you."

"I'm the one who should have been afraid," said François, rubbing his ribs.

Krista scrunched her eyebrows together. "Why?"

"Her black belt." His tone implied he assumed everyone knew.

"You have a black belt?" Krista asked.

"Yeah, in Taekwondo." She leaned further back into François.

"Amazing. Why am I only learning about this now?"

Darcy shrugged. "I don't know. There was never a reason for it to come up."

"What else can you tell us, François?" Krista asked. "We haven't had dinner yet, and already I've learned so much."

The timer for the lasagne went off, and Darcy ran to the kitchen.

"Looks like you're saved by the bell," Marco said.

Marco pushed his dessert plate away. "That was awesome. I am so stuffed."

"Me too," said François.

"Really?" Darcy asked him. "You're never full."

"It's not fair, right? How can men eat all they want and hardly gain any weight?" Krista said.

"I know better than to answer that," Marco said. He turned to François. "You think the Canadians have a chance at the cup this year?"

"Oh God, here we go with hockey," Krista said. "I hope you know a lot about hockey, François; otherwise, this guy will bore you to death."

"Of course I like hockey," François replied. His eyes caught Darcy's attention, and he gave her the subtlest shake of his head. Interesting. He didn't want Marco to know he played at a high level.

"You play? We're always looking for guys for our beer league. Games are Monday nights, ten or eleven."

"That sounds fun. Let me think about it."

Krista rolled her eyes. "Fine, talk hockey all you want. Me and Darcy are going to go play with the puppies." Krista walked over to the pen, reached in, and pulled out a puppy. "Do they have names yet?"

"No. Naming them would have been too personal, and we didn't want to get attached. We call them one, two, three, and four."

"Well, which one is this?"

"Three. He came out tail first. Which isn't surprising. He's a bit clumsy but makes up for it in cuteness."

"Is anyone interested in them yet?"

"No. We haven't advertised them. On Wednesday, they will have space for them at the shelter. We'll be dropping them off."

"And you're not going to keep any of them?"

"No. I don't think so. François brought up keeping Cookie a few times, but it's not a good idea." She'd been evasive whenever François asked about it. Just because she loved helping animals didn't mean she wanted one at home.

"Why's that? In case you split up, you don't know who'd keep her?"

"No." That problem never entered Darcy's mind. "Nothing like that. It has more to do with not knowing how long I'll be here." That was Darcy's go-to answer for avoiding long-term commitments. *Want to join the volleyball team/prom committee/environmental club/office lottery? Sorry, I don't know how long I'll be here.* It was also a lie because she had no intention of leaving.

"What's that mean?"

"I've always moved around. It's what I'm used to."

"Well, you can't go. We'll miss you."

"It's not like I have plans to move, but you never know what the future holds."

Krista put the puppy down and whispered conspiratorially to Darcy, "I'm going to work on Marco for one of these guys. He says he's not ready for a kid yet, so I'll guilt him into getting a puppy. Put in a good word for me at the shelter." She leaned back and took a drink of wine. "Oh hey, I almost forgot to show you this." She pulled down the waistband of her skirt to reveal a tattoo on her hip. "We each got one on our honeymoon. Since we went to Hawaii, I got a yellow hibiscus because it's their state flower, and Marco got a Kukui nut tree on his shoulder blade."

"Did it hurt? Mine hurt like crazy."

"Hell yeah. Way more than I thought it would. Where's yours?"

"Same as you."

"What is it?"

"A German symbol for luck."

"Let's see it."

Darcy showed her a tattoo of Glücksschwein.

"That is awesome. A pig in lederhosen. You're so funny!" Krista said and laughed so hard she got the hiccups.

Darcy's cheeks burned with embarrassment. That's what you get for sharing. "I'll get you some water." She stood, wanting to change the subject.

They walked into the kitchen, and Darcy poured Krista a glass of water.

"Thanks, Darce. I guess that serves me right. I hope I didn't offend you because I'm sure it has meaning. It wasn't what I expected, especially after hearing about the black belt." She stood behind Marco and put her hands on his shoulders. "Well, I hate to end the night, but we better get going. We're babysitting his niece and nephew tomorrow."

"*Our* niece and nephew," Marco said.

"Oops, you're right. I'm Aunt Krista. How crazy is that? Well, thanks for an awesome night. Next time at our place."

Once alone, Darcy collapsed on the couch beside François. Dinner turned out okay—not perfect. She did forget about the garlic bread, setting it on fire under the broiler and causing the fire alarm to sound, but she'd done it. Make that *they'd* done it.

She put her legs across François' lap. "So why didn't you want Marco to know about you playing hockey?"

"I don't know. People sometimes get excited. They ask about different players and the draft. Even though I didn't want to play professionally, it makes me embarrassed because I wasn't good enough." He sighed.

"And?"

"What makes you think there's an *and*?"

"A hunch."

He leaned his head back and shut his eyes. "And it makes me question myself. Would I have played in the NHL had I had the chance? Did I convince myself I didn't want to play because I knew I wouldn't be drafted?"

She'd never known her confident and optimistic François to be insecure. He cheered her up and comforted her. Now the tables were turned. She longed to say something wise and insightful; however, she had no words of wisdom. All she said was, "I get it. Thanks for telling me."

"You do?"

"Yeah. I think so. It bothers you that even though you're nine-ty-nine-point-nine percent certain you didn't want to make it a career, you'll never know for sure because you didn't have to choose. I'd probably feel the same way. You should play, though. Marco's a nice guy. It's also win-win for you. You like both hockey and beer."

"You got me there." He pulled her legs closer and gave her a look that suggested a gauntlet had been thrown down.

"What?"

"How about we make a deal?"

"Um, okay."

"I'll consider beer-league hockey if you consider joining a dojo. There's one a ten-minute walk from here."

"First of all, it's dojang. Dojo is Japanese. And second of all, why would I do that?"

"Because you like it and want to keep your skills up."

"Okay, besides that, smart ass?"

"So you can meet people with common interests in the neighborhood."

"I volunteer."

"Yeah, and it's awesome, but it's also across town. This way, you meet locals." He gently placed her legs on the sofa before entering the kitchen to finish filling the dishwasher.

Why the hell was he bringing this up? He knew her insecurities about belonging. She stared at him, frustration steeping like a strong tea. Her elation over the night was ruined, all because she'd asked him about hockey—wait. Of course. He was deflecting. Making it about her. Walking away to tackle a mindless activity. He'd ripped a page out of her playbook.

She changed from sharp and prickly to soft and squishy. "I'm an idiot."

"What?" François asked.

"Nothing. Talking to Cookie." Why did she love him even more, every time he did something less than perfect? Oops. Liked him even more. *Liked*.

13

On Wednesday, Darcy hit snooze on her alarm clock three times in a row. She'd been dreading this moment for a while now, and despite her hesitancy to start the day, it couldn't end soon enough.

"You okay?" François asked, facing her in bed and tucking a strand of hair behind her ear.

"I don't know. Dropping the dogs off will be harder than I originally thought."

François rolled onto his back, tucking his hands behind his head and sighing.

"What?" she asked. "Unless this is about keeping Cookie. I told you, I'm not keeping her" She thought she'd made that clear since the dinner party, no longer giving vague answers to the question of Cookie. "She needs to find her forever home."

"And that's not—"

"God, François," she said, cutting him off. "How many times do we need to go over this? No." Darcy pushed herself away from him, rolling onto her back. Great. Now both of them lay in silence, staring at the ceiling. Why did he have to bring it up again?

"You know, I wouldn't keep asking if I understood. You rescued her and brought her home. And knowing how much you love dogs, I'm surprised you aren't more attached. It's like you're afraid of making any emotional investment."

"Just stop, okay." Her words were abrupt and razor-sharp. Powered by a frustration that churned in her chest, she leaped out of bed, wanting to kick something. She needed to find a dojang. The sooner, the better.

Leaving him in the bedroom, she stormed into the kitchen. Her hands shook as she made coffee, slamming cupboards like they owed her money. She turned to the fridge and darn near died of a heart attack when she saw François leaning against the wall, arms crossed.

That guy could churn up her insides like an industrial blender. Why? *Emotional investment*. François' words popped into her head. God, that sucked. She pinched the bridge of her nose as her eye began to twitch. Her blood pressure could power a car. But she couldn't get those two words out of her head. *Emotional investment*. He seemed to know her better than herself at times, so why couldn't he understand this? "Getting attached means getting hurt. Nothing is permanent. Especially relationships."

"Do you really believe that?"

Darcy stilled. Oh God, did she say that out loud? Did part of her cling to that belief, regardless of her feelings for François? She was cornered, but instead of attacking like an injured animal would, his concerned expression melted her anger away. Her wound had opened, and she was bleeding out. Helpless, she allowed him to embrace her, her throat tightening—somehow, he'd become the balm that could heal her.

He held her in silence. No pressure to talk or explain. Offering only support. Against his bare chest, listening to his heartbeat, inhaling the scent of intimacy, and wrapped in warm nonjudgemental arms, the last of Darcy's armor fell away.

"I was eight when we left Germany. It was the first place I remember living. The first place I remember leaving." His arms tightened around her, and he kissed the top of her head. "It was devastating to leave my friends and the only home I knew." She sighed but kept going. "Several months before we moved, we found a stray dog and took him in. I called him Lucky and gave him a stuffed pig. It was supposed to be short-term until the owner was located, but after a few months, I assumed we could keep him. My parents looked into what documentation we needed to have him move with us—but we couldn't take him." She tried to swallow the emotion that made her voice shake, but it didn't work. Darcy could still feel the dog's fur brush her face as she clung to his neck, sobbing her goodbye, refusing to let go. Her father's large hands on her arms broke Darcy's grasp and pulled her away, only to have Lucky jump up one last time and lick the tears off her face. "It's not a tragic story. One of our neighbors adopted him, so I knew he went to a loving home. But not only did it hurt, I never got over the fact that I let a dog I loved so much go. Love wasn't enough. Love didn't last. Love only hurt."

Because being held by François magically opened Darcy's emotional vault, she needed distance for the next part. Pulling away, she stood at the counter and poured them both a cup of coffee. She had to focus on the facts. That's all. "Shortly after we arrived in our new home, I got a package from the family that adopted Lucky. It was Glücksschwein. Turns out, their youngest daughter fell out of a tree and bumped her head, knocking her out. Lucky raced back to their house and caused such a commotion that they followed him and found their daughter."

"That's incredible," François said softly.

"Yeah, it is, and as thanks, the family wanted me to have Glücksschwein so I'd always have a bit of Lucky's luck." She took a long drink of her coffee. "I was so happy that Lucky helped that family but losing him still hurt. Each night, I would tell Glücksschwein how much I loved and missed Lucky and that I would never get another dog because Lucky would take up my heart." She drank the remainder of her coffee, avoiding eye contact with François. "And yes, I know I was only a kid, but moving around made it an easy vow to keep. So there you have it. That's why I don't get attached."

Darcy tried to escape to the shower, but he blocked her path. "Getting another dog doesn't betray Lucky."

"Don't try to placate me."

"I'm not. Just think about it for a minute. Would you say that loving someone and having it not work out would stop you from loving someone else?"

"I don't know. Maybe."

"No, Darcy, it wouldn't." His words were cold, and something washed over his face she couldn't decipher, causing an uneasy feeling in her chest. "If that were the case, then a hell of a lot more people would be single."

"Do I have to pay you for the therapy session, or is the first one on the house?"

He opened his mouth, shut it, then walked away. Darcy longed to go after him. Instead, she let him go.

Darcy returned home from the shelter and changed into sweats, tossing her jeans on the bed. Peaches, sitting on François' pillow, stretched, then exited the room with her head high. Great. Snubbed by a cat. "I miss her too, you know," Darcy said to the cat's butt.

At least the worst part of the day was over. Now whether that was her morning conversation with François or dropping off the dogs had yet to be determined. Either way, they were going to have to talk. Something had shifted, although what exactly, escaped her.

Darcy checked the cooking schedule on the fridge. Sometimes François drew tiny pictures of food, and she'd guess at what he was making. But tonight's entry was blank. Oh. Right. She'd forgotten he was having dinner with a friend of his father's—one who might be able to help him find a job—so she was on her own. She took out some leftover lasagne and put it in the microwave. While it was heating, she hit play on the answering machine. There were two messages. Hopefully, the therapy dog charity wanted her for a second interview. Or, even better, a job offer.

"Hello, darling," her mother's recorded voice sang. "I forgot to ask you what your plans were for Thanksgiving when we talked the other day. I know it's short notice, but we'd love to see you. And bring your new beau. Call when you have a chance."

Her new beau. What decade did her mom pull that term from? Every time she did historical research, her mother always started using terms she discovered. Luckily, she didn't refer to François as her *suitor* or *fancy man*.

"Hello. This message is for François. This is Marie, we met last week. We were really impressed with your skills and enthusiasm. Unfortunately, our position in Montreal is already filled, but we would like to offer you the position we discussed in Quebec City. Please call me back when you get this message so I can go into more detail with you."

Darcy stopped the machine. Her knees gave out, and she slid down the wall, landing in a brokenhearted lump on the floor. Quebec City? He'd never mentioned applying for work out of town. Their morning argument replayed in her head. What had she missed?

Oh no. François had told her that losing someone shouldn't stop her from loving again. Was that a hint to prepare her for this?

The room blurred as she fought back tears. He was willing to leave Montreal. He was willing to leave *her*. Yes, their relationship moved fast, but she'd believed in their connection. She'd made an emotional investment (to use François' words), and he'd become part of her life. Like coffee. A habit. An addiction. Wanted. Needed. Couldn't he see that? Or maybe he could, but it didn't matter.

How could she have been so wrong? She'd thought he was...that they we re...oh God, she couldn't even think it. How had her instincts let her down? She'd been drawn to him from the first night they met. Everything about their relationship felt right.

Until now.

A knot formed in her stomach, the size of a bowling ball. She was going to be sick.

That primal instinct of fight or flight kicked in, and without hesitation, she chose flight. Was it childish? Maybe. Okay, yes. But she could only focus on protecting her now-broken heart. Even with a ninth-degree black belt, she wouldn't be strong enough to face him.

As soon as her bags were packed, Darcy took the coward's way out and left him a note.

Going to visit my parents. Not sure of my return date. Don't forget to feed Peaches.

D

14

Darcy had been at her parent's house for two weeks when the postcards started arriving. They were short, simple messages.

Wish you were here.

Miss you.

Thinking of you.

Call me.

???

The sixth, and, as it turned out, the last, was longer. François' messy handwriting filled the entire card.

I don't know what made you run. But you once told me people would promise to stay in touch and never did. Well, I've tried showing you that I miss you and care about you. You are the one not making any effort. But don't worry. I can take a hint. I just wish you followed your own advice and told me to my face to have a nice life. I deserved that much. I've moved out, so don't be afraid to come home. And yes, Peaches is fine.

Darcy's mom sat at the kitchen table, facing her. "What's going on?"

"You read my mail?"

"It's a postcard. Postcards are basically public property."

"It's nothing."

"Right. At least this explains why you showed up out of the blue and haven't left."

Darcy sighed, stood, and began to fill the sink with water.

"Talk to me. I was under the impression you were finally getting what you always wanted—a place to settle and build a life. You purchased a house, for Pete's sake, and this François of yours, he was the first boy you ever told us about. Why are you running away from that?"

"I'm not. Not exactly."

"Then what? And turn off the water. Keeping busy doesn't make your problems go away."

"Well, it should."

"Darcy Alexandra."

"Fine. God, I'm not a kid." She huffed, turned off the water, and faced her mom. "And you're right. About everything. Happy?" Her mother had a glare that could bring world leaders to their knees. "Oh, all right. I was beginning to make close friends and think about a permanent job, not just a contract. I love my place. Absolutely love it. And even though I wouldn't have moved in with someone this fast, living with François...it was better than anything I could have imagined. But François was offered a job in another city, and I don't know...I panicked. I thought we had something, but he was applying for jobs out of town and never told me."

Her mom placed her hands on Darcy's shoulders, so they faced one another dead on. "Did he take the job?"

"I didn't ask him." It came out as a mumble.

"You what?" Her mother's voice rose an octave, and she took a step back, releasing Darcy's shoulders.

"It's not like he was there. I heard a message for him on the answering machine."

"What on earth were you thinking?"

"I told you. I panicked." Now it was Darcy's turn to raise her voice. "I'm not proud of it, but that's what happened."

"Oh, my darling Darcy, you can't make a decision without all the facts. You know better than that."

"Jesus, Mom, it wasn't about facts."

Darcy's mom circled the kitchen before placing a casserole dish into the sink, exactly what she'd told Darcy to stop doing. Did her mom notice their similar behavior or just Darcy?

With the dish soaking, Darcy's mom stared out the kitchen window, her voice softer now. "Our life kept you moving around, and while it was what we wanted, you never had a choice. You were always so social and outgoing. You had to be to make friends, but we robbed you of experiencing the ups and downs of long-term friendships and relationships. It must be hard now, allowing yourself to open up and deal with challenges of the heart."

No kidding. Darcy leaned against the counter beside her. "How did you do it? The constant moving and starting over. Didn't you ever want to stop moving?"

"Sometimes, but I'm more of an introvert than you are. My home was wherever you and your dad were. That's all I needed."

"Oh my gosh, Mom. Could you be more cheesy?"

"Unlikely. I used something along those lines in an essay I recently wrote for a travel magazine, but it's true. I never needed a geographical place to anchor myself. It was about the people I loved."

"So what do I do? I don't want to choose between François and Montreal, providing I still have a choice to make."

"Well, you're not going to solve your problems from Yakima. Go back home and try to figure things out. You said it's not about facts, and you're right. It's not. But you do need all the information. Then, once you have it, allow yourself to listen to your heart."

Darcy agreed. If she ended up with nothing else, she still had a place to call home and friends she could lean on. Realizing that gave her an unfamiliar feeling of security and comfort. Whatever happened with François, she could handle it.

Or so she hoped.

15

With no direct route from Yakima to Montreal, plus a delay in Denver, Darcy traveled for nearly twenty-four hours. She couldn't wait to relax in her soaker tub with a good book. But finding Becks on the couch petting Peaches changed her plans.

"What are you doing here?" Darcy asked. "Taking care of Peaches?"

"Yes. Sort of, and I could ask you the same thing."

"I asked first. Just let me drop my stuff off in the bedroom. Except for this," she pulled a bag out of her backpack and waved it at Becks. "I bought some duty-free booze."

Becks gave a whoop and hopped off the couch.

Darcy's room welcomed her with warmth and comfort as if wrapping her in an invisible blanket. God, she loved it. The old wood floors. The exposed brick wall. The creaky bedroom door. She relaxed for the first time in weeks. Well, almost relaxed. François' absence haunted her like a ghost.

"Okay. So spill it," she said as she returned to the kitchen to find Becks pouring them each a drink from the cocktail shaker. "Thank you. God, have I missed your martinis. They are the best. Cheers, my friend."

Becks took a sip and then blurted out, "Turns out Jason has a love child. He's four."

Darcy nearly spat her sip onto the island. "Holy shit. He never told you?"

"He never knew."

"You're kidding."

"Nope. I always knew there was something in his past. I could sense it. It was like he wasn't always in the present with me."

"Wait. So Jason did know?"

Becks took a much longer sip, then began making a second drink. "No. It wasn't the kid. It was her. Lisa. His ex. He never got over her." She poured the gin without measuring like an experienced mixologist. "I dumped him within minutes of finding out. And, if I'm being honest, I was kind of a dick about it. Make that a huge dick, but I was hurt and humiliated. I didn't want him to see that."

"I'm sorry I wasn't here for you." Darcy meant it too. Like François, Becks had slipped under her radar and been there longer than Darcy realized.

"It's okay. I liked having the place to myself to lick my wounds. And to continue with my theme of full disclosure, I wasn't completely devastated, which says a lot. I guess it wasn't meant to be."

"You sound so smart and reasonable. I wish I was more like you."

"No, you don't. But now let's talk about you, and in case you're wondering, François was gone before I moved back in. He'd already called me about the cat."

Darcy looked into her glass. "I kind of acted like a jerk myself."

Becks leaned her elbows onto the kitchen island. "Don't stop there. What happened?"

"I heard a message for him on the machine and—"

"Another woman? I'll kill him."

"No. A job offer in Quebec City. I was devastated that he would consider moving without telling me—which I know sounds stupid because we weren't together that long, but everything felt so right, and because of that, I felt sucker-punched. So, I panicked and did the one thing I know how to do. Leave."

"You didn't talk to him first?"

"No."

"Oh shit." Her head dropped.

"I know."

"I don't think you do. That's the problem. Here. You're gonna need this." Becks poured them both a new drink. "I take it he didn't tell you about his ex."

Darcy's stomach hit the floor. "His ex? No. Never."

"Figures. I'm going to smack him for this, that's for sure." Becks shook her head. "So, okay, in a nutshell, François was engaged a few years ago, and right before the wedding, as in the day before, his bride-to-be took off. No warning. No nothing. Left him a note saying it was a mistake. He was left to cancel everything, let everyone know, and return the gifts. As soon as that was done, he took off traveling."

"Fuck me." Darcy collapsed onto a stool. "I did the exact same thing, including leaving a note. Oh my God. I'm such an idiot."

"It's not like you did the same thing on purpose. How could you have known?"

"I know, but still. I need to talk to him and fix this." Her mind raced. No wonder he didn't want to go to the wedding. But he did. For her. "Do you know where he went? I'm assuming he took that job."

"I don't know anything about any job. He didn't leave any forwarding information either. Try not to worry. He'll turn up sooner or later. He always does."

"I hope you're right." Darcy followed Becks to the couch and turned on the TV. Darcy no longer wanted that bath. She needed a friend and a stiff drink, and right now, she had both.

A couple hours later, Becks turned off the TV and went to bed, leaving Darcy alone and restless. She was bone-tired but not sleepy. Thinking about François would have to wait until tomorrow. Nothing would be solved tonight. She was resourceful and would figure out a way to find him. She had to.

To distract herself, she tidied the kitchen, then went through the phone messages Becks had written down.

Krista had called twice.

Carrie, once.

The shelter called to let her know all the puppies had been adopted. Even Cookie found a home.

There was a second message from the shelter, this one from Annique, asking her to call. Annique never called. That was the volunteer coordinator's job, so something must be wrong with the puppies or Cookie.

So much for sleep.

Darcy called the animal shelter as soon as they opened.

"Hi, Annique. It's Darcy. I got a message that you called. Are the puppies okay?"

"The what? Oh, right. They're fine. All at new homes. No, I'm calling because I'm leaving, and I recommended you for my job."

"Me?"

"Of course you. You would be amazing in this role. I know it. You know it. Hell, we all know it. I'll set up a meeting with the board for you. One evening this week would be preferable."

"I don't know."

"Seriously?"

"No. Yeah. I mean, go ahead. Anytime is fine."

"Great. And wow. So much change. Did you know we hired a new volunteer coordinator? Probably not, since you've been out of town. Okay, well, I'll be in touch, and honestly," Annique's voice lowered to a whisper, "unless you blow the interview, this is mostly a formality."

Darcy listened to the dial tone for a solid few seconds before realizing Annique had hung up. This couldn't be real, could it? That this gift of a job landing right on her lap? And not any old job either. She needed to tell someone. No, not someone. François.

16

One week later, Darcy pulled up to the shelter with five minutes to spare. She would have preferred to have arrived earlier but kept checking her appearance in the mirror. Jeans and a T-shirt were far from special, except this T-shirt said *Staff* on the back, and it was her first time wearing it.

At nine on the nose, Annique unlocked the main doors, so Darcy exited her car and walked toward the building, surprised by her stomach doing flips. She could do the job and do it well, so what was going on?

Annique only had two days to show her everything, so they would be a busy couple of days. "At least we don't have to waste time with a tour. You already know the staff, most volunteers, and where everything is. This morning, we'll set you up with staff logins and an email address. This afternoon, we'll go to the bank. Mostly you'll make deposits, but you'll also have some signing authority for small purchases, so you'll need to sign some paperwork."

"Sounds great." Darcy immediately got to work. At eleven, a new volunteer walked in. Annique introduced herself and Darcy. Turning to Darcy, she said, "Can you take Mariam to the staff room and find the volunteer coordinator?"

"No problem." Darcy walked around the desk. "Follow me." They began walking down the hall.

"How long have you worked here?" Mariam asked.

"Today is my first day on staff, but I started here as a volunteer. It's a great place. I'm sure you'll enjoy it here."

"Oh, I'm sure I will," said the older woman, "if it gives me a smile even close to yours."

Darcy blushed but couldn't deny the truth. "They should pay me for the free advertising," Darcy joked as she directed Mariam into the staff room, giving her a brief tour. "So this is where you come to begin your shift. Hang your coat in an empty locker and help yourself to anything. Coffee, tea, cookies, whatever we have. There's a sign-in book by the door, so we know who is in the building. Make yourself at home, and I'll have the volunteer coordinator meet you here."

"Thank you so much."

As she exited the room, she realized that she had yet to meet the new volunteer coordinator. She walked down the hall to their office. The door was ajar, so she knocked and entered.

The office was empty of people. However, a dog was curled up on a bed in the corner. A cone around its neck. Darcy's eyes nearly popped out of her head. "Cookie! Oh my gosh. "Cookie leaped off the bed, barking and licking Darcy, who had dropped to her knees. "Oh, my sweet girl. I've missed you so much! I thought you were adopted."

"She was. By me."

Darcy froze. You've got to be kidding. She whipped around to face François, her heart racing, then screeching to a halt, as she took in his face. That beautiful face with its scars, crooked nose, and soulful blue eyes stared blankly at her, devoid of emotion. That stung more than if he'd been mad.

"What happened to her?" was all Darcy could manage.

"Nice to see you too," François said, walking past her and petting Cookie. "Come on, sweet girl, back to bed."

Cookie listened and lay back down." I had her spayed. One set of puppies was enough."

"Makes sense. So volunteer coordinator, huh?" Was her voice shaking as much as her hands?

"Yup. And now you're the office manager."

"Kind of funny, isn't it?" She attempted a small smile.

François sat down at his desk without replying.

"What happened to that job in Quebec City?" Her voice, full of insecurity and remorse, wavered.

His expression revealed his confusion.

What did that mean? *Keep it together, Darcy.* "So, um, a new volunteer is waiting for you in the staff room, and, uh, obviously now is not the right time to talk, but maybe we can meet for lunch?"

François scratched the back of his neck. The silence felt like a hand pushing her out the door. Finally, he let out a sigh and glanced at his watch. "What time?"

"Twelve-thirty."

"Sure. I'll meet you at reception."

Darcy gave him a weak smile and walked back to her desk.

Luckily, she knew most of what Annique showed her because her mind was distracted. How could it not be? If things didn't work out between her and François, they'd have to work together.

Minutes felt like hours until finally, she looked up to see François standing in front of the desk. He raised his eyebrows. "Ready?"

"Yup." She turned to Annique. "I'll be back in half an hour." Annique nodded as Darcy grabbed her bag and walked out with François, neither saying a word. Darcy pulled out her car keys. "Where do you want to go for lunch?"

"Doesn't matter. I already ate."

She gave him a brief nod, wondering what he'd eaten and in whose kitchen he'd prepared it as they lowered themselves into her car. No small talk. No jokes. The air, so thick with tension, it was a miracle she could move her arm enough to poke Glücksschwein. *Don't let me down now.*

She took them to the nearest drive-through, ordered only for herself, and pulled into a parking spot away from most other cars.

With the weight of silence threatening to crush her car, she had no choice but to begin. "I know it was stupid to take off like that." She looked out the windshield, not at him. If she did, she would break down and cry, but before that happened, she wanted to tell him the truth. "I panicked. Things were going great. So great, it felt too good to be true. Then I heard the message offering you a position in Quebec City, and all my insecurities came rushing back. All I could think of was that you were leaving. It blocked out everything. Especially common sense."

"You should have talked to me. I told you before not to assume you knew what I was thinking."

"I know." She swallowed hard and turned toward him. "I can't undo what I did. I'd give anything to take it back. I really would. God, this is so embarrassing to admit, but I think I've clung to that childhood belief that love ends up as hurt, and because of that, I kept expecting the other shoe to drop. So when I heard that message..." Her voice trailed off, and she closed her eyes and kept them shut until summoning enough courage to continue. "I'm not going to beat around the bush. Right here. Right now. I'm going to lay everything on the line. And whatever happens, we'll find a way to work together."

Her food sat in a warm lump on her lap. There's no way she could eat it. "I don't believe in love at first sight, but you changed my life the moment I met you. Talking to you was...I don't know...the word comfortable doesn't do it justice. And then, when you moved in, even before things heated up between us, you helped me begin to build a life. This place started to feel like home. Something I've been searching for, for a long time. And when I heard the message, like I said, I panicked. Oh God, this is hard."

Her eyes tingled, and she desperately tried to blink back the tears. But then he went and placed a hand on hers, and tears began to roll down her cheeks. "My heart broke because I thought you were leaving me." She wiped at her face with a shaky hand. "But there's more. If you asked me to go with you, I would. I'd give up everything I'd built because I knew, in my gut, that life with you was home. That you were what I've been looking for." She took a deep breath and blew her nose on a napkin. "I'm sorry, I must sound like an idiot."

He released the hand he'd been holding and scratched the back of his neck. "You hurt me, Darce. A lot."

"I know. I'm sorry. Especially since, well, Becks told me about your ex. But it's not the same. On the surface, yeah, it does look like it, but I ran, not because I wasn't sure about you, but because I was absolutely one-hundred percent sure. I'm sorry, I'm making a mess of this." She scrubbed her face with her hands and then started the car. "Forget it. We need to get back."

"Hang on." He ran his fingers through his hair and exhaled loudly. "Once things began between us, I should have told you about my ex. I tried a few times, but quite frankly, I didn't want to think about it anymore, and also, let's face it, it embarrassed me. That issue I have with people assuming they know what I'm thinking? It's because her note said she knew I was thinking the same thing as her and that it'd been obvious for a while. That getting married would be a mistake. For the record, I did not think that but had we talked about it, things might have ended without as much pain." François took a deep breath. "Traveling cleared my head, and I wanted to move forward. I wasn't looking for anyone. I certainly didn't want a relationship, but you got under my skin from the moment we met. It was a mistake to think I could handle living with you as friends." He ran his palms up and down his thighs. "I thought you were different. And maybe you are because you came back." A spark of hope ignited in Darcy's heart as François grabbed the drink that came with her lunch and took a sip. "When you mentioned Quebec City in my office, it took me a minute to piece it together. I'm trying to understand why you didn't talk to me, but I think there's a chance I underestimated your insecurities. And in fairness, I never told you mine. And for the record, I wasn't planning on taking it—the job in Quebec City. I didn't even apply for it. They offered it to me because the position in Montreal was filled and this one was similar. Which makes this all the more frustrating. I want to stay mad at you and tell you to stay out of my life because being left like that for the second time hurt twice as much and made me wonder what's wrong with me that causes people to take off."

Darcy grabbed his arm. "No. Please don't think that. It was me. Stupid, stupid me."

He looked at her, his blue eyes moist with emotion. "I don't know what to do, Darcy. Now that you're here...I don't know. I can't tell you it's over because I love you too."

"I never said..."

"Yes, you did. Just in a roundabout way."

"Yeah, I guess I did." Her burst of relief had her smiling.

"So humor me and say the words."

"I love you, François. Madly. I truly do."

He smiled, but her heart dropped as it faded. What if her apology and her love couldn't undo the hurt she'd caused?

"There's something else you should know," he said.

"Okay." Why did it feel like she was about to get pushed out of an airplane with no parachute?

"I applied and took the job at the shelter to hurt you. I got to chatting when I came to adopt Cookie and heard about the position, and it went from there. I thought when you came back, *if* you came back, and found me working there, it would serve you right. I even felt that way when I heard you were starting there. But today, in my office, I felt like an asshole and decided to quit."

His words hung in the air, but she wasn't mad. They'd both done stupid things. Perhaps her village was meant to have two idiots. "Please tell me you didn't quit."

"No, not yet."

"Don't. That role is perfect for you, and I'm going to like being your boss."

"You're not my boss."

"Well, not technically."

They drove back in silence. This time though, the silence didn't suck all the air out of the car. It was golden, like the evening sun in her apartment.

Darcy turned off the car, and François opened his door. "François, wait." She grabbed his shirt with unparalleled urgency and pulled him into a kiss. It's a miracle the sparks didn't set the car on fire. "So? Are we good?"

"Yeah. I think so."

She kissed him again. It was soft. Gentle. Grateful.

"Okay. You can go now," she whispered.

François gave her a mock salute, then exited the car. Darcy waited for his door to close. "Thank you, Glücksschwein. I knew you wouldn't let me down." She gave him a little poke. If she didn't know better, she would have sworn he smiled.

JANET KOOPS

Six Weeks With You

Sometimes timing is everything

Prologue

Stupid tiara. I pull it off my eyes, having just knocked it on the car door frame as I slid in, and chuck it into the back. The sparkly headdress hits the edge of the seat, popping off the last zero of 2000, then falls to the floor. Well, Happy New Year to you too. I rub behind my ears, where the plastic has been pinching all night. Across the street, another party is still going strong. Yup, the electrical grid is alive and well. I guess the world as we know it didn't collapse as computers everywhere figured out what to do with all those zeros. I find it almost disappointing, though hardly surprising, that things usually stay the same when change is anticipated.

Kent drops heavily into the passenger seat, reeking of booze and cigars, and dangles the keys in front of my face. I start the car, then rub my hands together while the car warms. Our breath merges into an icy cloud and floats between us. I am grateful for the quiet car interior compared to the noise of the party, and I take a minute to close my eyes and lean my head back against the seat. My body, tense from standing in heels all night, begins to loosen. Soon I can take off these uncomfortable boots.

I am about to sit up when Kent's hand grabs me by the hair at the nape of my neck and turns me to face him. Instinctively, my hand grabs his arm. "What are you doing?" Despite the cold, a rush of heat floods through me, and I feel a wave of perspiration break out on my forehead. He is not ordinarily physical. We keep my bruising internal and private. What could I have done to provoke this?

He gives my head a slight shake. "Aren't you going to apologize?" He speaks slowly. Partly due to his anger—he likes to draw things out to make his point—and partly due to the alcohol.

"For what?"

"You don't know?"

"No. I had a nice evening. It was fun."

"Oh my God, Victoria, do you have any idea how you embarrassed me?"

He tightens his fist, pulling my hair harder, making me draw in a breath, but I know enough not to complain.

When I fail to answer, he continues. "You snorted."

"What?" I wince as he tightens his grip again.

"You snorted like a pig when you were talking to Samantha. Maxwell had just introduced me to Michael Greggs—you know how I want to be the contractor to remodel his house—then we hear this snort. We turn to see you covering your mouth and laughing. It was humiliating."

"I'm sorry. I don't even remember doing it. I was having a good time. Samantha's nice despite what an oaf her husband is."

"Who are you to judge Maxwell?"

Oh boy. Here it comes—his favorite mantra.

"Don't forget who you were when I found you. Waitressing in a cocktail bar and living in that dump. A cheap dye job and tarty makeup. Twenty pounds heavier. You were nothing. I saved you. I made you who you are. The least you can do is not embarrass me." Droplets of spit hit my face.

"I'm sorry. You're right. It won't happen again."

"Right. That's what you always say. I don't know why I keep you around."

A brave person would remind him that he was the one who started flirting with me—yes, me—even with my cheap dye job and extra twenty pounds.

He lets go of my hair, and I rub the back of my neck before pulling out of the driveway. Away from this night. Away from who I've turned out to be. Perhaps the apple didn't fall as far from the tree as I had hoped.

The roads are quiet, and he is asleep before I stop at the first red light. The route home unfolds before me. One I've taken so many times, I could do it with my eyes closed. Kent's voice echoes in my mind. I told you to go this way,

Vic-toooor-reee-a. It's the most direct, Vic-toooor-reee-a. There are fewer stops, Vic-toooor-reee-a.

Well, screw it.

Impulsively I take a left. The sudden turn causes Kent to shift in his seat.

"Where are you going?"

"I'm taking a different route."

"Don't be an idiot."

"Jesus, Kent. Despite what you think, I'm not stupid. Your way isn't the only way, you know. I know what I'm doing."

I steel myself for his scathing reply. But nothing happens. I quickly glance over. He is asleep again, barely aware of my first act of rebellion.

1

August 2000

WHILE MOST PEOPLE DON'T look forward to cleaning, for me, it means the end of another week, and that alone is cause for celebration. It also helps that my apartment is small, so there is not much to clean. So, once the bathroom is done, I check off another day on the calendar. Look at all those rows of red checkmarks. I've been in Montreal for four weeks.

I quickly shower and dress—so fun to wear old ripped jeans and running shoes for a change—then step out into the communal hall to sort the mail. Because this is an old house converted into apartments (which may or may not be legal), there is only one mail slot on the main door. The mail for all three flats drops into a pile on an old navy carpet, sitting in whatever people have dragged in off their shoes, and waits to get sorted by whoever comes across it first. Or not—one of my neighbors steps over it or on it. Not the end of the world, but flipping through a grocery flyer caked in mud is not pleasant, and I do like the grocery flyers. Maybe like is a strong word. Need is better, as in I need to save money where I can.

My neighbor above me in apartment two typically gets most of the mail. I have yet to run into the person in apartment three, but according to their mail, their name is C. Levesque, and they have an overdue bill or two. But no bills today for me, Vicki Meyers, in apartment one, but I will take these two flyers. Thank you very much.

Directly under the last flyer is a postcard of the Rideau Canal in Ottawa, my hometown. Fear grips me, tight, like a hand around my throat. I can't even touch it.

This is exactly the kind of thing he'd do to mess with my head. But how did he find me? I specifically didn't get a phone, so he wouldn't be able to call information or check online and locate me.

"Hey, is there any mail for me?"

The shock of her voice nearly causes me to drop my flyers, and I grab onto the radiator for support with my free hand. My upstairs neighbor stands in front of me on the landing. How did I not hear her coming?

"Are you okay? I didn't mean to startle you."

"Yeah, sure. I was lost in my thoughts and didn't hear you coming down the stairs."

"Hey, is that a postcard from Ottawa?"

"Yeah."

"Is it for me?"

"I don't know." She looks at me, waiting, or at least I assume she is since her eyes are hidden behind sunglasses. "Oh right. Sorry." I flip it over. To Karen Ho. "Yeah. Here." I'm too stunned to feel relief.

She takes it, gives it a quick look, and slips it into her purse. "My mom's so funny. She knows I collect postcards from around the world, so she always sends me one, even from somewhere close by."

"That's nice of her," I manage to say.

"Moms, right?"

"Yeah, moms."

"Well, have a good day."

"You too." While she bounds out the door, ponytail swinging high, I retreat to my apartment and lock the door. Why am I shaking? Nothing happened. Kent didn't send it. Relax. I brew some camomile tea, then pull out my sketch pad and draw. Breathe, Vicki, just breathe. Some people journal to express their feelings. I draw. My writing is messy, and my spelling is atrocious. No matter how hard I tried at school, my teachers always told me to try harder, so I came to hate writing. But drawing is different. My brain and hands work in unison, allowing me to release that which builds up inside me.

Today I sketch a woman with deep, hollow eyes. Don't they say the eyes are a gateway to the soul? She has her head tilted slightly back, her body stiff, hands clenched into fists so tight that were she to open them, nail marks would be embedded in her palms. Her mouth opens for a scream, but instead of sound, she expels her life like a poison. From a distance, it looks like swirls but up close, you can see tiny shapes and figures of the shame and regret that haunt her.

Across from her, an extended hand, palm up and open, offers to lead her away. Is it her past, or is it her future?

2

As I step outside into the crisp air of a September day, I wait on the landing until I hear the satisfying click of the front door lock. Not that I own anything worth stealing. Barely any furniture. No TV. No phone. My bed is a blow-up mattress with sheets from the thrift shop. I own two suitcases worth of clothes. If anyone steals anything, they are welcome to it as they are worse off than me.

No, my fixation over the lock is about safety. The landlord assured me the building was secure, and by secure, he was referring to the flimsy lock on the outer door that leads to the three apartments. This type of lock keeps honest people out, not someone determined to get in. Someone motivated. Someone like Kent.

Obsessing comes quickly when I have too much time on my hands. I'm not sure if idleness is the root of evil, but it is the quickest route to the darkest corner of your mind. Fortunately, the animal shelter is within walking distance from my apartment, saving me the bus fare, and today is my first volunteer shift. All positions needed, the sign read, and had pictures of someone walking a dog, answering a phone, unloading a truck. Knowing nothing about animals, never having owned a pet, not even a fish, I am a bit nervous, but it seems there is office work I can do. I know as much about working in an office as I do about animals, but an office won't bite me. Plus, the experience will only help me. Answering phones and filing would allow me to include clerical work on my resume and could lead to another part-time job or even a full-time one. A girl can dream.

Not that I am ungrateful for my waitressing job. But it is all I have ever done, and currently, I only work three days a week. They aren't good shifts either.

New employees work the Monday, Tuesday, and Wednesday lunch and evening shifts. Not a lot of opportunities for big tips. A rapidly dwindling amount of money sits in a savings account, but I try not to dip into it. If Mom taught me anything, it was to always have an escape plan. She was right. My secret bank account allowed me to leave Kent.

As I begin to walk, I pull up the collar of my peacoat to brace myself against the wind. Yesterday was warm and sunny, but fall weather in Montreal is unpredictable. One day warm, one day cold. Up and down the thermostat like stocks in an unstable market. Luckily, I don't have far to go.

The neighborhood quickly transitions from residential into an old industrial one, with narrow streets and cracked sidewalks. Some buildings are boarded up, others under renovation. The animal shelter is housed on the first floor of an old factory, its original purpose long abandoned. With red brick, sweeping arches, and large windows, the ghosts of overworked laborers, women weaving, and children knotting carpets hide in the interior. I enter through modern glass doors, functional but out of place against the arched entryway.

It smells a bit like pee, but compared to the outside, the inside is uplifting. The color on the walls is a surprisingly bold and fresh green, like early summer grass, and a big welcome sign hangs over the front desk. A cartoon silhouette of a cat head is on the wall in a bright blue with an arrow pointing left. My eyes turn in that direction, and sure enough, I see a wall of cat cages. Someone cleans one out while another holds a kitten and strokes it tenderly. The kitten nuzzles a grey and white head against the person's cheek, and the volunteer kisses it on the head. I recognize the actions as soothing and maternal, even though I never experienced them myself.

A large bulletin board is mounted on the wall to the right of the welcome desk and is covered in Polaroids of people and animals. Furever Families reads the sign. Cute.

Stepping toward the person at the reception desk is when the nerves hit, nearly causing me to run. But I want to do this. I can do this. What are the three basic rules for entering a new social situation? Oh right. One: Back straight. Two: Head up. Three: Appear friendly.

Here goes nothing.

The person at reception looks up and smiles. "Good morning. How can I help you?"

"Hi," I say with practiced brightness. "My name is Vicki. I'm here for my first volunteer shift."

"Oh, fantastic," she says as she stands up, placing a tiny dog with a big pink bow onto a pillow on the desk. She scratches the dog's head. "Céline likes a good cuddle, don't you, Céline?" The dog circles the cushion before laying down. "Céline here was found in a garbage bag, can you believe it? Some people, I swear. Okay. So, welcome. My name is Darcy. Come with me, and I'll take you to the staff room. You can hang up your coat, grab some coffee if you want, and then one of our volunteers will give you the grand tour."

"Sounds great. Thank you."

I follow her down the hallway opposite the cats. Darcy is about three inches taller than me, with gorgeous red hair pulled back into a ponytail, a smattering of light freckles, and an athlete's build. Everything about her is efficient and practical, from her clothes (faded jeans, a staff sweatshirt, and what I think are steel-toed boots) to her movements (economical and fast). She is a busy woman who doesn't waste time. Her walk is naturally confident, and I can't help but wonder what it is like to be so comfortable in your own skin.

We enter a room with a window overlooking a small, grassy, fenced-in yard. The room is warmer than the hallway and filled with the aroma of fresh coffee. There is a lunch table, a bulletin board, and a small kitchenette. On the opposite wall to the window stands a bank of lockers. A middle-aged woman with grey hair in a sleek bob hangs her coat up in a locker.

'Hi, Mariam. You're here already. Awesome. This is Vicki. She's a new volunteer, and today is her first shift. I was hoping you could give her the grand tour since François won't be in for another hour." She turns to me. "François is our volunteer coordinator."

"Good morning, Darcy. Of course, I can," Mariam says, smiling at me and extending her arm for a handshake as Darcy exits the room. Mariam is a woman accustomed to wealth. Her hands are soft and well-manicured, and I can't miss the sizable diamond ring and diamond-encrusted wedding band. Her clothes are functional for the shelter but well-tailored. Her broad smile, combined with how she leans toward me in genuine interest, makes her overall manner friendly, not ostentatious or flashy. I take her hand in mine. Remember eye contact, moderate pressure, confident poise.

"Sorry about the cold hands," she says. "Leather gloves look nice, but they don't keep you warm, do they?"

I'm pretty sure her question is rhetorical, so I smile and nod.

"Darcy introduced you in English, so I assume you want to speak English, or would you prefer French?"

"English."

"Do you speak French?"

"I do. My mother's French Canadian."

"Oh, perfect. That makes things much easier. Are you from here?"

"No. Ottawa. My mom is originally from Northern Ontario. Sudbury. I won't need to write in French, will I? We just spoke it at home. Especially when she was mad." Oh my God, Vicki. Shut up. Remember, pause—deep breath.

"You're so lucky to grow up in a bilingual home."

"Yeah. Lucky."

"Makes speaking two languages second nature. I need to translate everything in my head first. Now let's find you a volunteer t-shirt. Hmm, what size are you? I recommend a bigger size to fit comfortably over your clothes."

"Sure. Um, a medium, I guess."

She opens a cupboard and pulls out a blue shirt with a white silhouette of a dog and cat on the front. Volunteer is written across the back. Miriam takes one out of her bag and pulls it on. I slip mine on too. She writes me a name tag, and my tour begins.

Mariam is chatty. Not only does she seem to know everything that goes on here, she knows all the staff and volunteers and fills me in on bits of their lives without being too gossipy. Her easy manner helps me to relax, and I no longer sound like a babbling idiot.

Within five minutes, I know that Mariam moved to Montreal from British Columbia ten years ago. Her parents are of Loyalist descent, though family lore suggests that they only fought for England in the American Revolution to obtain free land. Her husband came to Canada with his parents in the 1950s, and they were some of the first immigrants from Hong Kong. When she married her husband in the mid-sixties, it was quite unconventional.

I am more familiar with her ancestry than my own. Not only that, my personal history is less impressive. I am from a single-parent home and moved to Montreal for a fresh start after ending things with my boyfriend. All true. Just with the unpleasant details omitted. No one wants to hear them, and I am not looking for pity, so I redirect the conversation by asking if she has any children.

Mariam is the mother of four sons she is proud of and enjoys discussing, the youngest having just left for university. "So, we are empty nesters now," she says, smiling. "When the right dog comes in here, I am going to snatch him up. Just don't tell my husband." She winks.

When the tour finishes, Darcy suggests I shadow Mariam for the remainder of the shift. That involves taking the dogs outside for a bathroom break and some playtime.

"Oh, um, I thought I could help with clerical work. You know, filing, answering phones, stuff like that. I don't know anything about animals. I don't think I'll be much help."

Mariam smiles and places a reassuring hand on my shoulder. "Don't worry. You're not the first person to have no experience. I'll show you what to do. And trust me, once you start working with the animals, you won't want to do anything else."

"I'm not so sure."

"It'll be fun. I promise. Now let's not keep these cuties waiting."

"Well, okay. I guess." If today turns into a disaster, I won't come back.

We walk through the kennel to the end of the farthest row to reach the first client of the day. A small placard with the dog's name, breed, age, health issues, and temperament is attached to each pen. A colored sticker in the corner provides extra information for volunteers and staff. A green sticker means the dog can go to the play yard with other dogs. Red signifies they need to go alone, and yellow, check with staff.

I read the dog's sign.

GUNNER. APPROX. FIVE YEARS
OLD. POSSIBLE HUSKY – PIT
BULL MIX. FOUND ABANDONED
AND STARVING IN AN EMPTY
APARTMENT. HE IS LOOKING FOR
A HOME FAMILIAR WITH DOGS
THAT CAN WORK WITH HIM TO
REBUILD TRUST.

A red sticker sits in the corner.

"Why does he have a red sticker? Is he going to bite us?"

"Oh no. Nothing like that. He is just very stressed out. But he is making progress. When he first came here, we couldn't get him out of the pen at all." Mariam opens the gate. "Hello, Gunner." Her voice is gentle. "This is Vicki. We are going to take you for a walk. Sound like a plan?"

Gunner is a grey and white ball of fur, curled up in the corner, as far away from us as possible. He is not even on the dog bed, and despite Mariam's coaxing, Gunner doesn't move.

"Oh, Gunner," Mariam sighs. "By the time someone found him, he was skin and bones. The floor covered in pee and poo. The poor guy would have died of dehydration had the toilet seat lid not been left up. He's suffered abuse and was possibly used as a bait dog in fighting. He has significant scarring and is wary of everyone and everything. I don't understand how anyone could do that."

I do.

"Needless to say, we need to rebuild his trust. Then he'll come out of his shell and find the home where he belongs." She reaches into her pocket and pulls out a small bag, shaking it. "My secret weapon, just for Gunner. Beef jerky."

"Come on, Gunner. Let's go." Her voice is still gentle but more commanding. She waves a piece of jerky in the air. Gunner's head pops up, his nose sniffing. He gets up, stretches, then slowly walks over.

What a beautiful dog.

His snout and build are that of a husky. But, instead of a thick coat, Gunner's fur is short, like a pit bull's, along with floppy ears. His eyes, the color of a turquoise gemstone, assess us with trepidation.

Mariam hooks up the leash. "Would you like to take him?"

I take a fearful step back. "I've never walked a dog before."

"Well honey, then it's time you learned. Gunner is a good dog to learn on. He's slow, and he never pulls."

She holds out the leash and waits patiently for me to take it from her. I move as slowly as Gunner did but eventually take it. Mariam's quiet persistence works on both untrusting dogs and humans, I guess.

We follow Mariam down the corridor, and with each step, my apprehension switches a little bit more towards excitement. Here I am, walking a dog! I contain it to a small smile. Gunner is less enthused, his head hanging low as if walking down death row.

Once outside, we enter the yard visible through the staff-room window. The lawn is bumpy, the grass dormant for winter. Three orange balls and a comically large plastic bone are scattered across the yard.

"Tell him to sit, unhook his leash, then say release."

"Sit."

Gunner sits with weary resignation.

I squat beside him to remove his leash and then scratch his head as Darcy had done to the tiny dog. "It's okay, Gunner. You're safe here. No one is going to hurt you now."

He makes brief eye contact with me, doubt in his eyes. I've been fooled before, they say.

Touché. Me too.

"Release."

He just sits there.

"Go on," Mariam orders.

Gunner looks at her and sighs. Sighs. Then wanders across the yard to do his business.

"Here." Mariam passes me some poop bags. "Always keep one in your pocket."

At the end of the shift, I meet with the volunteer coordinator. François is a giant. Well beyond six feet, he towers over me. He's pretty buff, too, and would not look out of place in a professional hockey team's starting lineup. Mariam mentioned during my tour that he and Darcy were a couple. Otherwise, I might be tempted to seek some temporary comfort in his body. Instead, he asks what I would like to do. I think of all the clerical experience I could gain but somehow find myself telling him I enjoyed working with the dogs. Before I know it, I'm signed up for three shifts a week, all in the kennel.

I guess Mariam was right—one shift with the dogs, and you don't want to do anything else. Too bad she couldn't help me get the rest of my life sorted out.

3

AFTER SEVERAL SHIFTS, THE routine of the animal shelter becomes familiar. So different from anything I've previously done, I become a sponge, learning everything I can, and after only three weeks, I am pretty confident in executing my tasks. Perhaps employment at a vet clinic is in my future.

There is no end to the animals arriving at the shelter, all abandoned, mistreated, or surrendered. The dedication of both staff and volunteers to rehome the animals is inspiring, and as a result, most are not there for long. Sometimes, however, there are exceptions, like Gunner.

When I'm not waitressing or at the shelter, I visit the library. The computers are always busy, so I read every book they have on dog training, even though I don't enjoy reading. I begin my shifts early and stay late, so I can spend extra time with Gunner and force myself to seek advice from experienced staff and volunteers. Soon everyone knows my project is to coax Gunner out of his shell and help him find a home.

The work is starting to pay off, but while Gunner and I have made progress, he remains shy and nervous around strangers. This makes him hard to relate to, and people struggle to connect with him. And when people can't make a connection, they look at other dogs. The poor guy must be so lonely.

Today, as I come in from walking him, I run into Darcy. Gunner darts behind me and pees on the floor.

"Well, at least we know he's getting enough to drink," Darcy says.

"Yes. I guess you could say that."

"So a bunch of us are going out for drinks later. Did you want to join us?"

"Thanks, but I can't tonight." The response is automatic. Kent insisted I check with him before agreeing to any social activity, and old habits die hard.

"Alright then, another time. We're a pretty fun bunch, you know. Unlike the cats, we don't bite."

I smile. "Oh, for sure, hopefully, next time." That's a lie too. Relationships are problematic. I'd rather keep to myself.

Gunner and I make our way back to his pen, and after removing his leash, I squat on the floor beside him. I give him a good scratch behind the ears while he looks me right in the eye, right into my soul. "What?" I ask him. His eyebrows go up and down. "Don't look at me like that. You don't trust people either. It's why we get along so well."

He leans forward and licks my face.

A week later, I am in the staff room putting on my coat when Darcy walks in. Her usual gate is modified, her shoulders down in defeat.

"Oh," she sighs, wiping a tear. "I'm glad you're here. I need to talk to you about Gunner since you often work with him. If we don't find an adoptive or foster family soon, the board of directors feels it would be best to put him down."

"What? Why?" My insides turn to liquid.

"He's been here a long time. Three months before you started with us. We are not set up to be a long-term home. Living as he does, curled up in that pen, all alone, day after day. Dogs are social animals. That is no way to live. He has no quality of life."

"That's awful." The tightness in my chest nearly prevents me from speaking.

"It is." She turns to me. "How is he doing? Any signs of improvement?"

"He looks at me when I say his name, and eventually, he comes over without bribery. And he always—" Panic closes my throat. It takes every ounce of energy to swallow it down and continue talking. "And he always waits for a scratch behind the ears when I return him to his pen."

"That's more than he's done for anyone else. Let's keep our fingers crossed that we find someone to adopt or foster him by Friday. I'll keep reaching out to other places and some of our past foster families. Hopefully, someone out there can help him." She gestures to what I assume is the universe and hope, beyond hope, that someone or something is listening because Gunner doesn't deserve this.

Then it hits me—the second blow in a one-two punch. She said Friday. "Oh my God. You mean this Friday? That's not much time. Is there anything I can do? There must be something."

For several seconds we face each other in melancholic silence before she reaches out to give my arm a squeeze.

"I'll let you know. Thanks." Darcy then takes a deep breath and a long drink of water before exiting the room.

Resisting the urge to run, I soon follow Darcy out of the staff room and return to Gunner's pen. "Hey, Gunner." He turns quickly, surprised by my voice. Weren't you just here? I imagine him thinking.

"It's time you and I had a serious talk, okay?" I enter the pen and sit down on the floor beside him. "You need to perk up and come out of your shell. I know it's hard, but people need to see the real you. And once they get to know you, they'll love you as much as I do."

Gunner moves toward me, lays his head on my lap, and my heart snaps in two.

4

IF YOU PHYSICALLY EXHAUST yourself, you don't lie awake at night, drowning in empty silence, questioning your every decision. So that's what I do: walking every day, often until my feet hurt, discovering new neighborhoods. But I have yet to hike up Mount Royal—until today.

A long road winds up the mountain from downtown to a lookout high above the city. Both the walk and the view are beautiful, or so I've been told, but the looming presence of the one-hundred-foot illuminated cross intimidates me, like the watchful eyes of Mrs. Beliveau, my fourth-grade teacher. The memory of her standing at the school entrance, erect, hands on her hips, lips tight, waiting for the students to form two neat lines remains fresh, even after all these years. As we entered the school, passing her in silence, she would scan us like a robot. But unlike an unfeeling robot, her eyes were judgmental. I always chose the line farthest from where she was standing, keeping my head down, and walking close to the person in front of me, longing to pass unnoticed. If I dared glance up, I'd catch her shaking her head as I passed. And those were the good days. Often, she would call me out of line. "Vicki, your clothes are dirty. Vicki, you should be wearing a hat. Vicki, there is a hole in your pants." As if the constant torment from the kids wasn't enough.

The grey sky matches my mood, nearly enough of a deterrent to make me turn around, but I force myself to begin the trail, having come this far.

Turns out it's not as far as I thought, and soon I reach the top. The lookout is nearly deserted, so I jump onto the wall and sit cross-legged, scanning the horizon for a certain je ne sais quoi. The city responds with dull grey silence.

I remain there, staring off into nothing until the sun begins to set behind distant clouds and cold seeps into my bones like a sponge wicking up water. Stretching my legs out, I notice that all the other visitors are gone, leaving me alone.

Being alone doesn't scare me. Not anymore. I prefer it. You're safer. You're in control. Unlike Gunner. He is alone but without control. How is that fair? He did nothing wrong other than be born into the wrong circumstances. Isn't it amazing how much in life boils down to chance?

No one is going to give Gunner a chance, though—unless it's me.

Oh my God, why didn't I think of that before? Why don't I foster Gunner? I leap off the wall, walking twice as fast as on the way up. The universe Darcy called out to must have listened because, at one point, the sun breaks through the clouds right at the horizon, turning the sky orange and red, while the wind scatters dried leaves like a kaleidoscope of butterflies. I'd be crazy not to take this as a sign I'm doing the right thing.

How can I wait until tomorrow to talk to Darcy?

At home, I draw a bed of butterflies, carrying Gunner like an Egyptian prince towards a person waiting with open arms in a grassy field under a blue sky. The colors I choose are ones I haven't touched in a long time. Bright colors. Happy colors. Green, blue, orange, yellow, red. This is the life Gunner deserves.

Other than this one picture, my notebook is filled with black, grey, white. Lines. Shapes. A sense of movement towards nothing. Suffocating emptiness.

Now, it's filled with life.

If all I am here for is to provide enough love to help one lost soul rebuild trust and confidence, I will have accomplished something worthwhile and filled a life with color.

Maybe that is enough.

5

Darcy jumps up and runs around her desk to hug me.

"This is the best news! Oh, you've made my day. No, my week. My month. Gunner is so lucky!"

People thank me all morning for fostering Gunner, but their appreciation makes me feel like a fraud. I don't know what I'm doing. Why trust me with him? I've never taken care of anything before. Kent didn't even like real plants—our houseplants were all fake.

Panic forces me to track down Darcy and run through a litany of questions.

"Is it okay that my place is small?"

"Well, I'm certain it's bigger than his pen here."

"What if I screw it up and make him worse?"

"The fact that you're concerned about what happens to him shows how much you care. You're aware of the alternative. It can't be worse than that."

"Yeah. I guess not. But if anyone contacts you and wants to foster him, I'll bring him back."

She draws her hands together with a loud clap, ignoring my last sentence. "Oh, this is so awesome. I'll get it all organized. I need to do some paperwork and then load you up with supplies. I will also print off a guide we give to all our foster families so that you know how to make him comfortable and things to work on. Come see me before your shift ends to get it all sorted." With that, she throws her arms open wide and draws me into another hug. "Thank you," she whispers against my ear. "You saved him, Vicki. You did it."

Holy cow. I did.

I hug her back.

⇒ · · + · · ⇐

Later that afternoon, Darcy drops me off at home with a dog bed and a bag of food.

"You can leave it on the porch. I'll carry it in," I say, not wanting her to see how small my apartment is.

"Nonsense. Let me help. We'll leave Gunner in the car for a minute while we set this up."

"Sure." I resign myself to her seeing my apartment, chewing the inside of my cheeks to prevent my nervous chatter.

Darcy grabs the huge bag of kibble, and I take the bed and bag of toys. We enter, and she drops the kibble down with a heavy thunk.

"Sorry. It's heavier than I thought. I better start lifting weights again. But don't tell Francois I said that, or soon he'll have an entire program mapped out for me." She rolls her eyes, but anyone could see her affection for him.

Would anyone look at me that way?

"Your place is so cute—it reminds me of a place I had a few years ago— and it's in such a great spot. There's a park nearby, plus you can walk to the shelter if you need us. Gunner's going to love it. Let's go get him."

I follow Darcy. Successful, confident Darcy, who had a place like mine once.

Gunner resists leaving the car, but we manage to pry him out; then Darcy waves goodbye, leaving us on the sidewalk.

"So, this is it, Gunner. Just the two of us."

We remain outside while he takes in the new surroundings with the help of his nose. It is a slow, cautious endeavor. Even with me beside him, his ears are back with fear, and he jumps and pees a little when someone slams their car door. And again, when a motorcycle drives by. I sense he wants to bolt and find a dark corner to hide in, but I try to be as calm and reassuring as possible.

He is equally fearful when I try to lead him inside. Finally coaxing him to the door, he sits down, afraid to enter.

I step inside first. "See? All clear. I know the carpet has seen better days, but it's not that bad. Now come on, Gunner. Let's go."

He looks up at me, eyes full of hard-earned trust, and takes a tentative step.

"Good boy, Gunner." I give him a treat. Then another with the next step, and soon we are in my apartment. I remove his leash and watch as he sniffs every inch of the place.

I put Gunner's bed beside mine, and as mine is only an air mattress, it will be easy to reach over and pet him if he is nervous. When Gunner finishes exploring, he finds the bed, sniffs it, circles it, and curls up.

"Good idea. It's been a long day," I tell him, then lay down beside him, gently stroking his head. He gives my hand a lick, and we both take a nap.

When I awake, Gunner is staring at me from across the mattress, and it's the best face I've ever woken up to. "Should we go outside?"

I put on his leash, but don't take him for a walk, just into the back yard, which is a tiny square of dirt where once there was grass, a broken BBQ, and a cracked terra cotta pot.

"Sorry the yard's not nicer. I don't normally come back here. Boy, it could do with a makeover, huh? If this were my place, I would put in a small stone patio, two chairs, some planters, maybe hang some plants by the back door. Impatiens will do well as there is not a lot of sun, but of course, it's fall. The summer might be different. This time of year, mums would be good, although it's maybe too late for those now, as the nights are so cold. Soon it will be time for the evergreen planters. Sorry, I'm sure you don't care, but that was one of my jobs, maintaining the garden. Curb appeal is important, Kent always said." Oh my gosh Vicki, he doesn't understand you. "You almost done? I didn't wear a coat."

He squats. Turns his head away as if seeking privacy, then poops. Maybe he does understand?

The following day, I climb out of bed and step into a puddle. Gunner is curled up far away from me and his bed, as if I'd be angry at him, so I give him a kiss before cleaning up the mess. "Don't worry about this. Accidents happen, and it's easy to clean up." Especially compared to cleaning dried-up vomit off your mother and the bed, but I don't tell Gunner that.

6

THE BEAUTY OF OCTOBER'S crisp blue skies and colorful autumn foliage pale in comparison to Gunner playing tug-of-war with me. What progress! To celebrate, I bake and decorate dog-bone-shaped sugar cookies and offer them to the humans at the animal shelter. As I'm leaving a plate of them in the staff room, Mariam walks in. She is thrilled to hear about Gunner's progress and then invites me over to her house for Thanksgiving dinner. Before I can say no, she informs me that Thanksgiving at her house is a formal affair and expects me there at six.

"I don't want to impose on such short notice. So thank you, but it wouldn't feel right."

"Don't be silly." She dismisses my reluctance with a two-handed sweeping gesture. "Now, let me get a pen and paper and give you my address."

There's nothing I want to do less than go to a formal Thanksgiving dinner, but due to her kindness, I feel obliged to agree. I can survive one dinner.

On my way home, I stop at a consignment shop selling used designer clothes. It is a tiny little place tucked into a side street off St. Catherine's, situated below a comic book store and beside a tattoo parlor. Quite unnoticeable. Luckily, another waitress at work told me about it.

I'd much rather be home with Gunner; not quite sure how the day ended with me here, shopping for a black dress. I had more than enough dresses in Ottawa, but I left them behind. It only takes a few minutes for the clerk to find me two dresses, one in black, the other purple, or aubergine, as she says. They're both beautiful, but I select the aubergine one knowing Kent would hate it. That alone makes the shopping trip worthwhile.

Three days later, on Thanksgiving Monday, the pub where I waitress is closed because it caters to grad students, and most are spending the long weekend with their families. So instead of working, I spend my time preparing for the party, beginning with a hostess gift. Etiquette 101: A beautiful tin of baked goods makes a thoughtful and personal hostess gift. Too bad I couldn't package up the aroma of baking gingerbread. It's heavenly and would be much cheaper. At least cookies are more cost-effective than wine—good wine, that is. And I do like baking, especially the decorating. It is art on an edible canvas.

Gunner and I play—yes, play—in the backyard while the cookies cool, then the fun begins. I start icing them in solid deep orange. Using a tiny paintbrush, I add dimension to the veining with varying shades of orange and red. They don't exactly look real, but they do look realistic.

With that complete, I work on myself with similar focus and intensity.

I sweep my hair into a top-knot bun and apply my make-up skillfully. Kent's preferences with make-up were specific, and he had me practice long hours in front of a mirror to please him, having even built me a custom makeup bureau. Early in our relationship, he hired a make-up artist for an in-home lesson. She commented how lucky I was to be so spoiled by my man.

The new dress is a stretchy fabric with a shimmer, and I love how the halter-style top hugs my curves. The aubergine contrasts nicely with both my pale skin and chestnut hair and makes my green eyes more prominent, along with my freckles—but it was never me who had a problem with them. For lipstick, I choose a deep red with purple undertones and found a similar color for my nails. I select a black beaded necklace and matching bracelet. My earrings are a muted silver, a collection of tiny triangles on a center chain; they flow almost like a feather. No one ever doubted Kent's sense of style.

"What do you think?" I say to Gunner, who has been watching me with his big blue eyes. "So good you're speechless, huh? Well, I'll take it. Now I just need to get through dinner." I kiss him, pass him a new chew toy and walk out the door.

The bus into Westmount drops me off a block from Mariam's house. Her home is a beautiful stone-front row house. Two grand wooden doors greet me. I ring the doorbell, and Mariam soon appears to usher me out of the cold, and as I pass her my coat, I witness her approving look as she takes in my hair and outfit and find myself relaxing. Little Vicki Meyers cleans up good.

Mariam, who makes jeans and a T-shirt look sophisticated, is wearing a wrap dress in cranberry red. On the one side, holding it closed, is a beautiful broach. The woman exudes simple elegance.

As we exit the foyer, I pass her the box of cookies and follow her through the second set of ornate wooden doors; a stained-glass dormer window sits atop them. Running my fingers over the old, refurbished wood, with dents and scratches from past histories, evokes memories of a different time, a different house.

The foyer leads us into the formal sitting room, where people are already engrossed in conversation. One wall has a fireplace with a hand-crafted mantel lovingly restored. The ceilings must be at least ten or eleven feet high with original crown moldings. The rounded openings leading from one room to the next are also clad with elaborate plaster cornices. It's the artwork, though, that holds my attention. They are actual paintings, not prints, and are modern and abstract.

I chicken out from asking her who the artists are. Instead, I say, "Wow, Mariam, your house is beautiful. I love the moldings, and the collar on that plinth block is quite unusual."

"You're surprisingly knowledgeable about Victorian architecture."

My cheeks heat up as I nod, "A bit. I used to live in a house around the same age as this one."

"How fun. Don't you just love the character, regardless of the crooked floors? Now come with me; let me introduce you to some of my family."

Placing her free hand on my elbow, she guides me to the kitchen. And I thought the foyer was large. The kitchen is bright, warmed by dark stained Shaker cabinets, a beige natural-stone countertop, and a tumbled travertine backsplash. I have a bit of appliance-envy over her gas stove, which has six burners, several of them currently in use, and I can smell the turkey in the oven.

In the center of the kitchen is an island, with pendant lighting above, a wine fridge below, and a small sink, where two men are preparing drinks.

Jazz plays through overhead speakers.

"Gentlemen, meet my friend Vicki. Vicki, this is my husband, Edward, and our son Daniel."

Edward is about two inches taller than Mariam, with a slender build. He has jet black hair with a few grey streaks at the temples and funky blue squarish glasses. He is every bit the professor Mariam said he was, and I wouldn't be surprised if he had a wine collection. He finishes shaking the martini shaker and pours the drink. He then wipes his hands on a towel before offering me his hand. "So nice to meet you, Vicki. Make yourself at home."

"Thank you for having me."

"Our pleasure."

I turn to Daniel. Whoa. He's cute. Taller than his father with the same slender build, they also share dark hair, but his face is more like Mariam's, rounder and with a broader nose. But it's his warm brown eyes that draw me in. Beyond friendly, they contain an ethereal quality, that, if I let them, could see deep into my soul. Then there's his wide and sincere smile lighting up the night like evening primrose.

Daniel takes my hand. We shake, then he wraps his other hand over mine. Heat flows up my bare arm like hot lava.

"Mom told us about you fostering a dog, so it's nice to put a face to the name. I'm glad you could make it."

"I am too." And for the first time since I walked through the door, I mean it.

7

Daniel sits down beside me on a royal blue loveseat. Did Mariam ask him to come over as I'm sitting alone? I had sought out the solitude, having spent the last half-hour mingling and making small talk in the living room with the other guests. Kent's gift of etiquette lessons really was a gift that keeps on giving. Now I can work a room like a champ, but it is exhausting, and I require frequent breaks.

"Vicki, right?"

"That's me."

"Having a good time?"

"Yeah. Your parent's friends seem nice."

"Yeah. They're not so bad. But what about you?"

"Me? I'm not so bad either." At least this elicits a laugh out of him, but oh my gosh, why on earth did I say that?

"I mean, tell me about yourself. Are you from Montreal?"

Normally, I would redirect the conversation away from myself, but the warmth of his broad smile sneaks over the cold obstacles I protect myself with. "No, I was born in Toronto, but my mother moved us to Ottawa when I was in grade three. I only moved to Montreal a few months ago."

"I know the city well. I went to the University of Ottawa."

"Oh yeah? I audited a few courses there, but it wasn't for me."

"You found something that suited you better?"

"Something like that."

"Well, good. Now tell me, are you as dog crazy as my mother? She loves it at the shelter. She would go every day if she had the chance."

"I don't blame her. The animals are great. But it's wonderful and sad at the same time. The dogs and cats deserve better. I guess that's why I decided to foster Gunner. He is so timid and nervous of everyone after being mistreated, but we've been taking things slowly. I won't be happy until I find him a home. He deserves to experience real love."

"Don't we all," Daniel says before finishing his drink. "But be careful. I hear it's easy to end up adopting them yourself."

"Oh, I couldn't do that."

"Why not?"

"I'm not a long-term solution. Just the middleman to help him on his way to a better home. Plus, you could fit my apartment in your foyer."

"Sounds like a place I had in Ottawa. I could sit on my bed and wash the dishes at the same time."

I raise an eyebrow at him.

"Okay, that's a bit of an exaggeration, but not by much. I had to stand to wash the dishes. So what brings you to Montreal? Work?"

"No. I just wanted a change."

"Oh yeah? What do you do?"

"I'm a waitress. I like it, but eventually I hope to find something else, preferably full-time. I like to draw, so I'd like to work in an art store and maybe take some classes." Where did that come from and why am I telling him?

"I'm jealous. I can't even draw a stick figure. What kind of drawings are in your portfolio?"

"A portfolio? I'm not quite there yet. What about you?"

He opens his mouth to speak, but I interrupt. "No, let me guess. Judging by the suit, I would say either hedge fund manager or international spy. Am I close?"

He tilts his head back and laughs. "Was forensic accountant your next guess?"

"After funeral home director."

He laughs again and is about to speak but is interrupted.

"Bonjour, Vicki." The words pop the magic bubble I was floating in with Daniel. I turn to see François and Darcy. Daniel and I stand to greet them, and I introduce them to Daniel.

"I think we met in the summer," Darcy says to him. "Your mother hosted a barbecue. You were here with your wife. I don't see her. Is she here?"

My stomach tightens. A wife?

"Right, yes. No, unfortunately, she couldn't make it. Well, would anyone like a drink? Mother will kill me if you are here more than five minutes without a drink in your hand. Vicki, another water?"

"Yes, please."

"I'll have red wine," says Darcy.

"Moi aussi," says François.

Daniel catches my eye, nods, and walks off.

So he's married. Am I relieved or disappointed?

I don't have much time to think about it before we are called into the dining room, and I am seated beside Daniel. We continue our conversation from earlier, and knowing he's married relaxes me. Yes, I find him attractive, but at this point in my life, friendship is a better option. Not that I am used to friendship, but I can ease into it with baby steps, like Gunner.

As I prepare to leave, Mariam insists Daniel drive me home and sends me off with some turkey for Gunner. That works for me, as it saves me the cab fare. And if the car ride is anything like dinner, it will be equally pleasant. As we pull up in front of my apartment, Daniel asks to come in and see some of my sketches.

"If you weren't married, I would take that as some kind of pickup line."

He laughs. "You think that would work?"

"Not a chance but you can come up anyway."

Compared to the luxury of his familial home, the sad state of my apartment is humiliating. Neat stacks of art supplies take up residence on the shelf above my bed. A small table I found on the street with a small chair from the thrift shop sits by my only window. Across the room from the window is my bed (a blow-up mattress and mismatched sheets). Near the foot of my bed are two doors. One, a surprisingly deep closet. The other, a bathroom. Next to that is the world's smallest galley kitchen.

"Oh my God." I drop my bag and coat on the floor and rush to Gunner, who sits in the center of my near-empty room, covered in blood. "Gunner, what's wrong? What happened?" I turn to Daniel, my heart beating in my throat. "What do I do? I think I nearly killed the dog." I crouch down and run my hands over him, making his tail wag. As I lean in closer, slightly confused, he licks my cheek.

What the...he smells sweet. Relief floods through me so fast, I start laughing. "The red icing. From the cookies. He got into the garbage."

Daniel squats down beside me and gives Gunner a scratch under his chin. "I like the icing too, big guy."

Because of the shock, I almost fail to notice Gunner doesn't pee as Daniel pets him. A few more seconds go by. Still no pee. At least this surprise is a good one. I grab Daniel's arm and slightly shake it. "He didn't pee."

He looks at me, eyebrows raised. "What do you mean?"

"He pees when he meets new people. He didn't pee just now. I don't believe it."

"It must mean he's feeling safe here. Or, you know, that I'm just incredibly charming."

"Yeah, that must be it." I give him a wry smile.

"Anything else in your garbage that he shouldn't be getting into, like chocolate?"

"Who throws away chocolate? Not this girl."

"No? Okay, good. Looks like it's only the mess you have to worry about." He walks into the kitchen and begins to clean up the garbage.

"Daniel, stop. I've got this. You should get going. Thanks for the ride."

I kiss Gunner on the head and then join Daniel in the kitchen. Red and orange icing is on the cupboards and on the floor, the rest of the garbage is strewn across the room. The seriousness of what could have happened had something dangerous been in the garbage hits me. I sink down to the ground with the weight of that realization and lean against the fridge. Banging the back of my head several times against the fridge door won't solve anything, but I do it anyway. "I knew this was a mistake. What if he ate something bad? What if he dies? I'm trying to prevent that from happening. Not speed it along. I'm such an idiot."

"I didn't take you for a drama queen."

"What?" My head jerks up, snapping me out of my anxiety spiral.

"I mean, just relax. Dogs get into stuff. It's what they do."

"But I should know better. I've read like a million books on dogs, all in the last month. I should anticipate stuff like this."

"Don't be so hard on yourself. I think Mom told us that you never had a dog before, is that right?"

"Yeah."

"So learn and move on...oh wow. If looks could kill, I'd be a dead man."

This makes me smile. "Without a doubt."

"Want me to clean him up for you?"

"I do now."

He turns to exit the kitchen.

"Daniel, I'm joking. I can clean my own dog. Just give me your hand. I need to get up, and this dress is stretchy, but not that stretchy." He pulls me up, and I brush off my dress. "At least it means that he was exploring instead of sitting curled up on his bed. I'll take it as a victory of sorts."

"That's a good way of looking at it."

"That's me. The eternal optimist. I better change and give him a bath."

"Aren't you forgetting something? Your sketches?"

"Still?"

"Yeah, I'm curious."

"Oh fine." I pull a sketchbook off my pile, then excuse myself to change before bathing Gunner. I return to the living room to find him flipping through my private sketchbook.

"I'm sorry." My hand darts out, covering the page he had it open to. "These are kind of ... experimental. I hadn't planned on anyone seeing them. This is so embarrassing."

"Are you kidding me? Don't be embarrassed. These are incredible. Seriously. They're so dark and haunting. I love this one." He moves my hand and flips back to the previous page. "How you've drawn her splayed out on the bed surrounded by rose petals. It's like she is adored, but when you look at her face, her eyes are empty. Almost sad. There is no love or passion or lust. Just resignation. I find it incredibly moving."

Heat rushes to my cheeks. "Thank you."

"You know, a friend of mine owns this martini bar and is always looking for stuff like this to put on the walls. Can I show them to her?"

I have a sinking feeling my mouth actually fell open. "What? You want to take these? I don't know about that. I never planned on anyone seeing them."

"But these are great. Real edgy. Can I take one, then if she likes it, you'll let me show her the entire book? Deal?"

What do I do? Do I want images of my raw emotions on display in a bar? Not that anyone would know it's me. All this worry before Daniel's friend even sees them. It's ridiculous. I did move here for a fresh start at life. It won't hurt to have him take one. "Um, okay, I guess. I'll rip one out. Just promise me something, please. You won't show it to your mom."

"Sure. Can you give me your number? I'll let you know what Nathalie thinks."

"I don't have a phone yet, but I'll give you the number where I work. You can leave me a message to call you back."

I put the sketch in a folder, writing my work number on the outside, and as he leaves, I thank him again.

"What do you know? She can smile after all," he says.

"What do you mean? I smile."

"This one was genuine."

My mouth opens, but nothing comes out. Busted.

Gunner and I walk Daniel to his car and stay on the street until his taillights disappear around a corner. A cold wind scatters the leaves that have fallen onto the sidewalk, but the warmth Daniel's given me remains. "Come on, Gunner. Let's get inside."

Minutes later, I am in the tub with Gunner, both of us soaking wet. "You ever think of professional wrestling for a career?" He tilts his head at me, trying to understand how the night unfolded and ended up as it did.

"Yeah. Tell me about it."

8

GUNNER AND I HEAD outside. Instead of walking beside the house and into the backyard, I turn the opposite way. He stops dead in his tracks.

I squat down and scratch his ears. "Trust me, okay? We're trying something new."

Darcy instructed me to take it slow. Only going a few meters in a new direction counts as progress. I take a step. Gunner doesn't move. "Come on, sweet boy." I hold a treat out. He walks forward to eat it, pushing through every startling noise. His eyes dart around, head continually surveying, ears twitching with each new sound. He is fearful and cautious, but he soldiers on. We repeat the step and treat process until we reach the road at the end of the block. "Good boy, Gunner. You're such a brave boy. You did it. Let's turn around and go home."

Gunner licks my face and looks as proud of himself as I am.

"Wait until we tell Darcy about our walk! She's going to be so happy," I tell him as I unlock the door.

"Vicki!"

My name called out hits me like a gunshot, and I nearly drop my key. Tell me he's not here. He can't be. Every bone in my body tenses, like a coiled spring, as I turn around.

Daniel jogs over from across the street. Daniel. Not Kent. Breathe, Vicki. You're okay. "Hi, Daniel, you surprised me. How are you?"

"I'm okay. I'm glad I caught you since you don't have a phone yet—I came by to let you know what Nathalie thought about your sketch."

"You did? You showed them to her?"

He tilts his head to one side, pulling his eyebrows together in a similar manner to Gunner. "Of course. I said I would, didn't I?"

"Well, yeah, but…"

"But nothing. Want to know what she said?"

"Yes. I think. Only if what she said is good. Or not. I guess. I don't know. Sorry. I'm nervous." No one has judged my work before. I would be lying if I said I didn't care what she thought.

His warm smile practically melts the snow beneath my feet. That's a good sign, right?

"Well, she loves it. Exactly what she's looking for, for a dark corner above a couch."

"Are you serious? She does? I mean, that's awesome." I can't imagine anyone wanting my self-contempt looming over them while sipping martinis.

"She was hoping she could keep the one I showed her and have you do two more with the same kind of vibe." He pulls out a piece of paper from inside his coat and passes it to me.

The wind picks up, so I grip the paper tight while Daniel pulls a toque out of his pocket and pulls it onto his head. It has a Montreal Canadians logo on it and a big pom-pom on top, reminding me of what kids wore in elementary school.

He catches me staring at it and gives me a goofy smile. "What? It's my favorite hat."

"Okay."

"Anyway, back to business." He stops, having caught me trying not to laugh, making his cheeks turn red. "Do I need to take the hat off? Is it that bad?"

"No, I'm teasing you. Please continue." He's so darn cute. His wife is one lucky lady.

Again, he gives me a sunshine-warm smile. "Okay, once the sketches are done, send them to her by courier. All the info is on that paper, along with her phone number if you have any questions. Include the bill, and she'll send you a cheque for expenses plus five hundred dollars if that is okay with you."

"Wait." I grab his arm. "She's *paying* me?" My words cause me to cringe, knowing I must sound like an idiot, but I hadn't considered payment. I never thought it would get this far.

"Yes. That's usually how it works. But if you don't want to be paid…"

"No. I do. I do. This is just the first time. I'm a bit overwhelmed. How can I thank you?"

"You don't have to thank me. It was my pleasure. One ex-Ottawa citizen to another. But you know, you should really get a phone."

"I'll think about it. Thanks again."

Daniel leans in and kisses me once on each cheek, then crosses the street to his car, leaving me with a peculiar feeling in my gut—happiness, yes, but also something unfamiliar and intangible and not unpleasant.

A while later, I climb into a hot bubble bath. Gunner inspects the bathwater and takes a lick. "Watch out buddy, or you're next." He retreats to the living room, where I hear him climb on my bed and sigh. If only I could relax like that. Instead, my mind is a hurricane. Thoughts crash and pummel each other. Perhaps I do have some talent. Or not. This was all Daniel's doing. But I let him take the drawing. That takes courage. Except I don't have courage. I operate on fear. And what about rejection? Can I handle people rejecting my art? Yes. Maybe. I'm no stranger to rejection. If I can survive my mother rejecting me, I can survive anything, right?

"Gunner, I think I'm losing my mind."

Taking a breath, I dunk under the water, drowning out my inner critic.

For the remainder of the week, I fight the urge to give up. Partly for myself, partly not to let Daniel down. But once I start the sketches, they flow out of me like blood from a deep wound, pulsating, painful, unstoppable. I finish each one, drained and near breathless. Natalie will now have three images. A woman empty. A woman broken. A woman determined.

9

A late-November storm blankets the city in snow, then ice rain. The sounds of ice scraped off windshields and shovels against concrete penetrate my apartment. I had always wanted to love winter. But wanting and doing are two different things.

Growing up, I was always too cold to enjoy it. Mom never planned ahead, by which I mean she was too busy looking for her next fix to notice the changing seasons or my growing body. Winter would hit us, and I'd be sent to school in a jacket I'd outgrown, or she'd put me in hers and send me out the door. No boots. No hat. No mitts. I was grateful if there was a hood. Sometimes, I'd put socks on my hands until I reached the schoolyard, then quickly tuck them into my pockets. Notes would go home regarding appropriate winter wear. Occasionally, a teacher would provide me with clothing abandoned in the lost and found.

But I had always liked the idea of winter. Skiing, skating, snowmen. Kent had given me a down coat, which made the cold bearable, but the hat, gloves, and boots were for fashion, not function. He is not the type to frolic.

I brought the down coat with me, and as I slip it on, I can only imagine Kent's horror as I pair it with accessories bought at a thrift shop.

Downtown is decorated for the holidays. Store windows are filled with cozy images, with mannequins dressed in fleece and wool celebrating on a carpet of artificial snow. Beautiful, but painful for those of us who merely want to get through the holiday season without constant reminders of loneliness.

But nothing can dampen my spirits today because I'm on my way to the art store, five hundred dollars richer, thanks to Daniel's friend.

Not that I'm going to spend it all, but a few new items as an early Christmas present won't hurt.

So many times have I walked past this art store, longing to go in but not daring to—wanting what you haven't got and can't afford leads to trouble. But today is different. Today is special.

Today, I go in.

The old floorboards creek a welcome at me, and the exposed brick and wooden shelves create a warmth, erasing the day's chill. Troubles left at the door, I wander past paper, pens, brushes, canvas. Pencils, charcoal, ink, paper, pallets, easels. Floor to ceiling potential, waiting for creative energy to be released.

I dream big but limit myself to paper and pencils. As I'm checking out, I see a sign for seasonal help. Emboldened by my recent success, I ask to speak to the manager.

A woman comes out from a back office, looking like she's on her way to a *Sex Pistols* concert. She vibrates with energy, constantly running her fingers through bright red spiky hair and punctuating her words with hand gestures. Paint splatters adorn her jeans which are tucked into tall black Doc Marten boots. The laces, plaid ribbon. She is a rainbow to my grey cloud.

She introduces herself as Isabelle, and we talk for at least fifteen minutes. I gather this is her way of learning how much I know. Then she thanks me for stopping by and asks me to drop off my resume. Instinct tells me I didn't nail the interview.

As I turn to leave, a tiny dog wanders out of the same back office Isabelle came from. "Oh my gosh. Is that Céline?"

Isabelle's eyes open wide with surprise. "Yes. How do you know that?"

"I volunteer at the animal shelter. I met Céline on my first day. Everybody loved Céline." I squat down, and Céline comes over. "Hi, sweetheart, you're looking as beautiful as ever." I pick her up, and she licks my face. "Thank you for the kisses. It's nice to see you too."

Isabelle laughs. "It looks like you have Céline's approval. I tell you what. I'll call the animal shelter, and if they give you a good reference, you have the job."

"Oh my gosh! That's amazing. Thank you. Um, there's one more thing. I don't have a phone yet, I'm having some installation issues, so if I do get the job, can you please leave a message at the shelter for me?"

"Sure. No problem."

I leave the art store dreaming of working there and float all the way home.

The following day Gunner and I arrive at the shelter to show Darcy how well he is doing.

"Check us out, Darcy. We walked all the way here."

"Why, Gunner, way to go. And oh my, what a handsome boy. I love your sweater." She comes out from behind her desk to pet him, and immediately he hides behind my legs and pees on the floor. "Don't worry, Gunner. Baby steps. At least you're moving in the right direction. Oh, by the way, some good news for your momma." She turns from Gunner to me. "Someone named Isabelle called. We talked a bit then she said to tell you, you got the job. Congratulations."

"Thank you, Darcy. Did she also tell you that she is the person who adopted Céline?"

"She did."

"You'd be so happy to see Céline there. She's having the time of her life."

She claps. "Oh, I do love a happy ending."

I just hope there is one for Gunner.

As a Christmas present for the animal shelter, I sketched a picture of the staff sitting in front of the building with a bunch of the animals I'd copied from the website and had it framed. To say that I am nervous about giving it to them is an understatement, but if Gunner can walk down the street, I can give them a painting. I am not in danger of anything but a blow to my self-esteem. Poor Gunner overcame a lot more than that.

Working with Gunner brings me an unexpected joy, plus I've met so many kind people I want to show my appreciation.

Darcy opens it and immediately hangs it in the front lobby, telling everyone who walks by that I drew it. Some of my nervous tension eases until Mariam approaches me later that day in the staffroom.

"Daniel told me you were talented. I had no idea how much."

"Thank you. I have something for you too." My hand shakes ever so slightly as I pull a package out of my locker and pass it to her. "You've been a good friend to me."

She wraps me in a hug. "Can I open it?"

"Sure," I say, although I'd rather not be there. What if she hates it? It's a sketch of her house, and knowing her taste in modern art, I experimented with something more abstract,

"Vicki, this is gorgeous. Thank you so much. I can't wait to show it to Edward."

Of course, she says she likes it; she's incredibly kind. But even if she doesn't, it's the thought that counts, right?

Finishing up my last shift at the art store on Christmas Eve breaks my heart. As does smiling and wishing everyone a Merry Christmas. The well-wishes are sincere, but my smile is not. I'm lonely. Yes, I know it's my fault. Over the past few weeks, I was invited out by co-workers at the pub, staff and volunteers at the animal shelter, and people at the art store. Each time, I declined. The ghosts of Christmas past haunt me. Mocking me for getting nothing from Santa. Insulting my clothes. Laughing, because I didn't bring anything to the class party. Always the outsider. Always the loner.

Time doesn't make pain go away. Time allows it to settle and dig deep roots. Kids who torment grow up to be adults. Do they outgrow their cruelty or merely hide it? I'm too afraid to find out because my heart can only handle so much rejection. So, I keep myself coated in a thin veneer of friendliness but forge no real connections.

At home, Gunner jumps up, excited to see me. He gives me a big lick on the face, and I hug him back, burying my face in his long neck, letting my tears disappear into his fur. Coming home to him is better than any Christmas present ever.

I leash him up, and we stroll to the shelter. There is only a skeleton crew to care for the adoptees, so we leave them some treats and some for the remaining dogs and cats, the lucky ones adopted as Christmas presents.

We pass numerous parties on the way home, reminding me of past Christmases spent with Kent and his family. We would drive to his family's hobby farm in the afternoon of Christmas Eve, decorate the tree, and have turkey dinner. Like Kent's house, the hobby farm was a restoration. It had good bones, Kent told me, and was worthy of the hard work and time it took to turn it from coal into a diamond.

I longed to show his parents I was a diamond too. In front of them, I worked hard to become Kent's vision, desperate to hide my life, my upbringing. I obsessed about finding the perfect gift, planned conversations in my head, agonized over my wardrobe. I sought their approval. Their acceptance. But never felt at home. Our interactions, while pleasant, were shallow. Each year, I would leave thinking I didn't try hard enough. But at least I wasn't alone.

We get home and have a late dinner. Soup for me, kibble for Gunner. He gets a belly rub, then we both go to bed. Despite my exhaustion from the busy day at the art store, I barely sleep. Before Kent, I had spent several Christmases alone. Why was this one so different?

Did I make a mistake?

By Christmas morning, I'm frantic. I tossed and turned all night, obsessing about my decision to come to Montreal. I need answers, and there is only one way to get them.

I walk Gunner, get him settled with a new bone, then take the bus to Ottawa, two hours away. If things go well, I won't be gone any longer than a weekend shift at the store.

Kent's house is an old red brick Victorian close to the canal. I face it from across the street like it's an adversary.

Inside, Kent, being a contractor who loved old architecture, had restored the hardwood floors and trim, but he also opened it up, added a main floor bathroom, and rewired the entire house. His changes didn't end there. The attic was converted into the master suite with a deck and luxury bathroom. Below on the second floor is Kent's office, one guest bedroom, and one multipurpose room. This is the room he assigned me to store whatever I needed to keep the house and myself pristine. It was an odd combination of cleaning supplies, seasonal home decor, makeup desk, and treadmill.

The heart of the first floor is the state-of-the-art kitchen, the entire floor magazine-worthy. And that's how I had to keep it.

Kent never let me forget how fortunate I was to live in such luxury.

Today, as expected, he's not here. The snow on his walkway remains untouched, and his car is gone. I make my way into his backyard and unlock the back door with the key I never gave back.

"Hello? Is anyone home? Kent?" Stepping inside, I quietly shut the door and walk into the kitchen without removing my boots. Ha! I run my hand across the cool granite countertop. Here, I learned to cook. Meals were healthy, packed full of nutrients, low in fat. Especially for me.

Passing through the living room, devoid of any holiday decorations, I reach the foyer. This is where Kent pinned me against the wall the first night we met. God, how I longed to be wanted and desired. He fulfilled that wish. And I was grateful. Too grateful.

I climb the stairs up to his room, past the stained-glass window, the creaky third stair, and ornate newel post. Spotless and perfect, it was always *his* room, even after sharing it for years. It looks no different with me gone. Kent doesn't clean, so he must hire someone or have another girlfriend. I peer into what used to be my closet. My clothes are not gone but removed from the shelves and hangers and put into neatly labeled boxes. Nothing has replaced them, so he must have a housekeeper.

Between our two closets is the master bath, with its Carrera marble, heated floors, and shower built for two where he would scrub away my past. I always preferred the clawfoot soaker tub under the window.

The pristine white enamel, the ornate feet, and restored fixtures draw me in. Even today. Especially today. So, I turn the water on, pour some bubble bath, strip down, and submerge myself back into this life.

Kent is skilled at recognizing a project. I was flattered by the desire of someone more successful and sophisticated. We both hated who I was, and both recognized a willingness in me to change. Soon I quit my job, stopped attending art class, moved in. Kent had plans for me. I was rough around the edges but had potential. No one had ever thought that before, so I let him tear me down in order to be built back up. And I was used to angry men, grateful he didn't use his fists on me.

"You're lucky, you know. Most men don't have my level of control."

My mother, bruised often by men, was proof he was telling the truth.

"You're right. I'm sorry. I'll do better."

"Good girl."

Sometimes he'd punch the wall and then make me help him repair it—it was my fault after all.

Would I still be here if I had been able to please him, to reach a point where he loved me? Yes.

But I never did, and I never would.

As I dry off and get dressed, it hits me that I'm still wearing clothes he bought, covering a body he shaped. My hair styled the way he preferred. I think of Darcy, of Isabelle, of Mariam. Their personalities are alive in each movement they make. While I am no longer exactly Kent's version of me, I am also not the girl I was before.

So who am I?

10

From Kent's house, I wander the streets, ending up in front of the building where I last lived with my mother. All I wanted was for her to love me. Perhaps she did. There are distant memories of fort building and playing with dolls. Under a bright summer sun, the two of us swinging high in the park. Side by side. Laughing. She was only fifteen years older than me.

But love doesn't always translate into care. We moved frequently. I went to five different schools in five years. She was too naïve. Too trusting. Exhausted. Overwhelmed. Sad.

Being a high school dropout made it hard to find a job to support two people. Sometimes between apartments, we slept at a shelter or on the street. Halfway through grade three, we moved to Ottawa. She had a distant relative who managed the building I'm facing now, and they let us stay in an apartment in the basement. Tiny, dark, but the first stable home I had.

After five years of avoiding not just this building but the entire street, I stand at the base of the stairs leading up to the entrance. Is she still here? Could she manage without me?

All I have to do is walk into the lobby and buzz the apartment. But my feet have become part of the landscape, frozen into the ground like an old tree stump.

I am hiding in the closet while she fights with a boyfriend. I am eating only stale crackers for dinner. I am alone, wondering if she's ever coming back. I am scared. I am waiting for the mail carrier to deliver her welfare check. I am paying the bills. I am listening to her breathe to make sure she is alive. I am walking out the door and never going back.

Words I thought I meant at the time. Now I am not so sure, but I'm not ready to confront those demons yet. Today, I need to keep moving forward. Otherwise, I have learned nothing.

I turn around and make my way to the bus depot.

Once at home, I discover that Gunner's chewed my air mattress like a toy. My sheets lay in a tangled mess. How can I figure out my own life when I can't take care of a dog?

11

IN THE TWILIGHT OF Boxing Day, I leave the lights off and light candles. The soft glow not only adds warmth to the sparse apartment but highlights shapes and contours otherwise unseen, allowing me to find insight into form and pattern.

I carry one candle into the bathroom and begin to fill the tub. Not as luxurious as Kent's, but more relaxing. As I am about to step in, the doorbell rings.

Must be a mistake. Who would come here? Unless...No. Kent wouldn't realize I'd been in his house. Would he? Oh my God, does he know where I am?

Another ring. Wrapping myself in my robe, I enter the shared hallway and open the door with trembling fingers. I need to know.

"Daniel?" My knees go weak with relief.

"Hi, Vicki. May I come in?" He looks me up and down, "Oh, did I come at a bad time?"

"No, it's fine. Come on in." I step back and allow him to enter. Cold air and snow escort him in, and I quickly close the door.

"So, what's up? Everything okay with your mom?"

"Oh yeah. She's fine. I have come to ask you for a favor." He enters my apartment and takes off his coat, silk scarf, and leather gloves. Underneath is a navy suit, white shirt, and a deep red and blue tie. "Boy, sure is hot in here."

"I don't have control over the heat, but once you spend a few winters in a cold apartment, you know better than to complain."

He nods in appreciation. Melted snow drips off his head and onto the floor as he bends down and pets Gunner. "Hey, big guy."

156

"About this favor. It must be important judging by your attire."

"Well, I wouldn't say important, but it is kind of formal. I was wondering if you would like to come to the ballet with me."

"The ballet?"

"Yeah. My parents received Nutcracker tickets for Christmas, but my sister-in-law went into labor out in Vancouver, and my parents have jumped on a flight and taken off. They left me with the two tickets. What do you think?" He wiggles his eyebrows up and down. "I'm not such a bad date."

"What about your wife?"

He sighs, looks out the window, down at the floor, then back at me. "We recently had our divorce finalized."

"Oh my God. I'm so sorry. I didn't realize..."

"Don't apologize. How could you know? Things were being negotiated around Thanksgiving, and I didn't want it to be a topic of discussion at my parent's party. She wouldn't have come anyway. She hates the ballet." He gives me a small smile. "So how about it? You wouldn't want me to sit there alone, would you?"

"No. I guess not." I smile back at him. "So your approach is the pity date, huh?" I don't know why I said that, but he seems like someone who can take a joke—Who might *need* a joke. It must be difficult watching your brother's family grow while yours disintegrates.

"At this point, I'll do whatever is necessary."

"Do I have time to have a quick shower?"

"Definitely. I came early, knowing you would need time to get ready if you agreed, of course. We should also have time to grab a bite to eat. You know, I am going to keep bugging you about getting a phone. It would have made this much easier."

"Phone. Schmone. Have a seat. I'll be out as quickly as I can."

"On what? You still have no furniture."

"Very funny. As you can see, I have one chair. That should do." Moving into the bathroom, I quickly shower, and instead of washing my hair, I pull it into a loose bun and put on the same dress he saw me in at Thanksgiving.

The Nutcracker with Daniel. Not a bad way to spend the evening.

As I'm finishing my makeup, he calls out that he's going to get us some pizza. I yell at him to take my keys from the table.

When he's back, he opens the door and walks in, "Hi honey, I'm home," he says and hands me the pizza box. "Wow, you look amazing."

"Thank you." Please don't let him see me blushing. "And you are the best-dressed pizza delivery man that's ever come to my door."

Daniel pulls out two bottles of wine, one from each pocket of his coat. "Only the best depanneur wine for my pity date."

"I'm so sorry, Daniel. I hope I didn't hurt your feelings with that."

"Quite the opposite. Everyone has been walking around on eggshells since I told them. A little levity is needed."

After our meal and we place our dirty dishes in the sink, Daniel jokes about how long it must take me to clean up. He looks through my cupboards. "One of everything. Talk about minimalist living. I guess you don't entertain much."

"If by much, you mean ever, you're right."

"So no phone, no dishes, no furniture. Are you hiding from someone or punishing yourself? I know where you can get a good quality hair shirt if you want."

I can't respond before he apologizes. "Vicki, I'm so sorry. I spoke without thinking. I don't even know you. I'm such a jerk."

"We're all good. Don't worry. I need a little levity too."

"Well, to change the subject, do you have a warm winter coat you can wear with that dress?"

"Yes."

"Awesome, because I was hoping we could walk."

"Walk? Are you kidding? In this weather?"

"The roads are terrible, and parking will be a disaster. Plus, I've drunk way more wine than I should have." He pauses. "You don't drink?"

So he'd noticed I didn't touch my wine.

"No. Addiction runs in my family. I play it safe."

"I'm sorry. I didn't know that."

"Don't worry. How would you? Besides, there are perks. For example, my ex-boyfriend found it useful to always have someone as the designated driver."

"That's only a perk for other people."

"I guess. But I liked being wanted for something."

We head out into the cold crisp night. Traffic is unusually light, and often the roads are silent. We are too, but it is comfortable. He lets me hold his arm for stability, and it is reassuring to not walk the street alone for the first time since I've moved here.

The ballet is magical. I lose myself in the artistry of it all, appreciating how a story can be conveyed through music, movement, and costume. I become inspired, already sketching a dancer in motion in my head.

As the lights come on and we prepare to leave, I give Daniel a quick little hug. "Thank you. I enjoyed that. It is something I would never have done on my own." Or could have afforded.

"You're welcome. I'll tell Mom you liked it."

Outside, Daniel takes my hand and leads me to a small, cozy-looking restaurant, almost hidden away down an alley, like a secret. An expensive secret.

"Daniel," I whisper, swallowing my pride, "I can't afford this place. I need to eat next week."

"Don't worry," he whispers back. "My parents are paying. Part of the deal for using their tickets."

"I don't know. I feel kind of awkward."

"Vicki, I invited you. I'm happy you came, now please let my parents buy you dinner."

We sit near the back. The restaurant is dimly lit, primarily by candlelight and small tabletop lanterns. A fireplace dominates the center of the restaurant, and the walls are exposed brick. No, not brick. Stone. Very old stone.

Daniel smiles at me from across the flickering light of our lantern, making my insides tingle. So handsome and sweet. And now single. Nope. Not going there. And yet, his invitation out is the only one I accepted—Darcy's, Isabelle's, I always declined. That must mean something.

He takes a sip of water. "So, if you don't mind me asking, this time with no jokes, how come you're here all alone? Did you go anywhere for Christmas?"

"No, I was indeed alone. It was okay, though. It's not the first one."

His eyebrows bunch together. "No family? Friends?"

"No family. No friends close enough to invite me over for Christmas."

"I'm sorry, Vicki."

"Don't be." I lean forward, my hands clasped together on the table. "My mother is a junkie, and I haven't seen her for five years. I came to Montreal to get away from my ex. Our relationship was, um, toxic."

"He didn't hit you, did he?"

"Jesus Daniel, you get straight to the point, don't you?"

"Sorry. I just...I don't know... I'm comfortable with you. Like we've been friends for a long time. Never mind, you don't have to answer."

"It's okay. I like talking to you too, but I don't want to scare you off."

"I'm a big boy."

I take a long drink of water as a stall tactic while I think of how to sum up my relationship with Kent. "To answer your question, no, he never hit me. His angle was psychological. He was controlling. He preyed upon my insecurities, and I let him—I let him because I believed the horrible things he said.

My childhood was hard. And we were dirt poor, my mom an addict. I didn't feel I had much to offer the world. Then I met Kent, and...never mind. It's embarrassing."

"Please, keep going. I'm not going to judge you."

Maybe I'm crazy, but I believe him. "I thought he was my knight in shining armor, helping me transform from a caterpillar to a butterfly. But nothing I did was ever good enough, and I tried, believe me, I tried. Then, a few months ago, I just couldn't do it anymore. I packed some bags and never looked back. But who I was with him still haunts me. Yesterday, I ... forget it."

"No. Go on, please." He reaches across the table and takes my hand in his, giving it an encouraging squeeze.

"Yesterday, I returned to his house, knowing he wouldn't be there. It was so stupid, but I went inside and looked around. I don't know what I was doing. I guess I was seeking closure of some sort. I think perhaps I found it, or if not closure, at least understanding." Feeling raw and exposed, I sit back and rub the palms of my hands along my thighs, trying to keep myself from running out of the restaurant. Maybe he'll be the one to run. "I'm sorry. I shouldn't have said anything. We can go if you want."

He looks me in the eye, unafraid of what he'll find there. "Relationships are complicated. You're really brave. I hope you know that."

"Brave? I don't know about that. Crazy maybe, or stupid."

"Is that why you don't have a phone? So he can't contact you?"

I nod. "There was also the expense. I spent a lot of money moving here and didn't want to pay the installation fee but enough about me. Would you mind if we changed the topic? Tell me about your Christmas. I hope it was better than mine."

He nods. "It probably was, but it was weird. Uncomfortable. I know everyone feels bad for me. I feel bad for me. Getting divorced sucks. And I'm so tired of people asking me if there is any way we can reconcile—as if that's a novel idea. And then there are those who look at me like I'm to blame. Sure, I'm not without fault, but I wasn't the one fucking everyone I could. Everyone except me, of course. She wouldn't touch me with a ten-foot pole...sorry, sorry. I'm sure that's too much information." He takes a long drink of water. "God, I'm a great date, aren't I?"

"Well, if it makes you feel any better, I think she's crazy. You're hot." Immediately, I cover my face with my hands, my cheeks burning. I peek out at him between fingers. "Did I just make it better or worse?"

He tilts his head back and laughs. "Much better. Trust me."

"Glad I could help." I lower my hands and give him a small smile.

"Well, at least next year should be better. I'll be far away from here, leaving this mess behind me."

"What do you mean?"

"I'm moving to Hong Kong."

"Hong Kong? Wow. You certainly want to be free of her."

"It's not quite like that. I thought we were going together. I knew we were having problems and thought this could be a fresh start. I always wanted to go to Hong Kong, and Kim knew that, just like she knew I was looking for opportunities there. I went there on vacation a very long time ago and loved it. Became obsessed with it. Then the summer before university, my parents sent me there as a graduation present. They had a friend, and I stayed with him, and I guess you could say I did a sort of internship for his company. I think they thought I would get it out of my system, but it had the opposite effect. I've wanted to return for so long. My whole career thus far has been dedicated to getting back there. My wife knew that. I thought she wanted it too. When my dream came true, you know what she said?"

I shake my head, knowing he needed to continue. Sensing I was the first one he told this to, and now that he was talking, he couldn't stop.

"She said, *Great, when are you leaving?* Not when are *we* leaving? She saw the shock on my face and said, *Oh, come on now. Surely you saw this coming.* I didn't, I swear to you, I didn't, but as I stood there, I saw it all. And she was right. It was as clear as day. How could I have been so stupid?"

That I understand.

"To make it worse, after the shock wore off, I realized I wasn't that sad. Kim and I had been distant for so long. It was hard to accept that my marriage was over, but I wasn't that sad it was over with Kim. This was even before I found out about all the fucking. God, do I sound like a terrible person?"

This time, I am the one to squeeze his hand. "You don't sound terrible at all. You just sound human, and as humans, we are capable of incredible stupidity."

"Thank you," he said. "I suspect you're humoring me, but I appreciate it."

"No—I'm not. Trust me. I take stupid to a whole new level. Do you not remember what I just told you?"

Our eyes lock, and suddenly, we're laughing—gut-wrenching, uncontrollable, eye-watering laughter. When we calm down, Daniel picks up his glass. "A toast."

"To what?"

"To us. To new beginnings."

"I like that. Cheers."

We stay talking until the restaurant closes. We discuss our fears, worries, favorite movies, worst teachers, childhood memories, and hopes for the future. Now that we have shared our biggest mistakes, we can't stop talking, and when the restaurant closes, we walk to a twenty-four-hour diner and talk some more. I have never felt so connected to anyone in my life. As each minute passes, we move closer. Our heads are almost touching as if conspiring. Our hands entwine. Our kiss as likely as our next breath.

Our dawn walk to my place is cold, but neither of us rushes. No fear exists of missing the moment, our union as sure as the rising sun.

Even in bed, we take our time. Is it passionate? Oh, yes. Our physical connection is as matched as our emotional one. We savor every moment, every touch. Hands, lips, limbs, flesh entwined, we dance a ballet of our own. But with no audience—I moved Gunner's bed to the kitchen.

Alone, we are two broken people, but together we are magic.

12

Waking up wrapped in the warmth of a good man is a wonderful way to start the day, even when it is well past morning.

"You're awake," Daniel whispers.

"I am." I sigh, taking his hand and holding it close against me. I kiss his fingers. "I don't want to get up yet."

"Even though we appear to be sleeping on the floor? Our enthusiasm seems to have popped your mattress."

I laugh. "No. That was Gunner. I put some duct tape on it, but it doesn't seem to have held."

"Well, it could have been us. We were pretty enthusiastic."

"I'll say."

Gunner is awake now and standing beside me. He licks my face and then walks to the door. "Shoot. He must need to go. I'll be right back. Don't go anywhere."

"Can't get enough of all this, huh?" He shakes his body at me as I climb out of bed.

Fifteen minutes later, Gunner and I return to find Daniel blowing up the bed with my hair dryer—another layer of duct tape covering the hole. I feed Gunner breakfast, then crawl back into bed.

"Are you working today?" he asks as he pulls the covers over me.

"Nope. I'm done at the art store, that job was temporary for the holidays, and the pub is closed until tomorrow since most students are not around." I roll over to face him and place my hand against the stubble on his cheeks. "What about you? Is there any place you need to be?" Please no.

"The only place I need to be is with you, hearing you beg and call out my name." His lips curl into a cocky smile.

My cheeks heat up. "I did do that, didn't I?"

"Uh-huh," he whispers in my ear before tracing its outline with his tongue. All coherent thoughts leave my brain. I am at the mercy of his touch. Our physical connection is electric. Desire and need flow through us, and the charge builds with such speed and intensity that I lose control.

The next time we wake up, it is dark.

"I should probably go home and shower," Daniel says, and my mood immediately dips.

I've had this man in my bed for hours—*hours*—and I still don't want him to leave. I sit up.

He pulls me back down and tucks a strand of hair behind my ear. "Tell me, sweetheart, what's wrong." He blushes from using a term of endearment.

Maybe I do too. *Sweetheart.* I close my eyes and savor it. No one has ever called me that. I run my fingers through his hair and stare into his eyes.

He cups my face with his hands, his voice a whisper, "Tell me, what does your heart want? I need to hear it."

He looks at me with open honesty. I see his need to be wanted and the risk he is taking to show me. My walls crumble. My defenses shatter. Daniel opens me up, draws me out, and I speak the truth. "I want to be with you. And I don't only mean today. I mean for every moment possible until you leave for Hong Kong. I want six weeks with you."

He nods and kisses me to seal the deal.

And for the first time in my life, I am not alone.

13

IN THE KITCHEN WHERE I first met Daniel, back in October, back when he was still a married man, we make clubhouse sandwiches from turkey leftovers and Daniel drinks micro-brewed beer. In the den, we light a fire and watch TV. Gunner, curled up at our feet, snores lightly. I shiver, not yet having shaken off the cold from walking Gunner earlier. Daniel pulls a blanket over me and draws me closer. With his arm around me, I snuggle against him. The rhythm of his breathing soothes me like a lullaby. The kind my mother never sang.

"If I were a cat, I'd be purring right now. There's no place in the world I'd rather be."

"Me neither," he whispers back and gently kisses the top of my head.

There is an odd noise, and suddenly, someone leaps over the couch. All three of us holler in surprise. Gunner jumps up and lands on my lap. The body bears a striking resemblance to Daniel.

The party crasher sits on the couch, panting, hand over his heart. "Shit, Dan. I'm sorry. I figured you'd be alone. I wanted to scare you."

"Well, you achieved that," I say and give Gunner a reassuring scratch on the head.

Daniel laughs. "Vicki, let me introduce you to my brother, Benjamin."

"Hi, Benjamin. Nice to meet you."

"Nice to meet you too." He smiles coyly at Daniel. "And who is this guy?" Ben leans in to let Gunner sniff him.

"This is Gunner. Not much of a guard dog, but at least he didn't pee on me," I say as Gunner licks my face.

"So, Ben, what brings you by?" asks Daniel. He turns to me, "Ben lives in the Plateau."

"Just came to hang with my big brother. Thought you might be needing company, but I guess I was wrong." He shrugs. "Plus, my power is out. Again."

"Want me to make you a sandwich? There is so much food. Mariam would hate it if you had to throw it away."

"Sure, I guess." He eyes me warily. "That would be great.'

On my way to the kitchen, Ben says, "Speaking of Mom, did she call you with any news of the baby?"

"Oh shit. I completely forgot. She didn't call you?"

"Me? You're the one living in her house. Surely she called here."

"I don't know. I wasn't there. I forgot to check the machine when I got home."

"You've been gone? Where...Oh." They both jump up and race for the phone. Daniel yells out that they had a girl, and they are going to call them.

I always wondered what it would be like to have a sibling or grandparents I could turn to. Soon Daniel and Ben return, taking for granted the gift they already have as well as the one they have just been given.

Daniel gets more beer, Ben carries his sandwich into the den, and the three of us spend some comfortable time together watching TV. Daniel's affection and Ben's easy manner draw me into their circle. Daniel has broken down my instinct to withdraw, and I push against my fear of rejection by engaging in earnest. That baby girl has no idea how lucky she is to be born into a family that wants and loves her. I'm lucky too. Even though my situation here is temporary, I get a glimpse inside a close, happy family, as if I was pulled inside a snow globe with a perfect family scene, existing there until the snow stops falling.

I'm okay with that, as it's more than I've ever had.

At around midnight, Ben goes to bed.

"I like your brother."

"Yeah, he's a good kid."

"A kid? He can't be much younger than you."

"My brother Michael, who had the baby, is the oldest at thirty. Matthew is twenty-eight. You already know I'm twenty-six. Ben is seven years younger than me. Only nineteen. My parents would never admit it, but the rest of us assume he was an accident. It drives him nuts when we say that. Can you believe he is the same age I was when I met Kim? Obviously, we didn't marry then, but still. God, did I really waste all those years?"

"Don't regret it, Daniel. You can't think of them as wasted. I'm sure there were good times. You loved her, and she loved you. It didn't work out, but at least you tried. And I'm sorry that it turned out that way, except that it brought you to me." I whisper that last part.

He pulls me close, leaning his forehead against mine. "Thank you."

We sit in silence a few minutes before he asks, "What about you? What happened to you that brought you to me? You've told me the key events, but I'd like to hear the whole story if that's okay with you."

That's a tough one. How far back does one go? "I told you I was working as a waitress, right? In Ottawa? I was doing that and auditing an art history class at the university. I was on my own, renting a small room in an old house—that room makes my place now seem like a palace. But at least I wasn't living with my mother anymore." I sat up straight and faced him. "You're sure you want to hear this?"

"I do. Keep going."

"Living with my mother was too hard. Her addiction was everything. I was scared and angry all the time. So, once I graduated high school, I moved out. I was working hard, determined to change my life, but I was exhausted and wanted what other people had. Security. Love." I snuggle in closer. "I had been on my own for about a year when Kent entered the bar where I worked. He was very flirty. I liked the attention. He was different from the guys I was used to. He was...polished. Driven. Successful. Before I knew it, I moved in with him. At first, it seemed like a dream come true. I lived in a beautiful house. I had a handsome man who said he adored me. But the dream slowly turned into a nightmare. He began to mention things I should change. Subtly, at first. Then not so subtle. He used my insecurities against me—the feeling that I was white trash. Like everyone was better than me. He had me quit my job and art class to care for him and his house. Everything had to be perfect. He made me feel like I owed him for taking me in. I convinced myself that he was helping me, and this was the price to pay for having someone love me." Needing a moment to summon the courage to continue, I pet Gunner. "The worst part was that no matter how hard I tried, I could never please him. I never would. I knew I had to leave, but it took a long time to work up the courage, months actually."

"I'm so sorry."

"Don't be." I shrug. "I can't change it."

"I need to ask this and be honest. Are you worried about your safety?"

"No. I don't think I am worth the effort to him. But at first, I was worried that if he contacted me, my insecurities would kick in, and I would give in and go back. When I returned at Christmas, I think I was testing myself. I'm not afraid of that anymore."

"I'm glad. And don't be insecure, okay? You're amazing."

Before I can protest, he pulls me close and kisses my doubts away.

"One more thing, I've said this before, and I'm sure it drives you crazy, but I really think it's time you got a phone. You can get a cell phone. Those numbers aren't listed."

I nod against his chest. "I thought they were too expensive, but I'll look into it. I promise. Although, not having a phone is now kind of my thing. Everyone knows me as the girl without a phone."

We lay in silence for a while, legs entwined, his hand gently stroking my back.

Suddenly his voice reverberates through his chest. "You know Vic, with Kent—that's not what love is."

I nod. I guess the question is, what is?

14

THE FOLLOWING MORNING I wake up alone—no Daniel, no Gunner. His room is the guest room, having left his apartment with Kim. Even though Daniel has been living here a while, the room lacks any personality. His personal belongings packed away somewhere in preparation for his leaving. It's a temporary space, and perhaps that's why, despite the comparative luxury, he wants to stay with me. Guaranteed privacy doesn't hurt either.

Muffled voices reach me from the kitchen and urge me to get up. Daniel is frying bacon, Ben is leaning against the counter beside him and drinking coffee, and Gunner is sitting beside Daniel, waiting for something to fall off the kitchen counter. So much for him being nervous. Their conversation is relaxed—just two brothers talking in the morning and something I've only ever seen on TV.

Daniel must hear me, for he turns and smiles. "Hey there, beautiful."

"Good morning." I kiss him on the cheek, then lean down and kiss Gunner. Daniel hands me a mug of coffee and pulls out one of the island stools for me.

"Okay. I'm out of here," Ben says. "The vibe here is so sweet I'm going to go into a sugar coma. I'm going home to see if my power is back on. If not, I'll be coming back. Just so you two know to expect me. I wouldn't want to interrupt."

"We will be back at Vicki's anyway. Right, Vic?

"If that's what you want, that's fine with me."

"Oh, God." Ben rolls his eyes. "And yes, you can take the futon. See ya."

"You're taking a futon to Hong Kong?" I ask Daniel.

"No, it's for you. You can't deny that you need a bed. This way, you'll also have something comfortable to sit on. We have one in the garage. My brother bought it as a couch, but he moved into a furnished place. He doesn't need it. I just thought I better ask before I took it. That is, if you want it, of course."

"I can't take your furniture."

"Yes, you can. Believe me. My parents will be glad to see it go." He puts his hands on my shoulders. "Be honest. Tell me if you don't want it. Sometimes I become overenthusiastic about an idea and kind of take over."

It wouldn't hurt to have something soft to sit on. "I do want it, but I don't like asking for help. I don't want charity."

"Is that what you think this is?"

I shrug.

"It's not. Can you trust me on that?"

"I guess." It takes everything I have to believe him. But I do.

Daniel wasn't lying about his enthusiasm. Furnishing my apartment becomes his project. Once we move the futon, we go to a second-hand store. We find a wooden dresser with a broken drawer that Daniel says he can fix. I select a chair so both of us can now sit at my table, and lastly, an ugly bedside table from the 1970s. Daniel questions my selection, but this time, I tell him to trust me. Still, despite my outward confidence, I battle old patterns of approval-seeking on every decision. Maybe even more than approval, direction. But Daniel leaves me to make my own choices, and even when he questions me, he's not belittling my decision. It's about understanding or making sure I am happy with my choice.

"You're sure? Those are bold colors." We are at the paint store.

I hold two paint swatches in my hand, aubergine (my new favorite color) and bubble-gum pink. "Yup, they are going to be perfect."

"Alright then. I am excited to see the results."

Back at home, we paint both chairs purple, except for the spindles, which are done in the pink. The side table is basically a big box with two ornate doors on the front. We remove those before painting the inner box hot pink, while the outside is done in purple.

"Wow," Daniel says. "The furniture turned out amazing. I couldn't picture it at first, but it's funky and fun. Kind of like you."

His comments make my cheeks warm. Fun and funky. Me? Why not.

The final purchase is of two large cork boards, which Daniel secures to my walls using his father's tools. The first things I pin up are two sketches of the men in my life.

Daniel.

Gunner.

We do all this before New Year's Eve.

15

MY SHIFT ON NEW Year's Eve is our first time apart. With Daniel not working and with the student pub being slow due to the holidays, I haven't worked either. If I remember high school science correctly, it's called mutualism. Two organisms living together for their mutual benefit. It should scare me. But nothing with Daniel scares me.

Well almost. All I want is a happy new year with Daniel. But what if he doesn't show up? Daniel walks me to work on his way to meet his brother. He says he will be back by eleven to spend midnight with me and gives me no reason to doubt him, but I have been let down too many times before. Work is busy, giving me little time to obsess, but I keep looking at the time. I even mix up a few orders, causing the bartender to ask if I am okay.

Finally, I see him walk in, seeking me out. There is an odd pricking in the corners of my eyes, and I wipe at them while making my way over. I sit Daniel at the bar while I keep serving tables. When I check on him, I find him behind the bar helping to serve drinks. He gives me a quick wink. As the countdown approaches, we find each other. He stands behind me and wraps me in his arms. When we kiss and toast in 2001, nothing feels real. How can so much change so fast? I bury my head under his chin to smell him, to touch him, and know I am not dreaming.

He lifts my chin. "Vic, look at me. Enjoy this moment together. I am. We're here together. Only think about that."

"How do you do that?"

"Do what?

"Guide me to where I want to be." Instead of answering with words, he kisses me again. His affection, the soil for my wayward roots, anchors me to the present. I am not used to this mix of affection and reliability. It gives me a buzz as my synapses forge new connections.

We get to my place and quietly enter so as not to wake Gunner. His head pops up, and he rolls over for a belly rub before returning to sleep. Daniel and I crawl into bed. He pulls my back against him, wrapping me in warmth.

I interlock my fingers with his and bring his hand to my mouth for a kiss.

"This has been the best week of my life."

He squeezes me and kisses the back of my head. We lie entwined, warmed by tenderness as the snow falls outside, watching Gunner sleep, the rise and fall of his chest, the twitchiness of his legs as he dreams.

If this was my last moment on earth, I would die happy.

16

I wake before Daniel and trace over his body with my finger. He stirs and, in sleep, pulls me closer. How do I deserve such a man? I thought I had relationships figured out. Relationships were not the stuff in movies. They only worked if one person earned their keep.

I still recall my mother's voice telling me to make myself useful by getting her this or doing that. In high school, people only wanted to be my friend if I got them drugs. I didn't, so I had none.

As a child, I was always hungry, so I occasionally stole food—until I turned ten, but only because I got caught.

The shopkeeper, a large woman with grey hair styled like the Queen, always wore a short-sleeved floral dress even in the winter, like she never felt the cold. I can still remember the heat from her hand as she grabbed my arm. I almost peed my pants as she dragged me into a tiny office at the back and pushed me down into a chair. Crying, I begged her not to call the police, as I would likely be removed from my mother's care. And as much as I hated her, she was my mother, and I was afraid to leave her. So the shopkeeper agreed to call my home, but the phone had been disconnected—another unpaid bill.

Ashamed, I stared at my shoes, trying to hide the rips in them by wrapping my feet around the legs of the chair, and sat on my hands to hide how much they were shaking.

After a silence that felt like years, she asked if I was hungry. I nodded. She let me keep the chocolate bar, saying I could pay for it by sweeping and taking out the garbage. The next day, I returned and did some more chores. This time, she paid me with soup and a sandwich.

I did this for two years. And then, one day, she was gone. Her shop went up for sale. I later found out that she'd had a stroke.

I believe that the shopkeeper let me work, so it didn't feel like I was getting charity. Still, Kent's behavior wasn't so different, even if perhaps the intentions were. I sit up, and Daniel opens his eyes, sensing my intensity.

"What are you thinking?"

"Nothing."

"I can see the smoke coming out of your ears."

I lie back down, one breath away from him. "Is there something you want from me?"

His dark, serious eyes lock onto mine. "You've already given it to me." He takes my hands, brings them to his lips, and pulls me close. "You gave me a chance."

Closing my eyes, I take a deep breath, hoping to inhale the air that carries those words so that they enter my bloodstream and replace the harmful waste I've carried for too long. When I open my eyes, I find Daniel still gazing at me. "You're kind of corny, you know that?"

"Another one of my flaws."

"I wouldn't call it a flaw. It's sweet."

That gets a smile out of him, then he rubs his morning stubble against my cheek. "It took a pity date for it to happen, but here we are."

Our laughing must have woken up Gunner because suddenly his head is on the bed, his big eyes staring at us.

"I think he needs to go out," says Daniel. "Want me to go?"

"No. I can do it. Stay here where it's warm."

Gunner and I exit the apartment into biting wind; thankfully, Gunner doesn't waste any time. We walk a block, and as soon as he does his business, we turn back. I pass a person on the street, and they give me a big smile as we make eye contact. At this moment, in the early glow of a winter morning where the air is so cold my eyelashes are frosty, I realize the happiness inside me has worked its way to the surface. The man was smiling back because of my wide grin.

We return to the apartment with a gust of cold air to find Daniel up and making coffee. I warm up quickly because the heat emanates from my heart.

Despite the cold, Daniel and I take Gunner for a long walk before my shift to tire him out. The more comfortable he gets with us, the more energy he seems to have.

"So, Gunner is part husky, right? They have a lot of energy," Daniel says. "You might want to start jogging."

"Jogging? I've only ever run on a treadmill." Kent made me do ten kilometers a day after he left for work. Heaven forbid I gain any weight.

"Well, you might want to try outside. I don't think Gunner would take to a treadmill, even if you could fit one in here."

"But look outside. Winter."

"Dress warmly."

"I don't see you volunteering."

"Is that a challenge?"

"Yes. It is."

"Challenge accepted. Tomorrow we run."

"I don't have running shoes."

"Well, I guess we better get you some."

"I have to work."

"Vic, tomorrow. Bright and early. No excuses."

"Fine." I surrender. "But I choose the route."

"Deal." He hugs me, and Gunner jumps up, wanting to get in on the hug by leaning on us and wagging his tail.

The next afternoon, the three of us head out on our first jog. Other than buying me shoes, our prep work included buying Gunner booties to prevent damage to his feet from the salt and cold. It took almost an entire bag of treats to coax him to put them on.

We run two kilometers before I need to stop and walk. Gunner is tired, too—finally. Whoo hoo.

And for the next few weeks, the three of us settle into a comfortable domestic routine. Breakfast, jogging, work for me, travel preparation for Daniel, late dinner, bed. I enjoy every moment that comes with being part of a family, no matter how temporary.

17

A WEEK BEFORE DANIEL'S departure, Mariam and Edward host a going-away party. It is a formal black-tie affair, and I wonder if his parents ever throw a casual party.

After taking Gunner for his morning jog, I send Daniel to his parent's home because I plan to spend the day getting ready for the party. With Gunner settled down for a nap, I go downtown for a manicure, with plenty of time to find a new dress. There is one I am focused on. I had spotted it in the store window a while back. And now, the dress is fifty percent off since it is past New Year's Eve. It is an evening sheath dress in black silk, with a sweetheart neckline and spaghetti straps. Along the left side of the gown, down to the floor, are white silk orchids.

It's perfect and bold and unlike anything I've worn before.

With my nails done and dress in hand, I return home with plenty of time to work on my hair and makeup. Gunner sits on the floor beside me, watching my every move with curiosity.

I keep my hair simple with a neat French twist and do my eyes with smoky cat-eye makeup (something Kent would never approve of, but a look I've always liked). A stunning plum lipstick matches my nails perfectly. Finally done, I kiss Gunner on the head, leaving a faint outline of my lips on his fur. I also pass him a new chew toy, so he is entertained while I am at the party.

As I knock on Mariam's door, I hope to hide my nerves under these clothes and makeup. I am not sure what Mariam thinks of my relationship with her son. We are friends, yes, but that is different. I imagine to her I am not that great of a catch. But Daniel is the only one who matters to me, so I swallow my inhibitions and put on a brave face.

Mariam answers the door, and we exchange pleasantries. I ask about her new granddaughter, which gets her talking and eases my nerves. As I pass her my coat, I see him. He is so stunning I think I might be swooning. Daniel is wearing a tuxedo. A tuxedo! His hair is slicked back, making it appear darker, like his father and brother. He has a drink in one hand and is telling a story. People are laughing along with him. I think he senses me staring, for he turns. Our eyes lock, and he smiles as I give a little wave. He excuses himself from his audience and makes his way to me. I am grateful to have his arms on me—they are the only things holding me down on earth.

He kisses me before speaking. "So this is why you kept me away today. You're breath-taking."

"So are you." I pull at his bowtie with both hands. "I think we need to buy Gunner one of these."

He takes me by the hand and begins the introductions. I will never remember all the names, not that it matters. They might remember mine, though. Daniel's new girlfriend. Is the ink even dry on his divorce papers? It's a tiny bit scandalous. And a tiny bit fun.

Daniel is explaining his new role to some of his dad's colleagues, so I slip away to refill our glasses. A woman walks in, and I can't remember if anyone introduced us. She comes up beside me, uncomfortably close.

"Can I help you?"

Ignoring my question, she says, "You mean nothing to him. You're just a rebound."

I freeze briefly, stunned, then turn to face the enemy head-on. "I'm sorry. Do I know you?"

"No. But I am a close friend of Dan's, and believe me, you're not his type."

"Considering we just met, that is an interesting comment."

"It doesn't take much to recognize some stupid gold-digging slut."

That one hits me like a punch to the gut. A mix of anger and humiliation flood my body. I want to slap her and pour the ice bucket over her head. The only thing stopping me is Daniel—I would never do anything to embarrass him.

"Listen, whoever you are, I don't care what you think about me, but how dare you come to this house as a guest and behave so rudely. What kind of friend are you to Daniel if you insult the person he is dating behind his back? His parents invited us all here to celebrate and wish him well. If you're not here to do that, maybe you should leave. Now, if you'll excuse me, Daniel will be wondering what's taking me so long."

I wear a mask of confidence. Behind it, I'm a trembling mess. My core is taught. My stomach is in knots. I might be sick. I pass Daniel his drink and then escape to the bathroom, leaning against the door, barely able to remain standing as my knees shake. Everything is okay. Just breathe. I did nothing wrong and handled myself well, speaking articulately. Turns out that the Toastmaster's club Kent sent me to finally paid off. I have nothing to be embarrassed about. Do I?

A knock. "Yeah, one sec."

I open the door to see Ben.

"You okay?" he asks. "I kind of heard the whole thing."

"Oh my gosh. I'm so sorry." My hands cover my burning cheeks.

"Don't be. I was going to intervene, but you were awesome. You really put her in her place. Although I was kind of hoping for a catfight."

"Thank you. I think. Who was that anyway?"

"I can't remember her name. I think she is an old roommate of Kim's or something. I know Dan tried to fix her up with one of his colleagues a while ago. He found she was over at their place too much—she's obviously interested in him. I'm not sure where Mom got the guest list. Dan wouldn't have invited her. Anywho, she's gone now. Dad asked her to leave."

"You told your father?" Will the humiliation never end?

"Only the highlights. Had I told Mom, she'd have slapped her."

"Perhaps I should just go. I don't want to embarrass your family."

"Don't be ridiculous. Come on, let me take you back to Dan."

I fight my instinct to flee. As soon as I am back with Daniel, he slips his arm around me and squeezes. The warmth of his fingers penetrates deep into my heart and allows the memory of the last few minutes to fade away.

He glances at me, smiling, then begins telling the small group we're standing with a story about training Gunner like we are part of his life.

What if six weeks isn't enough?

18

Daniel and I spend the day after his party in Old Montreal. Underneath the snow lies cobblestone roads, and the historic stone buildings line the streets like sentries on duty. Daniel thought to bring a camera, and we ask tourists to take our picture. Our need to document us as a couple is unspoken but hovers in the air like the misty clouds from our winter conversations.

We stroll along the St. Lawrence river, and Gunner is having the time of his life, smelling all the new smells. When a woman stops to pet him and tell him what a handsome boy he is, I would swear he is smiling. My boy has changed so much. Daniel and I smile like proud parents.

As we pass a gift shop, Daniel runs in and buys us matching T-shirts. *J'aime Montreal.* The word *aime* replaced by a heart. Daniel is my Montreal. French. English. Strong. Encompassing. Diverse. Embracing. Deep. Complex.

Romantic.

"Tu aime Montreal?"

"Oui. Je l'aime beaucoup."

Snow begins to fall as the early winter dusk envelopes us. Daniel and I climb into a horse-drawn caleche and snuggle under a blanket. With Gunner at our feet, we hold each other in silence. The city night lights up to the background rhythm of horse hooves, and snow lands on us in big fluffy flakes, like a shower of white petals. When Daniel leans in to kiss the top of my head, I realize that while life is far from perfect, there are indeed perfect moments, sprinkled throughout the years like stepping stones across an ancient river.

The next day, we walk side by side up the mountain trail. The city is in a deep freeze, making us nearly unrecognizable beneath layers and layers of winter clothes. Eyelashes become icy. Snow squeaks under each footfall. Even Gunner refused to spend more time outside than it took him to do his business today, so we left him at home. Other than one lone jogger, we are alone above the city.

"Come," Daniel says.

I follow. We are at the end of the stone lookout wall. He jumps over a large boulder and crouches down.

"What are you doing?"

"You'll see. Tell me if anyone is coming. I've always wanted to do something like this."

I take my job seriously, but it is easy. No one is out today. At my knees, a drilling sound. I had wondered what was in his backpack.

"There. All done." He stands up, blows on his cordless drill like a gun. "What do you think?"

He points at a rock. Etched onto the side facing the city D + V, I trace over it with my finger.

"No one's ever vandalized for me before."

"Glad I was your first."

I embrace him in a tight hug knocking him down into the snow. He pulls me with him. We laugh and make snow angels.

The day before he leaves, we run around picking up last-minute items and packing his suitcases. We eat dinner with his family before returning to my apartment for the last time. Gunner's bed is temporarily relocated to the kitchen so Daniel and I can be intimate without curious dog eyes staring at us.

We stay up all night, savoring each moment. Sometimes we love frantically. Sometimes it burns slowly. Most of the time, we just hold each other, entwined together like a complicated sailor's knot.

As the sun rises, Daniel writes Leonard Cohen lyrics on my torso with a sharpie.

I sketch us together.

And so it ends.

19

Daniel and I sit in the back of his parent's car as the four of us drive to the airport. The conversation hums around me as I look out the window. The tightness in my chest, and the swirling thoughts in my head, prevent me from joining in. What will I do without him?

We pull into short-term parking, and he and his dad lift his suitcases out of the trunk. I leave to find a luggage cart, letting his parents say goodbye without my presence. His parents are getting into their car as I return, and Mariam wipes away tears as they drive away.

As he pushes the luggage cart towards the airline check-in, I cling to his arm like a life raft from the Titanic. I can't let go. I have to touch him every second I can.

"I knew this would be hard," he says, looking at me.

I nod and lean my head on his shoulder.

Once his check-in is complete, we walk to the security checkpoint.

He wraps his arms around me tight. This is it fills our every gesture. We kiss tenderly. When the kiss ends, I pull back and remove an envelope from my purse. "Open this on Valentine's day."

He nods as he slips it into his breast pocket. Tears in his eyes match my own. We embrace one last time, then he turns and walks to the security gate.

"Daniel, wait!"

I run to him. I want to tell him that I love him. I have never said these words to anyone. Not my mother. Not Kent. I don't think I knew what they meant until now—until Daniel.

186

I don't need to say them. Our love is evident in every look, touch, and gesture, but I say it now because I want him to hear what those words sound like coming from me.

In the future, when he thinks of me, he'll think of me saying them and smile.

"I love you, Daniel."

He cups my face in his hands as he stares into my eyes. "I love you too, Vicki. So much."

We lean our heads together. If I ask him to stay, he will. If he asks me to go, I will. But each of us started a journey we need to finish, and our destinations are not the same.

There is nothing more to say. Our time is up. Daniel takes one step away, turns back, and kisses me one last time.

I hold onto his hand until he moves beyond my reach.

Then I let him go.

20

At home, Gunner jumps up to greet me. His warmth is both welcome and needed. Then he sits down and stares at the door expectantly, awaiting Daniel's arrival. Tilting his head, he listens for footfalls in the hallway. Where is the tall one?

Silence fills the apartment like a dense fog. It burns my throat. Sits heavy on my chest. I quickly change and get Gunner ready for a jog.

I can't outrun the pain, but perhaps I can exhaust it.

We run and run and run. Along city streets. Through parks. Under bridges. Up the mountain.

By the time we reach the top, my legs are burning and shaking with fatigue. I double over, and the contents of my stomach hit the snow, a splatter painting of pure grief. I am hot yet trembling with cold at the same time.

Gunner tilts his head at me, concerned.

"I'm okay, I'm okay," I pant out in an effort to assure him, although I might be lying. "But let's sit down."

I walk beside the wall until I reach the end and sit on the rock with Daniel's handiwork. I trace our love with my finger.

He pulled me in from the far side of love, exposing me to all its beauty and now its pain. Yet I wouldn't change a thing.

Gunner licks my face. I pull him close to my chest and hug him tight. "Okay. Let's go."

I stand up, staring out across at the city. The buildings. The river. The bridges. The streets where we walked arm in arm. Hand in hand.

Kissed.

Loved.

J'aime Montreal.

189

21

Valentine's Day comes one week after Daniel's departure. I am working, so I will be busy at least, but it will be a struggle to be surrounded by couples and not break into tears.

Valentine's Day is over in Hong Kong. The envelope I gave him contained two small pen and ink drawings, the size of postcards. One is a drawing of a photo taken the day we were in Old Montreal. Daniel, Gunner, and me looking like tourists and smiling like we hadn't a care in the world. The other is more personal. Daniel and me in bed, early morning. Heads on pillows, minds foggy with sleep. Our lips curving into smiles for the simple pleasure of being together.

With a few hours to kill before my shift, I grab Gunner, and we walk to the animal shelter. I've baked heart-shaped dog and cat treats and will drop them off with Darcy, along with some I've made for the humans. Those I decorated with red and pink icing. They say I woof you in white. Silly, but it kept me busy.

Walking home, I stop to buy milk and a pack of smokes. I haven't smoked for years, Kent made me quit, so I guess I can thank him for that. Instead of going inside, I sit on the apartment stairs as snow begins to fall and light up. One puff is all I can handle, so I turn the cigarette vertically and watch it burn down. When this is over, I start the process with another one. Gunner raises one eyebrow at me like I'm crazy and taps on the door to be let in.

He shakes snow all over me as I stand to open the door. We are both startled by a honk behind us.

I recognize the car. Daniel? The passenger window rolls down, and Mariam smiles at me.

190

"I didn't know you smoked," she says.

"I don't anymore. I guess I was hoping it might take the edge off."

"Well, let me help with that. Come get in the car. Daniel wants me to take you to lunch."

"Thanks, but I'm not up for going out."

"He made me promise. Now come on."

I nod in silent acquiescence, then take a moment to settle Gunner in the apartment before reluctantly climbing into the car. We say nothing on the drive. It's only when we pull up in front of the restaurant that I recognize where we are.

"Mariam, I can't do this. I can't go in there. This is too hard."

"Love is hard, Vicki. Certainly, you've both realized that by now. Now please, he planned this all out. Don't disappoint him."

Never. So I suggest just a drink.

Daniel has made a reservation, and we are seated at the same table where he and I sat the night of the ballet.

The waiter brings over a bottle of mineral water without us asking. Daniel has thought of everything. Mariam orders wine for herself. Never really knowing what she thought about my relationship with Daniel, I find it difficult to start a conversation.

She smooths out the tablecloth in front of her, then clasps her hands together. "You know, when I first heard about you and Daniel, I didn't know what to think. He's my son, and you are my friend. With his divorce and your recent breakup, I wasn't sure if what you were doing was, well, healthy. And then," she pauses as the waiter brings her wine. She takes a sip before continuing. "And then you came to his going away party. You were passing me your coat when you spotted him. You gasped and grabbed my arm to steady yourself. Did you know that?"

I shook my head.

"My word, you looked at him like no one else was in the room. And he was looking back at you the same way. I stood there, looking at you, looking at him. When you see someone looking at your child with such an open declaration of love, it's breathtaking. Knowing that your child is loved that much, well, it's more than a mother could ask."

She reaches across the table and squeezes my hand before passing me a small box.

"From Daniel."

I take it tentatively and open it. On top is a silver dog tag for Gunner with a note that says, Get a phone in case he gets lost.

Underneath is a silver wide-cuff bracelet. My hands shake as I pull it out. Inside is an inscription.

BEST PITY DATE EVER.

D+V

All at once, some of my heartache is replaced by not exactly happiness, for I still miss him, but warmth and tenderness. He's done it again. Brought me to the place I need to be.

I drink down my remaining water and run my finger over the inscription. Without looking at Mariam, I tell her what I have just realized from deep in my heart.

"Daniel and I shared more in a few weeks than some people share in a lifetime. We ended things without bitterness or anger and parted deeply in love. It's a wonderful feeling to know that out there, across the globe, someone is thinking of me the same way I am thinking of them. It's remarkable. A gift."

When we exit the restaurant, I insist on walking instead of getting into her car. I give her a big hug knowing that this is likely the end of our relationship too. "Thanks for everything you did for me. I don't know what I would have done without you."

She kisses me on both cheeks. "Take care of yourself, Vicki."

"He's the best thing to ever happen to me."

"You'll be okay, you know. You're stronger than you realize."

I nod, thinking she might actually be right. Pulling on Daniel's favorite toque, I walk away and disappear into the falling snow.

22

As Daniel suggested many times over, I finally get a phone and have the number engraved on Gunner's new tag. Now, if he wanders off, I can be reached. I only want what is best for him and can't imagine surviving the guilt over losing him.

Work is thrilled that I have a phone number.

"Glad you came in to let us know. We're not an answering service," says Tony, one of the managers.

"I know. I'm sorry. Thank you for your understanding."

"And by the way, someone named Isabelle called for you yesterday. They want you to drop by the art store."

"Oh? Okay. Thank you."

Gunner and I walk to the art store the following day. I haven't been there since my last shift. I tie him up outside and enter.

"Bring that sweetie inside. Don't leave him in the cold," Isabelle says.

"Really?"

"Oh, of course."

"Thank you."

Gunner comes in, enjoying the attention, and he rolls onto his back for belly rubs. Céline walks out from the back. She and Gunner sniff each other. I doubt they remember one another from the shelter because Céline was adopted long before Gunner began to come out of his shell, but Céline gives him her approval. She walks away, and Gunner follows.

"You got my message?"

"I did, and I came to give you this." I hand her a piece of paper with my new number on it. "I finally got a phone."

"Perfect." She puts it in her pocket. "Would you mind coming to the back with me? I'm sure Gunner will be okay there for a moment. It looks like Céline is giving him a tour."

"Sure."

We walk into her office, and she closes the door.

"I'll get straight to the point. You really fit in with us here before Christmas. Claudette resigned, and we have a full-time opening. Both Phillipe and Michelle are students and can't work full-time, so I thought of you. Would you like the job? It would be Saturdays and Sundays from ten to six and then Mondays, Tuesdays, and Fridays from one to nine. We have a modest drug and dental plan. You don't have to decide right now. I've printed out a contract. Take it home and review it. Just let me know by Friday."

"This is amazing. Thank you. I'll let you know tomorrow."

"Great."

I leave on a high, wishing I could share the news with Daniel.

Of course I take the job. There wasn't anything to consider. I would have signed the contract right then and there but wanted to appear professional. I drop the signed contract off at the art store the following day. From there, we go to the animal shelter so I can give Darcy my new phone number.

"Can you bring Gunner in tomorrow morning?" Darcy asks. "I think we have a potential adoption for him."

My mouth goes dry, and my throat constricts. "Yeah. Sure," I somehow manage to say.

I should be happy. This is what I always wanted for him.

That night I bathe Gunner and trim his nails. "We've got to get you all handsome, buddy. Tomorrow is a big day. We might find you a home. How wonderful would that be?"

Gunner licks at the tears running down my cheeks.

The next day I present him to Darcy.

"Why, hello, Gunner. My, aren't you a handsome boy? I love the bow tie."

Gunner wags his tail and then lays down for a belly rub.

"I can't believe what you've done for him," Darcy tells me.

"He just needed someone to believe in him."

She takes the leash and leads Gunner away. He turns to me, knowing something is up. What did I do wrong?

Shaking, I enter the staff room and pour a coffee. It hits my stomach like cement. Soon I see Gunner, another volunteer, and a middle-aged woman enter the play area. Gunner sits down. They throw a ball for him, but he doesn't move. He keeps looking around for me. For me!

That's when the panic hits. My heart can't take another loss.

I can't lose Gunner.

Letting Daniel go was the right thing to do, even though it hurts. But letting Gunner go is wrong. I can't let that happen.

I burst out of the staff room and run to the front desk. "Darcy! You have to help me."

She jumps up. "What is it? What's wrong?"

"I want to adopt Gunner. I can't let him go! I can't. Please, don't tell me I'm too late." My voice waivers, heavy with fear and panic.

She puts an arm around me and escorts me back into the staff room.

"Sit here. It'll be fine. I promise."

"No. It won't. Not if I lose Gunner. I love him. Please."

"I won't let that happen. Trust me." She walks out; time seems to stop. They are no longer in the play yard. Where are they? Where is Gunner?

I can't sit here and do nothing. I open the door just as Gunner and Darcy enter the hall.

"Gunner!"

He bursts away from Darcy, and the leash pulls free from her hand.

He knocks me over. I lay on the ground and hug him. He licks my face.

"Okay, you two," Darcy says, standing above us. "I'll start the paperwork." She scratches Gunner's head. "Looks like you found where you belong."

23

THE NEXT FEW WEEKS pass in a blur. I wake up each morning energized, knowing I am taking steps toward the life I want. Isabelle lets me train around my remaining waitressing shifts. When I assisted them over the holidays, I worked in customer service. I didn't even work the cash register. Now that I will be the only employee other than Isabelle to work full-time, she trains me on all aspects of running the store.

During my lunch breaks those first few shifts, I would race home and take Gunner for a quick walk. When Isabelle realized what I was doing, she suggested I bring Gunner to work with me. I couldn't believe my ears, but with Céline already in the store, Isabelle saw no reason not to bring Gunner.

Now, we run each morning before work, so he is tired out and spends the rest of his day curled up on a dog bed in the back office with Céline, occasionally wandering out to check on me. He is adored by staff and customers alike.

When I handed in my resignation to Tony, I also gave him a sketch of the bar as a thank you. The pub is in a historic mansion up on the mountainside, and I think my drawing in pencil crayon captures the age and stature of the building.

"You drew this?" Tony asked.

"Yes."

"Well then, no wonder you are leaving us to work in an art supply store. You have a lot of talent." He came from behind his desk and shook my hand. "All the best, Vicki."

"Thank you, Tony. I have enjoyed working here."

On my way home, I stopped in at the tattoo parlor Isabelle recommended to me after admiring her tattoos. On my hip, I got an outline of Montreal with a heart in the center. On my forearm, above where Daniel's bracelet sits, I got a tattoo of the word "Hallelujah," the title of the Leonard Cohen song. The words Daniel wrote on my torso our last night are long gone. This way, he will always be with me.

Two nights ago was the first night I closed up the store by myself. After I had gone through the end-of-day checklist, locked up the cash, and turned out the lights, Gunner and I took a moment to sit in the dark. The street noise was muffled through the windows and inside, the store creaked with age, and the radiator pipes occasionally banged in the walls. The streetlights illuminated the front row of supplies and cast the store's name in shadows on the floor. Along with the shelves full of supplies, the hanging industrial lights, the paint-splattered counter, the art on the walls, I felt that I, too, could become a fixture here. Me, little Vicki Meyers, has found where she belongs.

The runs Gunner and I take are up to ten kilometers now, and we follow our route up the mountain. We run by what I call our spot and touch the engraving Daniel made. The snow is beginning to melt, leaving puddles of slush on every corner, but we are undeterred. Each day the sun rises earlier and burns a bit warmer.

Gunner and I are getting ready to go running when the doorbell rings. No one ever comes by, so my mind can't help but think of Daniel.

As soon as I click the lock open, the door is pushed in with force, knocking me back.

"Good morning," Kent says. "It's been a while."

His presence shocks me like an electric current, and I jump back, coughing to clear my throat. "What are you doing here?"

"Let's go talk." His eyes are hard with anger, his body tense.

"I have nothing to say to you," I say as he grabs my arm and ushers me through my open door.

Gunner is standing by the door, alert, anxious.

Kent eyes him, shaking his head, but Gunner's presence is enough that Kent lets go of my arm, and I take a step away from him.

"Again, what are you doing here?"

"I figured I gave you more than enough time to learn your lesson. Surely, you must see by now that you are nothing without me, but I know that you have a lot of pride and would hesitate before begging me to take you back. So I thought I'd save you the embarrassment and come get you myself."

"I told you I was leaving. That means for good."

"Oh, Victoria. Don't waste my time."

"My name isn't Victoria. It's Vicki. V-I-C-K-I. It says so right on my birth certificate. You know that."

He shakes his head in disgust. "Whatever, babe, just get your stuff. And this thing," he motions his head toward Gunner, "stays here."

"Kent, I'm not leaving with you. It's been months. We're over. My life is here."

"Really? You call this a life? I mean, look at this place. What a shithole. And look at you, you're a mess. You've gained weight, and your hair needs a good stylist." He grabs my hands and pulls them towards him for inspection. "And your nails, God, when was the last time you had a manicure? Is that paint under your fingernails?" He turns my arm over, exposing Hallelujah. "Jesus Christ, you got a tattoo."

I yank my hands away.

"You have good reason to be embarrassed by that. It's proof of why I'm here. You need me."

I stare at the man I spent years with, realizing I feel nothing. Nothing! The power he had over me is gone. I don't feel inferior or worthless. Not shame. Not fear or anger. Not regret, finally recognizing it for all it was—a period of my life. I learned many lessons and will keep what is useful. It is nothing more than that.

"I'm sorry, Kent, but you're wrong. We are over. I am happy here. Now please leave."

"Don't mess with me. I'm not in the mood."

He still doesn't budge. Instead, he continues taking in the new me. He must sense a difference too. Gone is that weak, insecure girl. Before him stands a confident woman. He doesn't know what to do with her.

What he does do is a mistake.

Stepping aggressively towards me causes Gunner to respond.

He places himself between Kent and me. Teeth bared, he emits a deep, menacing growl, his body tenses, and his ears go back. The fur on his back stands on end.

Kent immediately steps back, yet he continues the stare down, trying to intimidate me—hate emanating from his every pore.

"Fuck you," he says, then turns and walks out of the apartment.

Gunner and I don't move until the exterior door shuts and locks behind him. Then I drop to my knees and hug him.

Thirty minutes later, we leave for our jog, nearly plowing into a woman moving in upstairs. After a quick hello, we take off, running up the mountain, leaving this morning behind us.

At the top, we stop at our spot. I look out across the city. The sky is grey, but the sun is breaking its way through. I close my eyes and breathe in the smell of melting snow, fresh mud, and the promise of spring. Gunner puts a muddy paw on my leg. I bend down and scratch his head.

"What a beautiful dog you have," a woman says, walking over.

She bends to pet Gunner, and as she gives him a scratch behind the ears, he moves his head in contentment and smiles.

"He's so friendly and sweet," the woman says.

"Thank you. He's pretty awesome," I reply.

She walks away, and I give him a squeeze. No one would ever believe this dog was afraid of the world a few months ago. "It's amazing what you can do when someone believes in you, isn't it, buddy." I kiss him, then kiss the palm of my hand and place it on the engraving.

"Come on. Time to go."

Gunner looks at me, looks at the engraving, then back at me. He barks, wags his tail, and we keep going.

JANET KOOPS
Rules of Disengagement
Sometimes rules get broken

1

The Mitchel Sisters' Guide to an Awesome Life—Rule no. 1:
Always be the one in control.

October 2000

IT MIGHT HAVE STOPPED snowing, but the wind has picked up, blowing snow across the road like sand on the beach right before a storm. At least on a beach, you don't need to wear toe-pinching boots. Knowing my luck, I'll wipe out on the way to the door, but at least when they find my frozen corpse in the morning, it will look good, thanks to these sexy, if somewhat uncomfortable, boots. The weather was fine when we went into the gig, but things can change fast in Montreal.

"Good night, Steph," Marc says through a yawn while scratching his beard. "Practice on Tuesday. Don't be late and remember the van money."

"Yes. Of course. Good night, Marc." I lower myself out of the van we drive to all our gigs. It smells of sweat, cigarettes, and motor oil, but it gets us there and back. With the other two band members already at home, I am Marc's last drop-off of the night.

I give a small wave as I turn and take small careful steps along the snow-dusted walkway.

"Hey, Steph."

A voice other than Marc's is so unexpected I stop abruptly, dropping my purse and teetering on my heels. My heart pounds, and pain pulses through my feet, causing my words to come out quickly. "Trev, you scared me half to death. Why are you sitting on the stairs? It's freezing. Get inside."

"I was waiting for you."

"Oh," I'm so touched, I almost forget about my aching feet. Unless he is helping us at a wedding, he is typically asleep when I get home from a gig. "Aren't you sweet, but you didn't have to wait outside. Come on, let's get out of the cold."

"Can we talk for a sec out here? I don't want to wake Bridgette."

"Of course." Heaven forbid we disturb his frumpy roommate, but what could be so important that we talk now? Unless...Oh my God, this is it. I knew it. He's been acting weird all week. I pull back my shoulders and uncross my arms. My hair has so much hair spray a tornado couldn't move it, so I know it's still gorgeous. I hope my new highlights are noticeable. I could do without being proposed to as my fingers go numb, but whatever. I'm ready.

A restaurant would have been preferable, but I understand why he chose this moment. The light dusting of snow covers the street's imperfections, and the cool light cast from a nearby streetlight causes the snow to sparkle like the diamond he is about to offer me. He takes my hands. His are warm despite the cold, and while it's not kneeling, it's close enough.

He takes a deep breath. "I think you should spend some time back at your apartment. I put your stuff in some boxes. I'll drive you home."

What the...? I yank my hands away as his words swirl in my head. I close my eyes, massaging a throbbing in my temple. This is not happening. No way. I open my eyes to see Trevor looking across the yard, to the street, as if planning his escape. My chest constricts as tears build and threaten to fall, but I would rather succumb to frostbite than have him see me cry.

He turns, ever so slightly, toward me. "I think we need...well, at least I need...more space. That's why I thought I'd take you back to your apartment tonight."

"My apartment? Are you kidding me? I don't have an apartment anymore. Is this some kind of joke?"

His eyebrows scrunch together. "What do you mean you don't have an apartment? We never talked about moving in together."

"Oh my God, Trevor. I've been spending every night here for the past few months, so I didn't bother to find anywhere new when my sublet ended. What did you think was going on? Why would I pay rent somewhere I'm not living?"

"You can't just...without talking...Jesus, Steph." He runs his fingers through his thinning hair.

"Oh, come on. Unless we're at work or I'm with the band, we're together. It makes sense to be living together."

He sighs.

"At least it makes sense if you love me." I soften my voice. "You do love me, Trevor, don't you?"

"Oh my God." He jumps, glaring at me, his face so close, his breath hits my cheek. "Stephanie, I can't do this anymore. I'm sorry, but this has to end. I can't keep giving you constant reassurance. No, you know what? It's more than that. You need me at your beck and call, and I'm tired of it."

His words fall on me like chains, tethering me to this horrible moment. Despite the anger surging its way through me, I can't move. I raise an eyebrow, and through clenched teeth, I manage, "Are you done?"

"Yes." He snaps then tilts his head up to the sky before facing me again. "I'm sorry. It wasn't meant to come out like that."

I search beyond him, for something—anything—to tell me what to do because my mind is as deserted as the late-night street. How could he do this to me? We've been together a year—an entire year during which I tolerated his bad puns and sat through countless documentaries on WWII. He said he adored me. He often told me how lucky he was because I was out of his league. Out of his league! So why is he dumping me?

Humiliation has caused a lump in my throat, but I swallow it down and focus instead on the practicalities. "And where exactly am I supposed to go?"

He shrugs. The distance between us as frosty as our exhaled breath. "What about your mom's place?" he says. "It's not far."

Mom's place. Not ideal, but it's not like I have another option. I pretend to brush some invisible dirt off my jacket. "Fine then, but when the day comes that you wake up and realize you've made a huge mistake, don't expect me to take you back. We're done." I turn and walk towards his car.

As I slide into his rattly old Saab, slamming the door, I can't help but hope it transforms into a time machine and I can begin the day again. Please let me have a do-over. Or even a sign that this is a bad dream? Please? Anything?

Nope. Nothing but my stupid annoying gum-popping ex-boyfriend, all my worldly possessions, and me en route to my mother's house a few hours before dawn.

Single and homeless. What a way to close out the first year of the new millennium. Yay me.

"You still have a key to her place, don't you?" Trevor asks, his voice like a sudden gunshot, causing me to jump.

"Of course."

"I mean, I'd feel bad if we had to wake her at this time of night."

"That is what you'd feel bad about?"

He lets out a huge sigh, and I perceive the accompanying head shake despite my refusal to look at him.

When we pull up in front of my mother's house after the most awkward fifteen minutes in my twenty-five-year life, I remain in my seat, arms crossed, looking straight ahead.

Trevor turns to me. "Well?"

"Well what? You put my shit into the car. You can take it out."

"Fine."

"Fine."

Only when the trunk slams shut do I finally open the door and step onto the street. Of course, my stupid boots slip on the ice because hey, why wouldn't they, it being the kind of day I'm having. Arms flailing while I try to regain my footing, Trevor reaches out to steady me, but I snatch my arm away, nearly losing my balance yet again—I'd prefer to land on my ass than have him help me.

"Do you want me to move your stuff inside?"

"No."

"Well then, I guess that's it." He leans in, arms open for a hug.

He can't be serious. My hand darts up between us. "Don't."

We stand in silence until he shrugs and walks around the car. "Take care of yourself, Steph." My back to the car, the engine starts behind me, and he drives out of my life.

"Take care of yourself, Steph," I mock. God, what an asshole.

At least no one witnessed my humiliation. Halloween decorations sway in the wind along the street, with jack-o-lanterns partially hidden under the early snowfall. No other people are around. The wind blows through my thin wool coat, and the sharp cold stings my ears. No hat, of course, but at least I look stylish, standing abandoned on the sidewalk. Then again, I could be mistaken for a hooker in these boots and the dramatic stage makeup.

This cannot be happening. I join my boxes on the porch and knock loudly, not knowing where my key is. Mom will wake up, won't she?

I knock again and am flooded with relief when the porch light comes on, even if it does nearly blind me. But instead of Mom, a man in a t-shirt and boxer shorts answers the door. I step back and check the house number. Yup, I'm at the right place.

"Is there a problem?" he asks. His voice thick with sleep, his hair—what little there is—a nest-like mess.

"I...I'm looking for my mom, Helen..."

"Stephanie! What on earth are you doing here at this hour?" Mom rushes down the stairs, tying up her pink terry cloth robe, before grabbing my shoulders and checking for wounds. "Are you okay?"

I don't answer her because, honestly, I don't know.

2

The Mitchel Sisters' Guide to an Awesome Life—Rule no. 2:
Always go out looking your best.

KNOCKING. WHAT'S WITH THE knocking? I reach over to prod Trevor, but my arm touches nothing but cold sheets. Oh. Right.

"Stephanie, can I come in?"

"Sure, Mom." I roll over, away from the door, greeting her with my back.

Estée Lauder *Pleasures* reaches me before her words do. "Bruce and I are going out. Is there anything you need before I go?"

A new boyfriend? A new life? "No."

"I'm sorry, sweetheart. I know you really liked this boy."

"We were living together. I thought we were going to get married. So yeah, I guess you could say I liked him."

"Yes, yes. I'm sorry. You know what I mean. I didn't realize you were living together, though."

Apparently, neither did Trevor. "Well, you didn't tell me you were seeing anyone."

The sudden depression of the mattress under her weight, plus the warmth of her hand on my shoulder, takes me back to a childhood I no longer think about. She gives me a little squeeze. "I guess you're right."

The weight of her affection makes me wince, so I pull the covers up over my head, effectively forcing her hand away. She doesn't move immediately, but when I make no sign of continuing the conversation, the mattress shifts, signaling her departure. The door shuts. Her footsteps retreat downstairs. Muffled voices float up from the foyer until the front door closes, leaving me in silence.

Hallelujah. Alone at last.

Poking my head out from under the covers, I scan the guest room. My boxes and suitcases stand in the corner against a bookcase and a pale blue wall. She's painted and hung gauzy white curtains since I last saw this room. Which was when? Still, would it kill her to hang some art or buy an area rug? In our old house, each room was a different color. They were strong colors. Bold colors. Now, the only thing with life in this room is me, and that's not saying much, considering twenty-five years of life can fit into six boxes and two suitcases. No wonder Trevor didn't realize I'd moved in. At least my instruments and gear are stored at Marc's place.

Well, now that I have the place to myself, it's time for some breakup food. I'm so hungry, I bet the neighbors can hear my stomach growling. A wintery gust rattles the window as I slide out of bed, the floor chilly under my feet. No wonder people retire to Florida. The comforter serves as a make-shift robe as I rush downstairs, pausing briefly in the front hall to slip my feet into Mom's still-warm slippers. She won't mind if I keep them. Don't women her age have hot flashes?

I rifle through all the cupboards in the kitchen, not knowing where Mom keeps everything. Crackers. Cereal. Bread. Peanut butter. Not bad, but maybe the fridge can do better. Yogurt. Fruit. Vegetables. Nope. Nothing breakup worthy. I hit the jackpot in the freezer, though—a bottle of vodka and a tub of ice cream. Oh yeah, baby, come to momma.

⋅⋅⋅ ⋅⋅⋅

The sun hitting me in the face like a cream pie is better than any alarm clock. Guess I forgot to shut the blinds. Those gauzy curtains do nothing to block out light. I glance at my watch. Eight-thirty. Work at ten unless I call in sick. I haven't taken a sick day in years, and it's a Monday. The store won't be that busy, so they can manage without me.

Sudden knocking reverberates behind my eyes like a gong. Last night's vodka doesn't help.

"Stephanie! Stephanie!"

I pull the covers over my head to disperse the noise. "What?" I call out, not attempting to hide my irritation.

"Didn't you say you had work today?"

"Yeah. So?"

"So, rise and shine. You don't want to be late."

What I wouldn't do for a sinkhole right now.

"Stephanie!"

"Okay, okay. I'm up. Geez."

"Hurry up, or you'll be late."

"I have time."

"Are you sure? It takes a while to get downtown. The buses don't come that frequently after rush hour."

"You're not driving me?"

"No. I have things to do before I go to work myself."

"You could have told me." Even with the door closed, there is no mistaking my mother's sigh.

"Stephanie, I know you are upset, but..."

"Oh my God. I get it, okay?" I slide out of bed and stomp around my room like a moody teenager. The suitcase contents are dumped on the floor as I search for my jeans and music store shirt. And how many days without showering am I up to now? Two? Plus, Trevor dumped me after a gig, so those two days included a performance. Urgh. I rush around, doing what I can to make myself presentable. *Presentable*? Since when do I settle for presentable? The box marked *Steph-Bathroom 1* in Trevor's neat little printing takes the brunt of my frustration as I tear into it in an attempt to find some hair supplies and makeup.

Oh God, what a disaster. All I have time for is a messy bun, some lip gloss, and mascara before I storm out without saying goodbye. Not my best move because I don't know what bus to take. Dammit.

Of course, I'm late. Of course, my colleagues stare at me, wondering what the hell is wrong. I'm always dressed to perfection. Perfect hair, perfect clothes, perfect makeup. Perfect. Perfect. Perfect. But not today. Nope, today I find the manager and ask if I can do anything in the back. Inventory? Organizing? Anything. She agrees without hesitation.

Perfect.

3

The Mitchel Sisters' Guide to an Awesome Life—Rule no. 3:
Always keep them guessing.

SO WORK WAS HELPFUL. I'll never admit that to Mom, but I shouldn't have been all that surprised. The store's old wooden door, creaky stairs, and uneven floor have welcomed me with open arms since I was a young girl learning to play the guitar. Even then, the black walls covered with instruments, merchandise, and posters drew me in. And sometimes, on good days, staff would let me wander behind the long glass counter at the front of the store, allowing me a close-up view of the signed guitars and old concert shirts that hung behind it.

So yeah, even working in the back, unloading deliveries and organizing inventory, was cathartic. That is why today, I rise when my alarm goes off to have plenty of time to shower. Rule no. 2 was broken yesterday by going out merely presentable. It won't happen again. That is not who Stephanie Mitchel is.

"Good morning, everyone," I say brightly in a sing-songy voice as I enter the break room.

"Hey Stephanie, you look better today. You must be feeling better," says Denis, the assistant manager. He stands in front of the coffee maker, waiting for it to finish brewing, his hands resting on his beer belly like a pregnant woman protecting her womb.

"You bet I am."

"So you don't need more time in the back?"

"No thanks, Denis. I'm ready to go."

"Sorry about Trevor," says Natalie, another salesclerk like me. Natalie could pass for a librarian with her thick glasses and a book always in hand. But that big brain of hers, hiding behind severe black bangs, probably stores more about the history of rock than the entire internet.

"Oh, thanks, Nat. It's always sad when a relationship ends, but I knew we weren't right for each other, so it's better to end things than to stay in a relationship that has no future."

"You seemed pretty upset."

"Oh, I was. I felt so bad for hurting Trevor. But he understands it's for the best. He'll be fine."

She smiles and nods, giving my arm a little squeeze as she walks past me.

I manage to beat Denis to the coffee, pour a cup, then punch in, relieved the questions are over. It's not like anyone here knows Trevor—I never invited him in or introduced him to my colleagues—so my version of events is assured.

The morning is slow with only a few customers, but that means more time with each one. I love helping customers. Well, helping is the wrong word. I love talking about music with them. Performers, teachers, students, it doesn't matter.

Early in the afternoon, a woman and her son enter the store. They both are looking around, unsure of what they need. You can always tell the music store novices because their eyes never focus on one section.

I walk over and smile. "Can I help you? Puis-je vous aider?"

"Oh yes," the woman replies, looking relieved. She's quite the urban mom, what with her black velour tracksuit, messy ponytail, and manicured nails clutching her Balenciaga City bag. "Can you help us rent a trombone?"

"Of course. Follow me." I lead them over to the rental area desk and pull out the binder where we keep the agreements. Usually, people interested in renting are students at the beginning of the school year or occasionally when someone's instrument is in for repair, so I am curious why they are here. "All right, why don't you tell me what kind of trombone you need? Then, I can see what we have in stock."

The mom turns to her kid then back at me. "We haven't got a clue. He asked for trombone lessons for his birthday. None of us play an instrument."

"Hmm. Okay." I give the boy a once-over. He's shorter than his mom, but not by much, and kind of scrawny. But he's got a head of thick wavy brown hair that a lot of girls will go crazy for in a few years. I raise my eyebrows, encouraging him to speak, but he remains silent.

"Well, typically, we recommend a straight tenor trombone for beginners. But why don't you tell me what it is about the trombone you like and why you asked for lessons. That way, we can figure out if the trombone is the right instrument for you. It's great that you want to learn to play an instrument, but I want to make sure your first experience is positive. The trombone isn't for everyone."

Finally, the kid speaks, but it's at the ground as if his shoes asked the question. "I don't know. It seems easy. You just blow and move your arm."

"Well, for starters, no instrument is easy. It takes a lot of practice. How about this: you tell me what kind of music you like to listen to and what kind of music you want to play, that way I can help you choose an instrument that will suit your tastes. That makes practice much more fun."

He turns to his mom and shrugs.

She is as silent as the boy. Cue the crickets.

"Well, for me, I started playing guitar because my dad was a big fan of Van Halen. He played their music all the time. My sister and I would pretend we were in the band. Then we dreamed of having our own band, performing at sold-out stadiums, people chanting our names and screaming how much they love us." The memory hits with such visceral intensity that the smoke from my dad's cigarette burns my throat, my feet sink into the plush carpet, and Chelsea chants her own name, fist-pumping the air. Chelsea! Chelsea! Chelsea!

No.

Coughing allows me to clear both my throat and my mind, sending Chelsea back where she belongs. "Where was I? Oh right. But that's not for everyone. My friend Jess, who works here, plays double bass in a jazz band, you know, one of those huge ones you need to stand behind. Anyway, he's always liked the deep sounds it makes because it reminds him of a train."

"Oh."

"Yeah, so what do you want to do? Play in the school orchestra or a marching band? The trombone would be perfect for that."

"I don't think so."

"I tell you what, if your mom gives me the okay, I'll show you five instruments that I think are good for beginners. I'll tell you why and where you can use them to perform. Then you can both decide what is best, and then we'll set you up and help you find some lessons. Sound like a plan?"

"Sure."

"Works for me," says the mom. "The last thing I want to do is drag Riley to lessons he doesn't want to go to."

The next hour flies by, and eventually, they decide on an acoustic guitar, which they buy instead of renting, and I sign them up for six months of lessons through the store. After they leave, the manager Diane comes up and thanks me.

"You make it look so easy."

"It is easy when you are talking about something you love." It's true. Music was, and is, my happy place. And not only performing, I was one of those kids who loved practicing. There was a time when I would practice until my fingers bled. Repetition blocked out the pain and yelling. Repetition filled the emptiness.

"Hel-lo-ho, earth to Stephanie."

"What? Oh, I'm sorry."

"You okay? You went into a world of your own there."

"Oh, yeah, sure. I was remembering how much I used to practice."

"How sweet. I'm glad you have such fond memories."

"Yeah. You bet."

From work, I go directly to Marc's house. Too bad there is no direct route by transit. Without Trevor to drive me, I take the metro and two busses. The long, crowded journey does not help my mood.

Mark opens the door, his stance challenging, barring my entrance, like a bouncer or a troll.

"Do I need a password now?"

He unfolds his tattooed arms—I don't think he owns a shirt with sleeves—and holds out one hand, palm up.

"I didn't forget." I dig into my bag and pull out the money I owe him, slapping it onto his palm. He still doesn't budge but arches an eyebrow, barely visible under his shaggy hair, questioning my late arrival.

I turn sideways and shimmy past him. "Yeah, I know. I know. I had to take the metro and not one, but two busses." I wave two fingers in front of his face. "Two. It took forever. You ever consider moving closer to downtown?"

"Sure, but then where would we keep all this stuff and practice? I don't see you volunteering any space."

"Alright, you made your point."

"Wait a second, did you just say you took transit here? You never take transit. Is Trevor busy?"

Bending down while taking off my shoes gives me a chance to plaster a fake everything-is-fine smile on my face. "Actually, we broke up. We decided things weren't working and needed to go our separate ways."

"Too bad. I liked him. Who are we going to get to help us take requests at weddings now?" Erin says while tuning her base. Her bright red lips give me a small smile.

"That's what you care about? What about me? I'm on my own again. Besides, I thought we all agreed to cut back on weddings if possible."

Erin flicks her straight jet-black hair behind her shoulders. "Maybe now you'll get your driver's license without him to take you everywhere."

"Wow. You guys are so supportive. Thanks a bunch."

"You're right. We're sorry, Steph," says Marc. "But maybe you can turn that heartache into a song. We need some new material."

"For the record, it's frustration, not heartache, and yeah, maybe."

Sébastien walks out from the kitchen. Beer in one hand, drumsticks in another. "All right then. Vas-y, vas-y, let's go. We play a bar on Friday and a wedding on Saturday. We don't have much time to practice."

"Do you guys know any Van Halen?" Did I really just ask that?

"Van Halen?" All three ask in unison like they are auditioning for a barbershop quartet.

"Yeah. I got a song in my head, and I can't shake it."

"Wow, you're full of surprises today, Steph," says Erin.

"I know, right?" If those memories of Van Halen don't bring me to tears, no one will be more surprised than me.

4

The Mitchel Sisters' Guide to an Awesome Life—Rule no. 4:
Don't let them know your weakness.

Five Months Later

I CURL UP ON the couch and settle in for another night in front of the television. Wet, heavy, spring snow has been falling for hours and with the power having flashed on and off several times, Bruce is assembling a small army of flashlights and lanterns.

"Helen," he calls out, "Do you remember where I put the extra batteries?"

"Top right drawer of the hutch," Mom yells from the hall.

"Oh, right." The sticky hutch drawer rattles open. "Found them, honey. Thank you."

Mom walks into the living room smiling. Her affection for him obvious in the way she gently shakes her head and the way her sigh is not one of frustration, as I am accustomed to, but one of contentment.

She sits down beside me, and I move my legs to give her more space while I flick through the channels. "There's nothing on."

"That's okay. I just want to talk."

I stop, leaving the TV on a French sitcom. She leans towards me, takes the remote from my hand, and turns it off. Oh super. We're going to have one of *those* talks.

"So, Stephanie," she begins, "You've been here about five months now. Any plans on getting your own place?"

Five months? It's only March. Discreetly, I count out the months on my fingers. She's right. Jesus. "Are you trying to get rid of me or something?" I try to keep my tone lighthearted, but years of insecurity create words that are hard and sharp.

"Oh Stephanie, come on. It's not that I'm trying to get rid of you, but you're a grown woman. You haven't lived at home for years. You need to start living your life again. Finding a place is the first step to getting you back on your feet. Moping around here and having me take care of you isn't helping."

Of course not. I'm not the one she liked taking care of. The tension is immediate, automatically putting me on the offensive, aiming for her weak spot. "Right. Like you're an expert on moving on."

Mom clasps her hands together. The veining on them more prominent than I remember, the skin, slightly crepey. She rubs them together as if massaging in invisible lotion. It leaves me feeling like a class A jerk, but I don't apologize.

"I know I fell apart after your father left. It took me a long time to recover. I don't want you making the same mistake. But I was with your father for twenty years. We had a life together. A family. We buried our eldest daughter. Not many couples face that level of stress or grief." She stops talking, puts her hands on her lap, and stares out the window into darkness.

Her name is never spoken. Doing so would create an acoustic wave and once received, our brains would not only perceive the sound of her name but her voice, her personality, her ghost. Rather, we substitute in generic terms. Daughter. Sister.

"How long were you with Trevor?" she asks.

"What? I don't know. About one year I guess."

"One year. I know that seems like a long time when you're young, but it's not. I'm not trying to belittle your relationship, but you need to start looking ahead. You've been without him for about half as long as you were together. It's time to move on."

It's not Trevor I'm hung up on, if I ever was. It's the routine I've established here. I've grown comfortable. Welcomed in each night to conversation and a homemade meal is soothing, like my old childhood blanket. Have I not earned the payout of these moments—moments that have been sitting in arrears for years? Surely, I am owed that much. But who am I kidding? Deep down, I knew it wouldn't last because I have never been enough to hold us together.

Hurt claws at my throat. If she thinks I'm still pining over Trevor, fine. I can play along. "Are you kidding me? I'm sitting here, heartbroken, and you tell me to get out. Thanks a lot. I'll move out. I'd hate to be in the way of your relationship."

"That's not fair," says a deep voice from the hallway.

"Bruce, don't. Please," my mother says.

Undeterred, he walks over to us and places a protective hand on Mom's shoulder. "I'm sorry, Helen, I said I wouldn't interfere, but I'm not going to stand here and listen to your ungrateful daughter hurt your feelings." He turns to me. "Your mother has done nothing but help and support you. All you do is take, take, take. You don't help with the dishes or the cooking. You expect her to do your laundry. You work full-time—have you offered a cent towards room and board?"

I say nothing.

"I didn't think so."

"I'm her child!"

"Yes, you are, but you are no longer *a* child. Grow up and take some responsibility for yourself."

"Oh my God. This is crazy. Thanks for nothing." The TV remote goes flying as I jump up and storm out of the room. Very mature, Steph. Next time, don't forget to add in a foot stomp. Upstairs my bedroom door slams shut, committing me fully to the role of immature child. And like a child, I lean against the door in silence and listen for my mother's footsteps. But she doesn't follow to apologize.

Only when her soft laughter mixes with Bruce's and canned laughter from the TV, do I admit she's not coming.

Stunned, my knees give out and I collapse onto the floor. Does no one want me around? Fuck! I grab one of my shoes and throw it across the floor. It goes sliding under the bed.

⊸⊶ ·•◆•· ⊷⊶

The snow fell all night, bringing with it school bus cancellations, buried cars, and slippery roads. Inside is equally frosty, as I find myself blanketed under deep disquiet.

Racing around, I shower and dress, desperate to avoid conversation with Mom and especially Bruce. If I leave quietly and without leaving a mess, I bet last night will be forgotten by the time I return home. To seal the deal, I'll buy Mom some flowers.

Where the hell is my shoe? Oh, right.

I lift the bed skirt to peer underneath. My shoe lies against a plastic storage bin labeled CHELSEA.

No. No way.

The room fills with a silence thicker than the fresh snow. CHELSEA. Nothing more than a name in black marker. Big. Bold. Just like she was in life. Her name blurs as the box is pulled from its hiding spot.

Covered in a thick layer of dust, it hasn't been opened for a long time. Do I dare?

No.

Yes.

No.

What items did Mom keep? Chelsea's journal was the only item I took. How did Mom make that choice? And why under the bed in the guest room? Out of sight but close by? Perhaps it is better left alone.

Chelsea's voice goads me, God, you're such a wuss. Open it.

221

The old plastic is stiff and brittle, but the lid comes off easily. I don't move or touch anything, instead, I close my eyes and breathe in the past. Dry paper. Stale tears.

When I finally summon the nerve to look, I find a stack of sympathy cards secured with an elastic, placed on top. Our Deepest Condolences in an embossed silver script faces me. I toss them aside. Cards are pointless, anyone can sign their name to a piece of paper picked up without thought at the drug store. What is the point?

Next, birth certificate. Secured to that with a paperclip, her death certificate. Birth. Death. Side by side but separated by eighteen years. Almost to the day. Under these are a few awards and plaques. Honor Student. Best Vocalist. Star Performance. Never a gracious winner, I remember when, called upon the stage to accept the Best Vocalist award, instead of thank you, she said, I told you all I'd win. The audience laughed. Classic Chelsea.

I flip through the photos. Chelsea as a newborn. Chelsea holding a baby blanket and sucking her thumb. Chelsea on stage. Chelsea going to prom. Chelsea at Christmas. Chelsea graduating. All pictures of Chelsea alone. None with her parents. None with her sister. Even in death, she is hogging the spotlight.

Good grades, good looks, good voice. She had it all until she didn't.

Across the bottom of the bin, her baby blanket. My fingers rub the frayed satin edge like a genie's bottle, and suddenly there's Chelsea in front of me, the blanket tied around her neck, like a cape, as she welcomed the neighbors into our backyard for one of our many performances—this time a play she had created, directed, and of course starred in. There were several roles for me and the girl next door to us, but they were supporting roles, of course. Even at eight years old, Chelsea liked to boss everyone around.

Underneath the blanket is a small velvet box. I don't have to open it to know that it's her silver bracelet, a simple and delicate cable chain, given to her by my parents on her sixteenth birthday. Now both Chelsea and the bracelet lie alone in the dark, on a bed of satin. They should be together. Chelsea never took it off and Mom insisted she be buried with it; she was frantic to find it, calling the morgue and Urgences-santé several times, turning Chelsea's room upside down, and sending Dad to inspect the damaged car, not once, but twice.

I found it one week too late.

Memories pound against the door where I keep them locked up. Nuh-uh. No way. I quickly shove everything back into the bin, seal it shut, and return it to its home under the bed where it belongs.

Pandora's Box should not have been opened.

My missing shoe gets tossed into my bag and I escape the house as if chased by a demon.

Thanks to today's discovery, Mom and Bruce will get what they want. I can't stay here knowing Chelsea's memories are in the room with me. Asking Mom to move it isn't an option, I can't ask her to choose.

They think I'm useless anyhow, *you don't help with the cooking or the dishes, blah, blah, blah.* Fine, I'll show them.

The apartment building is a short metro ride from work—okay, so apartment building is being generous—and even in the dark, it's disappointing. The snow has done nothing to mask the building's lack of curb appeal with cracked concrete stairs, rickety iron railing, peeling paint, and not a lot of love. Inside is not much better. The common hallway is decorated with an old musty carpet and scuffed paint, although the main floor apartment has a colorful wreath on the door and a welcome doormat. At least someone here cares.

The landlord directs me up the stairs of what was originally designed as a single-family house until someone, with more ideas than skill, divided it into three separate flats. He opens the door to a small semi-furnished one-bedroom apartment—small being the operative word. The only saving grace is the large windows. One is in the bedroom, two in the living room. Who knows what they overlook but they will let in a lot of natural light. Maybe I could buy a plant and it would survive. Of course, I'd have to remember to water it.

Hardly my dream home, but it is clean, comes with a couch, table, and chairs, and the utilities are included. Best of all, it's available immediately. It is also within walking distance to the metro and Atwater Market, which will be helpful as I am now living without access to a car. And someone to drive that car.

The landlord tells me a woman around my age is renting the apartment below mine. She's been there almost a year, and he never has any complaints from her or about her. There is someone in the third apartment, but they are moving out soon.

It checks all the boxes, and since I don't want to spend time looking at other apartments, the lease gets signed.

5

The Mitchel Sisters' Guide to an Awesome Life—Rule no. 5:
Why do something if someone else can do it for you.

THE FOLLOWING WEEKEND, BRUCE'S station wagon is parked in front of my new apartment. The trunk hatch serving as an ineffective awning, as the rain pelts down.

Bruce joins me at the car with perspiration on his brow and heavy breathing, his middle-aged body and smoker's lungs unaccustomed to manual labor. Not that I'm doing much better.

"I'm going to need your help. The bed side-rails aren't heavy but they are long and I don't want to damage any walls." This is the most he has said to me in a week.

I take the front end and we make it up to the second floor and into my bedroom. Mom is sitting on the floor holding the bed instructions in front of her.

"Oh. I thought you were cleaning," I said to Mom. She'd led the charge early this morning armed with a bucket, mop, sponges, and several bottles of cleaning products.

"I was going to, but this is a two-person job. You can manage the cleaning once we're gone."

"Yeah. Sure."

Leaving them to build the bed, I return to the car. Icy cold water oozes into my boots one last time as I grab the one remaining box. Stepping over the snowbank, I lose my footing and wipe out, landing on my ass.

Mom and Bruce's laughter floats down the stairs. Must be nice. I place the box on the radiator and am wiping slush off my backside and legs as the door to the first-floor apartment opens. A woman and a dog enter the narrow hallway, blocking my way upstairs.

"Oh, hi," she says, "I'm Vicki. This is Gunner. I take it you're moving in."

"Yup." Wow. Nothing gets by this cute little brunette with a big smile. Don't tell me she's one of those perpetually happy people.

"Well, if you need anything, don't hesitate to ask. I've been looking forward to having a new neighbor. That apartment has been vacant for at least a month now."

The woman and her dog—in booties—step around me. "Come on, Gunner, let's go."

They hit the street and jog away.

"She seems nice," my mother says as she and Bruce descend the stairs. Bruce passes me and goes outside for a cigarette.

"Yeah, I guess." A friendly, cheerful woman with a cute dog—exactly what I need right now. "Although, she could have offered to carry some boxes upstairs."

"Stephanie Alice Mitchel. What is wrong with you?"

"Well, it's true."

Her jaw clenches so tight, she could bite through metal. I notice a slight head shake as she takes a step towards the door, the old wooden floor creaks under her weight. "So, are there any more boxes?"

"Nope. This is everything. The phone guy and cable guy will be here next week. I guess that's it. See you later."

"My goodness, child. You could afford to be a bit more appreciative. And a bit more positive. This is the first time you've had a place all to yourself. It's a wonderful time to be young."

"Whatever, Mom. And thanks for your help. I appreciate it." I say without a drop of sincerity.

"I don't understand you, Stephanie. I honestly don't. You walk around like the world owes you something. I hope one day you realize that you only get out of life what you put into it, or you're going to be very lonely."

"Thanks for the pep talk."

Another head shake, this one not as subtle before she places a warm hand on my cold cheek. Leaning in, she gives me a quick kiss. "Let me know if you need anything, okay?"

I nod, remaining in the doorway. Bruce takes her hand and helps her over the snowbank, then into an embrace. She pulls back, wipes her face as if crying, then leans into him again.

Why am I such a bitch?

I slam the door with my foot and stomp up the stairs.

The bed is built, but not made. The empty boxes piled neatly in the corner. She didn't even open the mattress. Gee, thanks Mom. I lug it over to the bed, rip open the plastic with my bare hands and uncurl it like a Swiss roll. Luckily Vicki and her cute little dog are out, or she'd think the ceiling was caving in with the way I'm moving around the apartment.

Unpacking sucks. Before long, I give up and collapse on the couch. Blank white walls stare at me. I hear a muffled TV from another apartment, but it's drowned out by my mother's voice inside my head. *You walk around like the world owes you something.* Well, doesn't it? The world took my sister and destroyed my family.

This was such a mistake. A furnished sublet in a nicer building, like I usually choose, would have been a wiser choice. Sure, it requires frequent moving, and yeah, a roommate or two is a necessity, but at least my last place had a doorman and the apartment came with a dishwasher.

At least I wasn't alone.

I find the box labeled toiletries and head into the bathroom for a relaxing bath in the deep tub—one of the only good things in this place. Oh, right. It's not been cleaned. Thanks again, Mom.

The tub and sink are scrubbed with such channeled anger, it's a small miracle the porcelain isn't rubbed right off. I save the toilet for last. Lifting the seat,

I close my eyes and spray, then wipe it off with toilet paper, flush it away and throw the rubber gloves into the garbage. Gross.

With the water running and the scent of vanilla overpowering the scent of disinfectant, I search for my new towels. That's when I notice the spider plant and note.

WELCOME HOME. LOVE, MOM.

Hopefully, my salty tears don't kill it.

6

The Mitchel Sisters' Guide to an Awesome Life—Rule no. 6:
Don't do something unless you are the best.

April 2001

I AM RESTOCKING GUITAR strings, wanting to get finished so I can take a break, when a familiar-looking boy walks over to me.

"Excuse me," he says.

"How can I help you?" I answer with my standard customer service smile planted on my face.

He is holding a guitar case in his left hand that he lifts slightly by the handle. "You sold me this guitar for my birthday. I've been taking lessons for months now, but I still suck. I want to return it."

"Oh yeah. Riley, right?" I say, remembering his mess of brown hair and his velour-draped mom. "What happened?"

"I don't know. Nothing, I guess. I still can't play a song." He stares down at his mud-covered shoes.

"Follow me."

We wind our way to the back of the store, through glass doors, and into the guitar room. "Okay, sit here and show me what you've learned."

"Uh-uh. I don't want people to hear me play."

"It's soundproof. Don't worry."

He sighs, but removes his puffy jacket, sits down on a leather bench, then takes out his guitar and manages to strum a few off-sounding chords. His hands red from the cold.

"Hmm. You said you can't play any songs yet."

"No."

"Show me your hands."

He holds them out, and I inspect them with military precision. "Uh-huh. Just what I thought. No calluses. Now Riley, how often do you practice? Be honest."

He shrugged.

"So you don't practice."

His shoulders slump forward and he stares down at the guitar. "I thought it would be easier."

I nod and sit next to him, inspired by his Montreal Canadians jersey. "I take it you like hockey."

"Of course."

"Do you play hockey?"

"Yes."

"How often do you play?"

"One game a week plus two practices."

"And do you ever skate by yourself for fun?"

"My friends and I go a lot. We chase each other around and play shinny at the rink in the park." He sits up a bit straighter.

"So, would you say you are better now than last year?"

"Yeah. Of course." His voice slightly stronger.

"If you never practiced or played for fun, would you be as good?"

"No. Of course not."

"So why would the guitar be any different?"

Silence. He shrugs. "But we only do boring stuff."

"At hockey practice, do you play games, or do you do drills?"

"Drills."

"And did you have to learn to skate before you played hockey?"

"Yeah."

"Soooo?"

"So I need to learn the chords before I can play a song." The resignation in his voice fills the room.

"Right. But I think you need a song to work towards. I know your instructor. Let me talk to him. I'm positive you guys can work towards something you like."

"Okay."

"Before you go, I have one more question. Can you tell me what each string is tuned to? I'll start." I lean towards him and pluck the thinnest string. "E. Your turn."

He plucks the next one. "B?"

"Okay. What's next"

"Um. A? No wait, G?"

"Yes. Awesome save. You know, an easy way to remember them is to make up a phrase where each word begins with the first letter of the string name. Going in order from the thinnest to thickest, we have EBGDAE. So I always think: Every Boy Gets Donuts At Eight."

"That is easier."

"Now, your homework from me is to make up your own phrase for the reverse order, starting with the thickest string. Deal?"

"Deal," he agrees, smiling for the first time since he arrived.

"It won't take long to learn them. Trust me. I speak from experience. And if you ever need extra help, come in and ask me. We're not usually that busy Tuesday and Wednesday afternoons. Okay?"

"Yeah, thanks."

He walks away and I am left in the silence of the guitar room, basking in the glow of good vibrations.

"That was impressive," says a voice behind me, causing me to jump.

"I didn't hear you come in," I say to Diane, as she walks over to me.

"Well, if a teaching spot opens up, I know who to ask. Why didn't you tell me you were interested in teaching?"

"I'm not. I mean, I don't have any training for it or anything."

"Well, you certainly have a talent for it." She smiles, then brushes away some dust off her shirt. "Goodness, why did the new store shirts need to be black, they are dust magnets. Anyway, as I was saying, it would be a shame not to put your skills to use."

"Thanks, Diane. That's certainly something to think about."

That stupid blinking cursor is mocking me. Blink. Blink. Blink. Well? Well? Well? Why can I not write anymore? Lyrics used to form in my head faster than I could write them down. Now, that part of my brain is like a ghost town, the creative juices having left for better opportunities. Dammit.

I connect to the internet and type how to be a music teacher.

Dad had a friend who was a music teacher, and once, he took us to a music night at his school. They were raising funds for something, new instruments, a trip, I can't remember. The school orchestra and band were what you'd expect—kids making sounds only a parent should have to sit through—but the night closed in a fun way with the teacher's band doing a few cover songs. They were not spectacular, but everyone got up and danced, singing along.

Chelsea made fun of them—and me—for weeks. "I can't believe you want to be a teacher," she said. "I was so embarrassed for him."

"People had fun. And the kids are learning," I said.

"He's a teacher because he's a mediocre musician."

She was doing it to piss me off, but that didn't stop me from arguing with her. "Did you ever think that he likes teaching?"

"Whatever, but if I wasn't an amazing singer, I wouldn't do it at all."

"You don't love it? You wouldn't miss it?" This surprised me because I thought the love of music was something we shared.

"I love being the best, but hey, go settle for teaching. At least you're being realistic about your mediocre skills."

"I am not mediocre." My voice booms into the empty room. My shiny new laptop shuts with a click, and I reach for my guitar.

After thirty minutes of practice, I put the guitar down and stretch my fingers. When was the last time I worked them so hard? I'm even perspiring, but I feel better than I have in a long time. Perhaps now I can get past the writer's block.

The stairs creak outside my apartment. Has someone moved in across the hall? Even though I am now listening for noises, the sudden knocking startles me. I open my door to find my ever-smiling neighbor.

"Hi, remember me? I'm Vicki from downstairs."

She is wearing grey sweatpants and a long sleeve baggy T-shirt. Yellow. A warm, friendly color, just like her smile. And yet I'm irked. "Oh right. Hi."

"Um, anyway, I was baking some cookies and thought you might like some."

Interesting. Despite her confident appearance, her voice wavers slightly, betraying her. This causes me to soften a little.

"That's really kind of you. Thanks." Practicing must have caused a rush of endorphins, because there I am, stepping back and welcoming her into the apartment.

"I love your posters," she says.

"Thanks. I've never really had to decorate before, but I work at a music store, and these were lying in our storeroom collecting dust." The posters are a series of individual guitars in bold colors from a long-ago ad campaign. Nothing special, but they are my favorite guitar brand. As she looks around, I see the space through her eyes. The sad couch. The mismatching chairs at the small table. The old TV with the bunny ears—cable was way too expensive. Every mug I own is dirty, some left half-filled with old coffee, breakfast bowls and dinner plates sit on every horizontal surface like ceramic stepping stones. Humiliation rushes through me with more force than Old Faithful. Thank God, I am exceptionally groomed and not lounging around in my pajamas. Like last night.

"Well, you're faster at decorating than me. I didn't do anything for months, and even then someone had to push me. But I'm glad I did. It makes it feel a lot homier and reveals a bit of personality. You play too, right? At least I assume that was you playing—unless we have a ghost, since as of last week, we are the only two living here."

"Yes, no ghost. That was me. Just practicing."

"Well, it sounded great. I can't play a note. And trust me, you do not want to hear me sing."

I nod my head and give her a small smile. "Here, let me put those in the kitchen." Reaching towards her, I take the plate of cookies and carry them into the kitchen. She follows.

"Mind if I have one?"

"No, go ahead. Enjoy."

I pull back the tinfoil cover. "Holy shit." The cookies are flowers, tulips. Pink, yellow, orange. I can make out the individual petals and she's even iced in stamens for Pete's sake. "You made these? Are you serious? These could be in a bakery. Is that where you work?"

"Thanks," Vicki says. "I like to bake and I like to draw—the icing is simply another medium. The best part is that even if what I planned doesn't turn out perfectly, people are still more than willing to eat them."

I take a bite. "I can see why, these taste great and I'm not saying that to be polite."

Vicki smiles.

"You want one?"

"No. I may have sampled one or two already, you know, for quality control." She taps her stomach.

"Okay then, what about some wine? I got some as a housewarming present from my boss."

"None for me, thanks. I don't drink."

"How about a glass of water. I don't have anything else, and I'd hate to drink alone."

"Sure, that'd be great."

She carries her glass of tap water into the living room as I down most of my wine. I pour a refill before joining her.

"So what brings you to this neck of the woods?" she asks as she sits down at the table.

"The cheap rent."

"I know, right? I was so lucky to find this place. Good things come in small packages, don't they? And honestly, your place is palatial compared to mine. I have only one room and a kitchen. Plus a bathroom, of course. I fold up my bed each day—it's a Futon. It's a drag, but I don't like always sitting on my bed. My dog, on the other hand, would be more than happy to sleep on it all day."

"Your dog is cute. What kind of dog is he?"

"We think he is a husky-pit bull mix. He's a rescue, so we don't know his origins."

"You live with someone? I haven't seen them around."

"Oh, no, by we, I mean me and the animal shelter. I was volunteering there when I met Gunner. I still volunteer there when I can."

"Oh. Interesting. Where do you work?"

"I work at the art supply store on St. Catherine's. I haven't been there long. Before that, I used to waitress. I love it there but boy is it hard not to spend my paycheck on art supplies. At least I get a deal."

"I don't work far from there. I work at Just Music, a couple of blocks east. And I get it. I have the same problem."

"I know where you mean. Maybe we can meet for lunch one day. Gunner and I go for a walk at lunch. Sometimes we bring Céline with us. She is the store manager's dog. But she doesn't like to walk as far as Gunner. She's just a little thing." She holds up her hands, showing me the size of the dog. "In size only. Not personality."

"You take your dog to work?"

"Yeah. Crazy, right? Gunner and Céline hang out in the back office mostly, but occasionally they walk through the store. Everyone loves them. We joke that customers come back specifically to visit the dogs. Have you ever had a dog? Gunner's my first."

"No. I don't see myself as a dog person. I always thought a cat would be the kind of pet for me."

"Oh my gosh! Then you have to go to the shelter. It's close. You can walk there from here. We always have cats that need a home."

"I don't think so. I wouldn't make the best cat owner."

"You don't have to be the best, you just have to do your best." She laughs. "Wow. I should put that on a motivational poster at work. Or maybe that's where I read it. Sounds like something struggling artists would be told, doesn't it? Anyway, do you have a pen and paper? I'll give you the address."

I find what she needs, and she quickly scribbles it down.

"All right. There you go. Oh, I hope you find a cat. Pets are amazing. I can't imagine my life without Gunner." And with that, she stands up. "Well, I better go, the dishes aren't washing themselves and if I'm not careful, Gunner will have started on the prewash. Nice talking to you."

"Thanks again for the cookies." She leaves, and I sit in the empty stillness of the apartment, as if in the quiet aftermath of a tornado. She is quite the little ball of energy.

I glance longingly at my guitar, desperate to feel it in my hands again, then look around at the dirty dishes. Sadly, my dishes aren't washing themselves either. The moldy mug on the floor beside the couch is evidence of that. Resigning myself to domestic chores, I collect an armful and enter the kitchen. I hear Vicki talking to her dog through the floorboards. She was nothing but kind, yet her visit exhausted me.

Gunner barks and Vicki laughs.

I turn on the tap to try and drown them out.

7

May 2001

YOU CAN'T MISS THE giant cat sign when you walk into the shelter. A bright yellow arrow directs me down a hall and soon I am standing in front of a wall of cats, like an animal vending machine.

"Can I help you?" A woman in jeans, a shelter T-shirt, and flaming red hair in a ponytail greets me.

My back automatically straightens to match her confident stance. "My neighbor volunteers here. She said it's a good place to get a cat."

"Well, they were right. Who's your neighbor?"

"Vicki something. She also got her dog here. I don't know her last name."

Her smile broadens. "We don't need her last name. Everyone knows Vicki and Gunner. See that picture on the wall. She drew it for us."

I turn to where she's pointing. Wow. The girl has talent beyond cookies.

Darcy clasps her hands together in front of her chest. "I'm going to leave you here for a bit to look at our cats. I have to cover the front desk, but I will make sure one of our volunteers comes over to answer any questions you might have and to open one of our playrooms if you choose one to interact with. Sound like a plan?"

"Yeah. Thanks."

She walks away, ponytail swinging in the air to the beat of her steps, like a red metronome, leaving me under the buzz of fluorescent lighting, wondering where to begin. I take a step back to take it all in. Each cage has a little tag with the cat's name and general information. Some of the cats are meowing. Most are curled up asleep. The majority are alone, but in one cage, two kittens, named Spike and Trixie, are wrestling. Above them live Leo and Charlie. One is laying down, while his roommate is standing over him, looking out. Beside them, an energetic black and white one is lying on his side while scratching a carpeted post, his fur poking through the metal bars. The tag on his cage says his name is Bob. Bob? Who would name a cat Bob? I am reaching out to pet him through the cage when I hear footsteps behind me. I turn towards them.

"Hi. I'm Josh. I hear you're interested in a cat." His voice is as large as his body. I'm a healthy five foot six, but this guy is over six feet, and he's not just taller. He's girthier. Much girthier. Like he plays offensive tackle in college. No, make that high school.

"I think so." Sound confident, Stephanie. He's a kid. "I mean, yes. But how do you choose? There are so many here."

"I know, right? It's so sad, but we do everything we can to find them a good home." He wiggles his finger into Spike and Trixie's cage, and one of them swipes at it. He laughs and turns back to me. "What kind of cat are you looking for?"

"Well, I live alone and am out a lot, so I think I need a cat who is relaxed and not very high energy."

"Okay, now let me think." I watch as his eyes scan the cages. He takes a step toward the far-left cage. "We have Rocky here, he is about five and on the small side. He was abandoned when his family moved. The neighbors found him and brought him in. They would have kept him, but their dog doesn't like cats."

"People do that? Leave their pet behind?"

"Oh, all the time."

"Wow, that's cold."

"You'd be surprised what people are capable of." He unlocks the cage, reaches in and tries to coax Rocky towards us. Rocky gets up, turns around, and lays back down, this time his back toward us.

"Well, I guess Rocky is not up for visitors today," Josh says as he shuts the door. "Anyway, right next to Rocky is Jaws...."

"Wait," my hand darts up like a crossing guard's stopping traffic. "Why is he called that?"

"Apparently, he bites and chews on everything. That's why he was surrendered. He destroyed his owner's favorite chair. But, we checked him out. There's no physiological reason for the chewing. He was bored. I know you said you wanted a low energy cat, but I have a soft spot for the guy and thought I'd at least introduce him."

"It doesn't hurt to try, I guess." This guy, Josh, amazes me. I bet he could pull a locomotive with his teeth, yet he has a weakness for abandoned cats.

"No. I guess not. Now, Ginger over here might be more your speed. She is an orange tabby—hence the name—and came from a loving home. We only have her because her owner died and the landlord dropped her off, not knowing what else to do."

Ginger is curled up but lifts her head when she hears us talking. She is light orange with darker orange stripes, white paws, and green eyes. She sits up but instead of coming over, begins preening herself, licking her paws, and washing her face. I like her attitude. She follows rule number two. "She's beautiful."

"She is. And tabbies are notoriously low energy."

He opens the cage and gently lifts her out, cradling her against his arm. She sits there like she owns the place. "Would you like to spend some time with her in the playroom?"

I shrug. "Okay. Sure." Josh directs me to a small room with a loveseat and toy basket. I sit on the couch, and he gently places Ginger on the floor.

"I'll give you a few minutes alone." He walks out and shuts the door. One wall is glass, allowing me to watch Josh walk to the reception desk and talk to the redhead.

"So," I say to Ginger. "How are you?" Panic hits then. How can I take care of a cat? My plant is barely alive. Maybe I should have started with a fish. Or a rock. Yes, I could get a pet rock.

Is Josh coming back yet? He's no longer at the desk. Oh, where is he? This was such a stupid idea. I look at the cat, an apology on the tip of my tongue as if she could understand.

She is sitting upright on the floor in front of me, her big green eyes taking in the new surroundings. She lifts her paw and wipes her face, then stares at me. Our eyes lock. My brown ones to her green. My apology gets caught in my throat because I realize both of us have experienced life altering circumstances through loss.

I reach down and scratch her behind the ears. Her fur is soft and warm against my cold fingers. Ginger closes her eyes and leans into my hand, ever so slightly before leaping onto the couch and sitting beside me, curling her cute little white paws under her, as if making herself into a little package for me to pick up and carry out under my arm.

"How's it going in here?" Josh pokes his head in the door.

"This one. Ginger. I like her. She's the one for me."

"Oh, fantastic. But remember Ginger is old; we are guessing she's in her mid-teens. She's healthy, but she isn't the pet for you if you are looking for," he pauses, "a long-term relationship."

His meaning is clear, but I can't even think of another cat now that my mind has decided on her. I already picture her in my apartment sleeping on a windowsill in the sun. "I understand. It's fine."

"That's awesome. Ginger deserves a loving home." He picks her up and walks out. "Follow me."

We walk to the reception desk.

"Darcy, Ginger here has found a home. I'm going to get her ready to go."

Darcy smiles. "And I'll do the paperwork."

As Josh walks away talking sweetly to Ginger, Darcy presents me with a clipboard and pen. "If you could fill out the adoption form." Then she wipes a tear from her eye. "Sorry. I've been worried about Ginger finding a home. I'm so glad Vicki sent you. You've made my day."

Between Josh, Darcy, and the fluttering in my stomach, I can't help but wonder what's in the air of this place.

Ginger receives a kiss on the head and scratches behind her ears as I leave the apartment. I've been spending every spare moment since I brought her home last week watching her actions and movements. Since the first day when I opened the cardboard cat carrier and she came wandering out, she's walked about like she owns the place. She explored every corner, every nook and cranny then jumped up on the couch and went to sleep. I sat beside her and watched her chest move up and down until I eventually dozed off.

Leaving her for band practice is hard, but necessary. This week we play a bar on Friday and a wedding—one of the last, thank goodness—on Saturday.

As I walk into Marc's, the room goes silent. "What's going on?"

Marc and Sébastien both turn to stare at Erin. She flicks her hair back and picks up a piece of paper from atop her amp. "I got the info sheet back from the couple for the wedding this weekend."

"I can see that. So?" Nothing earth-shattering so far. We always collect basic information about the couple along with their requested songs for the first dance, as well as the type of music they like. "Do they want polka music or something?"

"The groom," Erin says, lifting her eyes to meet mine while scrunching up her nose. "It's Trevor."

"Trevor? You mean *my* Trevor?"

"Yeah. I'm sorry."

I snatch the paper out of her hand. No freaking way. It can't be. I scan the page. His name. His address. And the bride? Bridgette? His roommate. He's marrying his roommate? Are you kidding me? "How did this happen? This wedding was booked months ago." My side of his bed would hardly have been cold. "And why would he hire us?" He's a dick, but not like that. He's the one who dumped me, he wouldn't be seeking any type of revenge.

"Well, funny story. The wedding planner said the original couple canceled, but she had other clients who wanted to get married fast because the bride is..." she stops.

Her unspoken word wraps around my stomach and squeezes. "I can fill in the blank, Erin. Pregnant. The bride is pregnant. Go on."

Her eyes dart to Marc and then back to me. "Um, well, they took over the venue and everything else. Plus, with our new name on the contract and stuff..." Erin's voice trails off.

It's amazing I can hear her over the sound of blood rushing past my ears. Trevor and Bridgette. Plain ol' Bridgette. His friend since childhood. A knitter. A civil servant. A person who walks to work in a skirt with sneakers because they are comfortable. I never perceived her as a threat. Was she waiting for the right opportunity or was Trevor so lonely after we split, that he turned to her for comfort, so desperate that all thoughts of birth control went out the window? Images of them together flood my brain. I close my eyes to squeeze them out.

When I open my eyes again, the band is frozen in place, awaiting my reaction. Bile burns the back of my throat. Deep breath. Think. There must be a rule for this. Why can't I think of a rule?

Placing the paper back on Erin's amp, I toss my coat into the corner and pick up my guitar. Still, no one moves. "Wow. Okay. Everyone, relax. Stop staring at me. It will be fine. We broke up over six months ago. He was hardly the love of my life."

"You sure, Steph? We can find someone else for this gig if it's too hard for you. I already talked to someone and she's available."

Super. Someone else to replace me. Am I not good enough for anyone? "Thanks, but I'm fine." I can't not go now. I need to see this through.

"Steph..."

"Oh my God, I said I'm fine. Now can we move on?" Immediate survival depends on me digging deep into my diva toolbox. Sure, it pisses everyone off. So be it.

By the time I get home, I'm exhausted. My throat hurts. My fingers ache. Collapsing on the couch, I send a cloud of dust floating through a small beam of setting sun. "Men," I say to Ginger who had quietly strolled into the living room. "We don't need them right, Gingin?" She walks over to her new pink puffy bed then turns and jumps on the couch, leaning against me. Choosing me. Fuck you, Trevor. Ginger licks her paw and wipes it over her face as I wipe away my tears.

8

The Mitchel Sisters' Guide to an Awesome Life—Rule no. 8:
Always be out of their league.

ON THE DAY OF the wedding, I spend money I shouldn't at the salon and select the sequined tank top and the leather pants Trevor liked so much. This is what I wore the night we met. We were singing at Trevor's brother's wedding and as I scanned the guest tables, I noticed him watching. He wasn't just looking in my direction. His entire focus was on me.

Trevor wasn't the hottest guy there, he's average—my type exactly. Guys appreciate you more when you're hotter than they are. They work harder to get you and harder to keep you.

Our eyes locked and I gave him a little smile as encouragement. After our set, he walked over and introduced himself. The cut of his suit told me it was custom-tailored, not off the rack, and his shoes were classic black leather brogues, so I flirted. Why invest time on a poor guy when you can spend it on a rich guy? What wasn't revealed until later was how tight he was with money. Oh, he has money—but it's invested. He's a long-term planner saving diligently for retirement. Day to day, he lives like a student, hence the roommate—the one he knocked up and is marrying today.

Trevor is not a risk-taker. He is methodical. A planner. So the fact that he got Bridgette pregnant and is basically having a shotgun wedding is out of character. How will the cost of a newborn baby factor into all his charts and spreadsheets?

Serves him right for dumping me. And tonight, in this outfit, he will realize his mistake. While he pines after me, I will sing like I don't even know who he is.

As we are setting up, Trevor's brother approaches me—the very same brother whose wedding I met Trevor at. Why does this family always pick us for their weddings? We are hardly the only band in town.

"You're in the band?" he asks, not bothering with a polite, "Hi Steph." His jaw is clenched, arms tense. He didn't particularly like me when Trevor and I were dating, so seeing me here now must piss him off.

"Yeah. Crazy, huh?"

"What do you think you're doing?"

I rest my hand on his arm, in what I hope is a reassuring gesture, planning to play the part of the mature, non-bitter ex. "Ethan, we were booked by the other couple. We didn't realize it was Trevor's wedding until it was too late. But you have to believe me, I'm happy for them. Trevor is a good guy, and just because it didn't work out between us, doesn't mean I don't care about him. If he's found the right someone, I think that's great." And the Oscar goes to...Stephanie Mitchel.

He wipes his brow on the sleeve of his tuxedo while exhaling a long breath. "Okay, great. Thank you, Stephanie. Does Trevor know?"

"I don't know." I don't. I'm sure if he did, he'd have canceled us, even if he couldn't get a replacement.

He exhales loudly. "Oh boy. I better go find out. I'm sure he would have said something if he did. Thanks for being so professional about this."

I try my best to smile. Did I come here wanting him to notice me? Yes. Do I want him to miss me? Absolutely. But I'm not going to make a scene. A, I'm not crazy, and B, I have some self-esteem. My God, is that what people think of me?

Ladies and gentlemen, let's all welcome Mr. and Mrs. Robertson to the floor for their first dance," announces Marc in his velvety baritone voice. Despite my brave talk, I couldn't announce them as husband and wife. I know my limits.

The lighting dims and a disco ball scatters light across the room like a million tiny knives. Their chosen song is "At Last," a common wedding song, so my autopilot takes over. My strong, melodious voice fills the room while Trevor and his bride sway to the music. I scrutinize Trevor's face for any reaction to me being there. But the truth is, his eyes never leave his bride. He says something. She smiles. They kiss. People applaud. But the two of them are oblivious to everyone as if they are locked inside a private love bubble.

No one has ever looked at me like that.

This wedding isn't about a surprise pregnancy. This is about two people falling in love after years of being friends. At last—no freaking kidding.

After thirty minutes, we take a break. I don't usually drink while working, but tonight I make an exception. On my way to the bar, I stop short, suddenly facing him. Dammit.

"Stephanie, wait." He moves, blocking my getaway. "You sound great as always."

"Thank you," I reply, hoping to sound sincere. "And congratulations, on… everything." I make some lame gesture of a big belly with my hand.

"Oh, thank you. We're super excited." He looks down at the ground. "Um, I'm sorry about this. Everything happened so fast, and this opportunity came along. Had I known…I mean, the name change. It didn't occur to me—"

"Don't worry about it."

I am about to walk away when he begins talking again. "Steph, my brother told me all the nice things you said earlier. It means a lot and I want you to know that nothing happened with Bridgette while we were together, and it wasn't the reason we broke up. Everything happened after. I swear." He holds up one hand like some do-good Boy Scout and gives me a small lopsided smile.

"Okay, thanks." The truth is, I believe him. Trevor has a lot of faults but lying isn't one of them. He once returned to a restaurant two hours after we'd left because the server forgot to charge him for two drinks.

He leans in with a crooked bow tie and peach lipstick on his collar, and we hug awkwardly. "Well, I better go find the Mrs."

And with that, he walks off, my anger and resentment leaving with him. Without them supporting me, I deflate like an empty balloon.

"Looks like you need a drink. What can I get you? My treat."

I blink, trying to bring myself back into the present. "It's an open bar," I reply dryly to the man on my left. He's significantly taller than me and built like a truck. Something about him is familiar. "Do I know you?"

"We've met before. Briefly. I'm Trevor's cousin, Jake."

I still can't place him.

"I used to have a beard." He grabs his chin in case I am unfamiliar with where a beard grows. "I think it was at Rosie's Bar. You were performing, last summer sometime."

"Oh, right. Of course. Nice to see you again." I lean onto the bar and order a vodka soda.

"So this must be an uncomfortable night, huh."

I shrug. "Not really. We broke up a while ago. Plus, I can do weddings in my sleep."

"Well, good, because you can definitely do better than Trevor. He's...how can I say this...a little boring."

I nearly cough out the drink the bartender passed me. "What?"

"Seriously, you're better off without him. You're a creative person, right-brained and all that, he is not."

Any energy I might normally have had to flirt or at least smile, left during the first dance. Getting through the rest of tonight will require all my remaining strength. "Look, I'm just here to sing."

"What about after?"

"After what?"

"The wedding. Let's go grab a drink or something to eat. Then we can talk about Trevor all we want. Or not. Most things are more interesting than Trevor."

"You're kind of funny."

"I try. No one's writing this stuff for me." He drinks down whatever is in his glass in one gulp. I arch an eyebrow. "It's water. It's very hot in here."

"Uh-huh."

"It is." He runs his fingers through his hair. "Change of topic. Would it scare you if I told you I remember you singing at Ethan's wedding? The night you met Trevor."

"You do?"

"Yeah, I wanted to ask you out that night, but Trevor beat me to it."

"Right."

"No. I mean it."

"I'm flattered but I think I should cut my losses when it comes to your family. If I'm not careful, we'll date, and before long, I'll be singing at your wedding."

He tilts his head back and laughs. "We're related by marriage, not blood," he says, winking at me and walking away. "Think about it," he calls out over his shoulder.

I weave my way through the crowd, back to the stage.

"How you doing?" Erin asks.

"I told you guys it wasn't a problem. You don't have to baby me." I don't mean to snap, but my head is throbbing and all I want to do is curl up in bed with Ginger.

Erin holds up her hands defensively in front of her. "Fine. Take it easy. Sorry for caring."

"Let's just do this, okay?"

We begin the next set, this time taking requests. We usually get a few, but tonight we are inundated with slips of paper, all with the same handwriting.

"I Like You"

"You're the One that I Want"

"Take a Chance on Me"

"Sexy and I know it"

"I'd Rather be with You"

"Are you Gonna be my Girl"

Every so often, I catch Jake making his way to the tiny control table beside the stage where our tech collects the requests—the job that used to be Trevor's.

"The Way You Make Me Feel"

"You Really Got Me."

"There's Nothing Hold'n Me back."

"Then I Kissed Her"

"Celebration"

Near the end of the night, Jake walks over to the table again. His smile is playful as he writes down one more request. Instead of passing it to our tech, he hands it directly to me.

"First Date"

I turn to the band and show them the song. We don't usually do Blink-182 at weddings, but they all nod in agreement. When I turn back to Jake, he raises his eyebrows expectantly, and when the song starts, his warm smile softens the edges of a very prickly night.

9

The Mitchel Sisters' Guide to an Awesome Life—Rule no. 9:
Never let them see you cry.

TYPICALLY, THE BRIDE AND groom leave ahead of the guests. But not Trevor and Bridgette. Oh no, these two stay until the end and stand at the door in a reverse receiving line, thanking all the guests for coming. Jake is near the end of the line, chatting with the guests in front of him. Suddenly they all burst out laughing but the one most noticeable is Jake's laugh—the fundamental sound above the other laughter, so loud and deep, resonating across the emptying banquet hall, like an open E-string on Erin's bass guitar.

I have always been drawn to lower frequencies.

Once Jake has said his goodbyes and the happy couple move on to the next guest, he makes his way to the stage and helps us carry stuff out to the van until we're done and soon the hall is empty, save the hotel cleanup crew. The glitz and glamour of the night are gone, leaving us standing under unflattering fluorescent lights, so why does Jake strike me as more handsome than he was before? He shouldn't. He's actually a bit of a mess. His wavy blond hair is all mussed up, even looking a bit sweaty at the roots. His suit jacket is tossed over one shoulder, his tie loosened, and I think there might be a small stain on his shirt. Red wine? Sauce?

"Well, how about it?" he asks. "There's a twenty-four-hour diner close by."

Not quite ready to return to an empty apartment, I agree.

"Milady," he says, offering me his arm, elbow bent.

"Seriously?"

He nods and repeats the gesture.

"Fine. Let's do this." I take his arm, and we walk out into the night.

With the wedding having been at a downtown hotel, it is a quick walk to the diner.

We step back in time to linoleum floors, yellow walls, and a pale green counter. And chrome. Lots and lots of chrome. Jake orders a huge meal. A smoked meat sandwich, fries, onion rings, and spaghetti. I order a coffee.

"Good lord, don't tell me you're eating for two as well?"

He laughs that beautiful deep laugh. "No. I worked today, before the wedding. I barely had time to shower before I had to be at the church. I picked up something small on the way to the hotel, but not enough. The food at the reception was okay, but I didn't want to make a pig of myself. Plus, I figured that since you only ordered a coffee, you'd probably help yourself to my fries."

"You're awfully presumptuous."

He shrugs. "I have three sisters."

Sisters.

"What about you? You have any siblings?"

God, I hate this question. Why do people ask this? Why do people care? He takes a sip of water, his eyes still on me, waiting for an answer to what should be an easy yes or no question. CHELSEA in all caps. Hidden away.

The waitress brings my coffee and I wait until she leaves before I say, "I had a sister. But she was killed about eight years ago in a car accident."

He puts down his glass of water. "Oh my gosh. I'm so sorry."

"It was a long time ago." This is my standard response, even though it feels like yesterday. The hurt and the pain sitting in my chest like a parasite, slowly devouring me from the inside.

"Did you want to tell me about her or does it hurt too much?"

I half-spit out my mouthful of coffee. "What?"

"I'm sorry. I don't mean to pry. You just have such a pained look on your face."

A long time has passed since anyone has asked about her. And even if they do, I redirect the conversation. Other than speaking to the therapist my parents made me visit for a while right after the accident, I've not talked to anyone about it.

I take another sip of coffee, suppressing the urge to run. Then fold my hands calmly in front of me on the table, like I talk about it regularly. "What do you want to know?"

"Tell me about her. Was she older? Younger? Fun? Sporty? Serious?"

The door that locks her memory inside bursts open, like the lid on that dusty box, revealing what should remain hidden. "She was older, only by a year and a half. She was outgoing and beautiful and quite the diva. Everything had to be her way. She had to be the center of the universe. Sometimes she drove us all nuts." I draw my lips inside my mouth and bite down to stop myself from talking.

"But you miss her."

Why is he asking me this? My chest tightens, squeezing my resistance away, and forcing out words that were previously only memories. "Yeah, I do. We were fighting when she was killed. She had picked me up from work, and we were on the way home. I was mad because she was wearing my favorite scarf without asking. When I gave her a hard time, she laughed and said it looked better on her. I sat in my seat, angry and resentful because she always got her way. She was mocking me, so maybe she was looking at me instead of the road, or maybe she was speeding, or maybe it was simply bad luck, but we hit a patch of ice on the off-ramp and went into a spin. She made a whooping sound like it was fun." His eyes are on me, but I can't meet them. Nor can I stop talking. Now that the door is open, everything comes tumbling out like old junk in an overstuffed closet.

"Unfortunately, she couldn't control it and the car came to a sudden stop by hitting a pole. The driver's door was crushed in, killing her. I only had a few scrapes." I slide out of the booth. "Excuse me. I need to go to the bathroom."

"Stephanie," he calls out, but I don't turn around.

Inside the women's bathroom, my hands are shaking so much I can barely lock the stall. What the hell was I thinking, telling a complete stranger about

Chelsea? What the hell was I doing thinking about this? The sound of crunching metal. The spray of glass. The rush of cold air.

The silence.

The blood running down her face, soaking into that stupid, stupid, scarf.

Somehow, I managed to unbuckle and move closer to her, screaming her name until her eyelids fluttered open. She looked at me, and reached for my hand, lacing her fingers with mine. Then she closed her eyes again and died. Just like that. She freaking died.

On top of the grief, everything changed. People treated us differently. My parents divorced. We sold our house. We all drifted apart. Even though I lived with my mom, we were never close again. I see my dad once a year. My survival a constant reminder of loss.

Memories coil around me like a snake, squeezing until I lean over the toilet and wretch. When I exit the stall, Jake is standing there, right in the women's bathroom. Too weak to argue, I enter his awaiting embrace. His strong arms hold me together, preventing me from shattering like the driver side window that horrible night.

Singing at Trevor's wedding was a mistake. Pretending everything was fine was too emotionally draining and the fallout? Finding myself in this dumpy diner bathroom, seeking comfort from a giant. What am I doing wrong?

"Thanks for telling me. I'm sorry it upset you," he whispers against my head.

I can do nothing else but nod before gently pushing him away. "I'm okay. Thanks. Exhaustion does that to me. Quite the day."

"Want me to take you home?"

"Soon, but not yet." Small talk and noise from the late-night drunken diner crowd will help ground me back into my life and distract my thoughts, allowing me to once again bury the memories of Chelsea.

"Sure. You say when." He takes my hand and leads me back to the booth. Sitting in silence, he slowly pushes his plate of fries toward me. I take a few. Then a few more.

"Well," he says after his food marathon. "What do you want to do now?"

"I think I better go home. I'm pretty tired."

"Sure. No problem. I've been up since five so I'm kind of beat myself."

He pulls up in front of my apartment, but instead of watching me leave, he gets out of his truck and walks me to the door.

"I'm not inviting you in."

"I know, but my mother taught me to always walk a lady to her door."

"Is that so? Isn't that kind of old-fashioned?"

"It is, but I'm not going to be the one to tell her that. I know when to pick my battles. Thanks for a fun night." He leans down and plants a chaste kiss on my cheek before stepping down over the stairs with his long legs. He waits until I am inside the main door before waving and getting into his truck.

Ginger gives me a warm welcome. She purrs loudly and rubs herself against my leg. I pick her up, burying my face against her soft fur. I walk into my bedroom and place her gently on the bed. I take a quick shower to wash away the night, put on my coziest pajamas, and climb into bed. The room is filled with shadows from a streetlight, and I am gently rocked by the motion of Ginger cleaning herself against my leg.

The empty silence squeezes me like a vice. This isn't how I imagined my life. Where have I gone wrong? I turn the light back on and open the drawer to my bedside table. I pull out a folded piece of paper, soft from age and handling. The creases are so thin, they could rip at any moment. I have lived my life by this list. Followed it blindly towards a bright future, and yet, here I am.

But what would I do without it?

10

*The Mitchel Sisters' Updated Guide to an Awesome Life—Rule
no. 1: Sometimes you need to go with the flow.*

"Hi Stephanie, it's Jake. I was wondering if you were doing anything this weekend?"

"Oh, hi." Jake? Even though he asked for my number I never expected him to call, not after the bathroom incident. Part of me wants to run and hide. The other wants to show him I'm not a complete idiot. That part wins. "I'm working Saturday but not Sunday."

"Okay. Would you want to go out for lunch on Sunday?"

"Lunch? What are we, fifty?"

He laughs. "Come on, it will be fun."

Well, I guess I can impress him at lunch as easily as at dinner. "Yeah, sure."

"Fantastic. I'll pick you up around ten."

"Ten? So you mean brunch?"

"No. For what I have planned it will be lunch. See you then." And he hangs up before I can ask him what exactly is planned.

My buzzer rings exactly at ten on Sunday morning. I run downstairs, pausing in front of the door to compose myself, going for an expression Chelsea coined pleasantly indifferent. Jake greets me in jeans, a sweatshirt, and hiking boots. I am wearing a sexy red halter-neck top, denim miniskirt, and knee-high black boots. Clearly, we are not on the same page.

"Holy. Wow, Steph. You look amazing, but I think you might want to change. I was hoping we could go for a walk first."

"And you're telling me this now?"

He smiles apologetically, cheeks reddening. "Sorry. Didn't I say that? Still, you always get so dressed up for lunch?"

"That's rude."

He laughs, raising his hands up in front of his chest like a surrender. "Oh God, I'm sorry. Just deflecting my embarrassment. I didn't mean to be rude. Honestly. Before you slam the door in my face, I am going to start again." He walks down the stairs, all the way to the curb, then turns around and comes back to where I wait at the door. "Hi, Stephanie. You look fantastic but I might have forgotten to mention I was planning on a walk and a picnic. I hope you will still come with me, despite my idiotic behavior—provided you have comfortable footwear. It'll be worth it, I promise." He tilts his head and gazes at me with the same look in his eyes that Gunner has when Vicki makes him sit for a treat.

"Fine, but I'm holding you to that promise."

Back upstairs I grumble to Ginger as I make a quick change, copying his outfit of jeans and a sweatshirt. My running shoes are saved for carrying my clothes to the laundromat. Ginger—who tired of me griping and left the bedroom—doesn't glance up when I say goodbye. Outside, I find Jake leaning against his pickup truck while talking on the phone.

He hastily ends his conversation. "Sorry about that. Work never ends," he says and slips the phone into his pocket. "Thanks for changing—you still look amazing by the way—and I apologize again for the confusion. Shall we get going?"

"Sure."

As my fingers wrap around the door handle, I spot a large backpack in the bed of the truck. Kind of big for a picnic. "So what's that all about?" I ask, tilting my chin in its direction. "Is that backpack full of food or are you going to take me into the woods and kill me? How about you show me what's in it before I climb in." Murder isn't a concern, but something else he forgets to tell me is, like that we need to skydive to the picnic spot or scale a mountain.

"Smart lady, I like that." He reaches for the bag and opens it. Inside are wrapped sandwiches, drinks, containers full of cookies, a bag of chips, candy, some plates, and a blanket. Enough food for a few days.

"Well, I guess I shouldn't be surprised you need a bag that size based on how much you ate the other night. Fine. Let's go."

"I love your enthusiasm." A wry smile crossing his lips.

We drive for about twenty minutes, heading north out of the city. "Is this park anywhere near here?"

"Define near."

"In town."

"Not exactly. I'm taking you to Mont Tremblant."

"'What? Are you kidding me?"

"No. I thought we could do a short hike and have a picnic."

"So lunch has turned into a walk which has turned into a hike. Is it too late for me to change my mind?"

"Trust me, it will be fun."

I stare at the road ahead as we leave the city behind. What the hell am I doing here? A hike? A picnic? Being wined and dined at fancy restaurants for dinner, *not lunch*, is what I am accustomed to. Places where you don't wear sneakers.

I glance at my pristine running shoes. Please don't get too dirty.

Please be comfortable.

Nope. About thirty minutes into our hike, I start limping, knowing a blister is forming on my left foot. Dammit. I should have expected that a short hike to me and a short hike to Jake was not the same thing. In addition to my limping, my embarrassing behavior now includes heavy breathing and sweating. "Are we almost there?"

"Stop your whining," he teases. "You're what, mid-twenties, and you can't make it on a short hike? You need to work out more." Instead of being insulted, there is something disarming about the tone of his voice and the warmth of his hand as he grabs mine and pulls me over to a large log. The teasing is comfortable, like playful banter between two long-time friends. Not that I'd know. I've gone from boyfriend to boyfriend, socializing with their friends before moving on. I've known my bandmates for two years, but we're not close. They were already friends when they came into the music store to ask if they could post a flyer as they were looking for a singer. I told them I sang, played one gig with them, and stayed on. I saw it as work, and eventually, they stopped asking me to hang out socially. This is the longest I've been single. Is that why I've noticed?

"Sit." His voice reaches deep into my mind and snaps me back to the hiking trail.

"I'm sorry?"

"Sit down. Let me examine your foot. New shoes?"

"Not new. Hardly worn."

He shakes his head. "No worries. I have a first aid kit in my backpack."

"Of course you do."

He gives me another one of his disarming smiles. "You need to be prepared when hiking, Stephanie. You're quite the city girl, aren't you?"

"Yes, yes I am and proud of it, thank you very much. But, for your information, I spent many summers at a camp in northern Ontario. So, I've hiked before. I've even slept in a tent."

"Oh wow. You're a regular Grizzly Adams. But I'm guessing not for a while, huh?" I am about to remind him this was his idea when he holds up a hand. "I know. You were unprepared. All my fault. Now let me make it up to you by taking care of your foot."

He squats down in front of me and places my foot on his leg before untying my shoe, gently removing it, and peeling off my sock. On my heel is a blister the size of a dime, all white and squishy. "That is so gross."

"It's not so bad. At least it hasn't popped." From a side pocket on his backpack, he pulls out a first aid kit. Finding a bandage, he gently covers my blister. His fingers on my foot are warm against my cool skin as he pulls up my sock, causing me to shiver. He ties my shoe and squeezes my toes. All done."

"Thank you. You should have been a doctor."

"My parents think so too." He wipes his brow with his arm, slaps my knee, and stands up offering me his hand. "Tell you what, we're almost at the lookout. You carry my backpack, and I'll carry you piggyback."

"I'm not a kid. I don't need you to baby me."

"I know, but I don't want a blister to ruin your day. Let's give your foot a break."

"I'm not sure about this."

Stubborn, he holds out the backpack.

"Oh, fine." I snatch the bag out of his hand and slip it onto my back. Holy mackerel, it weighs a ton. Once I have it adjusted comfortably, he turns around and squats down, offering me his back.

"So this wasn't just a rouse to trick me into carrying the pack?"

"No ma'am. Now climb on."

When I still don't move, he tilts his head and smiles, those darn brown eyes eliciting trust. It doesn't hurt that, for the first time, I notice a small dimple on his right cheek. I'm a sucker for a guy with dimples.

"Trust me, I won't drop you."

With a sigh, I climb on and he grabs my legs while I wrap my arms around his neck. As he stands up, he begins to swagger and fall over. He's joking, of course, and I play along by screaming.

"Ready?" he asks.

"I am, now giddyup."

"I will as soon as you loosen your grip on my neck. I need to breathe."

"Oops. Sorry. That's what you get for toying with me."

My new vantage point provides an innocent yet oddly intimate closeness. The smell of his shampoo is both citrusy and woody and hidden behind his left ear is a missed smudge of shaving cream. On his cheek is a chickenpox scar. His breathing is heavier with my added weight, the motion of which is felt against several of my body parts. Arms, chest, thighs. His voice reverberates like a plucked guitar string resonating through his chest and into the air.

In less than five minutes we reach the top and the reason he chose this spot extends for miles. A million shades of green fan out around a deep blue lake and indigo sky. This is a view that could inspire poets, dreamers, and even the most challenged of songwriters.

"Thanks for the lift. Sorry to be such a burden."

"Don't be sorry. I'm glad you're here despite my ineptitude this morning. And thanks for not giving up. Here, have a well-earned drink."

He passes me a water bottle and proceeds to set out a blanket and buffet of food.

I dig in eagerly. "Maybe it's because I'm hungry, but these are the best sandwiches I've had in a long time. Where'd you buy them?"

"I made them."

"Shut up. You did not."

"I did. They're sandwiches, not soufflé. They're surprisingly simple to make. You take a slice of bread, top it with meat, cheese, lettuce, tomato, mayonnaise, pickles, or anything else you like. Then you top it with another piece of bread. Et voilà. A sandwich."

"Thanks smartass. I know how to make a sandwich."

He opens another container with carrot and celery sticks. Then one with hummus. "Don't tell me you made the hummus too?"

"Yup."

"I take it you like cooking?"

"I like eating."

"You can buy hummus."

"Sure, but I like to be aware of what goes into my food. I'm not a fan of anything artificial. I don't like a lot of preservatives and additives. My body is my temple," he says while patting his stomach. "Wait until you try my chocolate chip cookies. They are to die for."

"Oh my God, you bake. You're quite the catch, aren't you?"

He wiggles his eyebrows at me and pops a carrot stick into his mouth.

"How the hell are you related to Trevor?" Trevor would never have thought of this or been so laid back. At least not with me.

"Like I told you. We're related by marriage, not blood." He takes a drink of water. "So, you used to go to camp, huh. I'm having a hard time picturing you roughing it in the woods."

"We weren't exactly roughing it. We were in cabins and there was a dining hall. But, we did hiking and canoeing and stuff. The last two years I was there we did an overnight canoe trip. That's when I slept in a tent."

"Did you like it?"

"Hmm. Well, there were things I liked. I wasn't a huge fan of the scheduled activities, at least not all of them. But I liked the arts and crafts, and I liked singing around the campfire." A few of the counselors would bring their guitars and the night filled with magic as the music filled the warm circle under the black starry night. "During free time I would sit and read by the lake—I had a favorite spot under this huge birch tree—or I would try to write songs. They were awful, but I was only a kid. Wow. I haven't thought about that in years." The musty smell of the cabins, bug spray, campfire, the sound of sleeping bag zippers. "I loved reading in my sleeping bag with my flashlight. Most other kids would be up talking or sneaking out and meeting friends. And by friends, I mean boys. Not me. I just wanted to read. God, I was such a dork."

"I think you sound sweet."

The carrot stick thrown at him hits him in the chest. "Yeah, right. The last two summers there, my sister pretended not to know me. I ran into her in the showers once, and started a conversation—we were the only ones there—but she freaked out anyway. *What's your problem? I told you not to talk to me. I don't want anyone to know that such a loser is my sister.*" My hands dart up to cover my mouth. Anything to stop talking.

"Sounds like she had the problem. Not you."

"What do you mean?"

"Well, you weren't being a jerk or anything. You were just doing your own thing. What did it matter to her? But, I'm looking at it as an adult. And let's face it, we're all stupid when we're kids." Jake stretches out and lies down. "I think I ate too much."

"Is that even possible?"

"Hardy har, now come closer." He taps the blanket. "Lay beside me. Isn't the sky beautiful with the puffy clouds?"

I lay back, arms folded across my stomach, my head resting on his out-stretched arm. The sky is beautiful, but now that Chelsea is in my mind, she won't leave. She wasn't always so mean. As young children, we were inseparable. I remember us laying on the grass in the backyard, just like me and Jake right now. The grass was pricking the back of our legs and our hands were sticky from having eaten popsicles. She was watching an ant crawl over her hand as she talked about how when we were older we would live together in an apartment downtown and have a dog named Eddy. She was going to become a singer. I would write her music.

"Oh no. You're shivering. Are you cold?" Jake asks.

"I'm okay." Just shaking off the feelings that have surfaced.

"You want to get going?"

"No. Not yet."

He pulls me closer and kisses the top of my head. I am so comforted, tension seeps out of my body like blood from a wound.

"Hey sleepyhead, rise and shine."

"What?" My eyes blink open. "Oh my gosh. I fell asleep? For how long?"

"Not long. Five minutes or so."

"I am so sorry. I can't believe I did that."

"It was fine. Well, except for the snoring. Were you a lumberjack in your previous life or something? An elephant?"

"I don't snore."

"If you say so."

"I don't." He flinches as I poke him in the side. "I was not snoring."

He grabs my finger. "Okay, okay, whatever you say Stephelant."

"Stephelant? Did you seriously just call me Stephelant?"

"I did."

Reaching out, I pick up a water bottle. "Give me one reason why I shouldn't dump this over your head."

"Because I'm cute." He gives me a grin. "And your ride home...and you like me."

My cheeks heat up. Darn his cute little dimple.

He wraps his fingers around my hand holding the bottle. "And I only give nicknames to people I like."

With our faces only a few inches apart, we sit in silence, grinning goofily like adolescents, before leaning in for a sweet kiss. His lips are warm and soft and what it lacks in duration, it makes up for in electricity.

Little bees buzz and dance in my stomach as I lean my forehead against his. "You know, I recently read that chocolate chip cookies help prevent snoring so I guess I will be taking home the leftovers since my snoring is such a problem and all."

"Fair enough, but only if there are any left," he says popping one into his mouth as he begins to pack up the picnic.

Walking down the trail is easier on my foot, and while I can tell he is walking at a slower pace than he is used to, he doesn't complain. Instead of focusing on my sore foot, I think of the warmth of his hand around mine.

As he throws his pack into the back of the truck, Jake checks his watch. "It's still early. Do you want to go into the village?" he asks.

"Civilization? Hell yeah."

We drive into Tremblant village and wander around the touristy shops. Jake buys me a souvenir baseball hat and pulls it on my head.

"Hey, you're going to mess up my hair."

"You were asleep on the trail. Trust me. This won't make it any worse."

He flinches as I smack him in the stomach but I keep it on. Because, hey, I'm cute in hats.

Jake suggests we have dinner at one of the restaurants and I agree. Back in familiar wine-and-dine territory, I sip my martini and relax back into my seat. My turn to ask questions. "So, I told you about my sister. Let's hear about your family."

"Well, I'm kind of the black sheep."

"You? How so? Do you work for a drug cartel or something?"

He laughs. "No. I started a house painting business. I wasn't a fan of school and I didn't want to go to university. I started working for a painting company, one of those places run by students, and I liked it. I moved to a bigger company for a year or so, before starting my own. Just me at first, now I employ two guys full time and a few more when we have a lot of jobs. We also offer drywall repair, and hopefully one day, complete contractor services."

"Well, I'm impressed. And this makes you the black sheep, how?"

"I come from a long line of doctors. My stepdad is a surgeon, my mother is a professor of medicine. All my sisters are doctors. Then there's me. I never wanted to do it. All those years of school, not to mention the blood, no thanks."

"Wow. I can't imagine. That's a lot to live up to."

He takes a sip of his beer and shrugs. "It took a long time for my parents to come to terms with it, but eventually they did. They don't love it, but they accept it."

"So you must be related to Trevor through your stepdad, right?

"Yeah. My biological dad, who is also a doctor, surprise, surprise, lives in Europe now. We don't have much to do with him. My mom remarried when we were young, and my youngest sister is technically my half-sister. My uncle, step-uncle, didn't live far from us and since Trev and his brother are about the same age as us, we grew up with them."

"Is it weird for you, to go out with me knowing I was with him for a year?"

"If it did, would I have asked you out?

"No, but..."

"No buts. I really like you."

"Well, I am kind of hard not to like."

He tilts his head back and laughs. "Modest too."

We don't say much on the drive back to Montreal. The silence is comfortable. Jake is comfortable. Is it because he saw me at my worst and still called me? Who knows, but it's weird. And kind of scary. And kind of good—and that circles me back to scary.

When we pull up to my apartment, we both get out of the truck. Standing in front of the door, there is no awkwardness as he bends down and kisses me. His lips brush mine, a little tentatively, like he is holding back, but I don't have the patience. I remove the baseball hat and wrap my arm around his neck, pulling him close, my tongue against his lips until he opens his mouth and the kiss turns deep, from pleasant to passionate.

He moves back, separating us. "That was a great ending to a great day."

"It had its moments, despite the hiking."

He leans his forehead against mine. "I'll give you more warning about what I have planned next time. For example, right now, I'm going to lean down and kiss you again."

"I think it was me who kissed you, but I'll take it."

"I'll call you soon," he says when we finally pull apart.

"Sure, I'd like that."

He takes off, bounding down the stairs, leaving me breathless, if not a little confused as to why he didn't hint about an invitation to my apartment. A kiss like that is a sure sign of attraction, isn't it?

Upstairs, the baseball hat gets tossed onto my table as I make a cup of herbal tea. Ginger makes her presence known and I pick her up, giving her the attention she deserves. We relax on the couch, both of us stretched out.

"I really like this guy," I say to Ginger.

If I could just stop embarrassing myself with the tears, but Chelsea's memory insists on rising to the surface. I reach for my wallet and take out her picture, old and faded from being carried around everywhere I go. It's not the best photo, but there she is, looking at the camera like it was made for her, and her alone. Cropped out of the photo is me, sitting beside her on the porch railing, admiring her. How I longed to be like her, popular, bold, confident. She had a long list of guys vying for her attention. I would have been happy with just one.

Like the one I went out with today. She never would have gone out with Jake for a hike, let alone a picnic. His truck is not flashy enough. His clothes not expensive enough. But maybe that too would have been her problem.

11

*The Mitchel Sisters' Updated Guide to an Awesome
Life—Rule no. 2: Always go out looking your best but keep it
appropriate to the situation.*

ON MONDAY, I HOBBLE around work in flats—*flats*—thanks to the blister
on my heel. Even two bandages are not enough to stop the pain from
seeping through in every step I take. And this is from someone who often
sacrifices comfort for fashion. Normally though, I save those feet-killing
shoes to walk from the car to the restaurant table and back again. Not many
steps involved there. But I have been on my feet all day and completely
preoccupied with how soothing it will be to soak them in a bath at home.

Visions of Epsom salts dance in my head as the clock strikes six. Time to
clock out, baby.

"You hoo, excuse me." Velour-mom walks toward me like a woman on a
mission. "I don't know what kind of magic powers you have, but you are
the only one who can get through to him. Can you please be the one to
give him guitar lessons? The other lessons are a complete disaster."

"I'd love to help you, but I'm not an instructor here."

"I don't care. You can come to my house, or I'll bring him to yours. Here
is my phone number. Call me when you have a chance and we will work out
the details. I won't take no for an answer."

She strides out of the store, head held high like I've already agreed. Sorry to disappoint, I whisper to the paper as it's crumpled up, but my fingers won't release it into the garbage can. Instead, it's jammed into my pocket.

Unlike in school, where my chances of winning the lottery were greater than my chances of being asked out on a date, the last few years have more than made up for it. Until Trevor, of course. Prior to him, most dates were one-offs. Sometimes a man and I went out for several weeks, a few guys lasted several months. I chose guys who wanted to party. Guys who wanted me as arm candy. Guys who didn't want to talk. But by the time Trevor entered my life, the novelty of this lifestyle had worn off. I wanted something more. Looking back, it wasn't Trevor I longed for. It was a relationship.

Things feel different with Jake. I like him and want him to keep liking me, hence my panic on Thursday when no hot water comes out of my shower.

The shower water runs and runs as I beg for a miracle. My prayers go unanswered. Now what? Wearing only a robe and desperation, I knock on Vicki's door.

There is a muffled, "Gunner, sit," before the door opens.

"Hello, neighbor, I guess you noticed there is no hot water."

"Oh, no. You too? I was going to beg you to let me use your shower. What do I do?"

"Not much tonight. I called the landlord and miraculously, he answered. He's sending someone around tomorrow."

"But I need to shower. I have a date."

"Oh la la," she says, leaning against the door frame, "Where are you going?"

"To a movie. Nothing fancy." This time I was smart enough to ask.

"Why don't you put your hair in a ponytail or something."

"A ponytail? For a date? What if someone sees me?"

"It's a movie, not the red carpet."

"Easy for you to say. You always look good. Even when you come in from running."

Something washes over her face, although I am not sure what. "I was with a guy who only cared about appearances. Trust me, he's not worth it."

"It's not him. It's me. I can't go out like this. I've had my hair up in a bun all day at work. There might be dust in it because I was moving stuff around in the percussion area."

"Oh, come on now. Don't panic. I'm handy with a hairbrush. I'm sure I can do something that appears casual but is very well crafted. Would that help?"

"You'd do that for me?"

"Of course. It would be no problem at all."

"Are you always so nice?"

"I try to be."

"Why?"

"Why not?"

Assuming she is not expecting an answer, I turn and head up the stairs. Vicki shuts her door and follows, while Gunner lets out a sad whine.

The box that houses my hair supplies is dragged out of the bathroom. What a jumbled mess. Vicki begins to dig through it, but in order to speed things up, we dump it onto the table.

Once she begins, neither of us talk. Instead, she hums as she focuses on what she's doing. When she reaches in front of me to pick up an elastic from the table, I see a small word tattooed on her forearm. *Hallelujah.*

"What does the tattoo mean? I can read it, I know what it says, but why that word?"

She pauses what she's doing and gently traces the word with her fingers. "It's to remind me of someone special. Someone I miss." Her voice is soft and missing its usual upbeat tempo.

I long to ask her more about it but don't feel comfortable as we're neighbors, not friends, but I know I've triggered something as she no longer hums. The air feels heavier. Thicker. Like her memory is sitting in the room with us. Perhaps her life is not so perfect either.

"There, all done. Want me to do your makeup as well?"

"Yeah. Sure. It's kind of nice being pampered."

Ten minutes later, I hardly recognize myself. Typically, I select bolder eye-shadow colors, like pink or purple, but this makeup is natural-looking, using the neutral colors I ignore in eye shadow pallets. She's ironed my hair pin-straight and pulled it back into a sleek ponytail. Instead of the elastic being visible, a strand of my hair has been wrapped over it. I am familiar and foreign all at once.

"Thanks, Vicki. You did an amazing job."

"Well, I've had lots of practice. Glad to see it wasn't wasted." She glances down. "Oh my gosh, who is this cutie?" She bends over and strokes the cat.

"That's Ginger."

"You went to the shelter? Oh, what a beautiful girl you are. Gunner is going to go nuts when he smells you on me. He gets a bit jealous, but I can't help it. You deserve a head scratch, don't you?"

"Her owner died," I say, "Leaving her all alone. She's elderly, not many people want an elderly cat."

"Well, she's gorgeous and so sweet. You're very lucky."

I'm lucky? Isn't she the lucky one? I am the one who adopted her. Shouldn't I get some appreciation too?

As if Ginger reads my mind, she leaves Vicki and walks to me, all style and grace, and rubs her body against my leg. Her purring vibrates through the air and she looks up at me with warm eyes.

Well, okay, we're both lucky.

Vicki walks over to the door. "Thanks again," I tell her as she swings it open. "I appreciate your help."

"Anytime, neighbor. Have fun."

I pick up Ginger, burying my face into her fur. "What's with her always calling me neighbor? Oh shit, GinGin. Have I never told her my name?"

If I am to meet a guy somewhere instead of having them pick me up, I always show up fifteen minutes late. That way I am not left standing alone waiting for my date, plus it never hurts to keep them guessing. Their expression of relief when I do show up is rewarding.

Until today.

Jake is leaning against a wall outside the theatre doors, phone to his ear. When he sees me he stands up straight and puts the phone away.

"I just called your place to see if you forgot. We're almost late for the movie." He's more pissed than grateful.

My body stiffens. "Nice to see you too. Geez, I'm sorry. There was no hot water in my building and then it took longer to get here than I thought. I don't have a car, like you."

"I took the metro too. You try parking a truck downtown." He takes a deep breath while slightly shaking his head. "Steph, I'm sorry. I didn't intend on starting this date by snapping at you. I have this thing about being late. It's one of my pet peeves. I show up early for everything. But that's my issue, not yours." He runs his fingers through his hair. "I've been looking forward to seeing you. I'm glad you're here."

His honesty softens my anger, despite my desire to hold on to it, and when he leans in and kisses me, it leaves me altogether. He tastes of chocolate. No doubt, from the remains of some in the corner of his mouth. I wipe it away with my finger. "You already got a snack?"

"I was hungry. Sorry." He takes his hand and wipes his mouth.

"Don't worry, I got it." I grin up at him. "And I am sorry for being late."

"Thanks. I can be weird about it." He takes my hands in his, and we stare at one another in silence. Only for a few seconds but it feels like we are resetting the night.

He winks, letting go of one hand and pulling me with the other. "The movie we talked about is sold out, but there were tickets left for *Enemy at the Gate*. I hope that's okay."

"You're not one of those guys obsessed with war movies are you?"

"No, no. There weren't any other options."

"Well, okay then."

"Alright. Let's go. We still need to get some snacks."

As the credits scroll by, I wipe at my tears, praying the waterproof mascara will hold up. The last thing I need is for Jake to see me crying again.

He puts his arm around me and gives me a squeeze. "Quite the movie, huh? You okay?"

"Yeah, fine. Thanks." Dammit.

We exit the theatre and step out into a warm spring night. He takes my hand and we walk for about half a block in silence.

"Do you mind if I take you straight home? I have an early morning tomorrow."

"That's fine. I have to work too."

Instead of hailing a cab, he leads us to the nearest metro. No one has ever taken me home by public transit.

"You told me you work at a music store," he says after we pass through the turnstile. "Tell me about it. What do you do there?"

"I'm just a sales clerk. Not much to tell."

"Yeah but, you're a musician. I imagine it's fun to work around music all day, no?"

"It is. Talking to customers about music is the best part of my day. There's this kid Riley who I helped to pick out a guitar—he originally wanted a trombone. He's come back a few times asking for help. Now his mom wants me to give him music lessons."

"Oh, so you teach?"

"No."

"Is that something you're interested in?"

"I don't know. My manager thinks I should. And I'm considering helping Riley. Years ago I wanted to be a music teacher but..." my voice trails off. Jesus. This again?

"But what?"

"I dropped out of university after a year, so teacher's college is out of the question."

"There's more than one way to reach a goal. You shouldn't give up if that's what you want to do."

"I don't know."

"Yeah, I mean twenty-five. You're close to retirement. Better not start anything new now." The train pulls into the station, as I punch him in the arm. When we sit down, I lean in close and he puts his arm around me. We ride in silence until we reach my stop.

It's only a five-minute walk from the metro to my apartment but he insists on walking me to my door. Surely this time he will ask to come up. But he doesn't. We share a very passionate goodnight kiss and he walks back towards the metro.

I watch him walk away until he turns the corner. Is a late-night ride on the metro more appealing than a night with me? Surely not after that kiss. I slip off my heels so as not to wake Vicki as I climb the stairs to my apartment. Once inside I scoop up Ginger and give her a cuddle before placing her on my bed for the night. Right before I jump into bed, I open my wallet to make sure I still have Riley's number. It wouldn't hurt to try at least one lesson.

12

*The Mitchel Sisters' Updated Guide to an Awesome Life —Rule
no. 3: Sometimes you need to make the first move.*

THE RINGING PHONE PULLS me out of sleep. I lift up my sleep mask to check the time on the clock radio. Brilliant sunshine already fills the apartment, assaulting my sleepy eyes, but Ginger is enjoying it, curled up on a sunny spot at the foot of the bed. The clock reads eight-o-four.

I stumble my way to the living room and cough to clear my throat before I pick up the phone. "Hello," I croak out.

"Stephanie? It's Jake."

"Oh hi. Yeah. It's me."

"Sorry, you sounded different."

"The bar was exceptionally smoky last night. My throat is a bit hoarse. It'll clear in a minute."

"Oh my God, I woke you, didn't I?"

"Yeah. I only got in a few hours ago, but no worries."

"Shit, Steph. I'm sorry. I'm used to getting up early. Sometimes I forget that people are on such different schedules. I'll call back later."

"No, no. Now is fine. I needed to get up soon anyway." I cross my fingers. Please ask me out.

"Okay, well, since you're up, I was hoping you could help me with a job today."

273

Am I dreaming? He wants me to work? "A job? You want me to work for you?"

"Not work *for* me—*with* me. I'm stuck. I need this room painted and no one on my crew is available."

"And you're asking me? Someone who has never painted anything in her life? Well, I did do some finger painting in kindergarten, but after that, nada."

"I'll do all the hard stuff. But rolling is easy and I'm a decent teacher. So, what do you say? Pretty please."

"Painting, huh?" This is clearly not a date—it's...what? An unfamiliar tightness grips my chest. There's no rule for this. I sit down as if that will help me think better. This guy does nothing I'm used to. Yet, apparently, that's part of his charm because I hear myself agreeing. "Would noon work? I can't be there earlier because I'm teaching my first guitar lesson this morning at ten. Riley lives in Westmount, but I'll be done by eleven. Where will you be?"

"I'm about a five-minute walk from the Outremont metro station."

"Okay. It shouldn't take me too long. Let me grab a pen and write down the address. You do realize you will owe me for this."

"I know. I'll make it up to you. I promise."

He gives me the address and we hang up. No point in going back to bed. Ginger has made herself at home in the depression where I was sleeping anyway. An empty cavity replaced by warmth.

Chelsea used to cut out pictures in magazines of things she wanted. She'd done this since we were kids. Over time her focus changed from toys to clothes to houses and cars. She kept them in an accordion file, each section labeled in her pristine handwriting. *Houses – Exterior. Bedroom. Bathroom. Living Room. Kitchen. Sports cars. Luxury cars. SUVs.* Each year her tastes grew more extravagant. Mom would be furious if pages were missing from a magazine before she read it. Dad would tell her she had champagne taste on beer money. To that, she would roll her eyes. "Daddy, I already told you that I'm going to marry rich.

And if we divorce, I'll take him to the cleaners." Dad would shake his head and Chelsea would tilt her head back and laugh.

She wouldn't be laughing at the house I'm standing in front of now. Her jaw would drop. Riley doesn't live in a house. He lives in a mansion.

The house has a stone exterior and a three-car garage. You could play golf on the lawn. Located up on the mountain with a view of the skyline, his neighbors must be diplomats and politicians. Bank CEOs. People who owned distilleries, department stores, breweries. We're talking old money.

I walk up imposing stairs of honed concrete to face two castle-like wooden doors. Not intimidating at all.

I use the lion-head knocker, half expecting a butler to answer. Instead, Riley's mother greets me, all smiles and genuine friendliness. Today she is wearing jeans that probably cost more than my rent and a crisp white T-shirt that someone (unlikely her) has ironed. She escorts me into a palatial living room where Riley is waiting on a white sofa. He already has a scowl on his face.

"Hey, Riley. Are you ready to start?"

He shrugs. "I guess."

"All right. Let me set up."

My supplies include a pen and paper, a metronome, and a small cassette player. I pull them out of my bag and place them on the marble coffee table, which sits, of course, atop a cream area rug. Please don't let me spill or break anything. What am I doing here? I can't do this.

I smile at Riley and he looks at me expectantly. Can he tell I'm a nervous wreck? I pick up my guitar and run my fingers across the smooth wood and rough wire. Try to relax. Music is your happy place.

Riley turns away from me, toward the hall. A boy, who I assume to be his older brother, walks by in soccer gear, cleats included, right across the polished hardwood. If this were my place everyone would be walking around in those shoe covers surgeons wear.

"See ya, loser," Riley's brother yells as he walks out the door.

Riley's shoulders slump and I recognize the expression on his face because I wore a similar one for most of my childhood.

"Do you play soccer too?" I ask him.

"No. Just hockey. Dillan plays every sport he can and is always good. He's better than me at hockey too."

"Yeah, but he's also older than you."

"I guess."

"I bet he likes rubbing in how much better he is, doesn't he?"

His head bolts up. "How'd you know?"

I shrug. "I've been there. So don't worry about your brother. It's what older siblings do. You do what you like. My sister was always better than me at stuff, but there were things that I did and she didn't." What the hell is wrong with me? Why do I keep bringing her up?

"Is she better than you at guitar?"

"Now that was one of the things she didn't do, but she did sing. We both did, and I will concede that she was better." She sure was, securing the lead part in two school musicals. Not to mention, she was a soloist in the choir.

"Do you guys ever play together?"

"We used to when we were little. But not as teenagers. We could never agree on anything."

"What about now? My mom always says that me and Dillan will get along better when we're older. Is that true?"

"My mom always said the same thing too, but I never got to find out. My sister died a while ago."

"That sucks. I'm sorry."

"Yeah. Thanks." The prickle of perspiration begins on my forehead. Nothing like the blunt honesty of a kid. He's right. It does suck. It fucking sucks. But thinking about that now won't help me survive this lesson. "So, I don't know what your lessons were like before, but I have a bit of a fun idea. But first, tell me the names of the strings - did you remember to create a phrase to remember them by?"

"I did."

"All right. Tell me."

"Eight Angry Dogs Grab Boiled Eggs"

"Awesome, Riley. Now play some chords."

When he's done, we practice three chords and begin writing a song. Or at least try to.

His eyes open wide with alarm and his fingers freeze. "What? I can't do that."

Once we begin, he should relax and have fun but how do I convince him? Of course—hockey. "Don't panic. We'll keep it simple. Maybe we can make a song about hockey."

He rewards me with a reluctant nod.

We begin by practicing three chords. Then, I play the cassette so he can hear the simple tune I recorded last night. "We are going to strum the chords in time to the music. There will be time between strumming for you to move your fingers to the next chord. I'll show you what I mean." I go through the strumming. With the recorded music in the background, the strumming creates a harmony, so that it sounds like a song, not single notes. We practice that a few times and it goes remarkably well. Then every time we strum we say *hockey*. The next few times instead of strumming only down, we go down and up. After a few practices we add the words *he shoots, he scores* when we strum different chords, and all too soon, the lesson is over.

Riley remains practicing as I pick up my baggage and walk out the door, singing a happy little tune in my head.

Jake was right. The house in Outremont was a short walk from the metro station, even at my slow pace, it took five minutes. My backpack and guitar felt heavy in the oppressive humidity, and even with my hair up in a bun, my neck was slick from the heat, yet I buzzed with excitement all the way to the address Jake gave me, looking forward to sharing my morning with him.

The house in front of me is smaller and less ostentatious than Riley's house in Westmount, but still impressive. It's a two-story red brick semi-detached house, with a tall maple tree dead center of the small lawn both sides share. The address is for the one on the left.

Wooden steps lead to a small porch with rounded columns supporting a second-floor balcony. The trim, even around the windows is black. Unlike its twin, which is all in white. The thick wooden door is old and likely original but has been stripped of paint and varnished. In contrast, the window insert is newer, with the number of the house etched in the glass. Beside the door, the wall curves out, reminding me of a turret, to support a bay window on each floor. At the top of the house, the brick meets the roof with ornate wooden trim.

Music can be heard from the street. Heavy metal.

I climb the stairs and peer through the window on the door. The music blocks the sounds of my knocking. There is no doorbell, so I knock again, harder this time, but again it cannot compete with loud aggressive lyrics and distorted guitar.

Opening the door, I call out and walk in. Leaving my guitar in the foyer, I wander into the house and find him painting the dining room. The dining room table is covered with a tarp and the chairs are piled on top. He is kneeling on the floor, paint brush in hand, while singing off-key to the music.

I hesitate briefly before tapping him on the shoulder, enjoying this unedited version of himself.

"Steph, oh my God," he yells, placing a hand over his heart, "You scared the shit out of me."

"Sorry. I tried knocking but the music is very loud."

He nods, pulls a remote out of his pocket, and turns off the music, before standing up. Sticking his neck out like an ostrich, he kisses me "I don't want to get too close in case I have paint on me." He leans forward and kisses me again. "I'm glad you're here."

"Me too. It should be a fun way to spend the afternoon."

"Fun?"

"Yes, fun - I'm keeping an open mind. Don't question it, or I might change my mind."

"I won't. Did you bring clothes to change into? If not, I have some extras."

"No worries. I got that covered." I tap my backpack. "This time you gave me enough information to be prepared."

"Fantastic. Do you want anything to eat? Drink?" He juts his chin towards a pizza box sitting under the dining room table.

"No. Not right now. I grabbed something on the way over, but hey, nothing like floor pizza to really woo a girl."

"Very funny, smarty-pants, but after a few hours of hard labor, you'll change your mind."

"We will see about that." I hold up my backpack. "Where's the bathroom."

"On your left by the front door, but first tell me how your guitar lesson went this morning."

A rush of warmth floods through me, and I'm not sure if it is because he cares or because I had a good time.

"I can tell by your smile it went well."

"You can?"

"Yeah. You're...I don't know...lighter? No, that's not the right word."

"Well, I do feel good. He was still practicing when I left. I think things might have clicked for him." The entire morning bubbles out of me.

"I take it that you're going to continue with the lessons."

"We booked the next one."

"I think that's great. We should celebrate."

My cheeks turn hot. Have I made this into too much? "It's not that big of a deal."

"Hey, don't be embarrassed, especially around me." He reaches for my hand and links his fingers in mine. "You've started doing something that you enjoy and that you're good at. Why not recognize that as an accomplishment?

All I can do is shrug. One music lesson is nothing, but it was something I'd wanted to do for a long time, and Riley's new-found enthusiasm made it worth it. "I guess it wouldn't hurt to have a small celebration."

Before I know it, Jake is showing me how to roll out paint. I follow his movements by first making a W then rolling over where I missed. At one point Jake takes my hand, telling me to apply more pressure. "There, feel that? That's perfect. Up and down. That's it."

His sentence is dripping with sexual innuendo, at least to me. Jake is back to painting with the brush, all business. Are we ever going to sleep together?

We quickly finish one wall and Jake moves the supplies to another. "Jake, really? Are we painting all the walls? Not just a feature wall? This is a bold color." It's a deep brick, not red, but not brown either.

"It goes well with the exposed brick in the kitchen, uniting the spaces. Come. Follow me. I'll show you."

I put down my roller and follow him into the kitchen. One wall, the wall that both houses share, is exposed old brick with wood cupboards, black granite countertops, and black appliances.

"This place is awesome. It's so stylish."

"Glad you think so. I designed it."

"What? Wow." My face must show as much surprise as my voice because his cheeks flush with pink—so cute. I grab a fistful of his shirt and pull him against me so I can kiss him. "I guess there's more to you than paint."

"There is."

We kiss again before returning to the dining room. Jake turns the music back on and we finish painting the remaining walls, two of which have doorways to other rooms, so it doesn't take long. I step back to admire our work, feeling pleased with myself, until I see the first wall we painted. "Uh, Jake. It's kind of blotchy. Did I screw it up?"

He's squatting beside the paint can, hammering the lid on. "It's only the first coat. Don't worry."

"First coat. You mean we're not done?"

"We're half done. Want a tour while we wait for it to dry?"

"Sure. I guess. If that's okay." I feel awkward touring a stranger's house, but maybe Jake designed more rooms and he wants to show me them.

"Of course."

He takes my hand and guides me through the house. The exposed brick wall of the kitchen runs into the living room, where a dark brown leather couch takes up most of the space. Facing the couch is a large TV. The coffee table is a repurposed wagon. Not a kid's wagon. Something industrial.

Upstairs there are three bedrooms. One an office, one a guest room, and one the master. The master also has an exposed brick wall, but this one is painted grey. A king-size platform bed leans against the wall, flanked on either side with simple wooden side tables. Above the bed is an abstract and colorful piece of art—not a print, a painting. Light pours into the room through the bay window that faces the street, and plants are everywhere. Hanging from the ceiling, in pots on the floor, against the wall. It's like a jungle and unlike my plant (may it rest in peace) they are alive. The vibe is boho-chic.

The master bath doesn't disappoint either, with an expansive double vanity, walk-in shower, and a Victorian claw-foot tub. Again, there are plants.

"I know it's not going to win any style awards, but I wanted to keep it simple. The white is easy to clean, and I like the way it contrasts with the hardwood floor—which I know is a huge risk because of the potential for water damage—but worth it. I hope."

"Don't tell me you renovated this too?"

"I sure did."

"Is there anything you can't do?"

He shrugs and his cheeks turn light pink as he turns and walks back into the bedroom.

I follow him out and stand in front of the bed. "Let me guess. You also did the painting over the bed."

"No. I wish. I am not talented with paint in that regard. I bought it at an art show."

"You bought it?"

"Yeah. I liked it."

"So why didn't you keep it?"

"What do you mean?"

"I mean, put it in your house."

His eyebrows bunch together. "I'm confused."

Now I'm confused too. I replay our conversations since I arrived. Offering me a tour...the kitchen he designed...now the bathroom...That son of a gun. He did it again. I don't believe this. I step towards him and poke him in the ribs. "Is this *your* house? Did we just paint your freaking dining room?"

"Well, yeah." He says rubbing his chest.

"Oh come on, you could have said something. I feel like an idiot."

"I'm pretty sure I did."

"No. Trust me. I'd remember."

"Well, then...tada!" He waves his arms around. "Welcome to my house."

Frustration and humiliation whirl around in my head. "Jake, can we get something straight? You are, without a doubt, a great listener, but the worst—and I mean worst—communicator. You leave out key information. It's embarrassing for me to always be one step behind. Are you doing it on purpose?"

"No. I'm not. Honest." He sits down on the bed and runs his fingers through his hair. "You make me nervous."

"Me?"

"Yeah. I like you a lot and when we talk on the phone, I become all tongue-tied. So I keep it short. Apparently, too short."

Sitting down beside him, I take his hand in mine. "You don't have to be nervous around me. I like you too. I thought that was obvious."

He turns his head toward me, "You're hard to read. I'm glad you said that."

"I am? I mean I opened up to you about the most personal thing in my life the first night we went out. I cried on your shoulder. I talked about my sister, something I never used to do. How can I be more open than that?"

He scrubs his face with his free hand. "I always feel you keep me at arm's length. Yeah, you told me all that stuff, but you've never once called me to ask me out or ask how my day was, or to say hi. I instigate everything. I'm still trying to figure out where we stand."

I never called? Wow. He's right. "I didn't realize." We sit in silence holding hands. Maybe I need to make the next move. Maybe we haven't slept together because he wasn't sure I wanted to. Well, I'll show him. I'm going to instigate his socks off.

❖❱ ❱ ·•✦•· ❰ ❰❖

"Hey, Stephalent, you're snoring again."

"I am not." So much for post-coital bliss.

Jake props himself up on one elbow, while his other one wraps around me. "The paint is probably dry by now. Should we start the second coat?"

"Seriously? We just had amazing sex and you want to go finish painting? At least it was good for me....did you not like it?" I sit up, pulling the sheets around me.

He pulls me back down. "Um, you know I did."

"So then what's the rush?"

"There's no rush. I like to finish what I started. Plus, there's this girl I like, and I want to invite her over for dinner. I can't have her over with a blotchy dining room."

"Uh-huh," I mumble as I start to kiss him. His body warm from the sheets and love. My hands begin exploring inch by inch. I run my fingers across the tattoo on his shoulder, down his muscular arm, across his chest, over his appendix scar, and along his thigh, all the way down to the tattoo on his calf.

"What are you doing?" he whispers, eyes closed.

"Learning my way around." I bring my hand back up, eventually wrapping my fingers around his most sensitive area. "Feels like something is starting down here. I'd hate to leave it unfinished, especially since you want to impress the girl you were talking about."

"You're funny. If you think this will get you out of painting, you're wrong." He tries to tease but his voice is husky and his brown eyes, as they stare at me from across the pillow, say he wants the same thing I do.

We do, however, finish painting the wall—eventually. After which, we eat a late dinner on his back deck, surrounded by the scent of cherry blossoms and air too cool for mosquitoes.

He tucks a strand of my hair behind my ear. "Tell me you are going to stay tonight. I know you work tomorrow but I'll make sure you're home with lots of time to get ready. I promise."

Nodding,, I lean into him and watch as a cat jumps onto his fence and walks along it for the length of the backyard. "Shit." I jump up so fast, my chair tips over.

"Whoa. It's only a cat."

"No. I mean, I know. It reminded me about my cat. I have to go home and feed Ginger. How could I forget about her? She's going to be starving."

"What are you talking about?"

"Ginger. My cat. She's going to be so hungry."

"You have a cat?"

"Yes, I have a cat. Keep up. I need to go. Where's your phone? Can you call me a cab while I grab my stuff together?"

"I'm not going to call you a cab. I'll take you."

"It's fine. You don't have to."

"Steph, I'm going to drive you home."

Within half an hour, we are pulling up in front of my house.

"Want to come up and meet my cat?"

"I really hope that is some kind of euphemism." He wiggles his eyebrows at me.

"No. Yes. I mean, you're invited up to meet my cat and you know, for other stuff too. And from now on, you don't need an invitation. You're welcome to stay unless, of course, I kick you out."

We enter the apartment, greeted by one angry Ginger and she is not afraid to express her frustration. While I put some food into her dish, Jake makes himself at home, sitting on the couch, his feet on the coffee table.

At least my place is tidier than when Vicki first came by, but still, now that I have been to Jake's...he owns a house. I don't even own the couch.

Plopping down beside him, I pick at some loose threads on the arm of the couch.

"Okay. What's wrong?" Strong arms pull me onto his lap.

"This place...it's not as nice as yours."

"What's wrong with it?"

"I rent it. It's small and unstylish. The polar opposite to your *house*."

He leans his forehead next to mine. "I like it here because it's your place. Here's what it tells me about you. Music is your life. I already knew you were a musician, but now I see the extent of your passion. Everything in here that has to do with music is treated with care. Your guitars are hung on the wall. Your CDs are organized first by genre, then alphabetized. You have two framed pictures, both of them I am guessing, from the music store—and you're smiling. It's clear you love it there. Compare those items with your shoes, which are in a messy pile at the door. And then there's your cat. She obviously means a lot to you. The only book in here is on cat care, and look at the plush pink bed, it's fit for royalty. You didn't expect me here tonight, so I know this is the real you and I'm grateful you trust me enough to show me."

"How on earth did you notice all that?"

"I have an eye for detail." He gives my knee a gentle squeeze. "And I'm trying to learn more about you."

"Can you do me a favor then?"

"Sure."

"Go into that level of detail the next time we go on a date. That way, I'll be prepared."

He tilts his head back and laughs. "At least I haven't scared you off because all my place says is that I'm an anal-retentive neat freak who isn't afraid of color."

"Don't forget stylish. You're a stylish anal-retentive neat freak."

He laughs again, this time I join in, and suddenly the sad, lonely air that filled my apartment is replaced by a joy so bright I can almost see it.

I place my hand on his cheek and caress his dimple with my thumb. "Want to discover what my bedroom says about me?"

13

The Mitchel Sisters' Updated Guide to an Awesome Life
—Rule no. 4: Sharing is caring.

WHY THE HELL IS Jake's truck parked outside the music store? I didn't ask him to stop by and we don't have a date. I'm to be at Riley's in an hour.

He sees me marching over and rolls down his window.

"What are you doing here?" My words are sharp and prickly.

"Nice to see you too, Steph. I thought I'd give you a ride over to Riley's for your lesson."

"Oh." My fingernails dig into my palms. This is not a normal reaction to kindness.

"Did something happen today? You seem kind of pissed."

"No. It's fine. I'm...you surprised me. That's all." I take a deep breath, trying to be normal. "I need to grab my stuff. I'll only be a minute."

"Take your time."

"Why do you have to be so damn sweet?" I mutter.

"What's that?"

Dammit. "I said, did you want to come in? I can show you around."

"Yeah, I'd love that." Of course, he would.

My smile is forced as I take a step toward personal growth. This is what adults do, right? Share bits of themselves to those they care about. The squeeze he gives my hand as we walk into the store sends a reassuring warmth through my body. I can do this. Easy peasy.

We wind our way through the store, stopping every so often for introductions. They aren't brief introductions either. Jake engages in conversations. Each new tidbit about my life here peels back my outer layers. By the time we reach the staff room, I'm standing there exposed, as if naked under fluorescent lighting. And when is that flattering. God, am I ready for him to see all of me? My heart rate increases. I'm a cornered animal. Fight or flight?

Flight, definitely flight.

I grab my backpack and pick up my guitar. "Okay, let's go."

No sign of movement from Jake. He's found a bulletin board covered in pictures and is examining them closely. Darn his eye for detail.

"Wow," he says. "Some of these are old. Look at those bell bottoms. Oh my God, is that..."

"Yup. This place is an institution. Musicians always used to stop in when on tour. Things are different now, we're not big and flashy, but you still never know who might walk through the door." I grab his hand and pull, but he is immovable. A giant boulder preventing my escape.

"And is this you?" His finger taps on a faded picture near the top.

"Um, yeah. I just started working here."

"Your hair is so curly and...voluminous." He chuckles. "I'm sorry...it's just so..."

Releasing his hand, I place mine over the photo. "It was 1992, and I admit, I was slow to let go of my Hair Metal phase. From there I went right into Grunge, so I got a lot cooler. Well, you've had your laugh. Can we go now?"

"Not yet. I want to see more. You were so cute."

"Another time."

"Promise me."

"Nope. Now move it. I'd hate to be late meeting Riley." That should motivate Mr. Punctual.

Jake serenades me with Def Leopard all the way to his truck, and then some. Only stopping when we pull out into traffic.

"You done now?"

"Oh Steph, I'm sorry. I tell you what, next time I go to my parent's house, I'll bring you the three worst pictures of me as a teenager. I'll even let my sisters be the ones to choose them, okay?"

"Fine. How about you go visit them tonight."

"I can't. I have to go and give a client a quote, but soon. I promise." He gives my knees an affectionate squeeze. "You've worked there a long time, eh?"

"Yeah. It's the only place I've worked. Is that weird?"

"Weird, why would it be weird? You're a musician who works at a music store. It makes perfect sense." His hand slides off my knee and finds my hand, which he brings up to his lips and kisses. "Don't be embarrassed around me. I like getting to know you better."

Feeling like exposed film, I put on my sunglasses and hide in the dark.

Jake waits in the driveway until the door to Riley's house opens. He gives a brief honk then drives away. Waving is impossible because Riley's mom encircles me in a huge hug.

"Sorry," she says, finally backing away. "It's just that he's made so much progress in such a short amount of time and, best of all, he practices. *Without being asked*. I can't believe it. You have a gift. You should be a teacher."

My cheeks tingle with heat. Nothing could make me happier, and I almost hug her back with equal enthusiasm. "I'm glad to hear that. Practicing isn't a chore when you like what you're doing. We just had to find the right way."

There's no doubt the kid has grown on me. I want him to succeed so the fact that he's working hard is awesome. But as soon as I see him, my happy bubble deflates. His shoulders are drooping and his usual smile is gone.

"Everything okay, Riley?"

"Yeah. I guess. I don't know." He looks down at his hands. "I think I might quit the guitar."

"What? How come?" I put my bag and guitar down. "Your mom told me how much you've been practicing. You are getting so much better."

"I know." He shrugs, still avoiding eye contact with me. "But my brother said it nerdy, and I should be more like him, playing sports. He said girls like athletes."

Instead of taking my usual seat across from him, I sit beside him. "Well, I hope you told him that girls also like musicians. Hello—rock stars have women falling all over them, right? Has he never heard of a groupie?"

"Yeah. I guess they do. I forgot about that."

"And while that is a perk, play guitar because you like it. If you don't, quit. But don't stop because someone tells you it's stupid. Just because your brother tells you to do something, doesn't mean that you have to do it."

"What about you? Did your sister tell you what to do?"

Yikes. He's got me there. "Sure. She was older and more popular than me. Of course, I wanted to be like her. But I never quit guitar or writing music." Not really. Her voice echoes in my mind. *God Steph, you're such a dork, no wonder you've never had a boyfriend. Could you at least try to be a little more like me?* "Honestly, she would drive me nuts, sometimes."

"Did you guys ever fight?"

"Does every single day count?"

"What happened when she died?"

Don't kids ever shut up? A line of perspiration starts on my brow. "Can you get me a glass of water? I suddenly don't feel so good."

"Sure." He jumps up and runs to the kitchen.

What happened when she died? Everything changed. Without her at the center of the family, we had nothing to hold us together—*I* wasn't enough to hold us together. We drifted apart like planets that have lost the gravitational pull of the sun.

"Here you go." Riley hands me the water. "I put ice in it because it is always better colder." His kindness all but destroys what's left of my composure, so I drink the entire glass as a stall tactic.

If only it was something stronger.

14

*The Mitchel Sisters' Updated Guide to an Awesome Life—Rule
no. 5: Try something new.*

June 2001

I HAVEN'T FORGOTTEN ABOUT Jake telling me that I never called him or acted interested. Since then, I changed my ways by calling him on my lunch breaks to say hi. Today, I hope to take another step forward by catering to his stomach with a batch of homemade cookies. Unfortunately, I have no idea what I need. So I find myself knocking on Vicki's door for help. Again.

"Hey neighbor, what's up?" she says. Gunner comes over, smelling my pants with great enthusiasm.

When I give him a scratch on the head, he drops down, and rolls over, exposing his belly. I indulge him and bend down to rub his tummy; grateful I can look at the dog and not at Vicki. "Sorry to bother you again, but two things. First, I realized I never told you my name. It's Stephanie. I hope you forgive me for being such an idiot. And second, I need your help. I want to make some cookies, but I'm not a baker, as you know. I found an oatmeal-raisin recipe on the internet and bought the ingredients, and since your cookies were so awesome, I figured you can tell me what kind of bowls and stuff I need."

"You don't have anything?"

"Nope. I've never even turned on the oven."

Her eyes go wide. "What do you eat?"

"Soup. Microwaveable stuff."

"So you have no bakeware at all."

"None."

"Well, you're welcome to borrow my stuff. No sense in buying something if you are never going to use it again."

Tell that to my rollerblades. "You don't mind?"

"Nope. But if you do ever need anything, can I suggest that you go to a thrift store. The money you save for quality items is crazy." She laughs. "Okay. I can tell by your face, you don't normally shop at second-hand stores."

"Um, no."

"Well, if you're looking for a bargain, you can't beat it. Especially for house-wares. I understand some people are squeamish about second-hand clothes, but you're crazy to buy a lot of kitchen stuff new. Okay, I'll get off my soapbox now."

We carry her items up to my apartment and I make us some tea.

"Are these for the handsome guy with the pickup truck?" she asks, leaning against the counter.

"Yeah. How'd you know?"

"Thin walls."

Heat starts at my neck and quickly works its way up to my face.

She laughs. "I meant I can hear you guys as you climb the stairs. Have you been together long?"

"No. Not long at all. Funny story—I met him at my ex's wedding."

"You must be good friends with your ex."

"Not exactly. My band sings at weddings and the couple who hired us, canceled but their wedding planner had another couple who wanted to get married in a hurry. The groom in that couple is my ex. Anyway, they took over the original couple venue and everything and none of us realized until it was too late." All true-*ish*. "Did that make sense?"

"It did. And wow. What a story. I guess it worked out though because you met your new guy."

"Yeah. Jake is awesome and different from the guys I usually date."

"How so?"

How indeed? "He pushes me out of my comfort zone, like hiking and stuff. Okay, this is going to sound weird, but Jake is the first guy I'm...hmmm. I can't find the right words. I want to say equal to, but that's not quite it either. With Jake, I'm more of a partner, not a girlfriend. Does that make sense? I mean, no one's ever asked me to help them with anything before—like painting his house. It was kind of fun."

"I get it," she says, nodding. "Sometimes we all need a little push."

"What about you? You don't seem to need anything."

"It's all an illusion." She waves her hands in the air like a magician. "But seriously, a year ago, things were different. I made some changes and had some help along the way. It paid off. But it wasn't easy." Silence fills the room, then she stands up, and walks over to Ginger who has curled up on her bed. "Thanks for the tea. Let me know how the cookies turn out." She gives Ginger a scratch on the head before opening the door.

"I will. Thanks again. I'll be sure to bring everything back later." As the door shuts behind her, I jump up and flip through my CDs. What is good cookie baking music? How about something upbeat and fun?

Twenty minutes later, one batch is already in the oven, thank you very much. As I'm putting dough on the second baking sheet, the smell of warm cookies hits me, transporting me right back into our old kitchen. Mom is frantically baking dozens of cookies for the post-funeral reception. They're oatmeal-raisin too. Chelsea's favorite.

Dad walks in, stands behind her, and holds her still. "Honey, stop."

"I can't. I need to keep busy. If I stop moving, I'm afraid I'll never start again."

Dad turns her towards him, holding her tight to his chest. "Why did this have to happen?" She cries out against him. "Why Chelsea? Why?"

I return the baking supplies to Vicki later that night.

"How did it go?" she asks.

"I ruined them." My cookies. My family. Everything.

15

The Mitchel Sisters' Updated Guide to an Awesome Life—Most Important Rule Ever: NEVER GIVE THEM YOUR HEART.

I AM IN DESPERATE need of a sugar fix. Work was busy and in two hours I will be Jake's plus-one for some kind of local business-awards banquet. Please let them have an open bar; sugar won't help me relax when I meet his parents tonight.

Exiting the grocery store, I rummage through my bag looking for the gummies I purchased, too desperate to wait until home.

"Ouff."

"Oh, I'm sorry," I say, embarrassed to have run into someone while routing through a bag for candy. I look up with an apologetic smile, directly into the face of Bridgette. Well, isn't that super.

"Oh, hey, Stephanie, how are you?" She smiles like we are old friends, her hand gently rubbing her stomach.

"I'm fine. How are you?" Where's a sinkhole when you need one?

"Feeling great. My morning sickness has passed." Despite my lack of feelings for Trevor, it stings that she has the life I once thought would be mine. She flushes with embarrassment realizing her faux pas. I might not like her, but she wouldn't be insensitive on purpose. She's not that kind of person.

"Um, anyway," she continues. "Thanks for being so professional at the wedding. I'm sure it wasn't easy for you, but I guess Trevor didn't need to send Jake over to talk to you after all. It's awesome that you're still seeing him. Funny how things happen sometimes."

The cold starts in my chest, rushing outward, filling my entire body. Trevor sent him over? "How do you know this?"

"We're getting Jake to paint the baby's room. He was showing us colors recently. Jake wanted Trevor to know he was still seeing you. I'm glad it worked out."

"Yeah. Sure, but it's nothing serious. We're only fooling around."

"Oh? It didn't sound that way but, hey, whatever works, right?"

"Yeah. Well, I have to go. Best of luck with the baby." And give Trevor a big kick in the ass for me.

"Thanks. Bye."

As soon as I round the corner, I rip open that bag of gummies and swallow them by the handful. Trevor sent him over? Jake was a distraction? Was everything he said a lie? This can't be happening. I thought he was different. But no, he's nothing more than a big fat liar who was doing his cousin a freaking favor. Am I so pathetic that people need to be doing someone a favor to ask me out?

Vicki will think the house is collapsing, the way I'm stomping up the stairs. Like what the actual fuck? I pick up the hat Jake bought me and try to rip it apart. I'm not strong enough so I turn on the gas stove and light it on fire. It kind of melts more than burns and stinks up the entire place before I drop it in the sink. Dammit! I collapse on the bed, breathing so hard, I think I might pass out. Ginger jumps up and cuddles beside me.

At least someone wants to be with me.

My little black dress hangs in its dry-cleaning bag, the breeze from the window ruffling the plastic—mocking me. Tonight is important to Jake but how can I go now?

The phone rings and I ignore it, choosing to listen to the machine. "Hey, Steph. Erin. Hope you're not busy. We can play at Rosie's tonight. The scheduled band had their van breakdown somewhere near Quebec City. They can't make it, so the manager called us. Let me know ASAP. Ciao."

Five minutes pass before I open my bedside table drawer and pull out my new list of rules. I write: *NEVER GIVE THEM YOUR HEART* before dialing Erin's number.

⊰ ·•◦•· ⊱

I arrive home to the light on my answering machine blinking in morse code for Jake is pissed.

To end this day on a high, I hit play.

"Hey Steph, it's me. Just wanting to know what time you're getting here."

"Hey Steph, it's about to start. I'm going in."

"Hey, is everything okay?"

"I just checked my messages. You went to a gig. I can't believe you. You didn't even have the balls to call my cell. Thanks for nothing."

So what. He hurt me. I hurt him. We're even.

Then why do I feel so bad?

⊰ ·•◦•· ⊱

A day passes. Then a week. Radio silence. "I guess it truly was a fake relationship, Ginger. How can guys be such jerks? Hmmm? "At hearing her name, Ginger jumps up on my lap and settles down for a nap. I continue to watch TV and order a pizza.

When the doorbell rings, I grab my wallet and run downstairs to open the door. Jake is standing on the landing with my pizza.

"You take on a second job?"

"We arrived at the same time. I'm hoping we can talk."

"Sure." I turn around and walk up the stairs. He follows.

"Hey, Ginger," he says as he walks in, putting the pizza on the table before bending down to pet her. Ginger walks away. At least someone is on my side.

"So, are we not going to talk about last Friday?" he asks.

"What's to talk about?"

"Why are you acting like this? You stood me up at a formal banquet in front of my family. I felt like an idiot. That night meant a lot to me. I was nominated for an award."

"Now you know what it's like to be made a fool of."

"What are you talking about?"

"Trevor sent you over to me at his wedding. I guess you flirting with me was a way to make sure I didn't ruin his wedding. Nice to know you all think I'm that shallow."

Jake says nothing. Which means everything.

"Wow. You're not even going to deny it. I guess that sums it up perfectly. So why keep the ruse going? Why string me along like that? I liked you. A lot." My hands ball into fists to stop them from shaking.

"Yes, okay, he asked me to go talk to you, but it was true what I said about seeing you at his brother's wedding. I wanted to ask you out way back when."

"I'm sorry. I don't believe you."

"I should have told you, but at the time it didn't seem important." He scrubs his face with his hands. "Honestly, I thought we'd have a few drinks after the wedding. That's all. I wasn't looking for anything more. And why would I? You come across as this ice queen, but then, at the diner, when you talked about your sister, I thought maybe you had another side. I wanted to get to know you. But I guess I should have listened to Trev, he warned me you were selfish and super high maintenance. God, I was such an idiot to think we actually had something."

"High maintenance?"

"Yeah. He said everything had to be your way all the time. You always had to be the center of attention. He was right after all. I wanted you at the banquet to share that moment with me. But you couldn't do that, could you? You had to go perform where you *are* the center of attention."

"So you're saying I can't have a successful career? My only job is to support you?"

"Jesus, no. What I'm saying is that in a relationship people support each other. You're there for me, I'm there for you. I didn't ask you to miss a gig for me. I didn't say what I do is better than what you do. The fact is that you had nothing planned, you agreed to come with me, and then you stood me up."

"You were told to talk to me. You asked me out as a favor to someone else. I was a pity date."

"I could have explained it all, if you'd just asked me, like an adult in an adult relationship. Not like a stupid teenager. Yes, I should have been honest, but your self-esteem is so freaking fragile, that I knew something like this would happen."

Somewhere, a little voice tells me I should listen to his words and try to understand, but this fireball of anger, lodged deep in my heart, blocks out everything. "You still should have told me."

He lets out a big sigh and his shoulders relax. He runs his fingers through his hair. "I don't know what else to say, we're going in circles. But I'm sorry about not telling you, I really am. In hindsight, it was stupid."

Nothing like a sincere apology to extinguish some of the anger, and my body relaxes too, my voice, softer. "So now what?"

He shrugs and walks to the door. "I guess we have to decide if we have anything worth saving."

The door shuts behind him, leaving me barefoot among the broken shards of our relationship.

16

Rules are stupid. Everything sucks.

WORK, AS ALWAYS, IS my refuge. Keeping busy helps preoccupy my mind. I stock shelves, dust, rearrange drawers behind the cash desk, file rental agreements. Anything to avoid thoughts of Jake. Missing him this much is unexpected. When Trevor dumped me, I was flooded with embarrassment and surprise. I didn't really miss him. But with Jake, it's different. I miss his smile, his laugh, our conversations. I even miss him teasing me about my snoring. Not only did I open up to him, being vulnerable with him felt safe. This has left me hurt and exposed, like a turtle stuck on its back.

When Natalie asks how things are going with us, I lie. What possessed me to bring him into this part of my world?

Numb, and without alternatives, I maintain the facade that nothing is wrong and arrive at band practice, relieved for the chance to drown out my thoughts with music. But walking into Marc's house is like walking into soup, the tension is so thick.

"What's going on?" I ask.

"Um, hey Steph. We need to have a band meeting," Marc says.

"Okay. What about?"

"Well, we were talking—"

"By we, you mean everyone but me."

Marc and Sébastien both look at Erin. "Yeah. We were talking and we've decided to take the band in another direction."

Buzzing begins in my ears and I think I might pass out. "Let me save you the trouble, that direction doesn't include me."

"Yeah, sorry. We find that there is us and there is you. We want something more cohesive."

"I ditched Jake so I could play at Rosie's on short notice. Is that not putting the band first?"

"It's more complicated than that, Steph. One night doesn't change things. We're tired of you telling us what to do. We have music we want to write, songs we want to play. It doesn't work with you anymore. We're sorry."

Ice queen. High maintenance. Selfish. *There is us and there is you,* Erin said. Et tu, Brutis? I want to drop on my knees and beg them not to kick me out. I need this. I need them. But I also need to walk out with what's left of my dignity. Turn on bitch mode.

"Fine. Whatever. I'm better off without you people anyway."

"Steph..."

"No. I'm serious. I was doing you guys a favor. Good luck replacing me. You're going to need it." Of course they have someone lined up, they're not going to kick me out without someone ready to take my place, but I say it anyway.

I call a cab and load all my stuff into it. Two guitars, an amplifier, some pedals, and what's left of my self-esteem.

When I finish bringing everything up into my apartment I collapse on the couch. Where's Ginger? I usually get some kind of greeting. Oh God. Her food hasn't been eaten. Did I accidentally let her out?

"Ginger?" She is curled up on my pillow, but my relief is short-lived. Her breathing is fast. Too fast. I crouch down and stroke her, putting my face close to hers. "Ginger? Is everything okay?"

She opens her eyes and looks directly into mine. I'm not so self-absorbed that I can't tell when a cat is in distress but that doesn't help because I don't know what to do. I need a vet and fast. But I don't have a vet yet. I've never required one.

Wrapping her in a blanket I oh-so-gently pick her up. "It's okay, GinGin. We'll get you better."

We make our way downstairs and knock at Vicki's door. As soon as she opens it, the tears begin.

"What is it? What's wrong?"

"Ginger. She's sick. She needs a vet, where do I go?"

"Don't worry. Let me call mine."

With limbs as heavy as my heart, I hold on to Ginger with everything I have, talking to her, reassuring her, hoping she doesn't feel my fear.

"Okay, well, thanks anyway." Vicki's voice is a million miles away. "Don't worry," she calls out to me. "I have another idea—oh, hey, Darce, it's Vicki. I need your help with something."

Somehow we arrive at the animal shelter. Darcy, the redhead who did the paperwork for Ginger's adoption, greets us at the door.

"What's wrong?" she asks me.

"I came home and she didn't greet me. Then I noticed that she didn't eat anything all day. And she's breathing really fast."

"Did she go to the bathroom?"

"I didn't think to check."

"That's fine. Let's get her inside. The vet is waiting to see her."

We walk inside and follow Darcy through a set of doors into the back. The vet introduces himself as Dr. Tremblay and gently takes Ginger out of my arms. Vicki directs me to the staff room. We pass the wall covered in Polaroids of all the pet adoptions. Ours included. The ice queen awkwardly holding a cat. I have such a bitch-face, why did they let me take her home. I tear it off the wall.

Vicki brings me a glass of water. "I'm sure they won't be long."

I nod but can't speak, afraid the tears will start again.

Before too long, Dr. Tremblay comes in and sits beside me.

"Well, we did a thorough exam of Ginger, and I'm afraid the news is not good."

"What do you mean?" My voice is rough and gravelly.

He rests his hand on my arm. "Ginger is in her last stages of life."

"She's dying?"

"I'm afraid so. She's an elderly cat and this is her time."

"No. Please. There must be something we can do." I can't lose her. Not now.

"I'm afraid all we can do now is make her comfortable."

"How?" It's barely more than a whisper.

"Take her home. Surround her with the things she likes. Keep it quiet. Some cats become more affectionate. Some hide. Let her guide you."

"I can't. I can't do that. I'm sorry." I run out of the shelter and collapse on the sidewalk, against a fence.

Vicki comes out and sits beside me.

"What?" I snap.

"I'm sorry about Ginger."

I shrug. "It's not like I had her that long."

"Sometimes love happens quickly."

She's just a stupid old cat, but she's my cat. And Vicki's right. I love her. Dammit.

"You need to go back in and do the right thing. Otherwise, you will regret it."

"Will you go in for me and hold her?"

"No. This is something you need to do yourself." She sounds irritated.

"Why are you getting mad at me? Getting a cat was your idea."

"Ginger is *your* cat. You took on this responsibility when you adopted her. She needs you so you get off your ass and do the right thing."

A confusing ball of fear, anger, and grief, tightens and twists in my chest. "You don't understand. No one understands! I held my sister's hand as she died. Do you have any idea what that's like? Do you? To know when life leaves someone. I know this is a cat, but it's the same thing. I can't do it."

A long silence covers us like a blanket as we both stare ahead at the street. A bus drives by, then some kids on bikes.

"I'm sorry. I can't imagine what that was like."

"Not many people can."

"But don't you think it was better for her to have you with her than to die alone?"

Memories bubble to the top, ready to burst forth. The blood. Her raspy breath. Her fear. That night stole my sister and destroyed my family, bringing nothing but grief. But what if I did bring her comfort? I squeezed her fingers. Tight. *Don't worry. I'm right here. I got you.* She squeezed me back. That's when she opened her eyes. Her fear filled the car. But our eyes met before she closed them one last time. She knew she wasn't alone.

I take a deep breath, stand up, and walk back into the shelter.

At home, I put her favorite treats in her bowl, then gently place her on my pillow and curl up beside her. The night passes with me gently stroking her head while she sleeps.

In the morning I wake up to her warm body curled up against me. Neither of us moved the entire night. I gently rub her head and softly sing a song. She exhales a deep breath and then she is gone.

Finding myself in front of Vicki's door, I'm frozen, unable to knock. But I don't need to. She must have heard me on the stairs because she opens her door and says nothing while drawing me into an embrace. A few minutes later, I am sitting on her futon pretending to drink tea. Her voice floats around me as she makes cremation arrangements.

Later that evening, as I stare at the indentation of Ginger on my pillow, a riptide of sorrow and fatigue drags me down so low I'm afraid I may never see the surface again.

17

The Mitchel Sisters' Guide to Starting Over—Rule no. 1: Be true to yourself.

THE BREEZE FROM THE ceiling fan does nothing to ease the choking humidity. Unable to sleep any longer, I slip quietly down to the kitchen before anyone else is awake and make coffee. Cucumbers from Mom's garden are on the counter, so I slice off two slim pieces and place them over my puffy eyes. Soon I hear her light steps on the stairs and she joins me in the kitchen.

I remove the cucumbers as she sits down across from me. She reaches across the table, placing a hand on my arm. "How are you doing?"

"Okay."

"I'm sorry about your cat."

I nod. The coffee maker sputters to a stop, steam rising in the already hot kitchen. Mom turns her head, then starts to stand.

"It's okay. I got it."

"Oh," she says, unable to hide the surprise in her voice. "Thank you."

She sits back down and waits while I pour the coffee.

"It's nice to be served for a change." She says this without thinking, clenching her teeth awaiting my childish rebuttal. But my defensive knee-jerk reactions are gone. Instead, I see myself through her eyes. Her needy, dependent, lazy daughter.

I look down at my cup, readying for a conversation we should have had years ago. "Mom, I need to talk about Chelsea."

Ever so slightly, her body tenses. "What do you want to talk about?"

"Anything. Anything at all. We never talk about her. It's like life with her didn't exist. I need to talk about it."

She wraps both hands around her mug, as if seeking warmth, despite the summer heat. "Okay."

This simple agreement surprises me as I had been expecting reluctance. What I had planned to say now to convince her to talk seems moot, but I say because I don't know what else to do. "I found myself talking to Jake about her and it helped, like a release, you know? I don't know how to explain it. But, talking to him isn't enough. I don't want to upset you, but there are things I need to say."

She nods. "I understand. I talk to Bruce."

"You do?"

"Yes. I don't talk about it to you because you seem so fragile. Because you were in the car with her. I am afraid to bring back that trauma."

"Bring it back? It's never gone away. I've kept it lodged inside me for so long but it's all coming out, like I've sprung a leak. She was my sister. I worshipped the ground she walked on."

"You did? I'm surprised because she was never very nice to you, at least as a teenager."

"I know, but she was outgoing and popular—everything I wasn't. I was a quiet, mousy kid who disappeared into the background."

I stand up and pace around the kitchen, stopping in front of the window and looking out, focusing on the grass and the flowers. "Her death drew a lot of attention at school. Everyone saw me for the first time. Her friends, the popular kids, they gave me attention. I didn't want to lose that, but I knew they weren't my friends—so I became the person they missed. But I'm so lost now."

"Oh, honey"

"No." I hold up my hand without facing her. "Let me finish." My fingers wrap around the edge of the counter, holding me in place, because oh, how I want to run. "I just...I can't keep going on like this. I'm like a guitar with the wrong strings and finally, they're starting to snap. People call me an ice queen, and they're right. The band kicked me out. Jake broke up with me. My cat died. I'm a complete mess. The only time I am comfortable is when I'm at the music store or teaching Riley and Riley's gone for the summer."

She comes up beside me and puts an arm around me. "Oh darling, I'm so sorry you're hurting. I'm so sorry you felt like you had to be like her."

Anger boils to the surface, but I shrug her off. "No, you're not. Don't lie to me Mom. Not anymore. I heard you and Dad."

"Heard us? What do you mean?

"You were frantically baking cookies for the reception after the funeral and when Dad comforted you, you said, "Why Chelsea? Why? Why couldn't Stephanie have been driving?" Then Dad said, "I know what you mean." Well, I'm sorry I'm the one who survived. I'm sorry I'm not enough for you. I tried to give you what you both wanted but I can't do it anymore."

Mom collapses back onto a chair. Her head drops into her hands and she sits, unmoving until Bruce walks in.

"Everything, okay?"

Mom sits up, her eyes red. "Yes. We just need a few minutes." He raises his eyebrows at her. "It's okay, trust me." She gives him a small reassuring nod, then he turns and walks out.

She takes a deep breath, then stands up and walks over to me, looking pissed off. "My God, Stephanie, how could you ever think that? How? I want to grab you and shake some sense into you. I would never wish that. Nor would your father. How can you not see that we love you?"

We're face to face. I'm not even sure if I'm breathing. Suddenly, she grabs my shoulders as if she is actually going to shake me, but instead, she draws me close and bursts into tears. "We felt so lucky that we didn't lose you too. Every night for about a year, I would open your bedroom door in the middle of the night, to listen to you breathing, thanking God that you hadn't been taken from us too. I don't remember saying anything about you driving, but if I did, it certainly wasn't because we wanted you dead. You were a better driver than she was, even though you were younger. Dad and I always agreed on that. Chelsea was more...reckless." She releases me and looks up at me with puffy red eyes that match my own. "And as for your father, he wished *he* was the one who was driving. He was supposed to pick you up—you know that—but he wanted to watch the end of the hockey game, so he sent Chelsea. He's lived with that guilt all these years. Nothing I could say could help him. And now, you tell me this? Can you ever forgive us?"

My feet are rooted into the ground. All I can do is nod. The tight knot of fury and self-loathing I have harbored since her death suddenly releases and when Mom leans in to hug me again, I collapse against her. I am as worthy of their love as Chelsea. Me. Quiet little mousy Stephanie. The Stephanie who loved writing music. The Stephanie who practiced guitar for hours. The Stephanie who hoped that one day, she and Chelsea would be close again.

I allow myself to welcome the love in her embrace. A love that always existed and that I ignored. Its warmth penetrates every cell of my body and the last remnants of the ice queen melt away.

"I'm sorry," I whisper.

We draw apart again, and she takes both my hands in hers. "No. No more sorries. It's time we moved forward. Let's start a new chapter, okay?"

I nod.

"But Steph. You do need to talk to your father about this. Do you want me to call him for you?"

"No. Thanks. It's something I have to do myself."

She gives my hands a squeeze.

Mom drives me home later that morning. She said I could stay as long as I needed to, and it was tempting, but I need to return to my life and try to salvage what's left. My relationship with my dad isn't the only one that needs tending.

18

The Mitchel Sisters' Guide to Starting Over—Rule no. 2: Do the right thing even when it sucks.

THE SMALL PATCH OF grass in front of Jake's house is yellowing and dormant from the mid-summer heat. I knock, but since his truck is nowhere to be seen, I sit in the shade and wait for his arrival. To kill time, I deadhead his planter and brainstorm some song lyrics in my notebook.

I hear a vehicle pull up and a door slam shut. Looking up, I see Jake digging around the back of his truck, looking tired, with paint on his clothes. I stuff my notebook into my backpack and jump up.

"Oh geez, Stephanie. You startled me."

"I was hoping we could talk."

He nods and walks past me to open his door. I follow him inside.

"Let me go change."

"Sure."

A few minutes later, he comes back down the stairs in shorts while pulling a blue T-shirt over his chest. He motions to the living room.

He leans next to the window. I sit, then stand back up. Pacing back and forth. "I'm sorry for overreacting about the wedding thing. I was a jerk to stand you up."

"I'm the one who should apologize. I should have told you once things got going between us."

307

"Yeah, you should have, but you were right about my reaction. The truth is it doesn't matter anymore. I don't care how we got together, I'm just glad we did. Being with you was...amazing. But it also scared me. I knew standing you up would damage our relationship. I think I was looking for a reason to do just that."

"But why?"

"Like I said, I was scared. You are the first person I've ever opened up to. I broke all the rules, making me vulnerable. I was afraid of getting hurt. So I resorted to being rude and selfish and I'm deeply sorry."

"What rules?"

"Rules?"

"You said you broke all the rules."

"I did?"

"Yeah. And I'd really like to know what you're talking about."

"It's a long story."

"I have nowhere to be."

We sit down and I tell him everything, beginning with Ginger and the band before revealing more about the night of my sister's death. The misunderstanding with my parents. How I tried to be like Chelsea. "I found her journal and she had this list. The Mitchel Sisters' Guide to an Awesome Life—something I'd completely forgotten about. We came up with these rules one summer afternoon when I was twelve. They seemed ridiculous even then, but as I read her journal, I realized she was sticking to those crazy rules. So I did the same thing. It worked. At least in school, but as we've seen, as an adult—not so much."

He puts his arm around me and kisses the top of my head as I take a deep breath, summoning the courage to continue. "I think I liked having something to hide behind. My rules kept me safe because they kept everyone at a distance but you came along and changed all that. I guess my insecurities got the best of me, I panicked, and well, you know the rest." I turn to face him, looking into his brown eyes. "The truth is, I love you, Jake. I want a relationship with you, a real adult relationship, but I need to figure myself out first."

He swallows hard. "And you can't do that with me. That's what you're saying isn't it."

"Yeah."

He runs his hand up my back, cupping the back of my head and pulling me into a kiss.

Finally, I pull away. "I better go."

He leans his forehead against mine. "You don't have to. I don't want you to."

"I don't want to go either, but if there's any hope we can make this work, I need some time. I'm not asking you to wait for me, but if I don't do this, we don't stand a chance."

He closes his eyes, and leans back, giving me a small nod.

I grab my bag and walk out of his life.

19

The Mitchel Sisters' Guide to Starting Over—Rule no. 3:
Sometimes the bravest thing you can do is be yourself.

August 2001

CONVERSATIONS WITH MY DAD are brief. We talk on the phone three times a year. His birthday, my birthday, and Father's Day. I meet him for lunch every December 26th. Months can go by where I don't even think of him, so the surprise in his voice when I invite him over for dinner is not unexpected. Nor is the surprise in mine when he accepts.

We greet each other awkwardly when he arrives, having lost familial ease long ago. He is wearing jeans and a long-sleeved T-shirt despite the heat. His face, lined and wrinkled from sun damage and grief, ages him beyond his fifty-five years. He wears the expression of a broken man.

I want to show him how I've changed. My apartment is clean, the dishes are done. My laundry is folded and put away. I'm planning a future. But will he notice, because we are like distant relatives, not father and daughter?

It doesn't help that I made spaghetti. Boiled pasta and jarred sauce. Something a ten-year-old could make.

Relax, Steph. He's not here to judge your cooking.

Dad doesn't complain, and after a couple of bites, he asks about work and the band.

"The band kicked me out."

"But you have such a beautiful voice," he says.

"Yeah, but I wasn't much of a team player. They made the right decision."

His expression reveals his thoughts. What happened to his self-absorbed daughter?

"Come on, Dad. You know I always liked guitar better. Singing was Chelsea's thing." Will saying her name out loud hurt him?

"Yeah, I guess it was. But I hope this doesn't stop you from writing music. You loved doing that. I remember you spending all your weekends up in your room writing and composing. Even from such a young age. The other kids would be outside playing or hanging out at the mall when you got older of course. But not you. Such focus."

This memory hangs between us in the humid air. An almost imperceivable smile forms on his lips, triggering me to open up. Everything I told my mom pours out fast. Dad sits there, unmoving the entire time, staring at his half-eaten dinner. Fear shivers through me. What if Mom was wrong? What if he does wish I was the one who died?

"There were so many things we did wrong after the accident." His words pierce through years of silence. "We were all in shock. All mourning Chelsea. Nothing felt real. I went inside myself. Your mother and I fought about everything and nothing, not knowing how to deal with our grief. But we let you down. We weren't there for you. I would never wish for you to have changed places with Chelsea. Please believe that. I was the one who should have been driving that night. If I hadn't let her drive..." His voice trails off and he continues to stare at his plate.

We both pick at our food without eating any.

"You probably won't listen when I tell you not to blame yourself, but you shouldn't. Accidents happen, Dad. Stupid horrible accidents. I didn't bring it up to make you feel bad, I brought it up because I needed to tell you why I've been such a lousy daughter."

Finally, he turns to me. "You're not a lousy daughter, Steph. I'm a lousy father. I abandoned you and your mother." He places his hand on my arm and this simple caring gesture brings with it the realization that this is the first time we've touched in years.

"Dad..."

"Let me finish." He takes a sip of water. "One thing I've realized over the past few years, and what I regret the most, is that I only focused on what I had lost. Not what I still had. Things could have been so different, for all of us."

I place my hand on his and gently squeeze. "What I'm learning, Dad is that we all deal with loss in our own way. It's hard and it sucks and it takes time."

One side of his mouth lifts into a half-smile. "It really does."

Dad leaves shortly after dinner. No dessert. No coffee or tea. Yet, his presence lingers in my apartment. Cigarettes. Aftershave. Motor oil. We might never be close again, but the anger and hurt I've harbored since Chelsea's death is gone, leaving the door open to possibilities.

I make a vodka soda and go downstairs to sit outside on the steps. A few minutes later the door behind me opens and Vicki plops herself down beside me.

"You look like you could use a friend."

I nod and lean my head on her shoulder. I'm so lucky to have met her. I think she irked me so much when we first met because she was outgoing, friendly, talkative, and bold—the kind of person Chelsea might have become had she had the chance.

The maple tree in front of Marc's house is beginning to show signs of fall with a couple of leaves changing to yellow. The band's warm-up reaches me as I approach the door. A deep gravelly voice flows overtop, out the door, and into my brain. A voice so different from my own. They haven't only replaced me. They upgraded. Every instinct I have tells me to run. The sweat on my brow, the racing heartbeat. I turn to make my escape and slam into Sébastien.

"What are you doing here?"

Good question. Maybe personal growth is overrated. "I, uh, I wrote some songs I want to share with you guys."

"I don't know if that's a good idea, Steph." He stares down at me, his expression cold.

"Geez, you could turn people to stone with that look. Come on, I'm not here to beg you to let me back in the band. Can you honestly see me doing that?"

"No. I can't."

"Okay, so when I say I'm here to share these songs, I mean it. Now, are we going to go in or keep standing here?"

Sébastien opens the door and I trail behind him like he is my human shield.

"Look who I found," he says. The room goes quiet.

"I know, I know. You all missed me." While my bravado hides my fear, nothing masks the shock on all their faces. "Guys, come on. I'm joking. The reason I'm here is to share some songs."

"Yeah, right," says Marc.

"I'm serious. Honest. You were right to kick me out. I wasn't a team player. The truth is, I don't like singing. I don't hate it, but I would much rather play guitar and write music. That's why I'm here. I wrote these songs with you guys in mind, and from what I heard, your new singer will rock it out of the park." So I kind of mixed my metaphors, sue me. I'm nervous.

She's a tiny little thing, their new singer, in low-rise jeans and a Metallica crop top. "Hi." I offer my hand. "Stephanie."

"I figured," she says, and we shake. "Abby."

"So are we all going to stand around uncomfortably or can we get down to business?"

"Fine. Show us," Erin says.

"Well, with that ringing endorsement I guess I will." I walk over to a table and pull out my laptop. I open the first song and let them read it over my shoulder. Then I grab a guitar and play it for them. Abby moves directly behind me and joins in for the final chorus and outro.

"That's fucking awesome," Erin says.

"Thanks. There's still work to be done but when you guys have time, I thought we could flesh it out together. Like I said, I'm not interested in performing. I only want to make these songs the best they can be."

An hour later, I leave Marc's with a bunch of notes. Things went so well once we began, I almost forgot how nervous I was. I did channel some of the old me. I had to if I wanted to survive the night, but I think there was a good balance. Perhaps a bit of inner-Chelsea isn't a bad thing.

20

The Mitchel Sisters' Guide to Starting Over—Rule no. 4: Life is unpredictable. Tell people you love them.

September 2001

WHY IS IT THAT September always feels like the beginning of a new year? Sessions with Riley will be starting soon. The store is busy with rentals and lesson bookings, and I've applied for a teaching position on top of my store shifts. Marc and I have been collaborating on a few new songs. For the first time in a long time, by which I mean ever, I am thinking beyond the day-to-day. Teaching? Producing? My future excites me, and I spend nights on my laptop exploring college programs and career pathways. So many times, I've picked up the phone wanting to share my ideas with Jake but stopped.

I walk into work and am taking off my headphones when Denis steps out of the lunchroom. "Everyone, in here now," he yells. I'm working the early shift, so the store isn't open, it's only Natalie and me. Nat shrugs, not knowing what he wants, but something in his voice causes us to hurry.

We find him transfixed in front of the small TV. He says nothing. He doesn't have to. The horror unfolding in New York is beyond words.

The day continues with no sense of normalcy. There are few customers. Hardly any street traffic. The internet has crashed. The manager sends most of us home early. I walk, needing air and time to think.

Haunting images are burned into my mind. All those lives lost. All those families left behind. Life has already shown me that everything can change in a heartbeat, yet there is something about the horror and magnitude of this loss that amplifies it a hundred-fold. This loss will affect more than individual families. This loss will change the world.

Instead of going home, my feet take me to Jake's. His truck is parked on the road, and the realization that he is home releases the emotions I have tried to outwalk all day. Grief, pain, and fear pulse through my body as I pound on his door with desperate determination.

As soon as it opens, I throw myself into his arms. He staggers slightly then carries me inside, placing me gently on the sofa. He tucks a loose strand of my hair behind my ear, his cool hand against my hot, sweaty, face.

He turns off the TV then kisses the top of my head. "I'll be right back." Unable to speak, I simply nod, lean back, and close my eyes—a mistake because all I see are images from the morning.

Jake passes me a glass of water and I drink the entire glass in one go. "Want more?" he asks.

"I'm okay. I walked here. From work. I might have some blisters. Do you still have your first-aid kit?"

"Yeah. Don't worry."

"Jake...I..."

He places a warm hand on my cheek, tilting my head up to face him. "We don't have to talk. Having you here is enough."

"But I do. I need to tell you something."

He nods, wrapping his arm around me. "Whenever you're ready."

I lean into him, my head against his chest, and listen to his rhythmic breathing and the beating of his heart. "For about two years, I didn't even like Chelsea. She was a bitch. But I did love her. She was my sister and I held on to the belief that we would one day be close again. But that day is lost. Today made me realize that I was still pushing you away. Telling you I needed time was another way to keep my heart safe, but life can change too fast, and I don't want to take the chance that..." The remaining words lodge in my throat so I reach out, placing a hand on this cheek.

"Me neither," he whispers, then draws me closer. Our kiss is deep and warm and full of love.

As nightfall approaches, we remain in his living room, huddled together, grateful for each other and all that we have, as the silence of a world in shock brings with it the visceral awareness of collective grief.

Epilogue

The Mitchel Sisters' Guide to Starting Over—Rule no. 5:
Never be afraid to live life by your own rules.

TWO MONTHS LATER, I am carrying the last box of my stuff down the stairs and outside into Jake's truck. Vicki and Gunner walk over to me, and she passes me a gift bag. I pull out a framed drawing of Ginger curled up in a guitar case.

"I hope it doesn't make you sad. I just wanted you to have something to remember her by."

Yes, tears form, but they are the happy variety. "I love it."

We hug and Gunner jumps up to join in.

"I'm going to miss you," I say.

"Me too. Stay in touch. You have my number, right?"

"I do." I bend down to pet Gunner. "Be a good boy." He wags his tail.

"We ready?" Jake asks as I climb into the truck.

"Yeah, let's go."

Moving in together was his idea. He wants me with him, and I want to be there. For the first time, in a long time, I am comfortable with who I am. Yeah, yeah, I'm still growing and changing, and it hardly makes me unique, but maybe that's what life is, a continual journey of discovery. Okay, too cheesy, but I bet I can work it into a song.

Suddenly Jake turns in a direction away from his house.

"Did you make plans and forget to tell me about them? A quick bungee jump before dinner? Scuba diving in the St. Lawrence?"

"Very funny, no, but I did want to surprise you. I thought we might get a cat."

I hug the picture of Ginger close to my chest. "A cat? You'll be okay with the fur and potential mess?"

"Yes. You're not the only one who can grow, you know."

"Awesome. Then how about two cats? They can keep each other company while we're at work."

"Two? Twice the fur?"

"And twice the love."

"Yeah. Okay. Why not."

As soon as we pull up in front of the animal shelter, I step out of the truck into the cold fall air, but for some reason, I couldn't be warmer.

About Janet Koops

A former librarian, Janet is a happily married empty-nester who writes full-time from her home just east of the Rocky Mountains. When she is not writing, she can typically be found hiking with her Alaskan Husky or working on a DIY project. Janet is a hopeless romantic who loves writing about complex women, their emotional journeys, and the healing power of love. Explore Janet's literary world further by visiting her official website. There, you'll find a comprehensive list of her published works. Additionally, become a part of Janet's reading community by subscribing to her newsletter, where you'll receive updates, insights, and exclusive content directly from the author.

Scan the QR code
or visit https://janetkoops.com